This i
lates
peric
- Ph n
- Visit

Di

о́с

ЕВ.

June Gadsby was born in Felling, Tyne and Wear, into a mining family. Her first love has always been writing, though she is also an accomplished artist, and loves to cook, read, and listen to music. She makes her own herbal remedies from the plants she grows in her half-acre garden. She now lives in Gascony, south-west France with her photographer husband Brian, and her miniature Yorkshire terrier, Candy.

THE IRON MASTER

Newcastle, 1908: Turning down a proposal of marriage from her older employer is perhaps the first mistake in Ellie Martin's young life. Running back to a family in trouble is the second. A new beginning awaits them in Durham, but at what cost? Her mother, with a dark secret in her past, mysteriously obtains jobs for her men in an iron foundry — and Ellie finds the magic she dreams of with Adam, son of the iron master of ill-repute. However, the hatred harboured by Ellie's mother for the Rockwells leads Ellie to believe that she is in love with her half-brother. And so she returns to Newcastle and tries to ignore her heart . . .

Books by June Gadsby
Published by The House of Ulverscroft:

PRECIOUS LOVE
KISS TODAY GOODBYE
SECRET OBSESSIONS
THE ROSE CAROUSEL

JUNE GADSBY

THE IRON MASTER

Complete and Unabridged

ULVERSCROFT
Leicester

First published in Great Britain in 2003 by
Robert Hale Limited
London

First Large Print Edition
published 2004
by arrangement with
Robert Hale Limited
London

British Library CIP Data

Gadsby, June
The iron master.—Large print ed.—
Ulverscroft large print series: general fiction
1. Iron industry and trade—England—Durham—
Fiction 2. England, North East—Social life and
customs—Fiction 3. Love stories
4. Large type books
I. Title
823.9′2 [F]

ISBN 1–84395–352–8

Published by
F. A. Thorpe (Publishing)
Anstey, Leicestershire

Set by Words & Graphics Ltd.
Anstey, Leicestershire
Printed and bound in Great Britain by
T. J. International Ltd., Padstow, Cornwall

This book is printed on acid-free paper

Part I

1

Newcastle, Summer 1908

The sounds of Sunday morning drifted in through the open kitchen window where Ellie Martin was enjoying a leisurely breakfast. The air was full of busy bees and twittering birds. From the small, neat garden the heady perfume of roses reached her, together with the smell of newly cut grass. She loved Sundays, just as she loved everything about her life here at Vale House.

Smiling contentedly, she began to plan her day off. She would borrow the professor's old bicycle so she could pedal up to the edge of the town moor. It was so peaceful there. As usual, she would take a book and sit by the stream, listening to it as she read while it gurgled and plopped its way back to Jesmond Dene.

'Ellie, the professor wants to see you right away.'

Ellie looked up with a start as the sharp voice of the housekeeper penetrated her thoughts. 'What's wrong, Mrs Renney?'

Professor Graham rarely had need of her

on Sundays. He was not the kind of employer who took advantage of her spare time. Although he was not an overly religious man himself, he did believe in a day's rest at both ends of the working week.

'I don't know what it's about, hinny, but he seems a bit agitated, like.' Mrs Renney fixed Ellie with a beady eye that spoke volumes. 'You haven't been doing anything to upset him, have you?'

Ellie pushed back her plate and wiped her fingers on a napkin, all the while keeping her gaze on the housekeeper. The woman's small dark eyes shot accusing glances at her, making her heart skip slightly in anticipation. She had absolutely no reason whatsoever to feel guilty, but when Mrs Renney suspected trouble, that's usually what they got.

'I haven't done anything that I know of, Mrs Renney,' she said, but wondered if it might have something to do with the fact that she sang rather a lot when she was alone. Or maybe she spent too much time feeding the birds and the squirrels. And, of course, there was the starving fox cub she had looked after, which still visited, much to Mrs Renney's horror. Or was it that she took bread and dripping and raisins and fed it to a family of badgers in the wood? 'No, I'm sure I haven't done anything that would make him angry.'

4

In fact, in the ten years Ellie had worked for the Graham family she had never personally been on the raw end of Professor Graham's often unpredictable nature. Most of the time he was a shy, quiet, kind man and treated her like one of the family rather than a servant.

Hannah Renney heaved her heavy bosom up an inch or two with her tightly folded arms and a discreet creaking sound came from her stays. 'Well, we'll see. You'd better get yourself along to the study. I don't like the look in that man's eye this morning.'

Ellie shrugged and shook her head. The movement made the untameable, fiery-gold curls that framed her face bob like gossamer springs. Her fair eyebrows rose slightly and she gave an uncertain smile. Most of the time she got on well enough with the housekeeper, but Mrs Renney didn't approve of familiarities between employer and employee, which was why Ellie was sometimes out of favour with her. She didn't think it was jealousy. More a protective instinct that had grown over the many years she had served the Graham family. She had been with them since before Nicholas Graham was born. That fact alone, she truly believed, gave her a rank far superior to that of a mere housekeeper.

With reluctance, Ellie left her fried eggs and bacon and hurried upstairs to see what the professor wanted so urgently. Because her natural exuberance would not allow her to go anywhere sedately, she ran all the way and skidded to a halt outside the professor's study, her soft black leather house-slippers squeaking on the highly polished parquet flooring. She knew she should act with a little more decorum as befitted a young woman of her age, but she was positively bursting with the joy of life. Everybody told her she was too old to go cavorting about like an overactive child. Maybe they were right, but she shed their criticisms like water off a duck's back. Being still, she told them, was tantamount to being dead.

Ellie was of an age, she had to admit, when most young women were settling down to domestic bliss and motherhood. She would quite like to get married one day, but for marriage you had to have a man. There was Ted, the gardener with his runny nose; Jimmy, the butcher's boy who smelled more like the local abattoir on a warm day; or Frank, the baker's son who coughed all the time from ingesting flour and probably had consumption like the rest of his family before him. They had all shown keen interest, but it would take more than that to stir Ellie's heart in the direction of the altar.

She took a few deep breaths to calm herself and allow her cheeks to cool down, then she rapped her knuckles in a sharp tattoo on the partially open study door.

'Come in, Ellie!'

Ellie peered around the door and greeted the professor with a broad smile. There I go, she thought with an inner laugh. *Being familiar*. Mrs Renney wouldn't approve, but that's the way I am, I'm afraid, and too bad if people don't like it.

She had never been one to bow and scrape before her superiors. Even when she was much younger and only a scullery-maid, she absolutely refused to behave in a totally subservient manner. Politeness, she felt, was one thing — she always had plenty of that — but she was not going to be made to feel inferior. Not by anyone.

'How did you know it was me?' she asked the professor.

A pair of soft, dove-grey eyes turned on her as she stepped inside the thoroughly masculine room. As always, she took a moment to inhale the scent of the leather-upholstered furniture and a lingering smell of sweet Virginia pipe tobacco mingling with beeswax polish. One day, she promised herself, she would count the books lining the walls. There had to be hundreds of them. Thousands, perhaps.

There were also a lot of brasses. The professor liked brass and insisted on cleaning it himself. He said it was his therapy and helped him to think. This morning, with the sun streaming in, the brasses were gleaming like living, magical creatures.

'Nobody *rat-a-tat-tats* quite like you, my dear,' Professor Graham said with a laugh. 'Besides, I can't think that anyone else in this household is energetic enough to run at full pelt through this rambling old mausoleum. Mrs Renney is too old and too heavy. And that new scullery-maid of hers is too lazy. What's the dratted girl's name again?'

'Maud!' No matter how many times she told him, he always forgot.

'Maud, yes. Do come in, Ellie.'

The professor regarded her for a long moment, then turned to the mantelpiece behind him and took his favourite pipe from an ebony rack. He filled it with deliberate slowness from a porcelain Worcester vase painted with peacocks and exotic flowers. Ellie loved that vase. The professor was very fond of it too because it had belonged to his mother. Much as she had adored her only son, old Mrs Graham, Ellie was sure, would not have approved of her favourite ornament

8

being used as a container for his tobacco.

Ellie smiled at the memory of the old lady's words on the subject of her son's smoking. *Such a useless, brainless habit, smoking! He took it up when he was quite young. Said he thought it gave him an air of sophistication. It's nothing more nor less than a comforter. Just you watch. He reaches for that ridiculous pipe of his every time he has something on his mind he can't resolve.*

'Is something wrong, Professor?' Ellie asked and had to wait for Nicholas Graham to light and draw on his curved briar pipe, puffing out clouds of blue-grey smoke about his head as he sucked voraciously at it.

'Hmm?' He extinguished the match with a lot of vigorous wrist-movements and peered at her short-sightedly through the fug he had created between them. 'Wrong? No. Why do you ask that?'

'Mrs Renney seemed to think you were — um — agitated about something.'

The professor frowned, stared at the pipe in his hand and instantly put it out, tapping the bowl into the empty fire-grate, which all went to prove, Ellie decided, that he most certainly had something on his mind.

'Mrs Renney said what?' Professor Graham's arms and shoulders lifted in a negative attitude. 'Oh, that damned woman!'

Ellie clamped her mouth shut to prevent herself from laughing. Her eyes followed the professor as he started to stride about the room, a slender, dapper figure with slow, graceful movements. He finally came to stand with his back to the high casement window. The sunlight, coming in from behind, put his face into concealing shadow.

'I've been going through my — er — my dear late wife's papers,' he said after a long pause. 'When my mother died she passed on everything to do with the household to Charlotte. I did not familiarize myself with any of the domestic arrangements. I'm a tutor in the history and practice of art. I could probably tell you the birth date of every well-known artist from the Renaissance to the present day. However, I have never bothered myself with any kind of date — shall we say — closer to home.'

'No, Professor — I mean, yes . . . ?' Ellie shook her head. 'I'm afraid I don't understand.'

'Don't you? Really? Ah, well . . . ' Professor Graham relit his pipe with maddening tardiness. 'It seems, Ellie, that my mother was far better organized than either my wife or myself. She always remembered your birthday, didn't she, and gave you some small token?'

10

Ellie nodded slowly. 'Yes, she did, but . . . '

'There! You see!'

Old Mrs Graham had been extremely generous. The professor's wife, who had died two years ago from a cancer, had not carried on the tradition of presenting the staff with a small gift on their birthdays. It would never have entered her head to do so.

'Your mother was a very kind lady,' she said, surprised that the memory of that gracious old woman could still bring a lump to her throat when she thought of her. 'Even after all this time, I still miss her.'

'Me too, Ellie. Me too.' They both fell into a short silence of mutual respect, then Professor Graham sucked in a great lungful of air and cleared his throat noisily. 'What I'm trying to say, Ellie — and I'm not doing it very well — is that since it's your birthday today I'd like to offer you something . . . '

'My birthday! Oh, Professor Graham!'

'What's wrong?'

Ellie's hand had flown to her mouth and she was grinning at him from behind it. 'Is it *really* my birthday?' She was quite lost with the date, but she supposed he must be right.

The professor was pacing again, puffing intensely on his pipe. 'Look, since it's a beautiful day, I wondered . . . would you like to go out anywhere special?'

Ellie's jaw dropped. 'Are you sure you want to, sir?' She hardly ever called him 'sir', except when she wasn't sure of herself. 'I mean — people might talk and . . . '

'Let them! Dammit, girl, I wouldn't ask you if I wasn't sure, now would I? Come on. Where shall we go, eh? I need to get out and breathe some fresh air.'

'Well . . . '

'Yes? Yes? Go on.'

'Well, there is somewhere I'd like to go. Somewhere I've never been before, but I don't know that you'd like it.'

The professor shook his head in exasperation. 'Let's not concern ourselves about whether or not *I* would like it. Where is it, girl?'

'The Quayside,' she said quickly, peering at him from beneath lowered brows.

'The Quayside?'

'Yes. The Sunday-morning market.' Thinking that he didn't seem too enamoured of the idea, she quickly changed tack. 'Of course, we don't have to go there. Jesmond Dene, perhaps? Or Brandling Park . . . ? The sea, maybe — no, that's too far.'

His hands shot up in the air, one of them clutching the smoking pipe, sending flakes of charred tobacco-shreds flying about the room.

'You want to go to the Quayside, Ellie? Then you shall go. You've really never been there? How amazing! I used to spend every Sunday there, much to the chagrin of my parents who thought a growing boy ought to have better things to do with his time.' Then they were both laughing. The professor flapped a hand at her. 'Off you go. Come back ready for going out in half an hour.'

'Thank you, Professor. What should I tell Mrs Renney?'

'Tell her to be sure and make an extra special Sunday lunch and we'll all eat together at one o'clock in the dining-room. Even that silly kitchen maid, unless she's too scared. What's her name again?'

'Maud, sir.'

'Ah, yes! Run along, now.'

Ellie beamed at him. 'Thank you, Professor.'

She rushed off to get ready, imagining what they would say at home if they knew how she was about to spend her birthday.

Oh, well. I just won't tell them, she sighed to herself. What the eyes don't see, the heart can't grieve over. Isn't that what Granddad always says?

And Ellie was sufficiently like her grand-father to give herself a mischievous grin in the mirror as she pulled out her best silk dress and slithered into it, her fingers clumsy in her excitement as she fumbled with the tiny pearl buttons of the bodice. The dress had belonged to the professor's wife, though she had never worn it. When the professor offered it to Ellie, claiming that it would suit her better anyway, she was at first hesitant, but it was so beautiful and it seemed such a waste just to throw it away.

She sighed again as she pinned her hat in place. It was of blond straw, had a broad brim and a collection of daisies around the crown. She was particularly fond of it and didn't care that it made her look much younger than her twenty-three years — no, twenty-four years to the day!

Ellie stared in the mirror and groaned over the rogue curls that escaped like lively springs from the hat and refused to stay in place. She could hear the professor calling her impatiently from the bottom of the stairs and grimaced at her reflection. Hastily, she gave the curls one last prod and blew out her cheeks.

Oh, well, she told her reflection. That will have to do. You're no raving beauty, Ellie Martin, but you'll do at a pinch. Besides, who do you think you'll meet down there on The Quayside, eh? There'll be so many people milling about you won't even be noticed.

'El-lie! Where the deuce are you, girl?'

Well, really! Just listen to the man. You'd think he was my father or something.

'Coming!' she called back and smiled fondly as she went tripping down the stairs to meet him.

★   ★   ★

Ellie was breathless with anticipation long before they reached the river. For the occasion, the professor had borrowed his cousin's new Dennis motor car and they rode into the city in style, the hood down, the chrome shining and sumptuous green leather upholstery glowing in the morning sunlight. The leather creaked beneath her and smelled deliciously fresh, just like the little purse old Mrs Graham had given her after spending a few days on the Continent a few years ago.

The car travelled at a speed of almost twenty-five miles an hour, five miles more than the official speed limit. They kept dodging the big electric tramcars, frightening horses and a few suicidal pedestrians on the way. Ellie's heart was in her mouth several times, but the professor happily managed to avoid an accident.

People turned to watch the distinguished, middle-aged man and his young companion with great curiosity. As they drove through the Haymarket there were so many Sunday strollers that the professor had to slow down to a near walking pace.

They left the car in Grey Street, in the care of a shabby, but respectable-looking man who was obviously down on his luck. For the promise of a shilling the fellow gave his word that he would sit in the car until they came back. Then, continuing on foot, they made their way down the very steep hill of Dean Street which led directly to the river.

Ellie found the uneven cobbles exceedingly difficult to walk on. They were bevelled and slippery. Professor Graham, seeing her problem, promptly took her hand and tucked it into the crook of his elbow, giving her the support needed on the way down.

As they approached the Quayside a cacophony of noise rose to meet them and Ellie gasped when she saw how many people there were milling about. Like herself, the women were all dressed in their Sunday best. Children rode on the shoulders of their fathers, to see better and not get trodden underfoot.

There was an infinite number of events and stalls. Ellie stood fascinated before a crockery stall where a man with a rough Cockney accent juggled with plates and saucers and cups. While he juggled, tossing the china high in the air, his eyes twinkling wickedly, his wide mouth grinning, he auctioned off his wares at next to nothing in price.

His voice sang out, raucous and foreign to Ellie's ears. ''Ere yew are, my lovelies. China the likes yew'll only see on the tables of kings and queens. In London folk pay a bloomin' fortune to eat their dinner off of these lovely plites. What am I arskin'? Not a fiver — not two parnds. Not ten shillings, but two shillings and a tanner, lidy — an' just fer yew oi'll thraw in a milk jag an' a sugar bowl. Wot a bloomin' bargain, eh? For a quid oi'll even let yew 'ave the whole bloomin' service. Look at 'em, luv. Bone choina. Yew can see yer fingers through it. All 'and-pinted and gilded with eighteen-carat gawld. Go on, spoil yerselves. Impress the mother-in-law.'

There was an endless string of similar stands, the vendors all competing one with another. Ellie stood before them all, transfixed and dazzled. A novelty stand sold toys and gadgets and a man in a Red Indian outfit with a colourful headdress of feathers bartered with the public for his old, American folkloric remedies for everything from ingrown toenails to miracle cures for 'women's complaints'.

Food stalls filled the air with sweet and

savoury smells, toffee-apples, candyfloss, pork-and-stuffing rolls and saveloy gravy-dips. There were cakes and biscuits and every kind of candy imaginable to titillate the palate of young and old alike. Jewellery and clothing stalls attracted the women while the men inspected tools, rummaged through boxes of nails and screws and various oddments, and the children stood wide-eyed in front of pet-stalls which offered kittens and puppies, tweetering canaries and colourful parrots with their bawdy remarks and ear-splitting expletives.

As Ellie and the professor inched their way along through the crowds, they had to stand back frequently for performing acrobats, clowns, a hurdy-gurdy man with a live, chattering monkey and a dancing bear. Ellie had never witnessed such an incredible spectacle. She laughed delightedly and exclaimed in childish awe while Professor Graham looked on, smiling indulgently.

And all the time, boats were sliding up and down the Tyne through the Swing Bridge. The sailors on board, with red, black and blue pompoms on their caps and bellbottom trousers swaying jauntily, called out provoca-tively in a variety of foreign languages to the people mingling on the quay. Ellie thought that perhaps it was a good thing she didn't understand what it was they were saying. Judging by their crafty expressions it was nothing that respectable girls ought to hear, though she did notice one or two giggling young females egging the sailors on by showing off their ankles and dimpled smiles.

'Well, are you enjoying your first visit to the Quayside, Ellie?' Professor Graham asked.

'It's wonderful! I didn't think it would be anything like this. Oh, look! A Punch and Judy stand! I remember seeing one once when I was very small. Punch frightened me so much I had bad dreams for a week afterwards.'

The professor laughed heartily and guided her on. At the end of the quay, where the long concrete walkway joined the lower part of the old city, the stalls and the better-dressed people ceased. Further along, Ellie could see a mass of poor people sorting through piles of old clothes. Some of them fought jealously over their finds. Women pushed at each other, cursing and slapping their children and spoke with such common dialects that Ellie was hard put to understand them, despite her own working-class roots.

'This is where we turn back, Ellie,' Professor Graham said. He promptly did an about-turn and offered her his other arm. 'Even when I was young I made a point of never going near Paddy's Market.'

'Paddy's Market?' Ellie strained her neck to look over her shoulder at the human mêlée they were leaving behind. She had heard the name before. Her mother, Polly, when she was complaining about the untidy state of her house, would invariably liken it to Paddy's Market. It was a vast exaggeration. Polly Martin kept an impeccable house, even though she was a poor miner's wife.

'It's where the impoverished go to buy clothes for a penny — or less as the case may be,' Nicholas Graham smiled down at her. 'They steal them when they can. And they take home more than a change of clothes.'

'Oh?'

'Armies of fleas and lice, my dear. The clothes are rarely clean and they are very often stripped from the backs of dead people before the poor souls are cold.' He chuckled when Ellie shuddered. 'When you're that poor, Ellie, pride moves over to make space for fleas and disease. Only the strongest among them survive.'

Ellie knew what it was to live among poverty, but nothing as bad as those poor people fighting over such shabby clothing. She came from a mining family. Miners and their families were respectable people, but they had hard lives. Nobody got rich hacking out coal from those deep, dark tunnels underground. They wore themselves out making money for the owners, coughed up black phlegm and died before their time from chest complaints, broken backs and blindness.

She had a father and two brothers working down the pit and another brother nearly old enough to join them. She was glad she had been born a female. Scrubbing floors at thirteen was nothing compared to what boys so often found themselves doing at the same age.

'Ah! I was hoping I'd see this fellow,' Nicholas Graham was pressing forward through a crowd gathered in a circle around a figure sitting on a stool in front of an artist's easel. 'Come on, Ellie. How would you like your portrait done, eh? An extra birthday present.'

'Oh, heavens, I — I don't know, Professor!' Ellie hung back, but he pulled her with him.

'Come on. He won't eat you.'

But Ellie wasn't sure about that. The artist had already seen her and was staring at her with open interest, his dark eyes full of something she couldn't quite make out. Whatever it was, it left her feeling decidedly disconcerted.

The artist stood up as he recognized Professor Graham and extended his hand, though his gaze returned quickly to Ellie and she felt herself colouring as the effect he had on her intensified. He was the most impressive figure of a man she had ever laid eyes on. Not handsome like the pretty young men she had glimpsed from time to time strutting around the city like peacocks. She saw no fine-boned breeding and vanity in this man's features. Only rugged strength thinly disguised by a veneer of sophisticated arrogance.

'Rockwell!' There was faint surprise in the professor's tone as he shook the other man's hand. 'I didn't expect to see you here. Where's Salter?'

The man called Rockwell seemed to have difficulty dragging his eyes away from Ellie's face.

'Freddie met with an accident last week. A barroom brawl. Somebody cut him with a broken beer-bottle because they took exception to a sketch he had done.'

'Oh, dear! I'm sorry to hear that. Not badly hurt, is he?'

'A slash across his painting hand. Not too serious, but a little incapacitating for a while until it heals. He can't afford not to work. If he doesn't turn up here regularly, somebody else will soon take his pitch. So, I said I'd fill in for him.'

'That's a good-hearted gesture, Rockwell. Is he still in straitened circumstances?'

Rockwell nodded. 'He can barely afford to pay his rent and now his wife is sick and may lose the child she's carrying.'

'Here.' Professor Graham was handing over some money which he pressed into the artist's hand. Ellie saw that there were at least five one-pound notes. 'Give him this from me when you see him. And now, I would like you to sketch a portrait of this young lady. Oh, where are my manners? Ellie, this is a former student of mine, Adam Rockwell — though he prefers, these days, to be an iron master rather than explore his excellent talents as an artist.'

'And your young *companion*'s name?' The dark eyes again scoured her face and she felt a frisson of anger at the way he had stressed the word 'companion' like that.

'Oh, I'm sorry — yes — this is Miss Ellen Martin.' The professor was smiling graciously, but his feathers were decidedly ruffled. 'Ellie worked for my late mother, then became companion to my dear wife who also died recently.'

'Ah! I see! And now?'

'Now?' The professor seemed confused by

the point-blank question. 'Now she is — um — she works for me — um — as my assistant.'

'How fortunate — for both of you.'

'You'll do the portrait, then?'

Adam Rockwell nodded. 'Since I don't seem to have a string of clients, it would seem prudent to accept your business, Professor Graham. Miss Martin, it is Frederick Salter's name that will one day be famous. I merely sketch as a hobby.'

'Or when you're helping out a friend in need, Mr Rockwell,' Ellie spoke for the first time and saw a tiny frown crease his broad forehead. 'Be sure and put your own name on your work today. I'd hate it to be mistaken for a Salter original.'

A sardonic grin spread over the handsome face, showing strong, even white teeth, but his eyes remained mysterious and cold. 'I don't think there's any danger of that. Freddie's a much better artist than I will ever be.'

'Perhaps I should come back on another Sunday morning, when your friend is back at work and he can do a second portrait of me. It would be interesting to compare the two, don't you think, Professor?'

'Hmm?' Professor Graham had a vague look in his eyes. 'Yes! Yes, indeed. What a good idea. You must remind me to bring you in a week or two.'

The portrait, executed in pencil, was done fairly quickly, to Ellie's relief, since she was quite unaccustomed to being the centre of attention with an audience of strangers. In a matter of fifteen minutes the artist was signing his name at the bottom with a flourish.

Everyone peered at her curiously, comparing the real thing to the drawn image. There were admiring exclamations and people started applauding. Rockwell acknowledged the applause with a brief nod, then tore the sheet off his sketchpad and gave it to the professor. His attention returned immediately to Ellie and she felt a new surge of heat rushing to her cheeks.

'You must get Freddie to paint you in oils,' he said. 'He would do justice to that fine skin and your exquisite colouring. And you must always wear blue, though I have to admit that those eyes of yours would make any other blue look faded.'

'Thank you, Mr Rockwell.' Ellie burned at the outrageous flattery and saw how irritated the professor was becoming.

A further amount of money changed hands and they moved on. Professor Graham's face had undergone a sudden change as if dark thoughts were marring his good mood.

'Can I see my portrait, please?' Ellie said.

'What? Oh, yes — I'm sorry, Ellie! Here you are. I'll get it framed for you. I know an excellent man in High Bridge.'

'Oh! Oh, he's made me look . . . ' Ellie was gazing at the portrait, which was a life-size head and shoulders study. She hardly dared pronounce the word that came into her head because it would seem so conceited, but the face that stared out at her from the creamy velum page was nothing less than beautiful. 'It's very flattering, isn't it?'

'Hmm? Oh, yes. An excellent likeness, Ellie. Are you pleased?'

'Very! Thank you so much. I really don't know what to say. I mean, you didn't have to go to all this trouble, just because it's my birthday, you know. After all, I'm not . . . ' Ellie swallowed the words that would have embarrassed them both. She was neither his daughter nor his wife. Just a servant-girl whom he and his mother had taken in, educated and moulded into something better. She looked up at him and smiled. 'Thank you!'

'Not at all, my dear. I'm just a little disappointed that it wasn't Frederick Salter, but perhaps Rockwell was right. Salter would do an excellent job in oils. He excels in the medium, whereas Rockwell is perhaps the master of the graphic pencil. Anyway, that's what I always thought.'

'I can't imagine that Mr Salter could do any better than Mr Rockwell.'

'Rockwell was an excellent student who threw away his talents to follow in his father's footsteps. I suppose it was only to be expected in the circumstances, his being the only son of a steel baron. Such a waste of good talent.'

'You don't like Mr Rockwell much, do you?'

'Why do you assume that?'

Ellie glanced back down the length of the Quayside. She could still see the artist standing by his easel, so easy to spot because of his impressive build and the fact that he stood a head taller than the crowd around him.

'I just got a feeling, that's all.'

The professor sighed and took her arm, drawing her further onward.

'How perceptive you are, Ellie. It is not a question, exactly, of like or dislike. Adam Rockwell was a model student and quite a likeable young fellow. I don't know why I reacted the way I did just now. Resentment, perhaps, for the way he allowed his father to bully him into throwing away what could have been a brilliant career doing what he loved most of all.' He gave a small, angry snort. 'But that wasn't what bothered me. I can't explain it. It's years since he studied under me, but when I saw him there today I felt a sudden rush of something akin to panic. Distrust, fear — I don't know what.'

Ellie started to laugh, then changed her mind. 'But what on earth could Mr Rockwell do to make you afraid?' Then she did laugh. 'Anyway, if it makes you feel any better, he bothered me too, so there!'

'Ah!' was all that Nicolas Graham said and smiled discreetly.

The motor car was still safe, much to the professor's relief, though its temporary guardian had fallen asleep. Professor Graham thanked the man graciously and gave him a florin.

On arriving back in Jesmond, the professor dropped Ellie off at the house and returned the Dennis. As she stepped into the hall, Mrs Renney was there to greet her with a face long enough to trip her up.

'I'm sorry if we're late back, Mrs Renney,' Ellie said breathlessly, making sure she was the first to speak. 'The Quayside was so exciting! I didn't want to leave. And the professor asked an artist do a portrait of me.

Look! Isn't it wonderful! I hope the dinner didn't spoil!'

'No, but no doubt it will soon. Best beef joint and it'll go to waste.'

'What are you talking about, Mrs Renney?'

'Aye, well . . . ' Mrs Renney's eyes went even smaller as she tucked her chin into the folds of fat beneath it. 'I've got to say it, Ellie, I don't know what the man's doing taking out a member of his household staff. And a girl young enough to be his daughter at that.'

Ellie's own chin now stuck out stubbornly. 'I've done nothing to be ashamed of, Mrs Renney . . . '

She heard the housekeeper's large chest wheeze and saw the doughy face pucker.

'Never mind that now. You've had an urgent message delivered by special messenger.'

Ellie looked stunned. 'An urgent . . . ? For me?' She took the buff-coloured envelope from the housekeeper's outstretched hand and tore it open with shaking fingers. It could only mean bad news, she was sure, and she dreaded to read the words inscribed on the flimsy piece of paper she drew out. 'Here, Mrs Renney. You read it for me, please. I daren't.'

Mrs Renney took the paper from her and

held it in front of her nose, then at arm's length, then finally found a comfortable mid-way distance for her failing eyesight. 'There's been a death in the family and you've to go home at once.'

2

Adam Rockwell gathered up his materials on the first strike of midday from the clock of St. Nicholas' Cathedral. As if by magic the crowds drifted away and the stallholders packed up their wares, leaving the Quayside strewn with discarded newspapers, cartons, wooden crates and bits of food for the local scavenging dogs.

With his easel and sketching-block tucked under one arm and his pencils in his pocket, Adam made his way up from the river through the side-streets to Sandgate where the Salters lived in rented rooms above a pawn shop. It was a tall narrow building squeezed between a bakery on one side and a greengrocer's shop on the other.

The greengrocer was closed, permanently it seemed, for there were boards across the windows and the stench of rotting vegetables emanated from an untidy pile of crates stacked outside the door. The baker, however, was standing on his doorstep, large, red-faced and dusted from head to foot in flour.

'Good day to you, sir!' The man touched a

finger to his forelock and rocked on the balls of his feet.

Adam nodded back courteously. 'You wouldn't have some bread left from this morning's batch, would you?'

The man rubbed his chin reflectively and glanced over his shoulder. 'Well, now, there might be the odd loaf lurking in the kitchen.'

'It has to be fresh,' Adam told him with a challenging stare.

'Aye. It'd be fresh all right, sir.'

'And large with a good crust.'

'Would ye care to step inside until I see what I've got?'

Adam, already warm from the summer sun, eyed the interior of the bakery with its steamy windows. The smell of the place was appetizing, but the heat and the flour-dust on such a beautiful day held no appeal. He got enough heat and dust down at the foundry.

'I'll wait here. Bring the loaf to me, if you would.'

The baker nodded, disappeared into the fug behind him and reappeared almost immediately with a fat golden cob that was still slightly warm when it was placed in Adam's hands. He sniffed at it and was satisfied that it was perfectly fresh.

'That'll be twopence, if you please, sir — or

I can let you have yesterday's for a penny if you'd prefer?'

'This one will be fine,' Adam said, handing over two bright, shiny new pennies and wishing he'd thought to bring some more substantial food from the larder at home so that Freddie and his sickly wife would not starve, though he knew that Freddie's great pride would have meant he'd have a fight on his hands to make the man accept his charity.

The door to the lodging-house was open and as Adam stepped inside the dark passageway, lowering his head beneath the lintel, a waft of warm, stale air assailed him. He gritted his teeth and wrinkled his nose, appalled at the squalor in which some people were forced to live, as if it were still the Middle Ages instead of the beginning of the twentieth century.

The Salters lived on the second floor where the paint was peeling and the floor linoleum had hardened with age and misuse. Their door was next to a foul-smelling indoor toilet, which was considered a luxury by the tenants who shared it — perhaps four or five families in all. There had been a time when the houses at Sandgate had belonged to wealthy shipping magnates. Those times were long gone.

He rapped sharply on the shabby door. There was a quick burst of anxious muttering inside, then the door was opened wide and Freddie stood there, smiling a warm greeting.

'Adam! Come in, won't you?'

The two friends did not shake hands, but embraced somewhat clumsily in the manner of men who did not find this intimacy comfortable, but had the need to express their affection for one another.

Adam stepped inside, his long legs carrying him immediately to the centre of the tiny home of his old friend. There was a scrubbed deal table on which had been laid two sets of cutlery and plates, ready for the midday meal, though there was no appetizing aroma of meat and vegetables cooking. He placed the loaf of bread on the table and turned to the young woman propped up with pillows on a narrow bed in the corner.

Clara Salter was pale with dark shadows purpling the hollows beneath her eyes, but she smiled at him sweetly and held out a hand, which he took and bent low to touch his lips to the hot, clammy skin.

'I'm sorry about this, Adam,' she said and her voice sounded as weak as she looked. 'I'm afraid I was angry with Freddie just now because he hadn't told me that you were calling in. I've not been well lately, so the housework hasn't been done.'

'She didn't want me to let you in!' Freddie

came and perched on the end of the bed, putting his arm with the heavily bandaged hand around her thin shoulders. 'I assured her that you were the one person who would not care how the place looked. You're too good a friend for that, eh, Adam?'

Adam laughed softly, his eyes searching for an answer to his unvoiced questions. Freddie knew what was in his head and smiled back wryly.

'No, Adam. There's to be no child this time. It was taken from us yesterday. Happily I was here and not down at my studio, so I was able to bring the doctor to Clara.'

Clara's eyes filled with tears, but she held on to them and nestled her head against her husband.

'It's all right, Adam. The doctor says that I can still have children, but must wait until I'm stronger.'

'I'm so terribly sorry,' Adam said in all sincerity.

Freddie shook his head sadly and got up to offer Adam a tiny glass of sherry from a bottle that had been given to him in part payment for a sketch he had done last month.

'As I've told you before, Freddie,' Adam said, taking a sip of his wine and running a thumb over the rim of the glass. 'There's always a job waiting for you down at the foundry.'

Freddie stared at him for a long moment, then gulped back his own sherry and turned to look out of the square cracked panes of the window that gave on to the street outside and the leaning buildings across the way.

'I know you mean well, Adam, but the answer is still no.'

'But, Freddie . . . ' Adam took a step nearer his friend, reached out and touched the man's shoulder, but his hand was shrugged off.

'You've got my answer, Adam. Don't press the question any further. Clara knows how I feel and she agrees with me. I must try to make a living from my art. It's what I've always wanted. Damnation, Adam, I *live* for my art — the way you used to before you started to kowtow to your old man. I can't be like you, man! I can't put riches and inheritance before my God-given talent.'

Adam sighed and nodded slowly. He placed a handful of money on the table, side by side with the bread he had brought.

'I think perhaps both of us are wrong, Freddie,' he said grimly. 'You in your way, and me in mine. Still, I know you well enough to accept that you won't be persuaded once you've got your heels well dug in. This is the money I earned for you this morning. And it's possible you'll receive a commission for a portrait in oils.'

'A commission! Adam! This is good news!' Freddie hit out at Adam's chest with a playful punch. 'My God, man, you've not only earned more money in a morning than I ever do, you've brought me luck into the bargain. Who is the portrait to be of?'

Adam took a long time to reply. He was conjuring up the pretty face of Miss Ellen Martin, but at the same time he was struggling with feelings of anger he couldn't quite explain.

'It's a young woman I met this morning in the company of Professor Graham, our old tutor from college.'

'Is she pretty?'

'Too pretty for her own good, Freddie.'

'What was she like? Describe her to me.' Adam could see that Freddie was already getting excited at the prospect of some real work. He hoped he wouldn't be disappointed.

Adam rubbed the back of his neck where he suddenly felt the hairs rising. 'She's small. Not even as tall as Clara here. A good figure — you know — not straight up and down. Hardly the figure of a demure young lady, though I must admit her face had breeding and she spoke quite well. Plenty of spirit, I'd say. Certainly not the shy and retiring type.'

'Her face, man! What was her face like?'

Adam looked at his impatient friend and smiled. 'She had the face of an angel with the bluest eyes you've ever seen, Freddie. And her hair formed a halo of molten gold around her head. Not straight and thin or tamed sufficiently to lie flat against her head like most of the women seem to favour these days, but an explosion of wild curls that all the taming in the world would not make lie down. A blonde gypsy, if there is such a thing.'

Freddie laughed enthusiastically. 'She obviously made quite an impression on you, Adam. I can't wait to meet her.'

Adam frowned. Ellen Martin had certainly touched a nerve somewhere inside him. He had taken one look at her and felt as if he had been punched right in the soft part of his belly.

'They talked about coming back to the Quayside when your hand has healed in a week or two. No doubt the professor will speak to you then about a portrait. You know, he's quite well off since the death of both his mother and his wife. I suggest you put your asking price up. By the way, five pounds of that money is from him . . . ' He saw the proud lift of Freddie's chin and went on quickly before his friend could object. 'He'll be insulted if you don't accept it. Call it a down payment on the portrait if you like, but take it. God knows, you could do with it. Clara needs some good nourishing food inside her and some new clothes to cheer her up.'

'Oh, I'm all right, Adam,' Clara sang out from the bed where her colour seemed to have brightened slightly. 'Anyway, we owe some rent and Freddie needs a new stock of painting materials, not to mention new shoes if he's not to go to work barefoot.'

Adam remembered to enquire after the small studio Freddie was renting down on the docks. It was no more than a disused storeroom, but it served its purpose and got the foul-smelling oil paint out of their living quarters. He had obtained it at a peppercorn rent, the owner only too glad to have the place used.

'Oh, it's not ideal down there, you know,' Freddie pulled a face, then grinned, forever the optimist. 'But it'll do until I can afford something better. The winter's the hardest part with no heating. I have to paint wearing gloves. But it's all right, really. It's fine!'

Adam did not stay long. He could see how Clara was tiring in her attempt to be light-hearted and brave in front of him. He took his leave and turned towards Central Station where he would catch a train for Durham. His stepmother was entertaining friends at home that afternoon, it being the first Sunday of the month, and he had promised to join them later. He doubted, however, that any of the ladies would be half as interesting as Ellen Martin.

★　★　★

There was something about the silence of a house on the day of a funeral that seemed quite touchable. It filled every space like a solid, living thing, making conversation of any kind immaterial. And so it was in the Martin household the day they buried Ellie's grandfather.

Ellie felt she had been sitting there for ever with the other members of her immediate family while they waited for the time to go by and the hearse to arrive that would carry George Martin's remains to the church. Her mother, Polly, sat on the sofa beside her, her back as straight as a ramrod, her hands tightly knotted in her lap.

She was wearing her black felt cloche hat pulled down low on her small head. It shadowed a pair of eyes that were drained of colour and constantly wary. There was no relief in the fine black woollen dress she wore, ruched and buttoned with tiny neck and wrist frills that were an extravagance at variance with her plain, parchment-coloured face.

Polly did not move, did not speak. From time to time, when the boys fidgeted or cleared their throats and looked as if they wanted to say something, she shot them a chilly stare of reprimand. That was enough to keep them still for a few minutes more.

A sigh of impatience escaped Ellie as she continued to stare ahead of her.

The clock on the mantelpiece was the only thing that broke the monotony of the deathly silence of the house. Its slow *tock-tock-tock* was like the hollow dripping of water in some dark place. Ellie could close her eyes and imagine that she was completely alone down a mineshaft or one of those potholes people were so fond of exploring and getting themselves stuck in.

Finally, another sound added itself to the ticking of the clock. The steady *clip-clop* of horses' hoofs in the street outside signalled the arrival of the hearse. It drew up outside the front door, the horses snorting and pawing impatiently the minute they were drawn to a halt. Polly gathered her handbag to her and stood up.

'Right,' she said in a hushed voice. 'It's

time. Let them in, will you, Ben.'

The undertakers and their helpers came in with grim expressions and bowed heads, black bowlers clasped before them as they shook hands with the family and muttered official condolences. Then they were shown into the front room, where George Martin was laid out in his best Sunday suit. His black tie, bought specially for the occasion because he never wore one, was hidden by his favourite white silk muffler around his neck. Ellie and Ben had done that while Polly wasn't looking. As she had not gone near the coffin since the laying out, she was not going to notice the muffler now.

Through the short silence that ensued, there was the grinding sound of screws being tightened as the undertakers secured the lid of the coffin. A few minutes later they were joined by the two eldest Martin boys, Ben and Tommy, as additional pallbearers. Jack Martin, with his youngest son, Archie, stepped out into the street ahead of them so they could watch the old man's transfer into the hearse.

'Ah, Lord luv us!' one neighbour was heard to exclaim. 'One o' them horses has just dropped a load of oranges on the road. That's luck if ye like. Charlie! Gan and fetch the shovel. It's just the job to make yer dad's rhubarb grow down at the allotment.'

Archie peered beneath the horse in anticipation of seeing some juicy fruit and jumped back with a *pshaw!* as the stink from the steaming horse-droppings reached his nose.

'Keep back, sonny!' the head undertaker warned. 'We don't want you getting kicked on the day of your granddad's funeral, now do we?'

At only ten years of age, Archie was far more interested in the two horses with black ostrich plumes sprouting from their heads and their jingling brasses, to be too concerned about imminent danger, but he backed off anyway.

'Let's go, then,' Polly said brusquely from the doorway and started forward, not looking left or right.

Ellie walked with her mother, with her sister, Mary, hanging back behind them, snuffling into her hankie and not wanting to go at all.

Jack and Polly rode with the driver of the hearse, while the undertaker's men rode on the step that skirted the vehicle, their expressions as suitably dour as the grave itself. Ellie could see her mother's posture getting stiffer and stiffer and wondered if it had anything to do with having her back to her dead father-in-law, probably for the first time in her life. It was something she swore she would never do. She didn't trust any man where she couldn't see him and George had tried her patience sorely over the years.

They had hired a horse and trap from the undertaker's firm for the grand-children of George Martin to ride to his funeral in. Neither Ben nor Tommy liked the idea of sitting there out in the open for all to see. *Like bliddy exhibits!* That was how Ben had put it.

It was a bit of a crush in the trap with two grown men, two young women and a lad big for his age. Ben, the eldest, was as big as a mountain, taking up more than his share of the seating. Ellie found herself wedged in with him, while Mary and Archie shared their seat with Tommy, who was as skinny as his elder brother was broad.

'Gawd, I hope this journey isn't going to take long,' Ben complained in Ellie's ear as he eyed the crowd of neighbours milling around, yet keeping a respectful distance. 'Fancy me mam doing this. I'd rather have walked to the funeral. It's embarrassing having everybody stare like this.'

'Oh, don't be daft, Ben,' Ellie hissed back and smiled at an old woman in a black shawl who grasped her hand and offered her sympathies. 'Get out and walk if it's so important to you.'

'I would an' all, if me mam wouldn't make me pay for the rest of me life.'

Ellie hid a grin behind her hand. It was a slight exaggeration on her brother's part, but she knew what he meant. Most of the time they all did what Polly expected of them because it was a sight easier than going against her wishes. When you all lived crammed together in a small house it was a case of least said, soonest mended.

Ellie considered herself lucky that she lived with the professor in Newcastle and only got to see her family once a month on her weekend off. Those two days of communal living under the same roof as Polly Martin were enough to make her appreciate her independence. It was Polly's constant narrow-minded nagging that had driven her to take on work as far away across the River Tyne as possible.

'What do they do with the feathers afterwards?' Archie was straining his neck to look at the horses pulling the hearse. The huge beasts were jogging proudly, their black plumes undulating with every plodding step.

'I expect they use them again for another funeral,' Ellie told him. 'Sit still, Archie. You're squashing poor Mary.'

'D'ye mean to say we can't keep them?' Archie wasn't much concerned about squashing his sister. He had his eye on a treasure that was far more important.

'No, you can't keep them, so don't you go thinking that you can help yourself.'

'Aw, Ellie, leave the lad alone. One of them black feathers would make a grand souvenir, eh, Archie?' Ben grinned at his little brother and the lad grinned back and scrubbed at his snub nose with the palm of his hand.

'Ben, if you're planning on doing what I think you're planning . . . '

'Leave off, Ellie. You're beginning to sound like me mam.'

That silenced her. The last thing she wanted was to be thought of as a second Polly Martin. Screwing around in her seat, she fixed her eyes on the back of her father's grey head. She was worried about him. He'd not said a word all morning, which in itself wasn't too unusual, but she hadn't seen him read a page from the *Evening Chronicle* or even one of his beloved books. It hadn't occurred to her before, but now she thought about it he was perhaps more upset by his father's death than he showed.

'I hope me dad's all right,' she muttered half to herself and Ben squeezed her hand in a rough, brotherly show of affection. She loved all her family, but Ben was her favourite. They had always got on well. He was only a year older than she was, but he was big and as strong as an ox and he had looked out for her for as long as she could remember.

'Don't worry about me dad,' he said. 'He's got hisself brainwashed over the years so that things bounce off him like water off a duck's back.'

On the opposite side of the trap, Tommy laughed and shook his head and Mary shot Ben a black look of disapproval. They were all so different, Ellie thought. Small, big, dark, fair. The Martins must seem like quite an assortment to outsiders, yet she could see family resemblances in all of them. Ben was perhaps the odd one out with his height and bulk.

People had always laughed over Ben's size. He measured six foot at the age of sixteen and had grown a couple of inches since then. They used to say his mother must have bathed him in horse muck when he was a baby, a remark that never failed to whiten the face and tighten the thin lips of Polly Martin, who had no sense of humour to speak of and did not appreciate those who had.

The small funeral cortège arrived at the Christ Church chapel five minutes later than scheduled to looks of disdain and impatience from the other members of George Martin's family, none of whom got on with Polly and couldn't understand why Jack had married her.

Ignoring them, Polly was, as ever, in charge of the situation.

'Right, we're here,' she said as she gathered her husband and their children around her. 'Now, we sit together at the front and I don't want to hear a word from any of you until it's over, do you hear?'

Archie objected at being told he wasn't expected either to move or to talk while in the church, then hid a grin as he caught sight of Ben's mock salute behind his mother's back. Ellie gave her elder brother a sharp dig in the ribs and bit on her lips to stop herself from laughing. Ben was incorrigible. Nothing seemed to put him down. Maybe that was why she was so fond of him.

The church was cold and smelled damp. The vicar read out the funeral service in a bored monotone as the gathered Martins and their relatives stared blankly ahead of them. There was a slight flutter of animation as a few courageous voices joined together to sing two of George's favourite hymns, 'Fight the Good Fight' and 'Onward Christian Soldiers' with the organist hitting the wrong last note that ended like the screech of a badly tuned bagpipe.

'I bet that made Granddad stick his fingers in his ears!' Ben remarked and there was a round of throat-clearing as his voice echoed audibly from the vaulted ceiling above their heads. The vicar gave an ecclesiastic scowl over his reading glasses and carried on regardless.

When the collection basket was being passed around Archie got his wrist slapped as he dipped into it and tried to pocket some of the change. The organist passed on to a dirgelike rendition of 'Abide With Me' and the congregation formed a long column behind the coffin as it was taken to the cemetery for burial.

'I've never seen so many people at a funeral before,' Ellie said as they all walked back to the house together.

'Aye. Me granddad was well liked, even though he was a foreman. Did ye see all them old miners who came to pay their last respects, eh? The lads down the pit who still remember the old man swear he was the best foreman they ever had. Strict, but fair. Not like the bugger we've got now.'

'Language, Ben!' came Polly's sharp remonstration.

'Gawd, it's not even Sunday, Mam!' he said

49

tauntingly with a mischievous nudge at Ellie.

'It's the day of your granddad's funeral. Ye should have more respect. The Lord will strike you down, Benjamin Martin, one of these days.'

'Aye, well, it seems to me God strikes all of us down sooner or later. I just hope he kind of overlooks me for a while, even if I do singe his ears off with a few blasphemies from time to time.'

They heard their mother's *tut* of disapprobation sucked loudly through her teeth. 'Come on, the lot of you. I want to get back to make sure that woman is doing things properly.'

'That woman' was Nora Brown from down the street. She had been left in charge of putting the food out. And heaven help her, Ellie thought, if she uses an old plate or breaks a new one.

The house on Queen Victoria Street, as they approached, seemed to be sleeping with its curtains all drawn. A small, black-ribboned wreath of waxy white lilies hung on the door.

Polly ushered them all inside as if they were guilty of something much more sinister than attending a funeral.

'Inside and quick about it!' she said with a sweep of her hand. 'Ben. Make sure that door

50

is locked until I find out what still needs doing in the front room.'

Ben exchanged a pained look with Ellie. He shut the door and stood with his back pressed up against it, pulling at his ear and smiling secretively to himself.

'Eeh, there you are, hinnies,' Nora Brown appeared from the kitchen, a plate of ham and pease-pudding sandwiches in each hand. 'Nearly done! Now, how did the funeral go? Not a pleasant time for anybody, is it?'

'Especially not me granddad,' little Archie piped up, heading for the stairs.

'Archie!'

Archie stopped dead, but he didn't turn around to face his mother who had screamed at him from the hall.

'Aye?'

'Archibald Martin, what have you got stuffed down yer gansie?'

'Just me, Mam!'

'Let's give you a hand with them sandwiches, Mrs Brown.' Ben pushed himself forward and took the plates from the neighbour's hands before she could object.

'I'll go and get the rest, shall I?' Mrs Brown asked and when nobody replied she went and did it anyway.

'I'm off to the lav,' Mary said quickly, obviously sensing trouble.

Ellie's mouth was slowly opening as she saw the object of her mother's anger sticking out from the V-neck of Archie's pullover. He looked as though he had black fur sprouting from his chest.

'Oh, Archie!' She stifled a laugh and wished she had seen the funeral horse's black plume before her mother got sight of it.

'Come down here this minute, Archie!' Polly was seething, her pasty face turning red in angry blotches. 'And give me that thing.'

Archie turned and promptly sat down on the stairs. Inch by inch he slowly pulled the long, luxurious ostrich-feather from his pullover and when his mother grabbed it from him his chest heaved and his eyes filled with tears.

'I was going to put it with the rest,' he said, tearfully. 'With me granddad's collection.'

'And what collection would that be, indeed?'

Archie's face bunched up and his stubborn Martin chin jutted forward as he stared back at his mother, then glanced in Ellie's direction, his eyes pleading with her to intervene.

'Ellie?' Polly swung round to face her, but Ellie could only shrug.

'I don't know, Mam.'

'Jack? What did your father collect?'

'I don't know, Polly.'

'Whatever it is,' Polly fumed, 'it'll be a load of nonsense.'

'It's not nonsense!' Archie cried out. 'He collected feathers, that's what he collected. He's got all sorts of them up in the loft and he always said he'd not go to his grave happy unless he had an ostrich feather — and the man with the horses said that this was an ostrich feather, so I pinched it for Granddad — only he's dead and he won't never get to see it now and . . .'

Archie's voice faded out on a wavery note and two huge tears oozed out from the corners of his eyes and ran down to his chin.

'I know what I'll do with this!' Before anyone could stop her Polly marched into the kitchen and threw the feather on the fire. 'He won't be wanting it now, will he?'

Ellie followed her mother into the kitchen. Her heart ached to see Polly do such a spiteful thing to poor Archie, who was left clinging to the banister rail sobbing mournfully and he wasn't a lad who cried easily, even at the worst of times.

'Oh, Mam, you shouldn't have done that. Archie loved me granddad. It wouldn't have cost you anything to let him keep the feather.'

Polly rounded on her. 'Oh wouldn't it? I already paid dearly to hire that hearse, feathers and all. Now they'll be sending me a bill for a damned ostrich-plume.'

They had never heard Polly swear like that before. Ellie felt a tightness in her chest as she faced her mother's anger. It was an anger that none of them had ever understood, but it was always there beneath the surface, grudging and spiteful and very often, or so it seemed, without reason.

'Here!' Ellie found her purse and emptied out some coins on to the table. 'Let me pay for the stupid feather, if that's what's worrying you.'

Then she stormed off to join Ben and Mrs Brown in the front room, her fists clenching and unclenching as she tried to fix her smile back on to receive her grandfather's mourners as they began to file into the house.

As she kissed the family goodbye the next morning, Ellie thought what a pity it was that her granddad hadn't been there to enjoy the 'good send-off' his daughter-in-law had given him. Differences apart, she had to credit her mother for doing herself proud on the day.

Polly hadn't wanted Ellie to go back to Newcastle so soon, but Ellie couldn't wait to get back. She found the family home dreary and claustrophobic after the spacious comfort she was now used to.

'Ellie, my dear girl!' Professor Graham welcomed her with a look of relief plainly revealed on his face. 'I'm so glad to see you back.'

He drew her into the sitting-room and gave her a glass of sherry, chattering nervously all the while, until she was forced to ask him if he was feeling all right, convinced that something was wrong.

'I'm quite all right, thank you, Ellie, but I've done a lot of thinking while you were away and now I feel I really must speak out on a matter which has been troubling me for quite a long time.'

'Oh?' She had *known* there was something wrong. What on earth was he going to tell her? Was he, perhaps, going to dispense with her services? Was he thinking of selling the house and travelling abroad, which was what he often talked about? She hoped she was wrong on both counts. The idea of leaving him was hardly a pleasing one. In fact, she got quite depressed at the thought.

'Ellie — dear Ellie, I hope you won't take this the wrong way, but . . . '

The professor's words tailed off as he reached for his pipe, filled and lit it, then turned back to her with such an anxious expression on his face it filled her with foreboding.

'What is it, Professor?'

'My dear, I have something to say to you. Something very important and I want you to think about it very carefully before you give me your answer.'

As she listened to him, Ellie's heart didn't know whether to sink or swim. When he finished speaking and stood, waiting for some response, she sat there, turned to stone.

'Oh, Professor Graham!' she exclaimed in a hoarse whisper, her fingers flying to her mouth. 'Oh, dear!'

3

It was only two days after the funeral and Ellie was already making her way back to Felldene feeling a lot sadder than she had done on leaving it. Rather than dwell on the last few hours back in Newcastle, she concentrated on little, unimportant things. Young Archie pinching the black feather; her mother boasting proudly how she had buried her father-in-law with the Co-op's best ham; her dad locking himself in the lavatory because he couldn't bear to show his emotions and her, standing there in the yard in the rain, passing him cups of tea.

It was all so much better than recapitulating on what had happened with the Professor. When she finally knocked on the door of number seventeen her heart crash-landed and something gnawed away in the pit of her stomach as the reason for her being there rushed back into her head.

It was obvious to Ellie that she was the last person Polly Martin expected to find standing on her doorstep so soon after her departure.

'Ellie! Oh, dear Lord, what's wrong?'

'Oh, Mam!'

Ellie took one look at her mother and dissolved in great wet tears. She didn't like it, being the least emotional of the females in the family, but on this occasion she couldn't help herself. The tears just came.

'Come in, girl. And mind the step. I've just brick-bathed it.'

Ellie snuffled up a few ragged sobs and stepped into the small lobby. She dropped her bags and fumbled in her pocket for a handkerchief.

'I'm sorry, Mam!' Ellie's chest heaved but she managed to stem the salty flow immediately.

'Well, we'll see about that when I know what kind of trouble you've brought me, our Ellie.' Polly folded her arms beneath her small bosom and looked uneasy. 'You might as well add to the troubles of your family this day, for everybody else has.'

Ellie gave her mother a funny look, having no idea what the woman was talking about.

'What's happened, Mam?'

Polly jerked her chin towards the kitchen door. 'Go on in.'

When Ellie entered the kitchen she was met by numerous pairs of eyes turned mournfully in her direction. The whole family seemed to be there, including her three maiden aunts, Rose, Mabel and Priscilla. There wasn't a smiling face among them.

'Well, don't we all look happy!' she said, gulping back her own misery and trying to make light of whatever it was she was about to discover.

'Never mind them.' Polly pulled a chair up to the table and pointed to it. Ellie sat down obediently and her mother stood over her, her expression menacing. 'Well, then? What's brought you back home so fast and in such a state, my lass?'

'Professor Graham . . . ' was all she was able to get out before her mother pounced again.

'Dear God in Heaven, you haven't got yourself in the family way, have ye? Don't tell us ye've brought that shame down on me head, our Ellie.'

'Oh, woman, will ye stop badgerin' the lass.' Jack Martin put his newspaper down with an exasperated rattle and got to his feet.

'Aye, Mam.' Ben was now bending over Ellie, his big workman's hand gripping her shoulder supportively. 'Give her some breathin' space for goodness sake. Come on, Ellie, luv, let's hear what you have to say.'

There was a poignant silence, during which Ellie's moist eyes swept from one face to the next. She settled her gaze finally on her mother, licked her lips and swallowed hard.

'You're wrong,' she said with a rasping rawness to her voice. 'The professor has never laid a finger on me. He's much too nice and respectable a man for that.'

'Then what in God's name is it?' Polly demanded and everybody moved in closer, all ears to hear Ellie's news.

She waited, then took a deep breath. 'He asked me to marry him.'

If they had all been turned to stone they could not have looked any different, in Ellie's opinion. Eyes widened and mouths gaped open, but apart from that you could have heard a pin drop. It was her mother who recovered first. Polly blinked furiously, snapped shut her mouth and punched her fists into her hips. 'He what?'

'The old geezer asked her to marry him, Mam!' Archie squealed with laughter.

'Shut up, you!' Polly slapped out in his direction, but he dodged her hand and went to hide behind Ben. 'Now, miss. Did I hear right? Did I just hear you tell me that Professor Graham proposed to you?'

'That's right, Mam.' Ellie nodded miserably.

'The Lord moves in mysterious ways, that

he does!' Now it was Polly's turn to shed a small tear, which she brushed away with an impatient finger.

There were more murmurs of agreement from behind where Rose, Priscilla and Mabel were sitting in a huddle on the sofa like triplets joined at the hip.

'Well, of course, Polly,' Priscilla said sagely, 'your Ellie's not the type of girl to get herself into trouble with any man. You brought her up right.'

'Eeh, hinny!' Polly had her hands up to her face. 'Eeh, I've prayed for this, I have. And on this day of all days . . . '

There was a loud clearing of the throat from Ben. 'Mam, I should wait till you hear what our Ellie has to say. Something tells me she's not finished.'

'Don't be silly, lad. Of course she's finished. She's going to be Mrs Professor Graham. She's going to be rich. Our problems are solved. When does he want to have the wedding, Ellie?'

It was time for Ellie to take another deep breath. Thankfully, she was feeling more in control now, although there was still a sad brick the size of a mountain lying deep down inside her.

'I'm not . . . ' She didn't get any further.

'Of course, you can't be married in church,

him already being married before and all, but . . . '

'Mam . . . Mam! *I'm not getting married*,' Ellie reached out and touched her mother's arm.

'You're not what?'

'I turned him down, Mam.'

Ellie could hear air hissing through disbelieving lips.

'But you said it yourself . . . he's a nice man, a respectable man.'

'Yes.'

'You worship the ground he walks on!'

'No! Well, yes, but . . . '

'He's rich!'

'Yes . . . well, no . . . not exactly *rich*. Well off, but . . . '

'*And you said no when he proposed marriage?*'

'Yes, Mam, I did.'

'Ellie Martin, I didn't raise you to be a fool. You just get yourself right back to Newcastle and accept his offer. Do you hear me, girl? You get up off your backside and go tell him you really meant yes. Go on.'

As Polly was speaking, she had a hand hooked under Ellie's arm and was hauling her up on to her feet. Ellie felt a rush of anger towards her mother. She pulled away from her, roughly shaking off her hands as they tried to push her in the direction of the door.

'No, Mam! I won't go back there. I've given in my notice and that's an end to it. I'm very fond of the professor and I'll always be grateful to him, but I can't go on working there now. I thanked him very nicely and we agreed that it would be best if I found employment elsewhere.'

'You'll go back there, my girl, and tell him you've changed your mind,' Polly persisted, one finger stabbing the air just in front of Ellie's nose.

'I'll not do it, Mam. I won't marry *any* man until I find one that brings something . . . well, *magic* into my life.'

Mother and daughter locked eyes with one another. Polly's pointing finger finally sank down until it was pointing at the floor. 'Magic?'

'Yes, Mam. Magic. You know . . . love, romance. When I say yes to a man it's got to be because I feel something special — like rainbows and shooting stars and sunlight bouncing from rippling streams and . . . '

'Oh, our Ellie! What a load of rubbish you do talk. With all that fairytale nonsense going on inside your head you'll end up just like those three witches down the street . . . ' Her words tailed off abruptly as she realized the three she had been referring to were sitting only a few feet away, stabbing her with their eyes. 'You want too much, my girl, if you ask me.'

'Well, that's a turn-up for the books,' Ben said with a scathing laugh.

Polly sat down despairingly as if her legs could no longer support her weight. Her narrow shoulders slumped forward over hands that now lay limply in her lap.

'We're finished,' she whispered miserably; Jack, in a rare moment of compassion, came to pat his wife's shoulder.

'Don't worry, woman,' he said gruffly. 'We'll pull through somehow. It's early days yet. There may be a reprieve.'

Ellie looked at her two brothers for an explanation. 'What are they on about?'

Tommy turned away and went to lean on the mantelpiece, staring blankly into the cold grate.

'We've been laid off,' Ben said eventually.

'No!' Ellie cried, turning from one to the other. 'But why?'

'They're closing the pit down, lass,' her father supplied, his face tight with tension. 'We're not the only ones. Over a hundred and fifty men were paid off this morning.'

'How can they do that!' she exclaimed, not wanting to believe that she was hearing such

64

misfortune on top of her own disappointment.

'It's easy,' Ben gave a dry chuckle. 'What's the use of employing men when there's nowt for them to dig? The pit's run dry. There's no more coal left. We've been opening new seams left, right and centre, but the land's exhausted.'

'What about the other pits? There must be jobs going there.'

'Aye, there was, but by the time we got to them they were all snapped up.'

Polly's head came up, her small eyes stretched and staring. 'They'll throw us out of our home,' she announced as if the thought had just entered her mind in a blinding flash.

'Aye, well, you've got problems,' Priscilla said and all three aunts rose as one and headed for the street. 'We'll leave you be to sort them out between you.'

'You needn't worry,' Polly hissed after them. 'I'd rather go to the workhouse than move in with you.'

'Now, now, lass, it won't ever come to that,' Jack told her comfortingly, but his eyes said that he believed differently.

* * *

Ben and Ellie, always very close as brother and sister, sat up most of the night discussing the family situation. Ben had some shocking things to reveal to her. It seemed that their mother, with her pride and her impatience to have nice things, had sunk the family into debt up to their gills. And the fancy funeral she had given to her father-in-law had been, as Ben put it, the final nail in the coffin of their finances.

Polly was in debt to the tallyman as well as the ticket shop. There was no making do for her. When she wanted something, she had to have it and wouldn't be put off with anything less than quality merchandise. But she had gone too far. Recently, like a lot of other women of the time, she had been buying things on tick to pawn for ready cash to meet the rent and the household bills.

'I can't believe it of me mam.' Ellie shook her head in despair. 'She's so proud all the time and looks down her nose at women who do that type of thing.'

'Aye, well, it all came out last night when me dad asked her how much savings we had. Ye know how thrifty me dad is. He'd been giving her money to put on the side. It should have been a pretty good sum by now, but it was all gone.'

'Mam never could stand the thought of

being poor. Not after she spent the first years of her life in an orphanage. It's harder for her than most, you know, Ben.'

'Aye, I suppose ye're right, but I think if she was my wife I'd never find it in mesel' to forgive her.'

'We don't know what she went through, Ben, before she married me dad. Sometimes, I get the impression that something really bad happened to her. She won't ever talk about it, will she. But whatever it was, it soured her whole life.'

'Ye mean she *let* it sour her. I can't ever see anything souring you, luv!' Ben had reached out and stroked her cheek with remarkable gentleness for a rough man.

Ellie laughed softly and pushed his hand away. 'Aw, go on with you, our Ben! Anyway, I'm different from me mam.'

'Thank God for that!'

★ ★ ★

After breakfast the next morning, Ellie started clearing the dirty dishes away while Mary mopped the floor. For the first time in their lives, they saw their mother just sitting doing nothing, her mind in another world entirely.

It wasn't surprising, therefore, that they

should jump when she suddenly burst out of her silence and called the whole family around her.

'Mary, fetch me best coat and me new shoes,' she said, jumping to her feet. 'Ellie, hinny, can ye lend us a bit of money? A couple of pounds, if ye can spare it.'

'Two pounds!' It was Ben who objected, though Ellie simply took the money from her purse, which was full at the moment, the professor having paid her six months wages in lieu. 'But Mam, that's a hell of a lot of money.'

'Aye, lass,' Jack frowned, regarding his wife through half-closed eyes. 'What are you planning to do with our Ellie's money, eh?'

'It's none of your business, Jack Martin.' Polly grabbed the money and stuffed it in her purse. 'I'm going out and I don't know when I'll be back.'

'Where're you goin' Mam?' Archie asked.

'Never you mind. I've got a plan. I've been thinking about it all night and it's the only solution I can come up with so it had better work.'

She squeezed her feet into the smart but tight new shoes that she had worn for the funeral. She allowed Mary to help her into her coat and was jamming her hat squarely on to her head as she walked out of the house, with not another word to anybody.

'You never know what's going on in me mam's head.' Ellie sighed as the door closed.

'Is she coming back?' Archie asked and, ignoring his question, they all fell into an uncomfortable silence.

★　★　★

It was an odd coincidence that Polly had seen the name of the foundry in last night's *Evening Chronicle*. She wasn't much of a reader, but she had struggled through the long article, stumbling over words she didn't understand. By the time dawn was creeping through the curtains she knew what she had to do.

Polly took the train all the way to Durham. It was a long journey for a woman who hadn't moved outside her own small village for years. At Durham, she had to ask the way to the ironworks. There was a horse-drawn tram she could take nearly all the way. After that, because her feet were already throbbing in her shoes, she splurged out on a cab.

Long before she got to the works she was aware of the noise of machinery coming from the foundry and the air was thick with the dust and the fumes from the furnaces. But Polly was too uneasy to notice all this for long. At the main gates she asked where she could find Mr Rockwell.

The man in the office rubbed a weary hand around his face and looked at her as if she had asked to see God himself.

'He'll not see nobody without an arrangement,' he told her. 'You got an appointment, lady?'

'I will have when he hears me name,' Polly said, holding her head high and trying to look more important than she felt. 'You tell him that Polly — er — that Catherine Durham is here to see him.'

He scratched behind his ear, pulled on its grimy lobe and grinned through a mouthful of tombstone teeth that would have been better out and buried. 'Catherine Durham, is it? Is that Miss or Missus?'

'That's none of your business. Just you give him my name.'

'Aye, well, we'll see. You stay here, Miss or Missus Catherine Durham. Don't budge from that spot. Civilians and especially women are not allowed inside these gates.'

She seemed to wait for hours, but in reality it was closer to twenty minutes. Then she saw the same workman heading back her way, followed by a tall, broad-shouldered young man who could never have been mistaken for one of the workers, though he was wearing working clothes and was brushing dust from them as he walked towards her.

'Here she is, sir.' The man pointed before disappearing back into the gatehouse.

Polly's anxious eyes fell on the young man towering before her. He was staring at her speculatively. She stared back at him, wondering why she should find something familiar and disturbing in his handsome features and in his proud stance.

'I'm told you want to see me on some urgent matter. How can I help you?'

Polly shook her head vigorously, dislodging her hat. She had to grab at it to stop it from falling over her eyes.

'Oh, no! It wasn't you I wanted to see. I asked to see Mr Rockwell.'

'I am Mr Rockwell.'

'But you can't be!' Polly faltered as she saw his slow-dawning smile and the supercilious rise of his brows. Those piercing black eyes of his had the look of the Devil in them. She had only seen eyes like that once in her lifetime. The thought made her shudder.

'I can and I am,' he took a step back and, with his head to one side, he looked her up and down in a manner she found most disconcerting. 'I'm afraid there must be some mistake, Mrs Durham . . . it is *Mrs* Durham, isn't it? Anyway, I'm pretty certain that we have never met.'

'No, I'll give you that,' Polly admitted. 'You're definitely not Donald Rockwell.'

The smile turned into a grin, then a deep-throated laugh. 'No, by God, I'm not! I'm Adam Rockwell. Sir Donald is my father.'

'Oh!' She had forgotten the 'Sir' bit. That hadn't been attached to the name of Donald Rockwell when she had known him over twenty-five years ago.

And now she knew why she found this tall young man so familiar. He looked just like his father had looked all that time ago, though he was perhaps a little younger and fitter. And they *had* met before, though the high-spirited infant that this man then was could hardly be expected to remember her.

Polly swallowed back the dryness that gripped her throat in a strangulation hold. Her nerve was slipping and as a works hooter sounded close at hand it made her jump and gasp out loud. It seemed to add to the young man's enjoyment of the situation.

'In that case, I would like to see your father,' she said with all the imperiousness she could muster.

'My father doesn't see anybody.' Adam Rockwell had become serious again. 'I deal with all affairs . . . business and private, if it's to do with Rockwell Ironworks.'

'I assure you that I am one affair your father would want to handle personally.' Dear Lord, where was she getting all this eloquence from?

Adam Rockwell hesitated. His brows lowered as he regarded her with intense curiosity. 'What kind of business could you possibly have with my father?'

'Private business.'

There was another long hesitation, then he shrugged his broad shoulders and she saw rather than heard him sigh.

'Very well. I'll give him your name and . . . well, we shall see.'

'You can give him something else besides my name,' Polly said stiffly. 'You can tell him that he will be better off seeing me. Much better off.'

The corner of the young man's mouth twitched. He gave a short, sharp nod. 'I'll tell him,' he said and turned from her, striding away on long, muscular legs.

Your father, young man, Polly thought to herself as she watched him out of sight, never had your charm, but I bet you've got the same fire burning in your belly.

★   ★   ★

It was nine o'clock and Polly had been gone all day. Nobody had said much for hours, but Ellie could see that even her normally placid and non-committal father was agitated.

'Where's the silly woman got to?' Jack Martin had been pacing the floor since half past seven.

'I'm sure she's all right, Dad.' Ellie tried to sound reassuring, but she was beginning to doubt her own words.

'Here she is!' Mary announced suddenly, from her lonely vigil at the window in the front room.

Ben yanked the door open as Polly started to put her key in the lock. The whole family crowded behind him and almost got trampled on as he moved back to let his mother over the threshold.

'You've been a long time, Polly,' Jack said sulkily as she marched silently in and warmed her hands at the stove. 'It's not like you to desert yer family like this.'

'Who's talkin' about deserting?' Polly tossed the phrase carelessly over her shoulder.

She groaned and kicked off her shoes. 'Gawd, that's better. It's to be hoped I won't have to wear them again in a hurry.'

'So where've ye been, Mam?' Ben insisted, giving vent to the impatience they were all feeling.

'It doesn't matter,' she said slowly, a strange light in her eye. 'The fact is, we're leaving here the day after tomorrow. You have jobs to go to. It's all arranged.'

'Jobs? What sort of jobs, woman?' Jack looked nonplussed.

'Down on the banks of the River Wear and accommodation's thrown in.'

'The Wear! But that's miles away!' Ben shouted.

'Not to the people who live there,' Polly told him. 'As I say, there are jobs for you and the pay's good.'

'What pit's this, then Polly?' Jack demanded, his face creasing into a thousand worry lines.

'Not a pit,' Polly said, facing them at last. 'My family are finished working down the pit. You're going to be ironworkers. The Rockwell Ironworks is looking for men. It's all settled, so let's not waste time arguing about it.'

Ellie felt an uncomfortable flutter rise and fall in her stomach. 'Rockwell?' she whispered, her thoughts flying back to Sunday morning on the Quayside when a handsome young man by the name of Adam Rockwell had sketched her. The professor had said he was an iron master.

'Rockwell!' Jack exclaimed.

'Aye, Rockwell!'

'But Mam ... ' Ben blurted out after exchanging a quick glance with Tommy, 'I've heard tell that it's the hardest foundry in the country. The owners don't care about the workers as long as they get their quota of blood out of the stone they chuck into the furnaces.'

He started striding about the room. Ellie had never seen either of her brothers look so angry, nor her father so disturbed.

'I'll not go to work for that bastard!' Ben growled. 'I've heard about him. He's the worst of all the steel barons.'

Ellie stared at him. She didn't know why his words should upset her, but they did. The face of Adam Rockwell floated again before her eyes and she shuddered. She didn't want to know that he was connected in any way to the man they were talking about. And yet, there had been a hard — yes, a ruthless light in his penetrating eyes that had disturbed her more than his good looks.

'There's got to be something else,' she suggested, desperately.

'Well, hinny,' Polly said with a sigh, 'you could marry your professor. Though I doubt, now that I come to think of it, that he would want to support the whole family. Anyway, it would get you out of it.'

Ellie fixed her mother with a grim frown,

her blue eyes becoming glacial. 'We've already discussed that, Mam.'

'Aye,' Polly sighed. 'And more fool you, pet.'

★   ★   ★

Cynthia Rockwell was watching her husband curiously as she struggled to entertain their guests, wondering what had happened to put him so out of sorts. Sir Donald was drowning his thoughts in his fourth large goblet of burgundy wine. He had been in a foul mood all through dinner and there was hardly a soul around the table who hadn't noticed.

'What is wrong with your father, Adam?' Lady Rockwell found a brief opportunity to whisper in her stepson's ear between courses. 'He's acting very strangely. Did something untoward happen at the works today?'

Adam shrugged. 'Nothing more untoward than usual, Cynthia,' he told her with a small, artificial smile, then purposefully turned to the guest opposite and engaged the man in a conversation about greyhounds, which he obviously found more fascinating than the price of steel and the disputes among shareholders.

Cynthia had been more than fond of Donald in the days when she would visit his first wife, Jane, who was always of a delicate disposition. The master of the iron foundry had fascinated her to the point of indecency. To such an extent, in fact, that she had virtually thrown herself at him the moment he was out of mourning and became free to remarry.

She burned with shame every time she thought about it, for her passion had been short-lived. Because of her husband's cold lack of affection, Cynthia's interest soon passed from father to son. Now, despite her better judgement and ultra-respectable façade, it was her stepson Adam to whom she was drawn to the extent of heart-palpitating, sleepless nights.

The pity was that Adam, charming and courteous though he always was, appeared to harbour no thought for her beyond polite acceptance of her as his father's wife. She had, in effect, fallen between the Devil and his disciple.

At a convenient pause in her stepson's conversation with his companion, she took the opportunity to lay her fingers lightly on his arm to catch his attention once more.

'One of my committee ladies tells me that there was a strange woman at the works today. Patricia Beresford was visiting a family in South Street. You'll recall, Adam, that a man was killed last week by falling in the path of molten metal.'

Adam frowned and nodded. 'I remember the incident only too well, having not been more than a few yards from the man when it happened. Such a stupid accident. A moment's inattention as the flow surged through the channel. One minute he was standing there laughing. The next, he was a mass of screaming, melting flesh and blackened bones.'

'How horrible, but at least death must have been instantaneous?'

'Not instantaneous enough,' Adam said and drew pictures with the prongs of his fork in the white damask tablecloth. 'The poor devil suffered abominably. It was so damned unnecessary.'

'With seven children and a wife always needing the doctor,' Lady Rockwell informed him, 'there's barely enough insurance money to keep body and soul together.'

'I hope your association is taking care of that?' Adam regarded her with dark eyes.

'Well, of course, but we don't have limitless funds. I'm thinking of setting up some kind of system to teach these young wives and mothers how better to manage their affairs. What do you think, Adam?'

'I think it's an admirable idea, Cynthia.'

While he spoke, Adam whipped out a cheque book from his inside pocket and scribbled in it rapidly. 'Take this. It should help.'

She glanced at the amount on the cheque he handed her and gasped in astonishment. 'Oh, Adam! This is much too generous! I can't possibly . . .'

'What else do I have to spend it on? I trust you to put it to good use and I thank the Lord that I shall never be in the position to need the help of one of your little charity organizations.'

Lady Rockwell had followed on the tradition of many iron-foundry mistresses, in that she and her equally wealthy friends who were of charitable heart, ran a variety of enterprises, including social-work visits and advisory committees. It had become quite a passion with her and very fashionable with ladies of her social level, if they had the time to spare and the stamina to fulfil their duties.

Her stepdaughter, Grace, Adam's sister, was one of the leading figures in her entourage. Such a pity, Cynthia always thought, that the girl could not bring the same enthusiasm into her own private life. As Sir Donald was known to remark, his daughter was more cut out to be a nun and would most likely have taken vows, had she not been born into a Protestant family.

'Thank you, Adam. This will be a great help.' Her eyes wandered across the table to where her husband was sitting, morosely staring into space. 'So, you don't know who this woman was, then?'

Adam's brow creased. He looked decidedly uncomfortable about answering her question. The question, however, was not destined to be answered. At that precise moment, Dorothy Emmerson, pregnant with her first child, decided to throw a faint.

'Adam!' His father bellowed across the table. 'Kindly help Mr Emmerson remove his wife to a quieter place, would you. Then, ladies, perhaps you would withdraw so we menfolk can smoke in peace.'

There was a rush of ladies excusing themselves. The expectant father looked on helplessly as Adam picked up the prostrate young woman and took her through to the cooler, more relaxed atmosphere of the drawing-room, where he left her to the ministrations of the women already gathered there.

'Adam!' Sir Donald's voice rang out once more as he re-emerged into the great hall.

Adam had been thinking to excuse himself in order to wander alone with his thoughts through the orangery, since it was too late and too wet outside to contemplate a walk further afield.

'Yes, Father?' He hoped he had hidden his instinctive aversion to being summoned in his ageing parent's brusque and characteristic manner.

'A word in the library, if you please!'

Adam followed his father into the library. It was Adam's favourite room and where he preferred to be alone rather than with the family. He loved the ceiling-high bookshelves that covered the walls and spent many a pleasant hour there reading.

He loved the smell of the creaking old leather furniture, the lavender-scented beeswax polish that Mrs McKenzie, their housekeeper, buffed to a brilliant shine on the simple lines of the Georgian furniture.

The rest of the house was pleasant enough, but less manly, having been the choice of his mother, whose tastes went to rococo. Many of the more ornate pieces had been specially imported from Italy. It took a woman of refinement to appreciate them, Adam always thought. He was happier sticking with plainer, less frilly surroundings.

Sir Donald Rockwell closed the door behind him and went to stand in front of the Georgian fireplace, hands behind his broad back, legs spread wide.

'I had a visit today, Adam, as you know,' he

started hesitantly and his penetrating gaze wavered when Adam's eyebrows twitched in response to his words. 'From a woman of a certain class.'

'Catherine Durham,' Adam supplied.

His father looked suitably ruffled; his heavy jowls quivered and grew pink as he clenched his teeth and breathed profoundly through his aquiline nose. His florid complexion became more florid as he pondered on the memory of the visit. He plainly didn't want to say the woman's name.

'Hm — yes. There's no need for your stepmother to know about the visit. It is of no concern of hers, having to do with something that happened a long time ago.'

Adam perched on the corner of the huge leather-topped desk in the centre of the room, one long leg swinging slowly. He looked at his father speculatively.

'Cynthia already knows about Mrs Durham's visit,' he said. He saw his father stiffen visibly.

'You told her!'

'No. She heard it through one of her committee ladies.'

'Damn those infernal females! They have their noses in everywhere!'

'She knows nothing other than that the lady visited the works.'

'And that's all she ever will know, but I'm going to ask you to do something and keep it discreet.'

'And what is this great secret, Father?' Adam had long since grown out of being afraid of his father. He respected him for what he was, a successful iron master and a brilliant businessman, albeit ruthless. But he no longer stood to attention and bowed to the man's self-acclaimed superiority.

He had served long, arduous years beneath the eagle eye and the iron rod of Sir Donald. He had started at the bottom as a young boy. There wasn't a job in the foundry he hadn't tackled. He knew them all and knew what it took in terms of human strength and stamina to make them work efficiently.

Sir Donald had forced him to work in the foundry in the first instance as some sort of punishment for daring to be gentle and artistic. The man had despised the genes his son had inherited from his mother and thought they had bred a creature that was less than manly. Adam had taken his medicine courageously, hiding his fears and his weaknesses beneath a determination to prove his father wrong.

And he had done it. With the result that there was not a man in the foundry who did not respect Adam Rockwell, for he would

84

never order any man to do anything he had not already done himself.

'No need for you to know the details, Adam, but when the Martin men show up here at the signing on, I want to assign them myself.'

'You don't normally involve yourself in this way. That's something that's usually left to Whitfield or me. What's so special about the Martins?'

'I don't care to discuss it with you. Don't forget that I am still in charge at Rockwell. I gave you forty per cent of the business and you'll get the remaining sixty per cent when I die. Until then, I still expect you to adhere to my explicit instructions. If not ... ' Sir Donald shrugged and inspected his fingernails, which bore no trace of foundry grime and were neatly manicured.

Adam frowned. 'What about accommodation?'

'Whitfield has it all in hand.'

There was no love lost between Adam and the under-manager. As Adam had discovered on more than one occasion, Whitfield was not a man who could be trusted. He was hard on the men and disliked by them because he ran to Sir Donald at every opportunity, which had gained him the reputation of being a spy.

'There aren't any houses vacant at the moment.'

'There's a house at Northend that was occupied by a young stower.'

'If it's the house I'm thinking of, it's hardly fit for human habitation.' Adam's brow creased even more deeply. 'Besides, it's still occupied. I visited the widow of the workman the day he was killed about ten days ago. She's hardly more than an adolescent and she's pregnant with her first child. They hadn't been married more than a few months. She told me she had nowhere to go.'

'Then she lied, but I'll hear no more of it. You'll do as I say, Adam. That's an order. If you value your inheritance, don't interfere.'

Adam's jaw set like the iron they manufactured, but he didn't intend to go against his father and risk losing his inheritance over what seemed a trivial matter. He had put blood, sweat and a great deal more into securing it. Nothing was going to make him give it up now.

4

The hoofs of the carter's horse kicked up great clouds of dust that enveloped the family sitting wearily on the back of the cart, which bounced and joggled them down the rutted road between Durham and Rockwell. It was a June afternoon, warmer than most, and they were hot and sticky after their travels with bag and baggage, of which there was precious little, for what they couldn't sell or give away, they had had to leave behind.

None of them knew just what it was her mother had done to find work for them. Whatever it was, she wouldn't be drawn, which made it all the more mysterious.

'Hey, Mam,' Ben said, busily swatting flies. 'It's a hell of a long way to go if there's no job at the end of the day.'

'There's a job, I'm telling you,' Polly said, tight-lipped as ever, modestly pulling down her skirt as far as it would go to her thin ankles.

'Are you sure it's the right Rockwell, though?' Tommy asked. 'I mean, the one in the papers — Sir something-or-other?'

'There's only one, Tommy.' His brother

nodded. 'Hard bugger, by all accounts. It seems he owns the whole ruddy river in these parts and everything that comes up and down it or across it.'

Polly sighed. 'Hard bugger or not, he'll give you lot jobs or my name's not Catherine Durham. And don't you use language like that, our Ben!'

'You're name's not Catherine Durham.' Jack suddenly woke up to the banter. 'It's Polly Martin and don't you forget it, woman.'

'That's as may be, but I used to be Catherine Durham in the old days. Catherine Polly Durham, that's me . . . ' She launched herself into the short speech her family had heard many a time over, with every one of them mouthing the words with her: ' . . . a foundling on the steps of Durham Cathedral, which is how I got my name. I never knew me real parents, but I've done all right for meself and I'll see that me family do better, one way or another . . . '

The three boys and the two girls laughed and nudged one another, and even Jack Martin grinned. It lightened the situation considerably.

★ ★ ★

88

'What's that?' Archie stumbled back out of the bushes where he had been relieving his full bladder.

The others, all grateful for a moment's rest while the carter fed and watered his horses, looked up, straining their ears to listen to the distant thrumming that Archie had brought to their attention.

'It's weird,' Ellie remarked. 'I can even feel it vibrating through the soles of my feet.'

'Aye, what is it, man?' Ben collared the carter as the man hung bags of oats around his horses' heads. 'Can ye hear it? That noise. A sort of thumping, like.'

The carter scratched his nose, then swept off his cap and rubbed the back of his head. 'That's Rockwell.'

The Martin family exchanged puzzled looks.

'But it's miles away yet,' Tommy exclaimed.

The carter grinned. 'See that hill ower yonder?' He pointed with a crooked finger. 'If you climb that you can see the place from there. It's lying three miles due west of us in the valley.'

Archie set off at a gallop, followed by Ben and Tommy. At first, the girls hesitated, then Ellie nudged her sister and started out after them. Mary trailed reluctantly behind. Polly and Jack stayed with the cart. They had already lost most of their belongings, all Polly's beautiful furniture and carpets and china. They didn't fancy now losing the few personal items they were left with.

'God luv us!' Ben breathed out.

'What can you see, Ben?' Ellie was breathless from the climb, but glad to get her limbs moving after such a long time sitting in the back of the cart.

'Come and look at this, Ellie!' Tommy shouted, more animated than she had ever seen him.

Ben held out his hand to her and pulled her up the last few feet that rose steeply on to a grassy knoll. She followed the sweep of his broad arm and gasped in astonishment at the sight that unfolded itself on the landscape.

Down in the valley, they could see a town spread out like the legs of a spider. In the centre there were huge factory buildings and sheds and tall chimneys of a sort Ellie had never seen before. The chimneys belched out smoke that formed itself into a mushrooming pall of black and brown and grey over the town, so that the buildings appeared to be coming out of a mist.

As she looked, the wind changed and blew towards them. She wrinkled her nose. Ben sneezed and Tommy, because of his weak chest, coughed raucously as he breathed in sulphurous fumes.

'Argh! That's horrible,' Mary said, pulling a face and coughing too. 'What is it?'

'I suppose,' Ben said, 'that it's the foundry. They say it gives off a stink that's hard to live with.'

Ellie licked her lips and fancied she could taste the iron on her tongue. The air was full of dust and it burned her eyes enough to make them water.

I don't think I'll ever get used to this, she thought to herself, but to the others she said: 'Well, I suppose we'll have to get used to it, won't we?'

'Aye,' Ben nodded. 'Until something better comes along.'

There was a call from down below. The carter was waving his cap at them, indicating that it was time to get on and finish the journey.

★   ★   ★

The noise from the foundry steadily increased as they neared the town. First, they passed by long, straggling building sites where bands of Irish labourers called to each other as they cemented bricks and tiled roofs with slate in long, straight rows.

The houses they were constructing were

close together, the land in between the rows rough and rutted with dried mud, though in some places they were already laying cobbles and slate slabs. It was almost as noisy at the building sites as it was in the centre of the town where the foundry itself formed the throbbing heart of the community.

'I've never seen anything like it in me life!' Jack Martin gasped, shaking his head. 'Ye nivvor mentioned that it was like this, woman.'

Polly afforded him a look of practised disdain. 'If I'd told ye what it was like, would ye's have come?' she asked. 'Any one of ye?'

Her question was met by silence. She turned her head from their stupefied gazes and jumped down unaided from the cart, though her first steps were stiff and unsteady.

'Where're ye goin' Mam?' Archie shouted after her, his fair eyebrows shooting up into his hairline.

'Well, we can't spend the night on this here cart, now, can we? We've got to go and find our living-quarters. Pay the man, Ellie. I'll see ye right the morrow.'

'And where will ye find enough money the morrow to see our Ellie right, Mam?' Ben demanded with a touch of irony in his voice.

Polly adjusted her stance and seemed to shake out the stiffness in her shoulders. 'Ellie knows I'll pay her back when I can,' she said. 'But right now, any money that belongs to any one Martin belongs to the Martin family. We're all in this together. We either stand together or we fall apart. What's it to be?'

'I'll pay the carter gladly, Mam.' Ellie gave her mother a reassuring hug, but the woman drew away from her. She didn't like closeness.

Archie was digging around in his pockets, unearthing bits of string, a chewed crayon, a few biscuit crumbs and, finally, some coins. 'Here, our Ellie. Take this. It's me savings. It's only twopence three-farthings, but it's all I've got.'

Ellie's smile wavered as she shook her head and ran her fingers affectionately through his shock of hair. 'Go on, love, put it back in your pocket. Keep it for a real emergency, eh?'

They were standing in the middle of the dusty road just outside the foundry gates. The machinery that they couldn't see continued to throb deafeningly and incessantly. The vibrations seemed to penetrate their bodies, which was even more daunting.

'I think I'm going to be sick,' Mary announced, her hand covering her mouth as her slightly off-set eyes looked wildly about her.

'Ye'll not be making a fool of yourself here, my lass,' Polly hissed at her, pushing her youngest daughter to one side where there was a convenient privet bush. 'Go behind there and be quick about it.'

Ellie went with her sister. Poor Mary had never had a strong stomach. She always threw up when she was nervous.

'Ben,' Polly said, 'there's the foreman's hut over there. You go and tell him that we've arrived and we need to know where to go.'

The man that Ben came back with looked them over with curiosity and distaste. He was a sandy-haired fellow with pale-blue eyes that had a touch of ice in them. His shirtsleeves were rolled up above the elbow showing a pair of muscular arms that were covered in thick downy hair. It matched the tuft escaping from his open shirtfront bulging with a chest that looked overstuffed.

'I'm Mr Whitfield,' he said, and stood, legs and arms akimbo, eyeing them up and down. He didn't seem to like what he saw, until he came to Ellie, then his gaze lingered a little too long. 'You're the Martin family, the lad tells me.'

'Aye, we are,' Polly stepped in front of Ellie, elbowing the girl out of the way. 'And we're expected.'

The foreman nodded briefly. 'Aye, I know about ye's,' he said gruffly, his watery eyes sneaking another look at Ellie, who refastened the top button of her dress with hasty precision.

'Well, then?'

He sighed, looked about him and found a passing workman. 'Yo! Styles! Take these people to the ferry, will ye.'

The man called Styles, who had a livid scar down the side of one cheek, looked sullen. 'I've just come off me shift, boss.'

'That's ideal, then, isn't it?' the foreman chided. 'Now take the Martins here to the ferry, like I told ye.'

The man stuck his hands into his trouser-pockets, nodded, then studied the ground at his feet until his charges were ready to depart.

'Here.' Whitfield handed Ben a slip of grubby, crumpled paper. 'That's the address. It's at the far side. You'll have to ask directions when you get across the river.'

'What about the signing on?' Jack wanted to know and the man glared at him as he hitched up his trousers beneath an overhang of belly.

'Report at nine o'clock sharp tomorrow morning. The big chief hisself will see to ye, so no shenanigans. Ye'll show him respect and if he asks ye to kiss his ruddy arse, ye'll do it and make no bones about it.'

The man called Styles left them sitting

waiting for the ferry. They weren't alone. It was shift-changeover time and a lot of the people waiting with them were foundry men.

Ellie thought she had never seen such a sorry-looking bunch of individuals in all her life. They were dirty, covered in stone dust, iron dust and sweat. Unlike the miners, they had little conversation, what remaining strength they had being saved for the journey home.

So this was what her mother had brought them to. Ellie closed her eyes and heaved a sigh. It didn't seem quite so exciting now. Maybe they would all feel better for seeing the cottage they had been promised. And even if they did have to cross the river to get to the works and the town, they would be living a healthy step further away from the dust and the noise.

When the ferry arrived, the crowd surged forward, pushing and shoving. The Martins were lucky. After an initial hesitation, conscious that they were strangers, they managed to squeeze on before the ferryman declared the boat to be full.

In the great crush on board, Ellie and Mary somehow got separated from the others. There was a great deal of trampling of feet and one or two surreptitious glances. At one point, Mary stiffened with a little gasp.

'Eeh, Ellie! Somebody just pinched me bottom!'

'Well, there are three things you could do, Mary,' Ellie told her. 'You could thank him gratefully, slap his face, or just ignore it.'

Mary immediately sagged against her sister and cried quietly into her handkerchief for the rest of the way.

As the ferry docked and men started jumping out on to the rickety old jetty, Ellie gave Mary a little shove to set her in motion.

'Come on, Mary. You'll be all right once we get home, love. Look, there's our Ben and Tommy. They're already on the bank and waiting for us.'

'Where's me mam and dad — and Archie?' Mary sounded panicky as her eyes swivelled left and right, looking for the rest of the family.

At first Ellie couldn't find them, then she spotted them standing beneath a tree, her mother doing her best to look as if she wasn't there, her father looking tired and resigned. Archie was sprawled on the ground at their feet.

Once more reunited, they again formed a group and stood a little nonplussed, for there were no houses to be seen. Undaunted, they started to follow the straggle of workers as they disappeared through a line of trees and scrub.

'Hey, fella!' Ben grabbed a skinny, wrinkled man with a thatch of white hair grey with dust. 'We're new here. Any idea where we can find Northend?'

'We're all from there, son,' the man squinted up at Ben and then turned his weary gaze on the rest of the Martins. 'What part is it you're looking for?'

'Dunno, really,' Ben said, shrugging, and looking at his mother for assistance.

'We're told there's a house for us,' Polly spoke up. 'My men have come to work at the foundry.'

The man's eyebrows shot up and his head tilted. Then he nodded slowly. 'Aye, I think I know what house you mean, missus. Just follow the lane between the houses when you get past these trees. It's the last one along on the left.'

His expression had become blank. He stared at them some more, then shook his head, turned and wandered off.

'They're not very friendly in these parts are they?' Tommy remarked as they set out to follow him.

Ben shook his head and stared at his boots as he walked. 'I get the impression we're not exactly welcome around here for some reason.'

'It's probably because we come from north of the Wear,' Ellie suggested, but Ben went on shaking his head in a negative fashion.

'Nah! It's more than that.'

'Come on.' Polly gave him a push from behind and linked her arm through Ellie's, which proved how tired she was, but at least she wasn't wearing those crippling new shoes of hers. 'Let's find that house of ours and get the kettle on.'

The run of straggling houses they came to weren't much better than tumbledown shacks. The last house was the worst of all. Indeed, it looked in such desperate need of repairs they stood and gaped at it open-mouthed until a crash and a cry and shouting voices could be heard coming from inside.

'What the bloomin' Moses ... ' Ben exclaimed, taking a step or two back from the front doorstep.

'It can't be the right house,' Ellie said. 'We've made a mistake. Maybe it's the last house on the right or ... '

As she spoke, the door was pulled open so vigorously it came dislodged and hung precariously on one rusty hinge. A young woman, so thin she looked as if she might snap, shot out and rebounded from Ben's chest. He gave an astonished gasp as the breath was knocked out of him, but was able to catch the girl and save her from falling headlong into the mud and the gravel at their feet.

'Ye've been ordered to get out!' The voice of the man who followed her was rasping, his expression mean. He stopped short in his tracks and inspected the small group of people standing there in some surprise. 'What do you lot want then?'

'We're the Martins,' Polly held on to Ben's arm as she sensed his rising anger. 'We were told to come to the last house on the left at Northend.'

'Aye, well this is it.' He jerked a thick, calloused thumb over his shoulder and quickly refastened a broad leather belt with a big, shiny buckle around his waist.

Ben felt the girl in his arms tremble like a frightened bird. His eyes followed the man's every move and a low rumble of mounting rage sounded in his throat. He put the girl gently to one side, but kept a hand on her frail shoulder to stop her from swaying.

'Did he beat you with that thing?' he asked quickly, jabbing a thumb at the belt.

The girl shook her head and looked up at him with dark pleading eyes that seemed too big for her tiny face.

'No! No, please ... please don't get yourself in trouble over me!' she pleaded. 'He didn't touch me, honest!'

Ben growled some more as he saw the fear in her face and the growing red weals on her bare upper arms. Then his eyes slipped lower down to the small swollen belly that told him she was probably pregnant.

'The bastard!' he ground out, his head swivelling in the direction of the girl's aggressor.

'Ben ... hold on. Be careful!' Ellie warned at his elbow. 'We don't know what this is all about.'

'I know what it's about all right.' Ben hissed like a bomb with a short fuse, which was just about what he was when he saw cruelty being doled out, either to man or beast.

The scuffle that ensued was over almost before it began. The man was no match for Ben's bearlike strength and was floored with a neat sledgehammer blow to the jaw. As the fellow tried to rise, crawling on all fours, desperate to get away from this human thrashing-machine, Ben lashed out with his foot. The man sprawled his length in the mud and chewed gravel.

'That's enough, Ben!' Polly admonished sharply. 'It's not our business.'

The rescued girl herself was pulling frantically at Ben's arm and at last he turned away from the man, who half-crawled, half-ran away down the street, issuing sobbing threats about retribution.

'Are you all right, pet?' Ben asked the girl, and the great angry bear was instantly gone, turned into an unbelievable gentleness. 'Did he hurt you? What about the bairn?'

The girl was nodding and shaking her head rapidly, trying to force some words out, though finding it difficult through the emotion that gripped her throat.

'Please . . . ' was all she could say at first, then after a few gulps of air, she tried again. 'Please . . . I'm sorry about all this.'

'Just tell us what happened,' Ben prompted. 'Why was he trying to beat you?'

She looked at the other of the people gathered around her, then burst into tears. Ellie put an arm about her and held her close for a minute or two, until she had recovered.

'This was my home,' the girl said, snuffling into a handkerchief provided by Polly. 'W-we lived here nearly two years, ever since Joe was taken on at the foundry. Joe's . . . Joe *was* my husband. He was killed . . . ' She gulped back a packet of sobs and had difficulty going on. 'He didn't have much of a wage. He was only twenty-two . . . Anyway, there was little enough insurance — just enough to bury him — and he never earned enough for us to save. They came yesterday and ordered me to get out. Said the house was needed for a working family . . . Oh, I suppose that must be you?'

'Aye, lass,' Ben gently stroked her head and pushed a strand of tear-damp hair back behind her ear. 'I'm afraid so.'

'They said I had to go and live with my family, but . . . I can't . . . I just can't . . . '

'What family?' Ellie asked, her heart going out to the girl who seemed too young and fragile to be a widow and an expectant mother. 'Your parents, do you mean?'

'No. My parents are both dead. My stepfather — he married again as soon as my mother died. I was still very young . . . He used to beat us.'

'That fella I just sent packing — who was he?' Ben asked.

'My stepfather.'

'Well, that's set. You're not goin' back wi' him, lass.'

'I've got no choice . . . ' The young woman looked around her forlornly. 'And with a bairn on the way . . . ' She shrugged her shoulders and heaved a sigh.

Ben's brows shot up and he fixed his mother with a fierce glare. Polly looked back at him, her face a barren landscape, void of all feeling. And, as usual, Jack was saying nothing and pretending not to be a part of it.

'She can't go to that ugly bugger,' Ben said. 'How big's this house, then? It looks no better than a pigsty, but it's a roof and four walls.'

'It's not big enough to take a family of four let alone all of us,' Ellie whispered to him, but he shook his head and chose to ignore her.

'Mam, we can't see this lass out on the street just so we can have a roof over our heads. It's not proper. It's not right.'

'Is there anything right and proper in this world, our Ben,' Polly muttered half to herself. 'Well, come on, the lot of ye. I'm dying on me feet and I daresay there's at least a stove inside this godforsaken house.' Then she turned to the girl, fixing her with dead eyes. 'What's yer name, lass?'

'Margaret . . . Margaret Hill.'

'Well, Margaret Hill, I don't suppose one more will make all that much difference in this shoebox, but if ye stay ye'll be expected to do yer share of the housework, mind.'

'Thanks, Mam.' Ben nodded and the girl turned to him and burst out into a fresh explosion of weeping as he held her clutched protectively to his chest.

Ellie looked on, smiling. She had often wondered what it would take to get her big brother to notice the opposite sex. So, she thought, this is what it takes.

* * *

Sir Donald Rockwell was not the kind of man who was known to suffer from 'nerves'. In fact, it was said that he was so cold to the core that he had no feelings whatsoever. But when the Friday of the signing-on dawned, he had spent most of the night before tossing and turning.

His mind refused to admit that this unaccustomed insomnia was anything to do with that damned Durham woman and her family, but it was to her his thoughts kept returning. She hadn't even been a pretty little thing to make his male hormones stir. Not like the other girls he'd had in his employ over the years. Catherine was different, however, and maybe that was what had attracted him. She had been so proud and haughty and when she looked at him with those pale eyes of hers, he felt challenged, felt the need to knock the contempt out of her.

He had felt that same challenge when she'd come to the foundry a few days ago, threatening him with blackmail and demanding work for her men. His first instinct had been to stamp on her as he would a cockroach. But he found he couldn't do it. He couldn't risk being exposed and this woman, he felt, more than any of the others, had the ability to hurt him.

When she had presented herself to him out of the blue like that after a quarter of a century, he had not recognized her. Recognition had crept in slowly as she talked. He had been shocked to find what the ravages of time and a life of near hardship had done to little Catherine Durham, the orphan lass who had warmed his bed so admirably when he needed to satisfy the sexual urges that his first wife found so totally abhorrent.

She hadn't been the only one to be taken, not by any means. There had been others. Girls from all walks of life, though he preferred to keep his extramarital pursuits close to home. In that way, when the girls presented problems of any kind they were more easily dealt with.

It was a long time since he'd had any woman. Cynthia had satisfied him for a few years, but as he grew older and was not such a well man, he satisfied himself with the occasional flirtation and fumble below stairs, depending on his mood and the state of his health.

Catherine Durham, by God! Such a scared little mouse of a girl she was in those days, despite her display of arrogance that irritated him so much. She had only once refused an order from him. It was, he remembered, the day of the Durham Miners' Gala. The miners gathered together and political speeches were made, and marching, music and dancing were the order of the day and everybody brought their families to enjoy games and a picnic.

A few of the ironworkers had planned to join them on their day off, since a good many of them had been miners themselves before turning to iron rather than coal. On that day, Mr Donald Rockwell, as he was then, was an invited speaker among the local councillors and some important Members of Parliament.

'Mr Rockwell, I have to talk to you.' The tiny, melancholic face of Catherine Durham swam into his memory. 'You've planted a baby in me, Mr Rockwell. I'm four months gone.'

'So what do you want me to do, you stupid girl?' The news had cut the legs out from under him, but he had successfully carried off an air of unconcern. 'I didn't ask you to get pregnant.'

'No, sir, but I am and I want to know what you propose to do about it.'

He had glared at her hatefully, then had scribbled an address on a scrap of paper. He slipped it to her folded in a five-pound note. More money than she had seen at any one time in her life.

'Go to this address. They'll see to it for you.'

'Get rid of it, do you mean, sir?' Her face never changed, but her eyes grew small and cold and menacing.

'Well, what else would you do?'

She looked at him, looked at the paper and the money he held out to her. She reached out, pocketed the money and screwed the paper up into a ball before throwing it in his face.

'I'll keep the money for it's little enough to help me raise your bairn,' she said evenly.

She had then spun on her heel and marched out of the house. However, later that day, in the throng at the Gala, he caught sight of her making the acquaintance of a shy-looking individual among the miners.

'Well, good riddance,' he had thought, wiping all memory of the incident from his mind.

He had only seen her once more, quite by chance, a year or two later and then never again. Until this week, when Catherine Durham came back into his life and informed him that he had a bastard son and threatened all kinds of trouble for him if he did not fork out jobs and accommodation for her family. Jobs, indeed. She didn't even have the astuteness to demand money!

Any other man might not have risen to the bait, but Sir Donald could not afford to lose the fortune his present wife would one day soon inherit from her father. He had no wish to alienate Cynthia by having a piece of his sordid past laid before her and broadcast to all and sundry.

And there was another thing. He was curious to know what kind of son he had spawned with the little kitchen-maid.

★ ★ ★

'Have you assembled the men, Whitfield?' Sir Donald was already speaking to his under-manager as he alighted from his private cab.

Whitfield nodded and touched a finger to his peaked cap. 'Yes, sir. They're waiting inside.'

'What do they look like? Are there many of them?'

'About fifty. They're a motley-looking bunch if ever I saw one.'

'Did you take their details as I instructed you?'

'Aye, sir. Here they are.' Whitfield passed

over some sheets of foolscap paper on which he had hastily scribbled the name, age and experience of each man.

'Right! Let's get on with it. Adam?' He turned to his son who was following a few paces behind. 'As I told you, you leave this one to me.'

Sir Donald, his eyes skimming the list of names in his hand, sailed into the signing-on shed, looking neither to the right nor to the left of him where there was gathered a group of men of varying ages.

He seated himself behind a large desk, taking the only chair in the place. Adam took up position behind his left shoulder and studied the crowd of expectant faces. There was a sudden lull in the rumbling conversation. All attention was riveted on the big iron-boss, whose reputation was legend. He took a long time to inspect them, his astute gaze passing along the lines, searching out the one man he hoped to recognize among the rabble.

The silence was punctuated by the odd cough, a shuffling of impatient feet. At last, Sir Donald spoke.

'Men, the jobs we have vacant are for young men, strong men, men of good constitution. First of all, we're looking for experienced workers. Step forward those of you under the age of forty who have had previous experience working in an iron-foundry.'

About twenty men advanced into the centre of the shed and stood stiffly to attention before the iron master. Sir Donald checked their details. He then proceeded to dole out jobs. The men on the receiving end, on hearing their name called and what position they were to hold, immediately doffed their caps and bobbed their heads in gratitude for their good luck.

Sir Donald passed them over to Whitfield to be registered and receive relevant details pertaining to insurance, sick clubs, savings schemes and accommodation, though the last would still not be ready for some weeks. The men would simply have to make do with tents erected within the walls of the foundry itself.

'Now the non-skilled among you . . . ' At that moment Sir Donald's eyes picked out the tall, broad-shouldered young man standing somewhat apart from the others. Something fluttered inside his chest and he knew instantly he was looking for the first time at the son he had not known existed until a few days ago. 'You, lad! The tall fellow with the thatch of rusty hair.'

There was a titter of laughter as everyone turned to look at Ben, for in the suffused light

111

that was coming through the shed window his hair indeed took on the shade of rusted iron.

'Me, sir?' Ben pointed a finger at his own chest and looked uneasily from side to side. There was something about this Sir Donald Rockwell he didn't like. He didn't know what it was, but it was curdling in his gut.

'Yes, you, lad! Come forward. You look like a strong fellow. Think you'll do all right as an ironworker, eh?'

'Try me, sir!' Ben said with a proud upward tilt of his square chin.

'And me too.' Tommy pushed forward, willing his weak chest to behave, at least until the signing-on was done. 'I'm his brother. Name's Tommy Martin, sir. Tommy and Ben . . . er . . . beggin' yer pardon, sir . . . Thomas and Benjamin Martin is our rightful names.'

There were some laughing jeers from the remaining men.

'Take the big fellow, Father.' Adam bent low and whispered in Sir Donald's ear. 'I'm sure we could use him. But the other one doesn't look too strong.'

'Let me decide what's to be done here!' Sir Donald ground out through clenched teeth. 'Come forward you two. Right. Martin, Benjamin, aged twenty-five, nine years at the coal face. Well, now you're a pig-carrier in the stock yard.'

Ben's forehead creased and his eyes narrowed. 'I didn't know you dealt in animals, sir,' he said carefully, not quite sure what his new job was exactly. 'Where do I have to carry these pigs? Is there a farm or summat?'

There was an explosion of laughter. Sir Donald cringed inwardly that such a son of his should be so ignorant. Pig-ignorant, he thought. Oh, dear God!

'Be quiet, you lot!' He rose to his feet stiffly and glanced fleetingly at Adam, who was looking pensive and suspicious. 'So, Martin, we now know that you have a sense of the ridiculous as well as muscle. No doubt you are perfectly aware that I was speaking of pig-iron.'

'Ah . . . er . . . Just testing, sir!' Ben pulled out a bit of humour to cover his embarrassment.

'Right. You'll join a gang of stevedores on Monday morning down at the stockyard. All right men. That's all for today.'

'What about me, sir?' Tommy persisted, pushing himself forward and ignoring the boos and hisses he received from better and fitter men who had been passed over. 'And there's me dad, too. He's a good worker. You'll not regret taking on the Martin men . . . sir.'

Sir Donald hesitated. The Durham woman had insisted he give jobs to all her men. She was crazy if she thought this weakling son of hers could ever be a foundry-worker.

'There's always room in the sand pits,' Adam said quickly. 'It's not too strenuous as long as he can stand the heat from the molten metal.'

Still Sir Donald hesitated, but again Catherine Durham's mean little voice rang in his ears.

'Oh, very well . . . but there's no place for the father. About that I am adamant. Sign the two of them up Mr Whitfield.'

'Right. That's it, everybody.' Whitfield moved in and took charge. 'There'll be another signing-on next month. You two, over here.'

He gave them their official employment papers and turned to follow Sir Donald out of the shed.

'When do we start?' Ben shouted after him, but it was Adam who replied.

The iron master's son came and stood next to the man who was responsible for throwing the invincible Sir Donald Rockwell into turmoil. He wanted to get a better look at him.

'Most of the workers do an eight-hour shift,' he said, 'but the stevedores don't work to the shift system. They work till the job's done, loading the pig-iron. Report at five o'clock tomorrow morning. Your brother can come at the same time. I'll be here so you can report to me, then I'll hand you over to your foremen.'

'Aye, right ye are, mister . . . ?'

'Rockwell . . . Adam Rockwell.'

'Oh!'

The two men stared at one another and something strange passed between them. Adam was the taller by barely an inch, but Ben was bulkier in build. One was as dark as the other was fair, but the faces were so alike it was uncanny.

5

'Well?'

The expression on Polly's face was a broad mixture of pride, trepidation and expectation.

'We were taken on, Mam, like you said,' Tommy told her. 'I'm going to be working in the sandpits, tamping down the channels for the hot metal to run into. It doesn't sound very difficult and they're going to pay me fifteen shillings a week.'

'It's not a fortune,' Polly said slowly, chewing on every syllable. 'Couldn't they come up with anything better?'

'All the best jobs were given to experienced men,' Ben said. He sat down heavily at the newly scrubbed kitchen table and smiled at Margaret when she put a cup of tea in front of him. 'You're looking bonnie th' day, Margaret. You must be feelin' better, eh?'

The girl was as quiet as a mouse. Ben wondered if it might be because she was afraid if she made herself noticed it might prejudice her position. It must have been hard to have to give up her home like that to a family of strangers.

There was certainly no privacy. Not for any

of them. Three bedrooms and eight people made that pretty nigh impossible. Ben, Tommy and young Archie occupied the biggest bedroom, Ellie and Mary shared, while Margaret was tucked away in the tiny boxroom that was no bigger than a cupboard. Polly and Jack slept downstairs in the kitchen where there was a pull-down double bed disguised as a cupboard during the daytime.

Every floorboard and door in the house creaked and groaned. And the walls were so thin they could converse through them without raising their voices. And when they weren't talking, they could lie and listen to each other breathing and snoring and turning over fitfully in their sleep.

At the moment, they were obliged to put up with the old furniture and bedding that was already in the house and had been used by more than one set of occupants, according to Margaret. The mattresses were worn and stained and alive with lice, despite the good beating they had been given. Archie had come up in an itchy red rash, which he was going around proudly showing off to everybody he met, much to the horrified humiliation of his mother. They were all surreptitiously scratching like dogs with fleas.

'I'll get something from the chemist's just as soon as I can get into the town,' Polly had promised and Ellie handed over two florins.

'What about you, Ben?' Ellie asked. 'What will you be doing?'

Tommy started to laugh and Ben gave him a look, kicking out at his brother's shin under the table.

'Well, what is it, then?' Polly demanded, looking furious as usual. 'I take it you're not going to be the court jester, so what is it you're going to do that makes our Tommy laugh like a drain?'

'He's goin' to lift pigs,' Tommy spluttered out the words, then clamped both hands over his face as his brother raised a threatening fist in his direction.

'You're what!' The women gathered around, eyes wide with curiosity.

'It's not what you're thinkin', man!' Ben grimaced and took a long grateful gulp of tea. 'I'm goin' to be a stevedore and it means I have to heft bits of iron about in the stockyard . . . you know, transfer them from one place to another and stow them ready to be taken down to the wharf when the boat comes for them.'

'And how much are they paying you for that grand bit of work, pray?' Polly had her hands on her hips and was looking like somebody ready for a fight.

'I dunno, Mam.' Ben shook his head and

pulled a face. 'The stowers work in a gang and they get twenty shillings a ton shared out between them. So what I bring home at the end of the week depends on how much pig-iron the gang has shifted. It could be good money and not too hard a slog handling the little bits of iron. I mean, it's not like they was great big sows. They have cranes that do that.'

'What on earth are pigs and sows?' Mary wrinkled her nose.

Polly hit the table with the flat of her hand. 'I'll thank the lot o' ye not to mention that word under this roof again if ye don't want to bring the luck of the Devil hissel' on our heads.'

Archie grinned. 'Why not, Mam? I thought it was all right to say pig, unless it was Friday, and it isn't Friday today.'

Polly rolled her eyes to the ceiling. 'It's still unlucky. This family's had enough bad luck without tempting fate even further,' she said. 'Where's your father?'

There was a quick eye-to-eye exchange between Ben and Tommy.

'Well, I'm waiting,' Polly persisted. 'He went out with you this morning. Why is it he hasn't come back the same way?'

'Look, Mam . . . ' The muscles of Ben's broad back had tightened as he hunched

forward his massive shoulders. 'The fact
is . . . '

'Aye?'

'Well, two out of three's not bad when you
consider none of us has ever worked in a
foundry before.'

'What does that mean, then?'

'They were only taking on young men th'
day. All the older ones, men like me dad
. . . even the experienced ones . . . weren't
considered for the jobs going vacant. Anyway,
there were too many men and not enough
jobs, like it always is for the likes of us.'

'He didn't give Jack a job?' Polly's voice
trembled, but it was more from anger than
disappointment.

'No, but there's always next month's
signing-on. Maybe there'll be something . . . '

'Don't try to pull the wool over my eyes,
Ben Martin!'

Ben swerved round and fixed her with a
bright blue eye that was as angry as her own.
'I'm not! As I said, me dad's not alone in
being turned down. There were plenty others
more deserving than him. What makes you so
damned sure, Mam, that Sir Donald
Rockwell would want to take on every last
male member of *your* family?'

'Ben!' Ellie warned, seeing her mother's
face going grey around the edges.

But Ben was not to be stopped. He'd got his dander up. 'Just what is it you're holding over that bugger's head? There's something. I can tell. And he looked at me real funny-like while he dished out jobs, like God Almighty hissel'!'

Polly's head jerked and her whole face seemed to go into spasm. 'Don't ask questions that don't concern you,' she said in a low, barely controlled voice. 'You know all you need to know.'

'But that's just it, Mam, I don't. What I want to know . . . what we all want to know is, why we've come here in the first place.'

'It doesn't matter. You've got jobs, you and Tommy, and we've got a roof over our heads, such as it is. That's all that matters. It's just a pity Rockwell didn't see fit to take on your dad as well.'

'Who says that he didn't take me on?'

They all jumped and spun round as Jack Martin stumbled into the room. He looked as immaculate as he'd been when he left the house more than twelve hours earlier. There wasn't a mark on his best navy-blue suit and his white-silk miner's cravat was still neatly in place at his throat.

But Jack Martin was as drunk as a lord and his legs appeared to have turned to rubber beneath him. He advanced into the room, to sighs and breathy exclamations of horror from the women present.

'Jack Martin, you've been drinking!' Polly accused her husband and he was too far gone even to look sheepish. He simply closed his eyes and smiled inanely.

'S'right, Polly!'

'But you don't drink!'

'No, I don't! Well, 'cept on soshable 'cashions . . . ' He hiccuped, opened bleary eyes in surprise, then giggled. 'The lads brought me home.'

'Lads? What lads? Ben and Tommy have been home long since.'

Jack looked blearily at his two eldest sons and waved a hand in their direction. 'Not them, woman! The Micks from the building-site.'

Jack staggered slightly and Ellie, biting down on her lip for fear she would laugh out loud and invite even more of her mother's wrath, grabbed his arm and steered him to a chair.

'I'll make a pot of strong tea,' Margaret whispered and turned her back tactfully on family business that was none of her concern.

Jack continued to hiccup incessantly. Mary passed him a glass of water, which he spilled all over the floor while trying to drink out of the wrong side.

'Eeh, they're good lads, them Irish fellas.' Jack laughed between watery hiccups. 'Nivvor thought I'd like 'em, but they're good lads.'

'You've been hobnobbing with Irish workmen?' Polly couldn't believe her ears. 'Well, that's the best yet, I don't think. Roughnecks every last one of them with their drinkin' and their swearin' and . . . and . . . all them other things ye hear about that no respectable person would put up with.'

Ben left the window and went to squeeze his father's bony shoulder. He felt sorry for the man. If he couldn't be forgiven for getting drunk for one day at his time of life after a lifetime of being a saint, there was something sadly wrong with the world.

He and Tommy had looked for Jack after the signing-on. He had gone off with the others who weren't wanted that day. They had caught sight of him laughing and chatting amicably with a group of men from the construction site that abutted the gates of the foundry. Thinking he would simply follow them home when he was ready, they had gone on without him.

Margaret came forward with a mug of tea for Jack and refilled Ben's cup, her eyes smiling shyly into his. She smiled a lot at Ben. After all, he was her hero and seemed to be her self-appointed protector, for he was never slow in lending her a hand whenever he was available.

'Ta, Margaret.' He smiled back at her. 'That's grand, lass.'

Ellie was frowning, trying to recall her father's exact words as he had fallen into the room.

'Dad, what did you say before . . . about being taken on?'

Jack's eyebrows shot up into his hairline and he drew in a long gulp of air. His face cracked into a wide grin, a rare sight to behold, though it had taken a skinful of alcohol to produce it.

'Aye. Your Mr Rockwell caught up wi' me.'

'Sir Donald?' Polly's face froze and there was a fusion of deathly white and angry red surging beneath her skin.

Jack shook his head and licked dry lips, then he slurped a drink from his pint pot. 'Nah! Not him . . . the bugger! It was his son. Adam, his name is. Mr Adam Rockwell. Ye know, I thought at first he was a bit of a stuffed-shirt like his dad, but I changed me mind. He's all right. He gets a lot of respect from the men. That says a good deal for a man.'

'He gave you a job?' Ben couldn't hide his astonishment.

'Aye. I'm to get ten shillings a week for sweeping up.'

They all heard the air rush down through Polly's pinched nose. 'Ten shillings!' she repeated derisively. 'You got more than three times that in the pit, where you were somebody important. How dare he! I'll go and . . . '

'Ye'll do no such thing, woman.' Jack interrupted her flow. 'Whatever it is you're thinkin' of doin'. Just you settle down. I don't know what you did to secure us work with old Rockwell, but I'll tell ye this, Polly, I won't stand for any wife of mine putting her neb in on my behalf behind me back. No more, d'ye hear me?'

'Jack!' Polly got no further.

'Enough!' Jack held up a trembling finger and fixed her with an inebriated but wise stare. 'From now on you'll keep out of the affairs of us menfolk, like you're supposed to do. Now, is there any chance of a bite to eat? I'm clammin'.'

★   ★   ★

To the raucous jibes and cheers of the other members of his 'stowers' gang, Ben heaved the last pig of the day on to the wagon that was waiting to take the iron from the stockyard downriver to the estuary where the boats collected it for transportation.

Beads of sweat were standing out all over his aching body. Veins were popping at his temples. His great bull-neck and his biceps were straining to such an extent they could burst any minute. Every muscle throbbed and felt on the verge of deflating like a spent balloon.

When it had been explained to him originally that pig-iron consisted of the 'small' pieces of iron that were attached to the larger 'sows', he'd thought, well, *easy!* But how wrong could a person be.

The pieces of pig-iron weighed about a hundredweight. A bit like hefting Ellie with a full load of shopping. They had to be picked up by the ends, the middle resting on the stower's thigh, then thrown into the wagons. It took eighteen pigs to make up a ton of iron and you kept on working till you ran out of pigs. At the end of a working day you could come away with as little as two shillings in your pocket. Or as much as fifty shillings, depending on how much pig-iron the foundry manufactured.

It was obvious from the start that Ben's presence was resented in a gang of men who felt that there was no room for a non-ironworker, even if he was built like a bull and just as strong. It was for that reason, rather than any kind of amicable initiation, that the men stood back for much of the time and watched Ben work.

And he worked, heaving iron until he thought that every heave was his last. He worked with a smile on his face while they were watching him, and a painful grimace when they weren't. But he was not going to show them that a miner had less stamina than an ironworker.

At the end of the load for that day, the men drifted away, but not before they had clapped him on the back and nodded their approval. He had nearly killed himself in the attempt, but he had proved his worth and could hold his head up proudly. The men who had started out by deriding him were now filled with respect for their new team-mate.

It was coming up to eleven as he staggered like a drunken man to the wharf where the last ferry was waiting to board. People jostled each other, laughed, joked, exchanged news of jobs and family. Ben, hardly aware of it, propped himself up against the rail and tried not to fall asleep.

The sharp jolt that came when the big, flat, cumbrous ferry bounced its nose on the other bank, shook him back to consciousness. He managed to clamber his way through the dark, bouncing off trees, tripping over roots and shrubs that seemed to be lying in wait for him.

He didn't quite remember how he got to the little house at the end of the lane at Northend, but suddenly there it was with a yellow light showing in the curtainless window. As he fell upon the door with fist raised ready to knock, it swung back with a whining creak and Margaret was there, her face full of concern at his exhausted state.

'Come along in, Ben,' she whispered, for Polly and Jack were already sleeping soundly in the pull-down double bed.

Ben found suddenly that he couldn't move. He felt paralysed. He blinked and looked plaintively at the dark-haired girl the family had adopted. Her pretty face with the dark, haunting eyes, swam before his gaze.

'I can't move!' he managed to say and she came to him, placing her thin arm under his shoulders, and drew him into the house.

He fell into the one armchair in the room and watched with a kind of childlike helplessness as Margaret undid his bootlaces and pulled the boots off. His eyes, half-closed with sleep, followed her about as she moved quietly in the yellow glow from one oil-lamp. She warmed some milk in a pan and cut him some bread and a wedge of cheese.

'Drink this, Ben . . . and eat . . . you've got to eat or you'll not be fit for your work in the morning.'

Ben threw his head back and gave a sobbing groan. He felt sure he would never make it till morning. He would undoubtedly die in the night and then his mother would have to make do with the wages of poor, weak-chested Tommy and his father's meagre wage for being a sweeper.

'Come on now! I know what I'm saying.' Margaret was holding the cup to his lips, forcing some of the warm liquid into his mouth. It tasted good. Now she was pushing bread and cheese at him and he was eating and drinking mechanically like an invalid.

When the milk and bread and cheese were gone, Margaret started gently but firmly massaging some strong-smelling liniment into his aching limbs until some feeling started to return. The trouble was, the feeling was a lot more painful than the numbness.

'It'll wear off by morning,' she assured him and touched his cheek with the back of her cool hand.

'How come you know so much?' Ben asked with a tired grin.

Margaret looked at him through long, dark lashes and he saw her lips quiver. 'My husband was on the pig-iron when we first came here,' she told him, then turned from him so he couldn't see her tears.

At six the next morning, having thought he would never again see daylight, Ben was back at work, hefting more pig-iron. This time, however, the other men in the gang were pulling their own weight alongside him.

★ ★ ★

The next two weeks were hard on all of them, but particularly hard on Tommy whose weak chest soon gave out and he started coughing badly. He still worked diligently, coughing all the while, much to the annoyance of the other men. There were whispered comments behind his back. He heard the dreaded word 'consumption' and one by one the men started keeping their distance.

Then one day he just could not find the strength to rise from his bed. The effort brought on not only a bout of coughing, but an attack of wheezing, gasping breaths that threatened to choke the life out of him. Although it was cold in the bedroom, perspiration was pouring out of him as if the river itself was running through his pores.

'Ellie! Margaret!' Ben ran, semi-naked, into the small passageway that separated his room from the girls. 'One of you! Get in here. Tommy's bad.'

Ellie was the first to appear, blinking sleep drowsy eyes and looking scared.

'What it is, Ben? What's happened?'

'It's Tommy.' Ben panted as if he'd run a mile. 'He's having some kind of seizure. I don't know what to do.'

'What's wrong?' Margaret joined them and peered around Ben to the thrashing figure of Tommy, gasping and clutching at his chest and throat with trembling hands. 'Is it a heart attack, do you think?'

'I don't know, but I think he needs a doctor and quick,' Ellie decided on seeing the drastic state of her brother and noticing how blue his lips were.

'I'll go, but we're not paid up in any club or anything. It'll cost money for a visit.' Ben looked plaintively at Ellie, hating to say the words, but knowing that she was the only one among them still to have more than a penny to her name.

The foundry rules were that the workers had to put in two weeks before being paid. That way they weren't so likely to abscond, because they were always owed money.

'Don't worry. There's enough to cover us.' Ellie nodded and saw his eyes soften.

'Ye're a good lass, our Ellie. None better.

Do ye know where the doctor lives?'

She shook her head. 'There's none on this side of the river.'

Ben looked over his shoulder at his brother and knew real fear for the first time in his twenty-four years. Tommy was only twenty-one and he was the nicest fellow there was. He couldn't let him die.

'I'll run down to the ferry and see if I can rouse the ferryman, see if he'll take me over early. Do what you can for our Tommy.'

He gave Ellie a tight hug and Margaret a brief touch on her shoulder before galloping down the stairs three at a time and bursting out of the front door, not stopping to speak to his parents who were rousing and looking about them in a dazed fashion.

Mary wandered out of the girls' bedroom, removing wads of cotton from her ears. She had found that blocking her ears was the only way she could sleep.

'What's happened?' she asked.

'It's your brother,' Margaret told her gently, restraining the girl from going to Tommy's bedside. 'I've seen workers here before come down with something similar. Mary, go fetch some cold water and bring it up here. As much as you can carry. And some cloths or towels or something to bathe him with.'

'What can I do, Margaret?' Ellie turned frightened eyes on the pregnant girl who seemed to be taking control of the situation.

'Try to calm him and when Mary arrives with the water, we'll start putting cold water compresses on him. Especially the back of his neck and his forehead.'

A little over an hour later, the doctor, having been called from his bed by Ben, stood back and regarded his patient. Tommy's breathing had become a little less laboured by the time the doctor arrived, but he was still struggling.

'What's that you've got there, girl?' he asked Margaret, who was holding something close to Tommy's face, stroking his head as she spoke to him soothingly.

'It's only rosemary,' she told him, showing him the herbal bouquet she was warming in her hand. 'I've been trying to get him to inhale it.'

'It worked too,' Ellie said quickly when she saw the doctor's frown. 'Tommy's better than he was.'

'Hmm.' The doctor took the rosemary and sniffed at it, then put it down at the small bedside stand. 'Yes. Well done. That was quick thinking. Now, if you'll all stand back, I'd like to examine the patient.'

'What's he got, Doctor?' Polly asked

fearfully from the door of the bedroom. 'Has he caught some horrible disease from the foundry?'

The doctor took his stethoscope out of his ears and folded it thoughtfully. He bit back a caustic remark about the foundry being a disease in itself. Instead, he shook his head and slowly replaced his stethoscope and syringe in his black leather doctor's bag.

'Well, Mrs Martin.' The doctor frowned, his eyes passing from one to the other of them. 'Tommy has asthma. Very bad asthma. He should never be allowed to work where there is dust or heat. Certainly not in a foundry. On top of that . . . possibly because of it . . . he has a weak heart.'

'Oh, dear God!' Polly clamped a hand over her mouth and stifled a cry. Her husband put his hands on her shoulders and blinked damp and furious eyes in the light of the oil-lamp that flickered and sputtered.

'There's no reason why he can't lead a reasonably normal life,' the doctor continued. 'With care and attention to his diet, of course. Not too much exertion. Above all, he should keep calm at all times.'

'But I can't afford to be laid off,' came a weak, wheezing voice from the bed and everyone turned to stare at Tommy, who was attempting to raise himself on one elbow.

'They'll never survive on Ben's and Dad's wages.'

'If you go back to work right now, my lad,' the doctor said sharply, 'they'll have no choice. You'll be dead by the end of the month. Now, take my advice and rest. After a week or so you may be able to take on some kind of light work. But not in the foundry. It would be better if you could get away from this place completely. Miles away. It's a killer.'

He left a few minutes later, taking the ferry into the town with Ben. The four women sat down and stared at one another, listening to Tommy's ragged breathing as he slept peacefully now for the first time for days.

★ ★ ★

'Where're ye goin', our Ellie?'

Ellie nearly jumped out of her skin. She thought she'd got away clear without being spotted, but there was Archie running along behind her, dogging her hurried footsteps like a young Indian brave.

'Archie Martin, you go right back home and don't you say a word about what you've seen.' She rounded on him and stood with her hands on her hips as she panted breathlessly.

'Tell me where ye're goin' then!'

'It's none of your business.'

'Why are you all dressed up like a man? Aren't they me granddad's old clothes?'

Ellie sighed and cast about her with an exasperated expression. She was angry and disappointed that Archie should still recognize her, despite the old rough stuff jacket with the worn leather elbows and the heavy cords tied up with string to keep them from falling to her knees. She had managed to stuff her fair, flyaway hair under a greasy old cap and she really did think she could pass for a boy, as long as nobody looked too closely at her.

The fact that she squirmed and itched uncomfortably beneath her grandfather's clothes was of little importance next to that of her mission that day.

'Oh, all right, Archie, but you've got to promise not to say anything to the others. Especially me mam.'

'I promise,' Archie said, spitting on his fingers and blowing on the wet patch.

'Right . . . well, I'm going to the signing-on this morning.'

'At the foundry, d'ye mean?' His eyebrows shot up and he blew out a low whistle of air. 'You? But they don't sign girls on!'

'Well, *I* know that,' Ellie said. 'But how are they going to know I'm a girl? I bet I'm as fit as any of them.'

'Go on!' Her little brother grinned disbelievingly.

'Now, let me get on. I don't want to miss that ferry. Off you go, Archie, and keep that loud mouth of yours good and shut. At least until I get back home. This is our big secret, eh?'

'All right!' Archie shrugged a pair of surprisingly brawny shoulders for a ten year old.

She caught the ferry with a fraction of a minute to spare. Most of her fellow-passengers were women going into Rockwell to do the week's shopping. They didn't take too much notice of her, though one man leered at her as she passed him and she felt her skin crawl. She drew the edges of her grandfather's jacket together at the front, hoping that her breasts weren't showing themselves too obviously, though she had bound them as tightly as she could bear with some torn strips of an old pillowcase.

The thought of bed-linen reminded her of the reason for her doing this crazy thing. Her mother, unable to wait, had taken it upon herself to buy a number of items from the tallyman. Bed linen had figured largely in her purchases, together with some necessary pots and pans and various dishes and cutlery.

Ellie had seen the money in her purse dwindle until it was only a few pennies after paying for two more visits from the doctor. The doctor's bill she couldn't resent, but the other things could have waited until Ben and her father had started earning decent wages.

But Polly wasn't used to having to wait for anything and had become quite petulant when Ellie had remonstrated with her about her frivolous expenditure at a time when they were as poor as church mice.

As for looking for work, this had proved more difficult than she had imagined. There was none to be had. The women in the big houses took one look at her pretty face and pleasing figure and changed their minds about having a position to fill. And none of the shops had any vacancies.

At home, Polly was driven to taking in washing and ironing and Mary even went out doing housework, all for a few women who could ill afford to pay more than a few pennies an hour.

Margaret, they had found, was good at shirt-making, so Ellie had bought a bale of flannel, together with a selection of needles and cottons, and the girl was busily sewing and charging five shillings a shirt. This was a lot of money, but the shirts were good quality and undercut the commercially produced ones by nearly two shillings. And Margaret still made a nice little profit, which she generously shared among the family.

The ironworkers believed that wool was the only material that could withstand the conditions under which they worked. It absorbed the perspiration, kept out the cold and didn't rot like cotton did when exposed to the various fumes that hung in the atmosphere.

The ferry jerked to a standstill and Ellie grabbed the rail to steady herself as the ferryman pulled the boat into the bank on the other side of the river. On getting off, she instintively held out her hand to the ferryman's lad who was helping the ladies ashore. He grinned at her and she realized, red-faced, that it wasn't quite the thing expected of a 'young man'.

With a rising flurry of butterflies in her stomach, Ellie pulled down her cap firmly on her head, making sure the peak was well over her eyes, and entered the signing-on shed at the foundry with a lot of other young male hopefuls. If there were any curious glances, she didn't notice them.

'Right! Today we're looking for the follow- ing: gantrymen . . . two; stower . . . one; chargers . . . three; scarrer . . . one; mine-filler . . . one; slag-tippers . . . four; weighers

. . . two. Have we got any experienced men among you?'

Ellie dared to look at the man who was speaking and recognized Adam Rockwell. She hadn't before met anyone who could compare with Ben for height and width, but this man did surprisingly well. In fact, if anything, he was slightly taller.

Adam Rockwell started pacing before the crowd of job applicants. Each time he passed Ellie, who was on the front line, she was aware of only one thing. The tremendous muscularity of his thighs in legs as long as any she had come across. In fact, he filled out his clothes to an almost indecent degree, which made her whole body react in such a way it was shameful to say the least.

'Sir! Sir, I can do any of that!'

Ellie's eyes stretched as she recognized Archie's voice coming from somewhere behind her.

'Come forward, lad,' Adam Rockwell demanded in his deep, authoritarian voice that had just a tinge of northern dialect.

Archie pushed his way through to the front and positioned himself at Ellie's elbow. There was a tittering of suppressed laughter in the mixed crowd of men and boys, but Adam Rockwell held up his hand and they soon quietened down.

'So! You can do anything, can you? What's your experience?'

'I haven't got none, sir, but I'm very willing and I'm strong.' To prove his point, Archie held up his arms and flexed his biceps. There was more laughter at this point and Ellie could see an amused twitch starting at the corner of Adam's mouth. He had a nice mouth, she remembered, recalling the day he had sketched her.

'How old are you lad?' Adam said gently, looking down from his great height on Archie.

'I'm . . . er . . . *fourteen*, sir!'

'*Fourteen!*' More laughter ensued.

'I'm small for me age.'

'He's ten, Mr Rockwell, sir,' Ellie spoke out, lowering her voice so that it sounded as masculine as possible without straining her vocal chords to breaking point. 'He's my little brother.'

'I see!' Now Adam's attention was drawn away from the boy. Fascinated, he stared down at Ellie. 'And what is your name and your age?'

'El . . . er . . . Edward Martin, sir,' Ellie said gruffly, masking her mouth with her hand as she spoke, muffling the words. 'I'm . . . er . . . twenty-four.'

'Experience?' Adam demanded.

There was a silence as they all waited for Ellie to speak. ' . . . Er — none, sir . . . at least, none in a foundry, but you employ my brother and my father.'

'Aha! Martin, did you say? New arrivals at Rockwell, I believe.'

'Yes, sir.'

'You have a brother who is too sick to work, I believe?'

'Yes, sir, but I'm very strong and healthy. I could take his place if you like. He's told me all about the job.'

Adam's brow creased into a heavy frown. Suddenly, he spun around and swiped a hand at the cap that was covering Ellie's abundance of hair and part of her face. The thing flew into the air, revealing the young woman beneath it for all to see. The shed burst into raucous laugher and ribald remarks.

Ellie stood, red-faced and with her hair flowing all about her shoulders. Sir Donald Rockwell's son and heir threw back his head and laughed just as hard as the other men.

'I think,' he said at last, when peace was restored, 'that any experience of work you may have had, young woman, was more of the feminine kind. Go back to your embroidery. There's no place here in the foundry for you. Or your little brother, who ought to be in school for at least three more years.'

Ellie's nostrils flared and she flashed her blue eyes at Adam, who seemed to appreciate the action, for he laughed some more, then turned his back on her and proceeded to get on with the job of signing on real men.

6

'Oh, my goodness, Grace,' Lady Rockwell said to her stepdaughter as they picked their way delicately through the mud and the discarded household rubbish of Northend. Her nose wrinkled as she breathed in the foul smells that seemed to hang on the air. 'This place gets worse rather than better.'

'How can they live in such conditions?' Grace replied, getting out her handkerchief, which she had remembered to soak in lavender water before leaving home.

'They don't have a great deal of choice,' her stepmother said grimly and turned to encourage their reticent companion who was hanging behind them by a few steps. 'Come along, Patricia. Do stop dawdling.'

'Dawdling! Good Lord, Cynthia, that's the last thing you'll find me doing in this godforsaken place. I swore last time I would never come back here, but there you are. I let you persuade me against my better judgement.'

'Oh, must you always complain? Our work is little enough suffering compared to what these poor souls have to put up with. Once a month with your feet in the mud and the mire shouldn't be too onerous, surely.'

'Will things ever be improved here?' Grace asked, skirting around two starving mongrel dogs copulating in the middle of the street, watched by a small group of young children. Half the children had the bowed, crippled legs of rickets that came with the kind of malnourishment they suffered because their parents could not afford decent food.

'That's up to your father, Grace.' Lady Rockwell gave a small sigh. 'All we can do is try to educate them, show them how to cope better. Most of these young mothers don't know how to look after children properly. Some of them don't even know how to cook.'

'Well, I'm sorry, but I think it's going to take more than domestic education to put things right.' Patricia Beresford, now that they were past the worst of it, was forging on ahead, her pointed nose up in the air.

'Yes, we need more money to plough into our little venture. Adam's a great help, as always, but it's never enough and I feel guilty every time he gets out his cheque book. It should be my husband who does that, but I'm afraid Donald takes no interest in good causes of any kind and would be happier if I shared *his* view.'

In fact, she thought, he was getting more

and more adamant that she should not meddle in foundry affairs. That morning, he had been particularly remonstrative when he found out she was planning to visit the new family at Northend, almost to the point of forbidding her to go.

Grace gave her stepmother a sharp look for speaking of her father in such a way, but said nothing. The girl knew what it was like living with this man who was as hard-hearted and as tight-fisted as they came, inside as well as outside his own home.

The three women eventually came to a halt in front of the last cottage at the furthest tip of Northend. The last time they had seen the house it was shortly after the death of the young man who lived there. Now, it was occupied by another family far too large for the accommodation it afforded.

'There have been some improvements, I see,' Lady Rockwell announced as she fanned herself with her kid gloves, the day having turned quite warm. 'Everything looks so much cleaner and there are curtains at the windows.'

Her stepdaughter put a hand up to her throat, remembering their last visit only too well. 'I wonder what happened to that poor young woman. She was pregnant, wasn't she?'

Lady Rockwell shuddered, despite the heat. She remembered the heated argument she had had with her husband over the girl in question. He had insisted she must be evicted from the cottage immediately since she was not contributing to the income of the foundry. It was abominable the way he sometimes treated foundry families with such cruel indifference.

As she opened her mouth to reply to Grace's question as tactfully as she could, she caught sight of the dark-haired Margaret sitting outside the house in a patch of sunlight. She appeared to be sewing industriously, a small table piled high with cloth next to where she sat.

'Good heavens! Why, I do believe the girl is still here!' She advanced on the cottage, the other two women close at her heels. 'Good morning! It is Mrs Hill, is it not?'

Margaret looked up from her sewing, squinting in the sunlight. When she recognized the visitors she jumped up, scattering materials and reels of cotton from her lap.

'Oh! Oh, Lady Rockwell! I'm sorry, I was so carried away with me work I didn't hear you coming.'

Polly appeared at the open door, duster in one hand, tin of Zebra black-lead polish in the other. She looked embarrassed at being caught doing her household chores.

Inside the cottage, Mary's face could be seen peering through the panes of glass she was cleaning, while the sweet sound of singing issued forth from the kitchen where Ellie was preparing lunch. The singing was punctuated from time to time by the chesty cough of Tommy, who was lying in bed upstairs with the windows thrown wide to allow the air to circulate more freely.

On the doorstep itself, young Archie was sitting cross-legged whittling a stick. He seemed to have a way with wood, for it was already showing promise as a finely sculp-tured bird.

'You must be Mrs Martin.' Lady Rockwell, looking at Polly, was the first of the visitors to speak. 'I'm Cynthia Rockwell ... Sir Donald's wife ... '

Polly's jaw dropped. Her pale eyes lowered and she turned the duster over and over in her agitated hands before quickly putting it behind her back as if she was ashamed to be found with it. This visit was obviously something she had not bargained for, Lady Rockwell thought, noticing the woman's discomfort. And yet reports had it that Mrs Martin — or Catherine Durham as she had called herself — portrayed no sign of subservient attitude when she visited the foundry a month ago and spoke to Sir Donald.

Lady Rockwell put the questions that rose unbidden to the back of her mind and went on to introduce her colleagues from the Association of Foundry Workers Committee. She was met with a mute response, so she continued regardless.

'This is fine work you're doing, Mrs Hall,' she said, inspecting the shirt Margaret had dropped and which she had picked up from the ground. 'Do you by any chance take orders, because I know a lot of people who would buy them if the price is right?'

Margaret stuttered out the price to her, glancing at Polly, who seemed to be riveted to the spot.

'Good. I'll be in touch with you further on the subject. Now, what I've really come for is to speak to a young woman who is, I believe, the sister of Benjamin Martin and who took it upon herself to apply for a man's position at the foundry.'

Polly drew in a huge amount of air and flexed her shoulders in such a way that it made her appear larger than the little sparrow she was. She was finally able to look Cynthia Rockwell directly in the eye, but words were late in coming. Before she could think what to say, Ellie herself appeared, a ready smile on her lips, her pretty face flushed with her exertions in the kitchen.

'I'm Ellie Martin — Ben's sister,' she said without a qualm.

'Your name again, my dear . . . ?'

'Ellie . . . *Ellen* Martin . . . and I'm sorry I made a fool of myself the other day, but I was so desperate to find work . . . '

'Not at all my dear,' Lady Rockwell's face cracked into a slow, but sincere smile, though she was aware that her companions were looking down their noses at the young woman who spoke to her with such lack of proper decorum. 'I admire your courage and your tenacity. My stepson, Adam, told me about the incident. He seemed to think you merited my attention. I have a need for a lady's maid. It will mean you living in — that is, at Rockwell Hall. However, you will, of course, have time off to visit your family on a regular basis.'

Ellie gaped at the woman and swallowed hard. 'You . . . you're offering me a job?'

'Yes, I am. Let's see. Today is Thursday. Shall we say that you can start work at the Hall on this coming Monday?'

Ellie blinked furiously, her mouth opening and shutting, her eyes stretching. Suddenly, her mother was pushing her to one side.

'She's not going to work at the Hall!' Polly stated flatly.

Lady Rockwell could not believe what she was hearing. There they were in desperate straits and the woman was turning down good money.

'How much do you pay, Lady Rockwell?' Ellie demanded and fobbed off her mother's flapping hands.

'Well, I'm impressed that you volunteered yourself as a foundry worker. That took a lot of courage, so I'll pay you the wage of a gantry man, which means two pounds a week. And, just as pure interest, it's equivalent to a curate or a junior clerk in a government office. And the work is far less hazardous than that of a gantry man, I assure you.'

'It's very kind of you Lady Rockwell — very generous.' Ellie bit down on her lip and frowned for a moment, then decided to be even bolder. 'I have a brother who can no longer work because he has asthma and a weak heart. And my father earns very little as a sweeper. We have debts.'

'Ellie! That's enough! Back inside, girl!' Polly was pulling at her daughter's arm as if deranged. 'I won't have you discussing our private business with strangers.'

Ellie shook her off and stepped closer to

Lady Rockwell, who was watching the little scene with interest. 'Lady Rockwell, I'll come and be your lady's maid. But only if you will consider taking on my sister too. Mary doesn't look very strong, but she's a good worker. You'll not find a more willing girl and that's an honest fact.'

Lady Rockwell's eyes slid sideways to the pale, thin face that was peering at her through the half-cleaned window. Mary pulled back self-consciously.

'Well, I didn't come with the idea of taking on two young women,' she said slowly, then reflected on it, one finger touching her chin. 'Let me think about it. You shall have my decision by the weekend.'

'I'll wait to hear from you, then, Lady Rockwell,' Ellie said a little breathlessly.

Cynthia Rockwell nodded and gave a small, enigmatic smile. 'Right. Now, I believe you have an invalid in the house.'

'He's much better, thank you,' Polly said quickly through tightened jaws. 'The doctor says he should be ready to take on some light work in another week or so.'

'There isn't much in the way of light work in a foundry, Mrs Martin.' Lady Rockwell put her head to one side and regarded the little bird of a woman, wondering why she seemed so reluctant to look her in the eye, why her manner was so abrasive. 'However, I will keep him in mind and if anything suitable comes up I'll let you know. In the meantime, he needs proper nourishment to get him back on the road to recovery.'

She turned to her companions and beckoned them forward. Each woman came up to her with covered baskets that they had carried all the way from the ferry.

'I think you'll find enough here for the whole family, Mrs Martin . . . ' She started to uncover the first basket, which was filled with fresh vegetables.

'I don't want your charity!' Polly almost shouted, then tucked her chin into her thin chest and looked bashfully down at her feet. 'We're all right. We can manage, now that my husband and my son are being paid for their work.'

She said the last few words with a sour note of disdain in her voice, which did not go unnoticed.

'I do not make the rules inside the foundry, Mrs Martin. But I do have some control over what happens on the outside. We — our Association — have set up many groups to help the workers and, especially, their families. For instance, Mrs Hill here . . . ' She indicated Margaret, who had once more picked up her needle and cotton and was fitting a sleeve into a shirt. 'Mrs Hill can go to a class where she can be shown how to cope with a newborn baby and how to feed the child with the proper food.'

She then turned to Archie. 'Your little boy should be at school. There are two schools in the town, but we also run special classes for those children who need to catch up or — indeed, who show an aptitude for anything special, such as carpentry. I see he likes working with wood.'

Ellie grinned at the face Archie pulled and ruffled his mop of unruly hair. 'All my brothers are good with their hands. Tommy makes some nice furniture when he has the time.'

Lady Rockwell shook her head slightly. 'Then why on earth isn't he earning a living by being a carpenter?'

Ellie shrugged. She had often thought the same thing, every time Tommy had proudly shown off a finished table or sideboard. He never had any difficulty selling the furniture he made, but a lot of the time he would give it away for the cost of the wood, or not even that if he felt people couldn't afford to pay.

'He hasn't got much head for business, I suppose,' she said and held her hands out to take the basket of food from the serious-faced young woman who was holding it. 'We'll take the food and thank you very much, Lady Rockwell. Take no notice of me mam. She has too much pride, that's all.'

Lady Rockwell's smile deepened. She liked this girl. Somewhere along the line she had shed the rough edges that were normally found on the children of pitmen. And she shone with something that glowed from the inside. It was no wonder Adam had been so impressed.

She took the other basket, which contained fresh chicken and a joint of beef, bread and eggs. She placed it carefully at the feet of Polly Martin and saw the woman's shoulders work up and down; saw her clasped hands, red and roughened from the constant household chores, clench and unclench.

'Thank you!' Polly said stiffly, her gaze fixed on the other woman's bosom and the pearl buttons that fastened her fashionable dress.

'Do you have sufficient bed-linen?' Lady Rockwell asked gently. 'If not, we can . . . '

'We're all right for things like that, thank you very much,' Polly told her quickly.

'Mam's just bought some from the tallyman!' Archie said in a loud voice and received a black look from his mother.

'I see . . . well, I don't suppose you need me to tell you how careful you must be not to run up too much debt with such individuals.'

'That's right . . . er . . . milady . . . I don't need you to tell me that . . . '

'Oh, Mam!' Ellie shot an apologetic glance in Lady Rockwell's direction and received a nod of understanding in return.

'Well, we'll let you get on with your work. My congratulations, Mrs Martin. Even from here I can see how you run a clean household. There are plenty who could take a leaf out of your book. We'll look in and see you again in a month's time. In the meantime, if there's anything . . . '

'There won't be nothing.' Polly picked up one of the baskets and started to march, stiff-backed, into the house with it. 'We're not paupers. We're a proud and independent family . . . '

Her words tailed off to a low muttering as she drew away into the shadows of the interior of the house.

'Here ye are, missus! It's for you.' Archie jumped to his feet and presented Lady Rockwell with his finished carving of a woodpecker.

Cynthia Rockwell was taken by surprise. It was the first time any of the workers had offered her a gift so spontaneously. She showed her appreciation by patting his rosy cheek and giving him a penny in exchange. 'A gift must always be repaid,' she told him as he turned the money over in his grimy hand. 'Now we'll both be lucky.'

'Lady Rockwell!' Ellie ran after her as she departed with her stepdaughter and her friend. She stopped with a smile, but the other two continued on their way. Neither of them had opened their mouths once during the meeting.

'Yes, Ellen?'

'Lady Rockwell, you will — I mean — please, will you not forget about Mary? People don't usually like to employ her because of her eye, but honestly, you won't regret it.'

'I won't forget, dear.'

As she walked away, Cynthia Rockwell wondered why she should have a lump in her throat and tears stinging her eyelids. It was quite ridiculous, but this family — and the girl Ellen, in particular — had touched a soft spot in her. There was something different about this girl. Something very different.

* * *

Adam Rockwell paced the library floor with long, impatient steps. During dinner his father had made it clear that he wanted to see him about something important, something urgent. Well, the old devil had kept him waiting long enough.

Just as he was about to leave, Cynthia entered the room, a ready smile on her face. He liked Cynthia, but he was always uncomfortable in her presence when they were alone. He knew how difficult her life was with his father and he sympathized. Perhaps he would have been better advised to stay cool and aloof with her, for on one occasion when she was full of chagrin, he had made the mistake of taking her in his arms.

It had been nothing more than a filial embrace, a brotherly hug of comfort. Unfortunately, it had produced such a violently emotional reaction in Cynthia that he had thrust her away from him in mid-embrace as if she had gone up in flames and burned him. He had not realized how she felt, how vulnerable she was. Now, it was something of a lasting embarrassment between them.

'Cynthia? Where the devil is the old man? He asked me to wait for him here an hour ago and he still hasn't shown up.'

'He had far too much to drink again at dinner,' Cynthia told him, not that it was necessary for he had witnessed for himself his father's rapid inebriation at the table. Sir Donald's colour had changed from deathly grey to a hearty purplish red as he stuffed himself with food and washed it down with glass after glass of rich red claret.

'I take it, then, that there's no point in my hanging around any longer?'

'None at all. He's too far gone even to remember. I've left him sleeping it off on the *chaise-longue* in the dining-room. The servants know better than to disturb him. He'll no doubt come round sufficiently in the early hours of the morning to stagger to his bed. They can clear away tomorrow.'

'In that case I'll bid you good night, Cynthia.' He hesitated before leaning over and kissing her lightly on her forehead and felt her shoulder quiver beneath his hand. 'By the way, how is Mrs McKenzie's leg? Did she see the doctor?'

Cynthia took a second or two to compose herself, then gave him a trembling smile. 'It's so like you, Adam, to think of the welfare of others,' she said, wanting to hug him and not daring. 'Our housekeeper is getting old. The doctor says it's varicose veins from being on her feet too long. He's given her some ointment and strapped the leg up. She's limping, but still cheerful.'

Adam nodded. 'We must get her more help.'

'I've already thought of that, Adam.' Lady

Rockwell had recovered sufficiently now to smile properly. 'I went to see the Martin family today, as you suggested. That girl you mentioned is quite something, isn't she? A pretty little thing. And what a personality for someone of her background. I'd say she had a good supply of intelligence and common sense. I've decided to take her on as my lady's maid.'

'I'm glad.'

'And because she said she wouldn't consider the job unless I took her sister on too, I'm going to employ her younger sister as Mrs McKenzie's assistant.' Cynthia sighed loudly, her chest heaving up and down beneath the fine silk of her dress. 'It's a pity about the girl's eye, which is quite in the corner, but I'm assured by your Ellen Martin, that Mary is a good and willing worker.'

'*My* Ellen Martin?' Adam gave a short laugh.

'Well, you were impressed by her and the recommendation you gave me made it quite impossible for me not to take her on. I suppose it has nothing to do with that golden halo of hair and those incredibly big blue eyes? Or the *retroussé* nose, the pink, dimpled cheeks — not forgetting the sensuous rosebud mouth?'

Adam laughed again, then regarded her

through half-closed eyes while he let her words sink in and he turned them over in his head. Cynthia had no need to describe Ellie to him. Her likeness, which he had sketched with so much fervour, was forever imprinted on his brain.

'Don't be ridiculous, Cynthia!'

He spun on his heel and left the house like a sudden gust of wind, leaving Cynthia Rockwell feeling empty and alone.

★　★　★

The cab was waiting outside, the horses pawing impatiently at the gravel of the courtyard. The night was black as ink with a starry landscape to the north in comparison to the red glow of the throbbing foundry to the south.

'Jenner?' Adam shook the driver and saw the man start. 'Sorry, Jenner! Didn't mean to keep you waiting this long.'

'S'all reet, sor!' Jenner was Adam's personal 'man', silent and uncomplaining. Whatever Adam wanted, he was ready to oblige. Adam had pulled Jenner from an escaping stream of molten metal a few years ago. The man had spent months in agony with the burns sustained and it was thought he would never walk again. He had proved this wrong, with Adam's persistent support and encouragement.

Adam had occupied the next bed in the hospital ward, having had burns to his hands, but thankfully, they had healed with only minimal scarring. The two men had survived the catastrophe together and were now morally bound to one another.

'All right.' Adam slapped Jenner on the back and climbed into the back of the cab. The hood was already up and there were thick woollen blankets to put over his legs to keep out the evening chill.

'Usual place, Mr Adam?' Jenner asked as he tickled the horses into a sedate walk.

'Usual place, Jenner.'

Five minutes later the horses, now thoroughly warmed, were trotting ahead along a well-beaten track towards a nameless cottage where Adam knew he would receive a warm welcome.

He had been visiting Sarah Wells, the woman people referred to as 'the artist', since he had first felt the stirring of sexual desire. In fact, since his eighteenth birthday, when his father handed him a handful of money and told him to use it making a man of himself.

His father's idea of finding one's manhood had been an initiation course with the local prostitutes in Durham and Sunderland. It had been abhorrent to Adam at the time, as it still was now. He had gone no further than Sarah Wells and with Sarah he stayed and added to his education in the subjects of art and sex.

Sarah was his muse, his mentor, and his best friend.

'Why are you so tense tonight, Adam?' Sarah wanted to know when they settled down with a bottle of port between them and some Stilton cheese with crusty bread that Sarah had baked herself that morning. 'Have you had another disagreement with your father? Is that why you were late?'

Adam shook his head and sank back into the multitude of cushions on Sarah's huge sofa. 'No. I think my father intended to have some sort of argument, but . . . '

'But?' Sarah's bangles jingled as she pushed back the wide kimono sleeve of her capacious floral smock, which she always wore over a full skirt, making her look very much the Bohemian she was.

'He drank too much and fell asleep. I shouldn't have waited. I could see the way he was going.'

'Your father is slowly killing himself with alcohol,' Sarah stated, holding her glass of port to the flickering fire that glowed warmly in the grate. She twirled the glass reflectively, warming it, coaxing it into maturity as she had once done with Adam.

'Yes, I know,' Adam conceded.

Sarah smiled wisely and gave him a look. 'What about your stepmother? Is she still in love with you?'

'Don't!' Adam groaned and rubbed at his eyes wearily.

'She's a young, attractive woman. Younger than me by a good ten years.'

'What's that supposed to mean?'

Sarah shrugged. Then she laughed lightly. He liked the way she laughed. It was a deep-seated, throaty chuckle. 'Nothing! I'm feeling old this evening, that's all.'

'You'll never be old, Sarah.'

'That's a matter of opinion.' There was a long hesitation, and then she continued. 'I've come to a decision.'

'Oh? About what?'

'About us . . . our relationship.'

'Really?' He knew, before she spoke, what her decision would be.

'Adam,' Sarah reached out and gently grazed his cheek with her knuckles, 'it's time for us to separate.'

'Do you mean that?'

She held up a hand. 'Yes, Adam! I've been putting it off for a very long time, because I know that we can't go on like this for ever. I'd prefer us to part while we still have affection for each other.'

'Sarah, for goodness sake!' He gave a short laugh.

She silenced him again. 'Adam, I'm fifteen years older than you. I always knew that there was no future in our relationship. We have to end it now.' Adam started to speak, but she placed her cool fingers against his lips and shook her head. 'You know me, Adam. Once I've made a decision, I don't go back on it. You brought a joy into my life I thought I would never know, but it's time you found a nice young wife. A girl who will make you happy, give you children. Not somebody old and dried up whom you're ashamed to acknowledge publicly.'

Adam knew a moment's guilt. As always, she was right. Sarah knew about human beings, understood their emotions. She was under no illusions regarding their relationship. Other women might have expected him to marry them. Not Sarah. She was too much of a realist.

'So,' Adam faltered, not quite knowing how to handle the situation because his own emotions were in turmoil, 'tonight must be my last visit?'

'Yes, my darling.' Sarah momentarily

closed her eyes. 'But don't worry. I don't want you to make love to me. God knows, we haven't indulged in that little pleasure for quite some time now.'

'I hope we'll always be friends, Sarah.'

'That goes without saying.'

'Sarah, I . . . ' He was unable to think of the right words. He loved her, but if he were honest it was not the kind of love he would feel for the woman with whom he might want to share the rest of his life.

'Just hold me, Adam, that's all I ask,' Sarah pleaded. 'Just this once. For old time's sake. And then you must go.'

7

'I suppose it's too late to change me mind?' Mary whispered in Ellie's ear as they leaned against the rail of the morning ferryboat. It was still quite early, not yet eight o'clock, so the boat was almost empty, having disgorged its first batch of shift workers on the opposite bank more than two hours ago. And it was as yet too early for the people going into the town to do their shopping.

Ellie gave an exasperated sigh and turned to fix her younger sister with a dominant stare. 'You're not going to change your mind, Mary, and that's that! Where do you think we'll find work that pays as much as Lady Rockwell has offered us, eh?'

'Oh, I know, but working at Rockwell Hall! Ellie, I've never been near such a well-to-do place in me life. And me mam's dead set against the pair of us going there.'

Polly had put up a valiant fight against her daughters' going to work for the Rockwell family. She was particularly adamant with regard to Ellie, though she refused to be drawn further than to say the idea filled her full of foreboding. Ellie's arguments, with the solid backing of the rest of the family, had won the day however.

'I don't know what Mam could possibly have against the Rockwells,' Ellie sighed. 'After all, she was the one who brought us here and found jobs at the foundry for Ben and Tommy and me dad. She must have had some connection with the family before to be able to pull that one. I just wish I knew what it was.'

She stared at the dark, greasy river-water sliding past like liquid steel and pondered on her mother's strong objections, which seemed to have no foundation. All Polly kept repeating was that she was afraid she, Ellie, would bring shame on her family. As if she knew it was a foregone conclusion.

Just what kind of trouble did her mother think she was going to get herself into? Lady Rockwell was the nicest, kindest person imaginable. She wasn't a snob like some of the women in her position. She had certainly not looked down her nose at them as if they weren't worthy of her consideration.

Even Adam Rockwell had not done that and he . . .

Ellie suppressed a little shudder at the memory of the big man who had flipped off the disguising cap from her head, laughed then stared at her through half-closed, thoughtful eyes. She wasn't even sure that he remembered her from the portrait he had done. She couldn't tell.

Ellie admitted reluctantly and silently, as her eyes followed the flowing water and the bits of flotsam that went with it, that if anything the feeling she had experienced, with his eyes eating into her, was a mysterious kind of fear.

She shuddered again, then drew back from the rail as the body of a small white dog, stiff in death, floated by. Was it a sign? A portent of things to come, perhaps?

'What's wrong?' Mary asked, edging up as close as she could get to her sister, for they were nearing the opposite bank and she was nervous.

'Nothing!' Ellie patted Mary's cold hand and gave the girl a reassuring smile. 'Nothing at all.'

They managed to get a ride from the carter who had brought them to the foundry in the first place. He was a likeable sort and greeted them like old friends, asking after the various members of the family as if he knew them intimately.

Because they were kept in continuous conversation with him, it seemed as though no time at all had passed before he was depositing them at the main gates of Rockwell Hall.

'There ye's are.' He handed them down from the back of the dray and nodded towards the hall. 'Better you's than me workin' fer that bastard . . . sorry fer the bad language, ladies!'

'Well, we're not going to be working for Sir Donald,' Ellie informed him quickly. 'It's his wife who's employed us and she seems very nice.'

'Aye! Give the woman her due. She's all right, that one. But him. He's a very different kettle of fish. You steer clear of them Rockwell fellas, mind. That's my advice.'

Ellie looked at him and frowned. 'Why do you say that?'

The carter took off his cap and scratched his bald pate. 'Well, the son works mostly from the Hall these days, apparently, and ye know what they say, don't you?'

'No. What?'

'Like father like son,' the carter said and cast his eyes to one side and back again in a slow, swivelling motion, that made Ellie's frown deepen. 'There's more than one lass has left the Hall in the Devil's own hurry. Why, only last week the secretary was seen running from the house in tears. I know because I have a niece who works in the kitchens. She doesn't have a good thing to say about the Rockwells. So don't say you've not been warned, eh?'

He touched a finger to his forelock and gave a short, sharp bow before climbing back up behind his horses and flicking the reins to jostle up the restless animals.

'What do you think he meant by all that?' Mary asked querulously. She looked as if she was ready to bolt into a gallop herself.

'It's all just rumour, I'm sure,' Ellie said carefully, but a cold feeling was settling in the pit of her stomach. 'And you know what you should do about that, don't you, Mary?'

'What's that, Ellie?'

'You should ignore it.' Ellie linked her arm tightly with her sister's and urged the girl forward through the huge, wrought-iron gates that opened on to a wide driveway of stone-chippings that snaked its way up to Rockwell Hall.

'Well, I would ignore it, if I knew what he was talking about.'

'In that case, Mary,' Ellie smiled, 'you have nothing to ignore and you can make your own mind up, as and when the need arises. Come on. Best foot forward.'

★ ★ ★

Cynthia Rockwell watched the two girls approaching. She was standing at the small side window of the breakfast-room, a delicate porcelain teacup half-raised to her lips.

'I do believe my new lady's maid has arrived,' she said, tossing a smile over her shoulder at Adam who was helping himself to a copious breakfast from the silver serving dishes keeping warm on the huge Victorian sideboard.

'Hmm?' It was the vaguely disgruntled response of a man who was totally distracted by his own thoughts.

'The Martin girl and her sister . . . the one with the lazy eye.' Lady Rockwell turned and saw him regarding her with a vacant expression. 'Really, Adam, you can't have forgotten. You were the one who suggested her for the job.'

'Who? The girl with a lazy eye? I can't say I've ever — '

'Oh, Adam, not that one, silly! Ellen Martin — you know . . . ? Golden curls and immense blue eyes?'

'Oh!' He suddenly looked full of interest and joined her at the window to watch the girls' progress up the drive, hauling their belongings with them in large canvas holdalls. 'Oh, *that* girl. Yes. Sorry, I'm a little preoccupied this morning, Cynthia.'

'Evidently? Did you have a bad night? I thought I heard someone moving about in the early hours.' She looked at her stepson speculatively and kept a polite smile locked into her lips, though she felt more like weeping and ranting and raving after the sleepless night of sexual frustration she herself had endured.

'I'm sorry,' Adam apologized, then dragged his gaze back to the window, or to what was happening beyond. 'I didn't think my nocturnal meanderings would disturb anyone. I have a lot on my mind at the moment.'

Cynthia Rockwell did not think for one moment that Adam's preoccupation had anything to do with the rising prices of iron and steel or the new deals he was negotiating with the contractors who transported it from the river to the docks and beyond. Nor did she think it was the threatened strike of some of the workers who felt that they were being unfairly treated.

All that was merely foundry business and, as she was well aware, Adam was more than capable of dealing with it with the minimum of effort. That was the way he was. And that was the greatest difference between himself and his father. Sir Donald was a self-made man who had got where he was by being a talented engineer and a bully. Adam had been forced into the job, doing it against his will and his strongest desires. He did it to perfection, like he did everything he tackled. But he never trampled other men into the ground to get where he was going.

As Adam raised an eye to her, Lady Rockwell turned away sharply to hide the expression of unrequited love in her eyes.

'You've hired the two Martin girls?' he asked.

She reached out and rang a service bell, then went back to the breakfast table and sat down, pouring herself another cup of tea and taking toast and marmalade. 'Yes. *Your* Martin girl wouldn't come unless I took on her sister as well. I had no choice, Adam. I'm desperate for some help. Of course, the other girl will have to work below stairs, but . . . ' She shrugged and made an urgent business of scraping butter on her toast.

'Good idea. She'll be a help to Mrs McKenzie.'

As if on cue, the housekeeper appeared. She looked red-cheeked and flustered and she was limping rather badly, though trying not to show that it bothered her.

'Yes, madam? You rang?'

'Ah, Mrs McKenzie.' Lady Cynthia turned in her chair and smiled compassionately at the older woman who had been the Rockwell family's retainer since the age of about fifteen. 'There are two young women struggling up the drive with their luggage. Could you ask Thomas or Arthur or someone to help them? They've come to the Hall to work. Ellen Martin . . . she calls herself Ellie . . . will train to be my lady's maid. Her sister, Mary, is to be placed below stairs and will train as an assistant.'

'Yes, madam.' Mrs. McKenzie remained perfectly calm on the surface, but her eyes betrayed her. She didn't like the idea that her employers thought her no longer capable of coping with her own job. Sir Donald's first wife would never have suggested such a thing.

Adam stepped forward, his breakfast plate balanced in one hand. He put his free hand on her ample shoulder and gave her a winsome smile. Her expression softened. Young Mr Adam always had a way with him that she could not resist.

'It's only till your leg heals, Mrs. Mac!' he used the childhood name he had adopted for her as a boy, knowing it would have the desired effect. 'And it's by way of being a favour for me, since I'll be needing a good housekeeper one day. I can't think of anyone better than you to take the Martin girls in hand. You'll teach them well and . . . mind you stand no nonsense from either of them.'

'Yes, Mr Adam, sir!' She beamed at him and retreated, a little lighter of foot.

The sound of voices in the courtyard outside distracted him. Adam left the food getting cold on his plate and went to look out of the window. The two new arrivals were being greeted by Arthur, the family under-butler. He was a bright, brash young man and he already had the young women laughing with his joking banter.

Adam had not seen the younger sister before. She hovered shyly in the shadow of Ellen Martin. From where, he presumed a little unkindly, she was hardly ever likely to emerge. The girl would never have the strong personality or the character of her elder sister.

His eyes lingered on Ellie and something seemed to rise from his diaphragm and stick in his throat. My God, the girl was striking to look at. And right now the sun was streaming through her halo of hair, turning it to pure gold.

He was too far away to see the colour of her eyes, but he already knew them to be as blue as any exotic sea and that there was a risk of his drowning in them if he looked too closely. This sensation had already made its presence felt the day he had sketched her likeness. Since that day, he had made several copies from memory, feeling that he would never want to sketch another face as long as he lived. *She* was the cause of his present discomfort. It had absolutely nothing to do with Sarah.

Adam started at the sound of Cynthia's voice close behind him.

'Having met the mother, I am strongly of the opinion that both girls were strictly raised to the utmost level of respectability. I doubt if either one of them will be willing to stray from the path of righteousness.'

'What strange things you do say, Cynthia.' Adam smiled wanly.

'What strange thoughts you Rockwell men do have, Adam.' Lady Rockwell's smile was a little chilly around the edges and he felt the barb of her comment as sharply as any arrow.

★　★　★

Ellie and Mary looked at one another and smiled. They turned slowly in tandem, taking in the details of what was to be their new home.

It was a surprisingly spacious room, though the old housekeeper had been a touch on the apologetic side, excusing the fact that they would be expected to share.

Waist-high oak panelling went around the

whole room, above which there was an ornate wallpaper depicting pale-pink roses, creamy honeysuckle and green leaves on a dark, wine-red background.

Fortunately, the oppressiveness of the paper was offset by some pretty watercolours of pastoral scenes; and two large windows heavily draped with rose-coloured velvet curtains looked out on a green, undulating landscape beyond formal flower- and vegetable-gardens at the back of the house.

Ellie gazed out of one of the windows and sighed with relief. It was such a joy to be away from the constant booming of the industrial town and the sight of slum dwellings. From here you couldn't even see the kilns belching foul fumes into the atmosphere and there was no dust that got into the hair, the clothes and even the food.

'I think I'm going to like it here,' she sighed and turned back to her sister, who had let her smile fade and was looking about her like a small, lost sheep.

'I'm not sure about that,' Mary said sullenly and tugged at the edges of her light summer-weight jacket as if she were cold, though the day had warmed considerably on their way to the Hall.

'Goodness, Mary!' Ellie remonstrated. 'There's just no pleasing you! Here we are whisked away from nothing less than misery to living in sheer luxury and you're not sure you're going to like it! Really! Have you ever seen anything as sumptuous as this house? This room? Look at it!'

'It's all right,' Mary admitted reluctantly.

Ellie sighed again, this time in exasperation. 'Come on, let's get our things unpacked. Which bed do you want?'

Mary shrugged, looking from one frilled chintz bedcover to the other. 'I'd better take the one nearest the door,' she decided, 'since I'll be getting up first. Anyway, I don't like sleeping by a window.'

Ellie frowned and pursed her lips, thinking that there was a tinge of bitterness in her sister's words.

'Mary, you're not upset that Lady Rockwell chose me to be her lady's maid, are you?'

'I don't care what I do.' Mary shrugged again and started pulling items of clothing out of her bag. 'Which side of the wardrobe do you want?'

'You take the left side. It's nearer to your bed. Mary, what is it, then, if you're not jealous of my position here?'

'Jealous!' Mary's long, thin head shot up as if the thought had never entered into it. 'Don't be daft. What would I know about being something fancy like a lady's maid. I mean, you know all about it after working for the professor. I never got beyond scrubbing me own mam's doorstep. Aye, an' she was never satisfied with how I did that neither!'

Ellie saw the funny side of her sister's remark and burst out laughing then suddenly both girls were laughing and clinging together.

'Oh, Mary! You should know by now that nothing *anybody* does is good enough to satisfy Mam. She sets standards that are so high — well, if you attained them you'd get a nosebleed!'

That started them off laughing again. The ice was broken and they were feeling better. After a bath and some food and a good night's sleep in those soft, clean, comfortable beds, life would no doubt take on a brighter hue.

'I bet Margaret's feeling lonely right now, with us two gone.' Mary said thoughtfully.

Ellie leaned her forehead against a pane of glass as she watched a tall figure strolling about the gardens below. 'Oh, I don't know. I think it's only a matter of time before Ben speaks up.'

'Ben? And Margaret! Go on with you!'

'Haven't you noticed the way his eyes go all soft and follow her around all the time. And she likes him. I could tell that right from the start. Only she's got to keep up appearances. It wouldn't seem right to get involved with a man so soon after she's been made a widow.'

'I can't see our Ben taking on a wife and somebody else's bairn,' Mary burst out, obviously against the idea of her brother taking on another man's responsibilities, even if the man was dead. 'He's never been serious about any girl that I know of.'

'Then it's time he changed tack and settled down.'

'Mam will have something to say about that. Remember when that girl from Fell Street started hanging around Ben a couple of years back? Mam gave her such a tongue-lashing and chased her all over the Bankies threatening her with a fate worse than death if she ever showed her face again.'

'Ben was a fool to let her get away with that. The girl was all right. She would have made a good wife for him. Somehow, I don't think Mam will be able to get away with it a second time. Ben's older and more mature now. What's more, he's ready to settle down. I've seen it coming for a long time now.'

'What about you, Ellie?' Mary asked shyly. 'Do you want to settle down, get married and have bairns and all that . . . ?'

And all that. Mary meant sex. Their mother had raised them to shut out the more intimate side of life. She had drummed it into them day after day since the time they could understand her innuendos, that sex was something vile, unhealthy, sinful; and that no man was to be trusted. *Once you let a man touch you, you've let yourself in for trouble. It'll bring only shame and a lifetime of misery on your heads and on the heads of your family.*

Polly's voice echoed eerily in Ellie's head as her eyes followed Adam Rockwell while he strolled through the garden. As she looked down on him, the dark head lifted and just for an instant their eyes met. Ellie drew swiftly back into the room, her hand flying to her heart, which had skipped an uncomfortable beat.

$$\star \quad \star \quad \star$$

Adam had experienced the strange feeling of being watched. He looked up and saw a movement. In the fleeting second it took for her to remove herself guiltily from the window, he saw her lovely face and again something deep down inside him stirred.

He felt her eyes burning into him. Although he knew them to be of the brightest, clearest blue, they appeared dark as navy at that distance. He was almost sure her cheeks had flamed with the embarrassment of being caught spying on him, if that was indeed what she was doing. He couldn't quite make out her mouth, but felt those full lips were seductively parted and he almost heard her small gasp of alarm as their eyes met.

He tore at his bottom lip, then gave a short chuckle. Then he stuffed his hands in his trouser-pockets and moved on through the kitchen-gardens. He was taking a rare few hours off from foundry work. The weather was fine, the land dry and perfect for walking.

Adam gave a shrill whistle and two large dogs, a rust-coloured Gordon setter and a pure cream long-haired retriever came bounding joyfully towards him.

'Here Dougal! Come on, Scallion! It's time all three of us got some healthy exercise.

The man and the two dogs left the gardens and turned north towards meadowland and undulating hillside country that was unspoiled by blast-furnaces and molten metal. It was fresh and soft and green and Adam could lose himself in it.

★ ★ ★

Ben's bed creaked and groaned as he tossed from one side to another in the dark. It was after midnight and he still hadn't managed a wink of sleep. Finally, with a desperate grunt, he flung his legs out of the bed and stood up.

'Is me coughing keepin' ye awake, Ben?' Tommy asked hoarsely. 'I'm sorry.'

'It's nowt to do with yer coughin', Tommy,' Ben whispered. 'I'm well used to that by now.'

'What is it, then?'

'Ach, man!'

'Oh . . . er . . . aye, I see . . . well, I think I do . . . it's *her*, isn't it?'

'Keep yer voice down, Tommy. Ye'll wake our Archie.'

'That boy would sleep through anything. Just listen to him drivin' the pigs to market!'

Archie, for all his tender years, could snore like the best of men, and was doing just that as they spoke.

'The innocence of the young.' Ben smiled wryly through the dark.

'So?'

'So, what?'

'I asked ye a question afore. Is it *her* that's botherin' yer sleep?'

Ben gritted his teeth and heaved a loud sigh. 'Well, it's not me mither, our Tommy,' he growled like a disgruntled bear. 'Nor is it me dad or you or Archie or the girls who've left us to go an' work ower yonder at Rockwell Hall. An' it's certainly not the tallyman or his daughter with breasts like balloons and a bum like the rear end of an elephant.'

'I'd settle fine for that one,' Tommy chuckled through rasping efforts to breath easily. 'I'd like a bit o' comfort afore I go to the other place.'

'Don't talk rubbish, Tommy, lad!' Ben's response was sharp like a gunshot. So sharp that it disturbed Archie, who gave a strangled cry in his sleep and thrashed about until his head was buried deeper beneath the covers.

'Well, it's true.' Tommy managed a whisper. 'With this blasted chest o' mine and me dicky heart . . . '

'Stop it, I tell ye! Stop that talk right now. Ye're gonna be fine. Ye just have to take things a bit easy-like.'

'Easy like what, Ben? Like don't do a man's work, don't exert mesel', don't have . . . women. It's all right for the likes o' you wi' all yer brawn and yer muscle. Where did all that come from, I'd like to know. There certainly wasn't any left for me when I came along.'

'Are ye sayin' that it's my fault the way ye are, lad?' Ben's own voice was rising now and Archie, from the depths of his slumbers, was mumbling and whimpering.

'I'm sorry, Ben. Take no notice. You're not

185

the only one to be having a bad night. All my nights are bad.'

Ben shook his head and wiped a clammy hand over his face. It came away even wetter from the perspiration of his brow.

'I feel bad, Tommy,' he said. 'I feel real bad about all this, but I have to have her.'

'Even wi' a bairn in her belly that's not yours?'

'Aye. Even then.'

'Well, ye'd better go to her, then, but be canny about it or me mam'll be at ye wi' a carvin' knife if she hears ye provin' yer manhood through the wall.'

'Aye. It was a sight better before they decided to put themselves into the girls' room, but at least we don't have me dad snoring in the kitchen all day long.'

Fumbling in the dark, Ben pulled on a long clean work shirt over his naked body. He was glad it was so dark in the room, for he would have been embarrassed to have his desperate state of excitement seen by his younger brother. He quickly and clumsily buttoned the shirt and crept, barefooted out of the room, across the creaking landing and stationed himself outside Margaret's room.

He waited for what seemed an interminable time, then scratched like a dog on the door, rather than rap his knuckles and have it wake the whole house.

At first there was nothing but a soft purr of breathing, then even that stopped and there was absolute silence from the room. He scratched again and he thought he heard a small gasping sound. Then there was a pad of bare feet on hard linoleum.

'Margaret!' he called softly through the closed door.

'Who is it?' she called back, her voice barely audible and sounding scared.

'It's me — Ben!' Ben's heart started to thud so loudly in his chest he could hardly hear himself speak.

The latch grated and the door swung open a couple of inches. Margaret's pale face showed in the gap, caught by a stray moonbeam coming in from the landing window. 'What do you want?'

Ben waited. He looked about him and listened. Nobody in the house was stirring. It was now or never.

'God forgive me,' he said gruffly. 'but I want you, hinny — if ye'll have me?'

The door swung slowly back. He caught his breath and held it for as many seconds as it took Margaret to step forward and throw herself at his big, barrel chest. 'Oh, Ben,' she whispered weakly against his bare throat. 'Oh, my lovely Ben!'

He felt the small, swollen round of her belly pressing against him with its precious cargo that he had had no hand in creating and he didn't care. At that moment he didn't care about anything but the passion that was rising in him enough to engulf him. And Margaret seemed to be of the same mind.

8

Ellie subdued a sigh of boredom. Her fingers ached from an hour of cleaning silver. She hated the smell of the cloying salad oil she was rubbing into the tarnished metal. The odour clung to her clothes and came up at her in sickening waves.

'There must be some other way to clean silver!' she complained, out of Mrs McKenzie's hearing.

'There is,' Mary muttered, 'but Sir Donald claims we use too much whisky, so we do it this way instead just to keep him happy.'

'Whisky!'

'Aye.' Mary grinned surreptitiously. 'He claimed that the kitchen staff in the past used to clean the silver a bit too often for his liking and were known to be falling over drunk by teatime.'

'What do you do with the whisky, then?' Ellie asked, thinking that she could probably stand the alcoholic fumes better than she was coping with the salad-oil.

'Well, first off, you don't drink it, our Ellie! You mix it with whitening, rub it into the silver and when it dries you have to brush it

189

off with a soft brush.'

Ellie considered that one method seemed as bad as the other, in that she had fallen foul of whitening in the past when her mother used it. It had made her sneeze and cough so much she couldn't see out of her eyes for hours.

'I think I'll just stick to the salad-oil,' she sighed.

She had offered to help Mary in the task, not because Mary was overworked, but because she, herself, had so little to occupy her time.

They had been at the Hall for nearly four weeks and were looking forward to their first weekend off in a few days' time.

Ellie's heart flipped as she suddenly found herself with a bad case of nostalgia for her life with Professor Graham. Maybe she should have stayed and married him, after all. Even without the 'magic' she dreamed of, they might have been happy.

'Oh, no!'

'Ellie, what on earth are you thinking about!' Mary cried, jumping to her feet and running for a cloth to mop up the salad-oil that was flowing like liquid satin across the whitewood kitchen table.

'Sorry!' Ellie shook her head, not believing that she could possibly have been so clumsy.

It wasn't like her at all.

'Now I'll have to scrub the table and I only just got it clean after all the cooking that went on this morning.'

'I'll do it. I spilled the stuff, after all,' Ellie told her, grabbing the cloth and wiping the mess from her fingers.

'You're not even supposed to be down here,' Mary complained, though Ellie knew that her sister had been glad of her company up until that moment.

'I have to do something to occupy my time, Mary,' Ellie told her with a grimace. 'Lady Rockwell is so undemanding, I'm often left with time on my hands and I find it particularly boring because I have to be seen to be busy. Otherwise they're going to think I don't earn my wages.'

Both young women kept their voices down since they were surrounded by the rest of the kitchen staff bustling over a variety of kitchen chores and cooking. A great cauldron of soup was simmering nicely, imparting a mixture of delicious aromas. And on the spit two suckling pigs sizzled as they were turned and basted every few minutes, their short porcine legs sticking out stiffly as if in supplication.

And Mrs McKenzie wandered in and out, supervising in the gentle, yet authoritarian way she had. She found no objection to having Ellie taking up space in the kitchen. She liked the girl immensely. They had very soon become firm friends, despite the difference in their ages.

Ellie rescued the few remaining pieces of silver, transferring them to another, smaller table, while Mary fetched a bowl of hot water with dissolved soda laced with a little vinegar and started scrubbing down the table vigorously with a stiff bristle brush.

She glanced at the big wall clock with its black Roman numerals and decided it was time to lay out their mistress's clothes for the evening ahead. It was to be a special dinner party in honour of Sir Donald's sixty-fifth birthday. Lady Rockwell had been twittering on about it for days, worried in case things did not go smoothly.

'Aye, lassie!' Mrs McKenzie tapped her on the shoulder. 'Ye'd better be getting yersel' above stairs to see to her ladyship. What colour frock has she chosen to wear?'

'She couldn't make up her mind so she said she would leave it up to me. She has so many, I hardly know where to start.' Ellie pulled a face and the old housekeeper chuckled.

'Take a tip from me and put out the emerald-green one with the dipped hemline and the black feathers. It has a row of black sequins around the neck and to the edge of the matching coat. She hasn't worn it yet, to my knowledge, and I happen to know that green is Sir Donald's favourite colour.'

'Oh, thank you, Mrs Mac!' Ellie beamed happily now that her job had been made easier. 'And it will match her eyes, too. Yes, that's an excellent idea.'

She turned to hurry out of the kitchen, but found her way blocked by a solid male form. She didn't have time to see who the man was before colliding with him and the impact almost knocked the breath out of her. A pair of strong hands steadied her and she looked up into the handsome but unsmiling face of Adam Rockwell.

'Oh! Oh, I'm sorry! I-I . . . ' She clamped her mouth shut and bit on her lips as a slow smile spread across his face and, just for a brief moment, lit up his eyes. Then the smile faded just as quickly.

'You'll do yourself an injury dashing about like that, young lady.' The deep, mellow voice was the voice she listened for constantly as she went about her duties. It was the voice she heard, more than the face she saw, for he was hardly ever near enough to her to reach out and touch.

Ellie quivered to the core of her being at the thought of ever being able to touch Adam

Rockwell. She pulled herself up short, flashed her blue eyes at him and told herself she would have to make do with occasionally bouncing off him accidentally in doorways.

'Run along, Ellie.' Mrs McKenzie had come forward and was frowning at her master's son, her eyes narrowed with curiosity. 'Her ladyship will be waiting for you, no doubt.'

'Yes, Mrs Mac,' Ellie said a little breathlessly, then with one more glance up at Adam, she excused herself huskily and pushed past him through the doorway. She had to push her way through, because he showed no sign of moving.

With her cheeks burning, she hurried down the corridor and up the servants' back staircase to her room, where she changed into her smarter brown silk frock and white frilled apron, which Lady Rockwell preferred her to wear in the evenings, being somewhat less formal than her daytime black outfit. Despite the fine materials used, neither dress pleased her. The colours did nothing for her colouring, being too dark and drab.

Ellie longed to wear the kind of dresses that were to be found hanging in Lady Rockwell's dressing-room. The blues in particular, the greens, the golds and the rubies. All the colours of precious gems, rather than the colours of damp earth, clay and peat.

She sighed and made her way to Lady Rockwell's private rooms, telling herself that she was ungrateful and should learn to be more content with what life and fate threw her way.

★　★　★

'Now, then, Mr Adam,' Mrs McKenzie was fixing Adam with a stern eye and he could see that her mother-hen feathers were a little ruffled, 'what are you doing down here below stairs again? You know it's not fitting for the young master of the house to be found in the kitchen. Now you keep away from those suckling pigs or you'll get yourself splashed with fat.'

'Not to mention my fingers slapped, eh?'

Adam smilingly ignored her warning and, taking a long carving knife, snipped off a slice of crispy crackling and succulent pork. One of the maids quickly provided him with a plate. Another produced a napkin and they watched, wide-eyed as he picked up the meat in his fingers and devoured it before them with great gusto.

'Go back to your room, Mr Adam and I'll have a plate sent up to you, then you won't disturb my work — or my girls.'

The girls in question kept glancing at Adam over their shoulders and giggling uncontrollably behind their hands as they stirred sauces, chopped vegetables and whipped cream. Mrs McKenzie turned a beady eye on them and they bowed their heads over their work, stifling their laughter. They all liked the housekeeper, but she could be severe when she wanted to be.

'All right, Mrs Mac.' Adam turned to go, then spun back, pulling something out of his pocket. 'Oh, I almost forgot why I came here in the first place. Do you recognize this chain and medallion by any chance? I found it in the kitchen garden a little while ago. It looks as if it may have some value.'

Mrs McKenzie glanced at the silver pendant swinging from Adam's fingers, then she called to Mary.

'Mary, would this be the chain I've seen your sister wearing?' she asked.

Mary came shyly over and peered at the pendant, then nodded. 'Yes, Mrs McKenzie. It's our Ellie's. She'll be very upset when she realizes she's lost it.'

'Well, it's fortunate I happened to be strolling in the kitchen gardens and found it, so no harm done.' Adam looked down at the girl who was so different from her sister it was unbelievable. One would say they belonged to very different worlds.

Mary shifted her stance self-consciously and tried to avoid his penetrating gaze as she reached out to take the necklace, but he withdrew it from her fingers.

'It's all right, sir,' Mary spoke up finally. 'I'll take it back to her. We share the same room — '

'Don't bother about that. I'll return it to her myself, seeing that she should by now be with my stepmother and that's exactly where I'm heading. Don't worry, child! I'm not going to steal it.'

'No, sir.'

'Come along, Mary.' The housekeeper was looking a trifle flustered and impatient. 'Let Mr Adam return Ellie's necklace if that's what he wants to do. Now, I need you to come and help me to spin some sugar for the sweet pudding.'

Adam nodded, gave her a lopsided smile, then left the women to their various occupations.

★　★　★

Lady Rockwell was rather nervous and tetchy that evening. Ellie deduced that at the moment she arrived at her mistress's suite. She was only a minute late, but the woman was already pacing the floor and wringing her hands.

'Ellen! Thank goodness you're here at last. Where have you been, girl?'

'I'm sorry, madam, but — '

'No, don't bother me with excuses now. What do you think I should wear this evening? For the life of me I still can't make up my mind. The occasion is far too important and I have a lot on my mind.'

'Well, madam . . . ' Ellie hesitated as she saw Lady Rockwell watching her expectantly. 'I think this one would be perfect.'

Ellie took down the green dress and held it up for Lady Rockwell to inspect. The woman did so with a doubting frown.

'The green? Are you sure?'

'Yes, madam.' Ellie nodded and draped the dress over the *chaise-longue* which was upholstered in pale-gold-and-maroon Regency satin. The colour stood out well against such a distinguished background. 'I have it on the highest authority that it's Sir Donald's favourite colour and . . . well, if I might suggest, madam, it will go very well with your eyes and your creamy complexion.'

'Hmm.' Lady Rockwell sighed and picked up the hem of the dress, fingering it thoughtfully. 'I bought this for a special occasion and never wore it . . . All right! Why not? And let's hope I haven't put on weight since I bought it. Help me, would you, Ellen?'

Lady Rockwell was standing in her undergarments when a light tap sounded on the door and she called out immediately to whoever it was to enter.

When the door swung open and Adam Rockwell stood silhouetted against the yellow glow of the landing light, both women gasped their surprise and flushed with embarrassment. Ellie immediately stepped in front of her mistress to hide her state of undress.

'Adam!' Lady Rockwell snapped at him angrily, yet made no effort to cover herself. 'When I told you to come in I thought you were one of the maids or at the very most my husband.'

'Well, now, Cynthia,' Adam's eyes were dancing with humour and his mouth twitched into a wicked smile which he switched from his stepmother to Ellie, 'as you see, I am neither.'

'Then what are you doing here in my dressing-room? Go away!'

'I came simply to ask you whether you had considered setting Colonel Remington next to my father at dinner. I know he has rather urgent business to discuss and he's quite apt to shout it across the table while he slurps his soup. I thought it might be . . . shall we say

'. . . propitious . . . to avoid such a possibility.'

Ellie could feel the heat of her mistress's body burning into her back, could even feel the beat of the woman's heart, the agitated twitching of her hands. Could there, she wondered, be something going on between these two? How ridiculous. The woman was Adam Rockwell's stepmother — but she *was* only about five years older.

She clamped her teeth down on her lower lip and fixed Adam with a curious stare. When he returned it her heart missed a beat. And when his smile widened and seemed to be for her and her alone, she felt something give inside and the fluttering in her stomach swooped low, startling into life a sensation between her legs that seemed frightening and wicked, but at the same time so exciting she could hardly control her breathing.

'Well now, little Ellen,' he said, his dark eyes mocking her and she wished he would not refer to her as if she were a child. 'Have you by any chance noticed that something belonging to you is missing?'

Ellie lowered her brows and, automatically, her hand went to her chest, feeling the bareness beneath her robe. The professor's silver locket was gone. She gave a small gasp. It was the only thing of value she possessed and, despite the final outcome of their relationship, it had great sentimental value.

'My locket!' she said as Adam held out the necklace, dangling it before her eyes. 'Oh, thank goodness! Where did you find it, sir?'

'It was adorning a rather ornate cabbage in the kitchen garden,' Adam said, watching her carefully. 'I feel that the cabbage will never wear it with as much dignity as its real owner, however. Where did you acquire such a pretty object?'

He had still not passed over the pendant, but was turning it over in his fingers, scrutinizing the inscription engraved on the back.

'It was a present, sir,' Ellie told him quickly, reaching out once more, but having it snatched away from her. 'From my previous employer.'

'I see.' Adam's eyebrows rose and fell like two black raven's wings. He stared at the inscription a while longer, then looked at her with renewed interest as he recited the words he had seen engraved there: '*To dear Ellie, in gratitude, N.G.* You must have indeed been a valued employee. What did you do to earn this *bijou*?'

'Adam, must you put the girl through some sort of inquisition just to satisfy your bizarre curiosity? Do go away and let me get dressed.

I'm starting to get goose-bumps, it's so cold in here.'

Lady Rockwell had moved away from Ellie's protective stance and was wandering unselfconsciously across the room in her chemise, which was extremely skimpy and short and showed a pair of very elegant lace garters holding up her silk stockings.

Ellie's jaw dropped at the sight of what appeared, to her naïve and inexperienced mind, a touch of unexpected decadence on the part of the mistress of Rockwell Hall. She drew in a gulp of shocked air and heard a low-throated chuckle a little too close to her ear for comfort.

Adam Rockwell had taken a step forward and was standing almost touching her. She could smell his very special odour of freshly washed skin, musky and warm.

'Here you are, careless child,' he muttered, thrusting the pendant at her in what seemed to be an angry gesture, then he turned on his heel and marched out of the room without bothering to close the door behind him.

Slipping the pendant into her pocket, Ellie went to close the door. By the time she turned back into the room, Lady Rockwell was already wearing the green dress and was admiring herself before the tall cheval mirror.

'My stepson is *the* most irritating man,' she

was saying to her reflection as she smoothed her hands over her bosom and her hips, obviously highly pleased with what she saw. 'Pay him no mind, Ellen. One never knows exactly what is going on in that head of his and I find that so infuriating. His father, on the other hand, never leaves me in any doubt whatsoever. This was a good choice of dress for this evening, Ellen. Thank you, my dear. Now, will you find me some shoes and an evening bag that will go with it.'

'Yes, madam. I thought the black patent slippers and the beaded evening bag with the little motif of encrusted pearls.'

'Perfect. You're an absolute gem. Already, I hardly know what I would do without you. Now, run along. I shan't need you again until tomorrow when I think I'll take you with me on one of my Committee visits into the town.'

'Yes, madam. Thank you very much. I hope you have an enjoyable dinner party.'

'Hmm?' Lady Rockwell was sitting gazing at herself in the dressing-table mirror, holding a triple string of pearls at her throat. 'Oh, yes . . . yes, of course. Good evening, Ellen.'

Ellie left the room and made her way to the dining room where she had promised Mrs McKenzie she would give her a hand with the table. It was an extra special occasion and the poor woman was a bit fraught in case things went wrong.

The dining-room was all hustle and bustle when she arrived, with Mrs McKenzie in the centre of it all, issuing instructions to her staff like a sergeant-major in the army.

'Ellie! Oh, am I glad to see you, hinny! I'm really pushed. Are you sure you won't mind helping me out a bit tonight?'

'Of course, Mrs McKenzie.' Ellie brightened at the prospect of having her hands occupied.

'I know I can count on you to do a good job. The girls are so nervous they'll like as not lay the cutlery back to front and get the place-names all in the wrong order to boot.'

Forty-five minutes later, all was ready. Mrs McKenzie disappeared to the kitchen to supervise what remained to be done to the food. The other girls had already drifted away to their various duties. For a while, Ellie was alone in the great room with its brilliant crystal chandeliers and the heavy, luxurious flock wallpaper with vines, bunches of grapes and doves.

As she took one last look at the dining table, laden down with a huge central floral display, candles and the best silver, her gaze became almost mesmerized. She imagined what it would be like to dine here and maybe to dance to a small orchestra on occasion, locked in someone's arms, swaying to the music. She was so immersed in these very private thoughts she did not hear the soft tread on the thick Aubusson carpet.

Only a fraction of a second before he spoke was she aware that she was not alone after all. She could smell his cologne, then feel his warmth, feel his breath on her ear, wafting the stray curls that always lurked there so waywardly no matter what she did to pin them up neatly.

'What dreams are passing through that pretty head of yours and giving you such a rapt expression?'

Ellie whipped around, swallowing back a gasp of astonishment.

'You shouldn't creep up on people like that — sir!' she admonished, then flushed crimson to the roots of her hair as she realized to whom she was speaking. 'I'm sorry, sir. I shouldn't have spoken like that, but — but you took me by surprise.'

Adam ignored her admonishment, as he did her apology. 'So what *were* you thinking about just then?'

Ellie dragged her eyes from his face before he could read something in her expression that would give her racing pulses away. It was so unfair of him to do this to her. It was cruel, wicked.

But it's not his fault! He is totally unaware of how his presence affects you. You're a fool, Ellie Martin.

She fixed her gaze back on the table. 'I was admiring the table,' she told him in a small, weak voice that made her want to stamp her foot angrily and kick out at something.

'It is certainly not to be commended for its simplicity,' he said.

It was a sarcastic comment that made her afford him a sideways glance and she saw again his sly smile and mocking eyes and wished they wouldn't play tricks with her emotions. How was it possible to have two conflicting emotions about the same person both at the same time?

But that was exactly what she had about Adam Rockwell. While one part of her was deciding that she disliked him intensely because of the way he made her feel, another quite separate part of her was drawn irrevocably towards him. There was no getting away from it. Adam Rockwell was the most devilishly attractive man she had ever met and her growing desire for him was doing all manner of weird and wonderful things to her body.

'What have you done with your pendant?'

'It's here,' she said, bringing out the silver locket from her pocket. It gleamed brightly in the light from the chandeliers. 'I'm very grateful to you for finding it, sir. It would have upset me to lose it.'

'Then you should wear it always, but make sure the clasp is properly fastened. Here, let me do it for you.'

Before she knew what was happening, Adam had taken the pendant from her and was fastening it about her neck. When she felt the light touch of his fingers nudging her she was seized with a strange rippling sensation that ended in a shudder.

Adam, the necklace securely fastened, turned her to face him, fingering the silver locket thoughtfully before stepping back and smiling at her. 'There. Now your true love is back near your heart.'

'Oh, but . . . ' Ellie instinctively clasped the locket in a hand that was slippery it was perspiring so much. 'It wasn't like that, sir! I mean, the professor was — a *gentleman*. A very *nice* man. He showed me nothing but respect.'

'Then why did you not stay with him? There was surely no need for you to give up your job just because your family were moving away?'

'No, that's true, sir. That wasn't the reason

I came with them to Rockwell.' Ellie blinked up at him, feeling as always, quite dwarfed by his size.

'Then how was it?'

'We had a slight difference of opinion — something personal . . . '

'You were in love with him, perhaps. Is that why you left him? The unrequited love of a servant girl for her master?'

She had to hold back the sudden impulse to slap his face. He was being insulting and for some reason she believed that he was doing it on purpose. He was trying to get her to react in some way to his careless words, as if daring her to answer him back as an equal.

'On the contrary, Mr Rockwell,' she said coolly, though her chest heaved and her heart seemed to be beating a slow but echoing tattoo against her ribs. 'He was more like a father to me, you see. He taught me things . . . about music, art, history, geography. He taught me to play the piano, though I doubt if I was his best pupil. He even taught me to use his typewriting machine. So you see, sir, I was much more than a simple maid in Professor Martin's house. I was his companion, his pupil and his secretary.' She found herself smiling fondly at her memories. 'Sometimes, when he invited people to lunch or dinner, he would insist that I sit down at table with them, as the hostess. He never treated me like a servant.'

'Quite a speech, Ellie!' Adam leaned back on his heels and applauded her slowly, clapping his long, tapering hands together, the sound reverberating around the walls of the empty dining-room. 'So, with all that, at the end of the day you simply walked out on the poor soul?'

She stared at him, a crease forming between her eyes. He waited patiently as she chewed on the side of her mouth. 'It . . . it was personal, sir,' she repeated at last and stared at one tiny pearl button on his dress shirt.

'Ah! The poor fellow was in love with *you*, was he? Tried to take advantage of your pleasant nature, no doubt?'

'No! He would never do that — he asked me to marry him.' There, she thought, it was out. I never meant to tell him, but I have and he's got a queer light in his eye. 'I could hardly continue working for him after I refused his proposal. Things would never have been the same between us. Never!'

'So, he never got to know the charms of Miss Ellen Martin,' Adam whispered stepping closer until she had to strain her neck to look up at him. 'Never sampled those tender lips, never knew what it was like to hold her, touch her, love her. He must be a very sad individual these days, Ellie.'

'Perhaps.'

'Don't you feel guilty about that?'

'Yes, in a way, but I could never have married him.'

'No? Why not? He could have kept you in a manner far beyond the dreams of a miner's daughter.'

'That may be true, Mr Rockwell, but I still couldn't have married the professor, because I wasn't in love with him.'

'I had not thought to discover such principles in a pretty young woman who offers such exciting promise.'

As he was speaking his fingers locked around her upper arms and he was drawing her closer, ever closer, until she was pressed hard against his chest and it was difficult to breathe. Ellie's throat tightened, though whether from fear or excitement she could not tell.

'What would it be like, I wonder, to sample the delights of Ellie Martin?'

She caught a waft of whisky on his breath and jerked her head away as his face descended, his lips searching for hers, his fingers digging ever deeper into her flesh. In a flash she remembered what the carter had told her and Mary when he brought them to

Rockwell. *Like father like son*. Was that how it was to be?

'Stop it! Stop it at once!' Ellie pushed at his chest, wincing at the pain his hold on her arms brought her. 'How dare you! You've been drinking and I'm not going to let you take advantage of me, even if you are *Mister* Adam Rockwell . . . *sir!*'

He released her so suddenly she almost fell. With his hand to his perspiring forehead, he half-turned from her, spitting out a harsh expletive under his breath. Then he straightened and looked immediately sober, though his eyes were troubled.

'You're quite right. I'm sorry, Ellie. Please . . . ' he held out one hand in her direction, palm towards her. 'Please forgive me. I have never — *never* done that before. How very stupid of me! I don't know what came over me. For one crazy moment, all I could think of was . . . '

His words tailed off and she watched him silently as he cast her a ravaged glance. Then he went from the room, the epitome of a man in torment and filled with remorse. And he left behind him a young woman filled with a confusion of thoughts and feelings that she thought she would never untangle.

On legs that were almost too weak to carry her, Ellie made her way to her room. There was only one thought that circled in her head like a spinning top. It was a thought that made her burn with anguish and guilt.

Oh, God, I wish I had let him kiss me! Just once! At least then I would know how it felt to be in his arms, have his lips on mine.

She flung open the door of the room she shared with her sister. Tears were near the surface, but she refused them access, stamped on them angrily and ordered them to go away. Weeping was something she resented bitterly. Besides, it made her look so ugly.

Mary, however, had no such prejudice against weeping. She was sitting on her bed sobbing her heart out, scissors in one hand, a hank of tangled hair in the other.

'Goodness, Mary! What on earth have you done?'

'Oh, Ellie! I was helping Mrs Mac spin some sugar for the sweet course th' night. I was doing so well and it looked ever so pretty, but somehow, it all got clagged in me hair! Look!'

She turned her head and showed Ellie a bare patch of skull where she had cut away the congealed toffee. Ellie, her own problems minimized by her younger sister's distress, sat down beside the girl and hugged her tightly, kissing the wet cheek.

'Well, it's better this way than have your

hair end up in the pudding!' she grinned and then both girls were laughing merrily together. 'Never mind. It'll soon grow back in. You'll just have to wear your cap at a more jaunty angle, eh?'

9

Adam was vaguely aware of a growing crescendo of conversation around the table. What had begun as a stilted, if polite, exchange of words, was quickly becoming animated as the guests thawed themselves out on the excellent wine. His father was no connoisseur, but he kept a well-stocked cellar that would impress the most discerning of wine drinkers.

'I'd give more than a penny to know what's going on in that handsome head of yours, Adam!'

The papery-thin voice of Stella Dunstable cut through the cacophony like a fretsaw. Adam jerked his head and blinked in her direction. She sat across the table from him, to the right of her uncle and guardian, the Reverend Wilbert Rawlins.

The vicar of the Rockwell Evangelist Church was a long, thin, spidery man with a shock of white hair and a face like a rather suspicious rat. In fact, all his movements suggested a rodentlike personality, so quick and precise were they. His eyes darted to and fro with a rapidity that disconcerted many of his parishioners. People avoided him when they could, for he was wont to tell them in no uncertain terms that they would certainly go to hell because of some misdemeanour they might or might not have committed.

Adam felt that the man's unfortunate niece would end up in much the same way if she lived in the shadow of his strict and misguided beliefs for very much longer. It was not just for that reason that he made it his business to stay out of her way. It was common knowledge among the community that the young woman was desperately searching for a mate and that her eye was on the iron-baron's son. Pretty enough though she might be, the thought of having any kind of intimate relationship with Stella left him quite cold.

He smiled wanly at her now, not wishing to offend, but determined not to give her any false encouragement.

'I shouldn't bother yourself over my thoughts, Stella,' he said 'It is doubtful whether you would understand them. I certainly don't.'

'You underestimate me, Adam.' She gave him a coy smile that on another woman might have seemed either brash or enticing. 'I'm torn to guess between two contradictory notions and I'm intrigued to know which one is correct.'

'Really?' Adam leaned his elbows on the table on either side of his untouched meal of roast pheasant. 'And what, pray, are these two notions?'

She flexed her shoulders at him and wriggled in her seat, casting a wary eye at her uncle before speaking. However, the Reverend Rawlins was in deep, spiritual conversation with Patricia Beresford on his left, who seemed to be giving him her whole-hearted attention.

'Well, I think you are either deeply troubled by something very personal ... ' Stella hesitated, glancing again in her uncle's direction and bit her lips before continuing, 'or you are entertaining thoughts of a young lady. A young lady who has become rather special to you, perhaps. Of course, I might be entirely wrong.'

'You are, as you surmised, Stella, entirely wrong on both counts.' Adam looked her straight in the eye, his gaze unwavering, though inside he experienced an uncomfortable stirring of guilt, for he had indeed been thinking of a young woman in that moment before Stella had baited him. The face that still floated like an ethereal spirit through his mind was that of Ellen Martin, his stepmother's maid. *Ridiculous! Absolutely ridiculous! What am I coming to, being drawn to a member of the household staff?*

Liaisons of that sort were things Adam despised. He had watched his father work his way through a multitude of employees over the years and had hated him for it. Even now, when Sir Donald was of an avuncular age, when he should be thinking of growing old gracefully and wisely, he was still seeking out girls from below stairs. Girls who had to please him or lose their precious jobs.

'But Adam, you can't leave it like that!' Stella was insisting, her face full of avid curiosity. 'What is it that's stirring inside that iron heart of yours to make you look so serious?'

Adam raised an eyebrow. His mouth twitched into the semblance of a smile. 'Nothing, Stella — absolutely nothing,' he said with a small shake of his head and saw a cloud of disappointment pass over her face.

'We really must invite you to tea one day soon,' she said.

'Adam is far too busy these days to go socializing!'

The brief, snappy retort came from Cynthia, who had just turned from a half-hearted conversation with a rather boring young man sporting a drooping moustache and sleepy eyes. Her eyes flashed from Stella to Adam and back again. He saw Stella shrink back visibly.

'Besides,' Cynthia continued, her voice softening considerably as she must have realized how much of her feelings she might have given away, 'he's not really interested in women, are you, Adam?'

'Really, Cynthia!' Adam expostulated. 'You make me sound like some sort of pervert.'

He wiped at his own mouth with his napkin and flung it down beside his barely touched plate. Cynthia gave him a sidelong glance, then dropped her eyes until Sir Donald bellowed out that it was surely time to bring out the puddings. There was nothing sweet about his father, Adam thought, except the man's sweet tooth.

There was, of course, the grand birthday-cake alight with candles, which Sir Donald grumbled about, but blew them out anyway in three attempts and with help from his nearest table-companions. And everyone sang 'Happy Birthday', raising glasses of sparkling champagne.

Sir Donald, Adam saw, was plainly irritated by the fuss. However, he put on a pained smile, mumbled his thanks, and announced that there was some entertainment laid on in the drawing-room for the ladies while the men could discuss more important matters over port and cigars.

Cynthia was instantly on her feet, clapping her hands and ushering her female guests and one or two non-business, non-smoking, non-drinking males into the drawing-room. Then she sought out Adam, a worried expression creasing her face. She had seemed agitated all evening, but now she looked positively panic-stricken.

'Adam, what on earth are we going to do?' She grabbed his arm and hissed in his ear, a solidly frozen smile locked on her face for the benefit of those close to them. 'Mrs. Ruby Penfold and her ladies' choir were supposed to be here half an hour ago, but as yet there's no sign of them.'

Adam tried not to smile too broadly. He had heard the ladies in question on a number of occasions. Heard them and seen them. Personally, he thought that their non-appearance was something of a boon.

'Somehow, Cynthia,' he said, patting her arm. 'I don't think our guests will be too disappointed. You can always ask Patricia Beresford to render something operatic.'

'Heaven forbid, Adam! I know she's my dearest friend, but I wouldn't want to inflict such torture on this gathering. There are some very important ladies present. I'm hoping to enlist their help on my committees. Or at the very least the help of their husbands' cheque books.'

'Ah! Well, in that case, perhaps Patricia was a bad second choice.'

'Go and see if you can see them, Adam, there's a dear. In the meantime, I'll try and organize some card games, or charades, even.'

Adam was crossing the hall, heading for the front door when he spotted Ellie slipping out of the library. She didn't see him until it was too late and almost bounced off him as she turned, dropping the leather-bound volume she had been carrying.

'Well now! What do we have here?' Adam's mouth twisted into an amused smile at Ellie's rosy-cheeked guilt. He bent down and retrieved the book that had fallen at his feet. 'Aha! Dickens. *Nicholas Nickleby*! Are you a devotee of Mr Dickens's works, Ellie?'

'Yes, I am . . . sir,' Ellie lifted her chin proudly.

'Have you read many of them?' Adam had her paralysed into immobility by the penetrating gaze of his dark eyes.

'All of them . . . except this one . . . sir.'

'And so you thought you'd borrow it? Perhaps it might have been wiser to ask permission first. Otherwise you might be accused of stealing . . . '

Ellie's chin lifted even higher. 'I've never stolen anything in my life, Mr Rockwell, I assure you. In my last employment I was allowed to read all of the professor's books and he had a library almost as big as yours. The fact is . . . '

'Yes?'

'I asked Lady Rockwell earlier if I could borrow this book.' Ellie swallowed with difficulty and wished he would take his eyes away from hers just one second to let her catch her breath. 'My sister is unwell and I thought it might cheer her if I read to her for a while.'

He stared at her for a long time without speaking, then drew in a deep breath.

'Well, in future, Ellie, you must ask me, since all the books in this room are mine and some of them are rather valuable.' He looked at her slowly and thoughtfully, his head cocked to one side, so that Ellie felt her knees turn to jelly. 'On second thoughts, you may borrow whatever takes your fancy. You have my permission. But I want a favour in return.'

Ellie took the volume of Dickens from him and clutched it to her chest, but her forehead creased and her eyes grew worried when she realized what he had said.

'What kind of favour, Mr Rockwell?'

He hesitated for effect, then gave a low, wicked chuckle as he read her mind. 'No, nothing like that, Ellen. I don't buy my personal favours from the staff of this household . . . or from anyone else for that matter. And it's no good you looking innocent and coy and pretending you don't know what I mean.'

'I know exactly what you mean, Mr Rockwell — especially after your behaviour earlier, but please go on. What do I have to do to earn your permission to borrow your books?'

He couldn't help admire her dauntless attitude. No other household employee, to his memory, had ever shown such character. Not even that silly secretary who had fled the place in tears because in a moment of weakness she had admitted her love for him. A love that was totally wasted and he had told her so in no uncertain terms.

'Ah, yes! My behaviour was unforgivable,' he said with a small frown. 'I can only apologize profusely and assure you it will never happen again.'

'I'll take your word for that, sir. So, what is the favour you want me to do?'

'The ladies' choir has failed to show up, Ellen. I want you to come into the drawing-room and entertain our guests.

Would you please do that for me? For Lady Rockwell?'

'Me! But I've never — I — oh, no, Mr Rockwell, I couldn't possibly.'

'Nonsense, girl. Of course you could and you will, or you won't lay a finger on *any* of my books, including the one you are clutching so desperately to your chest right now.'

'But I — what can I do?'

'You've already told me that you play the piano. That the professor taught you. Isn't that so?'

'Yes, but — '

'And I've heard you, myself, singing like a lark, putting the blackbirds to shame.'

'You — you've heard me singing? Oh, goodness.' Ellie shook her head in embarrassment. 'I never thought anybody was listening or I wouldn't have . . . oh, dear!'

'Never mind all that now. For your information I find it a singularly pleasant experience to wake up to your delightful voice every morning. Now, will you do as I say? The sooner you get it over with the sooner you can go back to your sister and read to her from Mr Dickens.'

'Well, I . . . '

Before she could resist any longer, Adam had grabbed her wrist and was heading for the drawing-room, dragging her along in his wake. She had to run to keep up with his long strides and he only slowed down as he entered the room where all the ladies of the company and one or two of the gentlemen were already gathered.

All eyes turned and stared as he marched her across the room and her face became like living flame beneath their scrutiny.

'Here we are,' he said, placing her before a grand piano the like of which she had only once seen when the professor had taken her to a concert by a famous pianist. She could no longer remember the pianist's name, but he had played a medley of pieces by Mozart, Chopin and Liszt that she had never forgotten.

'Adam! What are you doing? Why have you brought Ellen in here?' Lady Rockwell was staring wide-eyed at the two of them and whispering frantically across the shiny body of the piano.

Adam smiled benignly and held up his hands, ready to address an already interested audience.

'Ladies and gentlemen. Can I beg your silence for our young entertainer, Miss Ellen Martin. It seems we are harbouring some considerable talent here at Rockwell Hall. Ellen, what are you going to play for us?'

Ellie gagged slightly, her mouth opening and shutting as she met his expectant eyes. Adam's fingers gripped her upper arm and it somehow gave her the courage to continue.

'I — I can play a medley of — of light classical music,' she suggested in a small, shaky voice. 'If you like — sir?'

'Off you go then!' He smiled broadly.

Ellie sat down at the piano and placed her trembling fingers on the smooth ivory keys. She closed her eyes and took a few deep breaths, praying that she wouldn't hit too many wrong notes and make an utter fool of herself. As she struck the first key, a brief image flashed through her mind of the professor smiling and nodding his encouragement. It was all she needed to gain the confidence necessary to perform in front of her curious audience.

She played surprisingly well, but put it down mainly to the perfect pitch of the piano, so different from the old upright she had been accustomed to. There was a grand ovation with more than twenty pairs of hands clapping a sincere appreciation.

Adam was again there at her side, adding his applause. He looked decidedly smug and pleased with himself as if she was his very own creation. Ellie couldn't help but smile.

The applause died down and Adam had

the attention of the audience yet again. 'Now, for an encore, Miss Martin will give us a rendering of Vilia from Franz Lehar's Merry Widow.' He leaned towards her and whispered: 'I do know you are familiar with this one, since you sing it all the time.'

Again, Ellie's mouth opened and closed and she had to swallow several times before she dared play the introductory notes to her song. She was nervous at first. It wasn't quite the same as just playing the piano. The sound of her own voice echoed in her ears and she faltered slightly when Adam Rockwell leaned on the piano and smiled down at her, his handsome face hovering so close to her own.

It was incredible how she suddenly overcame her fears, however. Her singing was suddenly as clear as a bell and a hush had fallen over her audience. When she came to the last note and let it fade away the burst of applause was deafening. She turned to acknowledge it and saw that the other men, including Sir Donald himself, had come into the room and were standing near the door.

Adam came around the piano, offered her his hand and pulled her into the middle of the floor where everyone could see her. She bobbed her head by way of taking a bow and was acutely aware of Adam's eyes and his smile that made her melt slowly from the inside out.

Lady Rockwell's eyes were not quite so warm, and the smile she was wearing appeared to have frozen on her face as she briefly thanked Ellie and turned abruptly away, calling for people to form themselves into groups of four in order to play a little bridge.

'Oh, Adam, do come and be my partner! Daddy's such a bad loser!' Stella Dunstable was tugging at him.

'Sorry, Stella,' Adam said, gently patting her hand. 'But I have business elsewhere this evening, so you'll just have to win without me. Anyway, you know how I hate card-games.'

'Well, I thought, just this once . . . ' Stella pouted sulkily, but got only a raised eyebrow for her pains.

'Come on, Ellie,' Adam whispered urgently in Ellie's ear. 'Let's escape before someone else tries to buttonhole me.' He guided her out of the room, one proprietorial hand lightly placed in the middle of her back. It hardly touched her, yet it seemed to sear her skin like white-hot metal, turning her whole body into a mass of live nerve-endings.

Outside in the hall, with the drawing-room door closed firmly behind them, Ellie turned to Adam and bit down reflectively on her lips.

'I don't think Lady Rockwell was very pleased to have her lady's maid entertaining her guests,' she said wistfully.

'Don't worry about it,' he said, bowing slightly from the waist. 'You were magnificent. Far better than even I thought you might be. And thank you for entertaining us — for entertaining me in particular. I was in a bad mood and the thought of those damned women belting out dreary dirges all evening . . . Ach, it doesn't bear thinking about.'

Ellie was suddenly laughing up at him. All was forgiven. And, for the moment, she was forgetting that he was her employer and she nothing but a lady's maid. They were, in that brief passage of time, conspirators occupying the same plateau.

'I was so scared!' she told him, her hand clasped to her chest.

'You played and sang beautifully. Thank you, Ellie. Don't forget Mr Dickens.' He retrieved the book from the table in the centre of the hall, where he had placed it temporarily. 'There you are. My apologies for keeping you from your sister. I hope whatever ails her isn't too serious.'

'Oh, no.' Ellie was laughing again. 'She's just miserable because she got all tangled up in the spun sugar she made for the pudding.

It had to be cut out of her hair and now she has a bald spot right here.'

She pointed to the side of her own head and stemmed more laughter that was threatening to turn into helpless giggles.

Adam grinned beneath lowered brows and narrowed eyes. 'Well, you tell her that those sugar-strands were delicious nevertheless and I didn't hear one person complain that they had a hair in their pudding.'

They were laughing together like two ordinary people and it was a good feeling. Then suddenly, the laughter stopped. Ellie saw a darkness descend over Adam's face, his eyes become shadowed, veiled in mystery. She looked at him, her humour fading, wondering what was going on in that head of his that he could be so joyful one minute and so grim the next.

'Well, good night, Ellie.' He gave her a short, sharp nod, effectively dismissing her. With the book tucked firmly under one arm she headed for the back stairs, aware of his brooding eyes following her all the way.

★ ★ ★

Ben didn't know which was worse, working down below among the furnaces with the intense heat, or up on the high gantry, which

229

was completely without shelter and exposed to all the elements.

He was up there now on the main gantry and had been there for the last seven and a half hours, stopping only for a ten-minute break to eat his bait. Most of that time he had been shovelling coal on top of the ironstone in the kiln for which he was responsible, keeping it going.

He had to use his own judgement when to throw the coal on. That wasn't the difficult part of the job. The difficult part was keeping his balance in the face of a howling gale that brought with it dust and fumes.

There was always wind up on the gantry platform, but tonight it was particularly vicious. It had started raining an hour or so ago. Heavy sheets of the stuff that zigged this way, zagged that, until he was soaked to the skin and shivering convulsively in between shovelling. On more than one occasion, Ben thought he would prefer to go back to humping pig iron. It meant less money and it was hard work, but at least you had your feet firmly planted on the ground and the men were friendlier.

It had been Adam's order that made him a gantry man as opposed to a stower. When Ben had queried the sudden change, Rockwell had simply laughed and told him not to worry, that by the time he was finished there wouldn't be any job in the foundry he couldn't do.

That was all very well, but some of the men — the other gantry men in particular — seemed to resent his presence among them. He had somehow got himself into the position of a favourite with the young iron master. They didn't like that. Besides, as they were heard to remark behind his back rather than to his face, there were plenty of experienced men who should have got the job ahead of him.

Ben didn't argue with that, but it wasn't his decision, after all. He just did what he was told. And the money was steady. He took home around two pounds a week, every week, after deductions. That was as much as he'd ever earned as a miner at the coalface and there was no risk of being buried under-ground.

Ben had just relaxed after tipping a load of black shiny coal down into his kiln when he was aware of a body staggering along the platform, hanging on to the rail. The man was bowed forward into the driving wind and seemed to be having difficulty in staying upright.

He didn't take much notice of him, thinking it to be one of the checkers the foundry employed to go around poking their noses in everywhere to make sure the men were doing their jobs properly. It was, therefore, a surprise to recognize the broad, ugly face of the under-manager, as he pulled up before Ben, with the usual sneer and the smell of beer strong on him.

'Ah! Martin! Everything all right up here, is it?'

'Fine! Everything's all right!'

They had to shout to be heard over the wind and the foundry noises. Whitfield nodded and wiped his nose with the back of a hand.

'Some of the lads claim you're not pulling your weight, Martin. For that, I'm taking Jones off. You can look after his kiln as well as your own. I'm sure a big bull of a fella like you are can manage to do that, eh?'

'I don't say that I canna do it, Mr Whitfield, but it's not a fair order and you know it.' Ben's knuckles showed white on the handle of his shovel as he clasped it hard, wishing he could crash it over Whitfield's head. It wasn't the first time the man had tried to make things difficult for him.

'Are you refusing an order from a superior, Martin? Because if you are, you're out of here right now. This foundry only employs willing workers and I've already found you to be belligerent and lacking in respect, so you'd better do as I say or — '

'Or what? You'll report me to the owner? It's the owner's son who put me in this job, Mr Whitfield, and don't you forget it. I daresay, if I was to have a word in Mr Rockwell's ear about the way you treat *his* employees, he'd have a bit to say to ye an' no mistake!'

Whitfield's pale eyes opened wide, then narrowed and his mouth set in a mean, thin line. 'I hear that sister of yours is getting herself well in ower yonder in the Hall. And that's another thing the folk around here don't like. Just you tell her to watch it, my lad. She's not the first lass to lose her flower-head to them Rockwells, though I have to say she looks as if she lost it a long time ago!'

Ben stiffened with anger and the shovel rose a few inches, then stopped as the under-manager grabbed hold of it and gave one harsh laugh.

'I wouldn't mind having meself a bite of that one and I will, one day, so tell her to look out.'

Again, Ben drew the shovel up, but the man was hanging on to it too solidly and they were both swaying in the wind, with the gantry platform moving precariously beneath them.

'Ye bugger! I'll do for you if you lay a finger on Ellie — or Mary . . . '

He was vaguely aware of the other gantry-men, along the long line of kilns along the platform, sensing trouble. Their faces were a dusty, windswept blur, but he imagined they were grinning and hoping for a fight.

Whitfield was a strong man, muscle-bound and bulky. He was in his forties, but that didn't stop him being able to thrash the life out of any man half his age who got on his wrong side. Ben had seen him do it on more than one occasion. The men he fought never got up and walked away whistling the way Whitfield did.

He didn't know what his chances were against the under-manager, but he had a feeling they were pretty evenly matched. Except that Whitfield tended to fight dirty and that wasn't Ben's way at all.

The moment had passed. Whitfield, with another sickly grin, released Ben's shovel with a sharp push so that Ben landed heavily against the thin iron safety-rail that went around the platform. He felt it give beneath his weight and heard a grating sound as the tired metal moved against worn stanchions.

Whitfield walked further on to the next but one kiln. He stood a few minutes head to head with the gantry-man working there. The man looked surprised, but nodded and the pair of them came back towards Ben.

'Go on, Jones,' Whitfield said loudly as they approached. 'Get yerself off now. Martin! Take over Jones's kiln, will you?'

Edward Jones nodded to Ben as he passed and spoke quickly out of the side of his mouth. 'Look out fer yersel', lad!'

At least, that was what Ben thought he heard. Jones had been the only one of the gantry-men, so far, to show him any sign of friendliness. He was a quiet family man and, unlike some of the men along the platforms, he was not known to be one of Whitfield's men. Ben was slowly finding out what that meant.

Whitfield's men were in the minority, but they were hard men with, Ben suspected, a cruel streak that gave them pleasure when they carried out the under-manager's orders. Orders that were issued in private and were not meant to get back to the management. One young fella had not understood the unwritten foundry rules and had threatened Whitfield with exposure. Ben, and a few of the others, had never really believed that he fell accidentally into the furnace he was filling.

Ben was so busy with his thoughts and

watching the undulating gait of Jones as he made his way cautiously along the platform that he was caught off-guard when Whitfield bumped into him with the full force of his body.

The iron guard-rail, which was only as high as Ben's thigh, gave way completely and Ben was flung out, shovel and all, legs and arms flailing. He heard the clatter of the shovel landing ahead of him, then his fingers had latched on to something and he gripped it tightly.

The old loop of heavy-duty rope had been there a long time, but it was securely fastened and it took the weight of Ben's fall. He felt the jolt to his shoulder- and chest-muscles as he dropped and swung in mid-air, swearing into the wind that was buffeting him against the stanchions and supports that held up the platform.

There were shouts from above and below. He saw faces looking up at him from the ground as he twirled dizzily round and round like a puppet on a string.

Suddenly, hands were reaching out from above, grappling with the rope, pulling him up until they could grasp him and haul him to safety. Jones was one of his rescuers. Another two lads were with him. It took all three to get him back on to the platform.

When he finally stood, shakily and breathlessly back on his own two feet, Ben saw that Whitfield was standing behind the men, grinning in that sadistic way he had.

'Bloody amateurs!' he shouted for all to hear. 'I told ye to be more careful, Martin! Next time you might not be so lucky!'

Ben exchanged a glance with Jones and the others. Nobody said anything, but it was plain on their faces that they knew as well as Ben did, that it wasn't a careless accident. Whitfield had bumped him on purpose, expecting him to go over.

'Thanks,' Ben said to Jones and nodded to the other two, who were watching him, white-faced. 'All of ye! Ye saved me life. I'll not forget that.'

They gave short, sharp nods and went about their business. All of them had to rush back to their individual kilns and catch up on the business of shovelling coal into them. For Ben it was a busy last hour to his shift with two kilns to feed, but the excitement that was flowing because of the Whitfield incident kept him going until he was eventually relieved by the late-shift men.

He wouldn't give Whitfield another opportunity like that. Next time, he would be ready for the bugger.

10

Sarah Wells was surprised to see Adam. Surprised and a little worried. They had said their goodbyes. Now, in no time at all, he was back knocking on her door and she didn't like the wild, black look in his expressive eyes.

'Come in, Adam,' she said softly and no further words were spoken until she had placed a large whisky in front of him and he downed a good half of it.

'This is unforgivable of me, Sarah,' Adam said finally. 'I apologize and I wouldn't blame you if you threw me out.'

Sarah sighed long and loud. She viewed him from across the room, not trusting herself to get closer to him. She needed to know, first, what had brought him to her in the early hours of the morning.

'I would never do that, Adam,' she told him softly. 'We've been through good times and bad times together over too many years. I know you almost as well as I know myself.' She shrugged and gave a wry smile. 'Maybe even better, if the truth were known.'

'I didn't want to come here, Sarah.' Adam looked at her, then lowered his head into his hands and she heard him take a deep, drowning man's breath. She held on to her silence. Saying nothing was very often the best way to find out what was going on.

'Oh, God, I believed I could organize my life better than this, but I'm not as strong as I thought I was. I know I ought not to have come here, but you are my only true friend. Who else could I talk to about what ails me?'

'Tell me about it.' Sarah perched on the arm of a chair, placed a cigarette in a long holder and lit it, inhaling deeply and blowing out dragon-puffs of smoke from pinched nostrils.

Adam was lying back on the sofa amidst a multitude of soft, feather-filled cushions. They had exhausted mutual passions on this sofa over a number of years, every ensuing year a bonus in her life. She did not know exactly what it had meant for him. Not the same as for her, of that she was sure.

Sarah moved behind Adam. She leaned over the back of the sofa, careful to avoid seeing her own lined reflection in the mirror over the fireplace. It would be too hurtful to her pride for him to look upon this aging woman lusting after a man almost young enough to be her son. As long as she could only see him and could block her mind to her own image, she could be as young as she felt, as young as she wished.

Adam gave a slight groan of pleasure as her fingers massaged his head, his temples, the base of his neck. She always knew what to do to soothe him.

'Do you remember how I used to do this when you were a boy?'

'Mm. Not a boy, Sarah. I was eighteen, almost a man.'

'A boy! A very mature boy, I will admit, but a boy nonetheless. And I? I was a desperate young widow without friends. You were good for me.'

Adam stirred, captured one of her hands and kissed the inside of her wrist, making her squirm with desire.

'We were good for each other, Sarah, my love.'

'But now it's over,' she said, pulling her hand away from him and stepping back. 'Now, the boy is a man, and the man has already fled the nest. And not before time. Tell me what troubles you, Adam.'

When he finally spoke, he did not look at her, but stared at the empty grate and the remnants of a long-dead fire. Like their love, she thought.

'Oh, God!' he groaned.

'If you're about to tell me that you've been

on the rampage and deflowered all the virgins in Rockwell I shan't believe you. Adam, you are no more like your father in that respect than . . . than the bloody curate is. You run a mile if any young woman casts an eye in your direction.'

A small laugh escaped Adam's lips. 'Oh, Sarah, you do have a fine way of putting things,' he said in a low, languid voice. 'And in a way you're perfectly correct. I do back off. But there's none of the curate in me, I assure you. I have no preference for my own sex. The problem is, my body is in confusion with my mind.' He swallowed loudly and shook his head. 'I saw too much of what my father was like when I was a boy. What he still is, even today, though this evening we celebrated his sixty-fifth birthday. I don't want to end up like him, Sarah, yet I can't deny the physical things that are happening to me at the moment.'

'You're a man, Adam. It's perfectly natural to feel desire. If you don't satisfy it you explode — pouf! Like one of your slag-balls at the foundry. Heaven help anybody who is in the firing-line at the time. So who is it you are about to explode over, eh? Not me, I know that.'

She watched his reaction closely, her heart beating heavily inside her breast, but her face giving nothing away. He showed no more than a slight deepening of his permanent frown and he regarded her through eyes that were no more than slits.

'There is a girl,' he said slowly, sitting up and propping his chin up with his clenched fists.

'Ah!'

'It's not how you think, Sarah. I haven't — I mean, we haven't . . . ' His chest heaved and he rubbed his hands over his weary face. 'There's nothing happening between us. Not physically at least. The thing is, there's some mystery surrounding her and her family. Her mother came to see my father and after a short discussion with him he was ordering me to sign up the men of the family for work. We had to create jobs to accommodate them. They're inexperienced in the foundry field, being miners.'

'So?'

'I look at the eldest son, Sarah, and I see myself a few years ago, though he's as fair as I'm dark.'

'You see yourself? You mean — he has the same character, personality or what?'

'A bit of both, but we look alike too. We could even be brothers. In fact, I suspect we are.'

'And the girl? The boy's sister, I presume?'

'Ellie, yes. She's Ben's sister — younger by less than a year.'

'And?'

'She fascinates me, Sarah. It's not just a passing interest. It goes a lot deeper than that. She's beautiful, she's talented — surprisingly so for a simple working-class lass. She has some inner quality that shines out of her and draws me to her like a moth to a flame. I took one look at her and I've wanted her so badly ever since it's like an unbearable pain that won't go away.

'I try to keep out of her way, yet the more I try the more I find myself where she will be at any given moment of the day. I've even prowled about my own home and the grounds just for the opportunity of seeing her, bumping into her, speaking with her. I feel as if I'm going out of my mind.'

'I don't see the problem.' Sarah rose and paced the floor before him, staring down at her hands, which had become like agitated butterflies. 'If the girl is all you say she is and she likes you . . .'

'It's not that. In fact, if I read the signals right, she more than likes me, though I won't go so far as to say that either of us are harbouring ideas of love. There's too much that separates us.'

'Mutual lust can also be something

beautiful and good as well as gratifying,' Sarah said archly, reminding him of their long-standing relationship.

'You don't understand.' Adam leaned further forward, dangling his long arms between his knees, staring down at his feet. 'What if she's my half-sister, Sarah? What then? Maybe it didn't stop with Ben.'

Sarah's eyebrows shot up as she whirled to face him.

'If that's the case, then you certainly have a problem, Adam. I suggest you forget all about this girl and find yourself someone else to appease your sexual appetite.'

Adam got up. Now he was pacing the floor with her. They passed mid-way like sentries on guard duty.

'I tried that. Tonight. I went down into town. I chose a girl, paid highly for her services. I've never done that before. I couldn't perform, Sarah. I was impotent. The very thought of sleeping with anyone who was not special to me — I got sick, made a fool of myself and ran from her like a scared schoolboy.'

'My poor love.' Sarah spoke softly.

'Sarah, what am I going to do, for God's sake?'

She went to him then, ran her fingers up his broad chest and placed them on his shoulders. 'You must get at the truth, one way or the other. Or you must forget this girl and find another.'

'I don't want another.'

'Adam, you will soon become the only iron master at Rockwell. You will be rich beyond your dreams and very influential. A good wife is going to be very necessary.'

'But I don't . . . '

'I'm not talking about love, Adam. I'm suggesting you find the right candidate for the post and form a partnership. Afterwards, you will be able to do what all you great business magnates do. Find a mistress and enjoy the physical side of things while the good wife provides you with a family, a solid foundation and respectability.'

'That's what my father did, Sarah. I don't believe he loved my mother any more than he loves Cynthia. They were just essentials. Business assets. When I was as young as fourteen, I swore I would never be like him. It's a promise made to myself that I will never break.'

Sarah drew back a little, regarding him as though she had never really seen him before. 'In that case, Adam, my dear boy, you will perish in a hell of your own making and not even I will be able to save you.'

$$\star \quad \star \quad \star$$

Ellie looked down at her sister with a frown, noticing how dishevelled and unfresh she looked. 'Mary? Have you forgotten it's our weekend off and we're due to visit Mam and Dad?'

'No, of course I haven't forgotten.'

'But you haven't even washed!'

'I had a bit of a dabble last night. It'll do till we get home.'

'You'll have a good wash right now, Mary Martin,' Ellie ordered, 'or you'll not sit beside me in the cab going home. I'll make you sit up with the driver where the fresh air can blow away the smell.'

'I'll wash me face and hands, just to please you,' Mary said huffily.

Ellie shook her head in exasperation. She clambered quickly into her travelling clothes, pulling on a clean white blouse and a full, long skirt of navy blue that Lady Rockwell had given her, bought at a committee jumble sale last week. The garments fitted her surprisingly well and looked rather too good for travelling in, but Ellie was determined to look as much a lady as possible on her first visit back home after four weeks at the Hall.

'I'll go and leave you to it, then. And mind you wash behind your ears and your neck.

I've seen the odd tidemark there and you ought to be ashamed.'

'Ooh, our Ellie, you sound just like me mam!' Mary complained bitterly. 'Where're you off to in such a rush, anyhow?'

'To the kitchen-garden. Lady Rockwell says we can take a basket of vegetables with us and a ham from the kitchen.'

'You like her, don't you?'

'Yes, I do. She's always very kind to me, even though she seems a bit stiff and starchy at times, but then I would be stiff and starchy if I was married to Sir Donald.'

Mary shuddered. 'He gives me the creeps,' she said, pulling a long face. 'I don't like Mr Adam, neither.'

Ellie glanced at her sister over her shoulder as she went through the door into the dark passageway beyond. 'He's all right,' she said after a moment's hesitation. 'In fact, he's very nice, really.'

Mary's face set rigid as she choked back a derisive laugh. 'You be careful of him, our Ellie. I've seen the way he looks at you. Ugh! It makes me go funny all over.'

Ellie closed her eyes and shuddered too, only her shudder was a delicious sensation and she gave a secret smile, thinking how wicked all these sensations were. And how wonderful.

'I'll see you at the cab in half an hour,' she said, feeling a little breathless. 'Would you bring my hold-all with yours? I don't want to have to come back upstairs again.'

'Aye, all right.'

Ellie left her sister to wash whichever parts of her she deemed important. She hoped she would look clean enough to pass muster with their mother. At the thought of spending time with her mother, Ellie sighed deeply. She wasn't looking forward to the visit. It would be nice to see her dad and her three brothers, but Polly always managed to make things so unpleasant.

The gardeners were already hard at work in the kitchen-plots, digging and weeding beneath a pale sun that strove to burn its way through the damp morning mist. The hillsides were no more than milky silhouettes fading off into the distance.

One day, Ellie dreamed, she would like to walk out there into the hills, get as far away as possible from the foundry town which could still be seen and sometimes heard from the south wing of the Hall. Though she was thankful that the noise was muffled by the distance between them and there was not the dust that the inhabitants of Rockwell had to put up with unless there was a strong south-westerly wind.

'Mornin' Ellie!' Albert, the head gardener peered at her short-sightedly through his pebble eyeglasses. His dry, parchment face wrinkled with pleasure when she smiled back at him.

'Good morning, Albert. What do you think the weather's going to do today?'

Albert whipped off his cloth cap and scratched his balding pate. His slack old mouth gathered itself up into a rucked moue and he shook his head solemnly.

'Hard to tell,' he said sagely. 'Could be good. Could be bad. I'd put me money on middling if I was a betting man. Always safe to hedge yer bets. You off to Northend today then?'

She nodded. 'Lady Rockwell told me to take what I wanted from the garden. Is that all right with you, Albert?'

'God luv us, hinny! 'Course it is. You can come and help yersel' any time you want. There's plenty for all. Here, you gimme yer basket and we'll see what we can find fer ye. You stay on the path, lass. It's a bit muddy after the rain. Wouldn't want ye to get yersel' all dirty for seein' yer ma and da.'

Ellie thanked him profusely and handed her basket over. He went off whistling gaily, trudging along on slightly bowed legs and a back rounded from a lifetime of digging. His

249

two young assistants nodded to her shyly, touching their forelocks deferentially, then returned to their toil.

As she stood waiting for Albert to return to her with a full basket of garden produce, Ellie gazed out at the hazy hillsides and was surprised to see a figure walking towards her through the mist. She recognized the large, dark silhouette of Adam Rockwell almost instantly and her heart leapt.

What on earth was he doing out there, she wondered curiously? Surely he had not been walking all night, for it was still only eight o'clock in the morning and the rest of the household was hardly awake.

But there he was striding purposefully towards the house on those long legs of his, the two dogs at his side. He spent less and less time, it seemed, at the foundry these days. She was forever bumping into him. Not that she minded that, or that it was any business of hers. What did bother her was the way his mood could change so abruptly, almost as if he forgot himself, then remembered who he was before he could get too friendly.

It was an attitude she found quite disturbing. Just when she thought he liked her, he suddenly behaved as if she had done something wrong. Like last night after she had sung to the dinner guests at his insistence.

Her heart missed another beat and her stomach turned over as she thought of how he had been last night. And how she felt this morning just thinking about it. Almost as if her feelings were on show for all to see, Ellie flushed a deep scarlet just as Adam approached.

'So, Ellie . . . ' He pulled up short right in front of her. His forehead was moist with perspiration and he was breathing a little heavily so she assumed he had been walking briskly for some time. 'You were quite a success last night. Even my father and his friends were impressed by your performance.'

'I would have preferred to have had more notice,' she said by way of a mild rebuke and felt her pulses shiver into life at the sight of the amused smile it brought to his serious countenance.

'Yes, I'm sorry about that. I was a bit of a bully, wasn't I? It won't happen again, I assure you. Next time, you will be given as much notice as is necessary — though it's possible that you would have taken fright and not performed at all if the idea had been put to you beforehand.'

She tried to match his mischievous expression without looking too provocative, though his very presence brought out something in her that was shameful. 'I think you may be right, sir. It was very unfair of you to take advantage of my position.'

'Consider me well and truly rebuked. But you played so well,' he said, throwing his head back and looking at her down his nose. 'And you sang like an angel.'

'I was terrified,' Ellie admitted, then turned to take the basket of vegetables from Albert, who touched a finger to his cap and nodded a greeting to Adam. 'Ah, thank you Albert. That looks wonderful.'

'Have a good weekend, Ellie.' Albert winked at her and cocked an eye at his master's son. 'We hear the lass here was a success last night, sir. Better not let the ladies of that choir hear about it. They'll want to poach her.'

'They won't do that Albert, much as they could do with her talents in their midst.' Adam laughed and the sun finally got through, shining on his hair, turning it to blue-black and lighting up his eyes to a warm, sherry-brown. 'In fact, I'll see to it personally that they don't. Ellie, let me walk you to the cab. I presume it's waiting by the side entrance? Give me that basket, girl. It's far too heavy for you to carry.'

He took the basket from her hands, his

fingers brushing against hers. She blinked up at him in embarrassed confusion. His mood was definitely lighter this morning. This was the man in him she liked, but it was also the man who attracted her so much it frightened her. She felt much safer with the dark, brooding, ill-tempered Adam Rockwell who was far less of a threat to her emotions.

Mary was already waiting impatiently by the cab. At the sight of her sister with Adam Rockwell she stopped her fidgeting and stood staring at the pair of them as if turned to stone. How like their mother, Mary was, Ellie mused. How timid and disapproving all in the same small package.

'Mr Rockwell was kind enough to help me with the basket,' she explained to her sister, who stood rigidly to attention and stared fixedly ahead as if Adam weren't there. Ellie turned to him, straining her neck and shading her eyes from the sun. 'Thank you, Mr Rockwell.'

She was holding out her hands to take the basket, but he didn't seem to notice. He was frowning slightly. She put her head to one side and waited. Now what, she wondered?

Adam looked to see who the driver of the cab was, recognized the fellow and called him by name, ordering him to take charge of the basket of garden produce.

'Ellen, I have a proposition to put to you,' Adam said, when his attention finally returned to Ellie. 'I don't want you to give me your response now. I want you to go home to your family, think about it, and tell me what you've decided when you return to your duties on Monday morning.'

'What sort of proposition, sir?' Ellie demanded, her eyes narrowing.

'You're always so suspicious of my intentions,' he objected with a light laugh that sent no humour to his eyes.

'Perhaps I have reason,' she told him without rancour, but looking him directly in the eye so that he could be in no doubt what she meant.

'No, Ellie, you definitely do not have reason! I promise you.'

Mary was tugging at her sister's sleeve and looking rather afraid.

'Get in the cab, girl,' Adam ordered and Mary blinked furiously at him, her lazy eye getting even lazier until it rested right in the inside corner. 'I need to speak to your sister in private and she can't possibly think straight with you tugging at her clothing.'

Ellie inclined her head in her sister's direction and Mary, with one last look of discontent, mounted the steps into the cab just as the horse decided to take itself and its cab a few yards down the lane to a fresher, more succulent patch of grass.

Adam grinned at Mary's gasp of dismay as she was carried off out of earshot. Ellie stifled her own laughter and looked again at Adam, waiting for an explanation.

'You were saying, Mr Rockwell?'

'Ah — yes.' Adam straightened his waistcoat and ran his long fingers through his hair. 'You told me once, Ellen, that you did secretarial work for your professor.'

'Professor Graham — not *my* professor please. It makes it sound — well — not very respectable.'

'Really?'

'Yes, sir. And I assure you, my relationship with the professor was very regular, very respectable.'

'And he never . . . ?'

'No, sir. He never — never did what it is you're thinking.'

'He never touched you?'

'Never! It — he wasn't a man like that — not like . . . ' Ellie's voice trailed off as she remembered to whom she was speaking. 'Not like some employers who — you know . . . '

'Yes, Ellie,' Adam's mouth twisted into a lopsided smile. 'I know what you're inferring.'

There was a sudden protracted silence between them. Adam seemed to have forgotten what he had been about to say. Ellie felt herself being locked into his gaze, not able to move, or to speak. But she could feel. And she was feeling a lot just at that moment.

'Sir . . . ?' she managed to force out that one small word.

'Yes? Oh! I'm sorry, Ellen, I'm keeping you from your family and you must be anxious to see them after four whole weeks away.'

'What was it you were going to ask me?'

There was a moment's hesitation that seemed to last for ever and she thought he had changed his mind. But no. His shoulders rose and fell and he seemed to find something of ultimate interest in the tendril of hair that the breeze was playing with.

'I did wonder if you would consider being *my* secretary, Ellie,' he said at last. 'Of course, it would mean you giving up your position as my stepmother's maid, but . . . I'm sure we could all come to some amicable arrangement.'

Ellie felt her eyes widen and was sure they were probably sticking out like, as her father would have said, chapel hatpegs.

'I — I . . . ' She clamped her mouth shut and swallowed deeply.

'Think about it over the weekend. If you decide not to take up my offer I will have to advertise, of course. And, of course, there will be a rise in your salary if you agree to become my secretary.'

Ellie looked about her, flustered, her brain in turmoil, her heart leaping inside her like a rubber ball on a string.

'Of course,' she heard herself say stiffly as she climbed into the cab beside Mary on legs that had become wooden. 'Thank you, Mr Rockwell. I . . . I'll let you know my decision . . . on Monday.'

Then the driver was flicking his whip and the horse set off at a brisk trot, leaving a trail of dust behind its flying hoofs. Ellie sat erect in her seat, not daring to look back, for she knew he would be standing there still, and her glance might be construed as flirtatious.

'What was all that about, our Ellie?' Mary's voice broke the spell.

Ellie closed her eyes tightly and gripped Mary's hand. 'I'll tell you later,' she said in a breathy whisper. 'You won't believe it. *I* don't believe it.'

★   ★   ★

Ben surprised them by being there to meet them on the other side of the river when the ferry docked. He worked the second shift, from two in the afternoon till ten at night now that he had been promoted to gantry-man and spent his days teetering along a wooden planking a hundred feet from the ground.

'Well, just look at ye!' He laughed and held Ellie at arm's length before swinging her off her feet in a great bear hug, then turning to give a less demonstrative hug to Mary. 'What a sight for sore eyes, eh?'

'Our Ellie's getting to be even more posh than before, if that's what ye mean, Ben.' Mary sniffed and threw her head in the air as she walked out in front of them along the rough track through the tiny community of Northend.

'What's up wi' her, then?' Ben nudged Ellie and pulled a sour face at his younger sister's rigid back. 'You two had a barney or something?'

Ellie sighed and shook her head with a sad little smile. 'No, Ben. I think she's a bit put out because she's just a scullery-maid and — well, she's not made any friends at the Hall.'

'Snooty lot, are they?'

'Not at all. They're all quite nice, really, but Mary keeps herself to herself. You know what she's like, Ben.'

'Aye.' Ben sighed and brushed a big, rough knuckle along the side of her jaw. 'She's like me mam, in more ways than one. But at least she doesn't go about spending money she hasn't got. That's something to be thankful for, eh?'

'How are things at home?'

'Oh . . . ' He blew out air from pursed lips and shrugged his big shoulders. 'Mam's got a bad back, but she won't see the doctor about it. Dad's as silent as ever. Gets on with life without complaint. Tommy's doing all right. He's got a bit of a job. You know how good he is with wood? Well, the folks around here are paying him to make things — coffins mainly. But he takes it easy and he seems satisfied with the work. It brings in a bit extra money.'

'And Archie?'

Ben laughed, a huge belly guffaw that only he could do. 'Oh, aye, Archie! That bliddy little rascal is actually going to school in the town. Your Lady Rockwell organized it. 'Course, he had to be dragged there the first few times, but now he seems to enjoy it, except when he takes it into his head to do something else that appeals to him more. You know, like poachin' the odd chicken or rabbit or just sittin' by the river whittlin' away on a piece of soft wood.'

'Lady Rockwell still has that bird he gave her,' Ellie remembered. 'I think she quite took to him. Anyway, I'm glad he's getting some education. I've been on at our Mary to join one of the evening classes. You know, she still can't read . . . Ben? You haven't mentioned Margaret. How is she? Is she still living with us?'

Ben's square head dropped and he studied the ground before him as they walked. 'Oh, aye, she's canny, ye know. Good days and bad days, like.'

'Well, I suppose that's normal in the circumstances.' Ellie looked sideways at her brother and wondered what it was that was bothering him. Had he and Margaret had a disagreement? 'How's the baby. Is it all right?'

He nodded silently, then rasped a hand over his unshaven chin. 'Apparently. It's beginning to show more these days. She's about six months.'

They walked some more in silence, but as they got within sight of the small cottage Ben stopped and pulled at Ellie's arm, his face clouded with anxiety.

'Ellie — Ellie, I asked her to marry me — you know — Margaret.'

'Yes, Ben. Mam wrote and told me. I gather she isn't in favour, but don't take any notice. If you and Margaret love each other, that's the important thing. Not what Mam or Dad or anybody else thinks.'

'Aye, well — that's mebbe so, but . . . '

'But what, Ben? Is there another problem?'

He started to shake his head, then changed his mind. 'Aye, there is, lass. I've got awful mixed feelings inside me about this — this business about her carryin' another fella's bairn. You know? I didn't think it mattered, at first. I was so taken wi' the lass. Now, I'm not so sure. She's different too. And then there's Tommy ... Ach, Ellie, I'm all confused inside, you know?'

Ellie nodded slowly and slipped her arm into his, hugging it to her side. She had enough confusion going on in her own mind without trying to sort out her brother's emotional problems. But she smiled at him sympathetically anyway.

'What about Tommy?'

Ben pulled in air in a great long sniff and sucked on his teeth for a while. 'I think he's in love with Margaret. Dammit, Ellie, just what am I going to do?'

Ellie was a great believer in sitting tight when the way ahead seemed irrevocably blocked and she told Ben so. He didn't seem to get much solace from her words, but they had arrived at their own front door by then and Polly was there to greet them, her expression tight and strained, her smile forced.

Mam doesn't change, Ellie thought. She's

always the family martyr.

'Hello, Mam.' she put her arms about her mother's sparely built frame and hugged her, while Mary simply passed into the house as if she had never been away.

11

The house, Ellie remarked to herself as she helped her mother and Margaret clear away the lunch dishes, was looking decidedly smarter. It was still basic and shabby, but here and there she noticed new acquisitions. A sofa, some new china, table-linen. And curtains. Her mother could never exist without curtains at her windows.

It looked as though Polly was yet again joining forces with the tallyman and buying things on tick. There had been no savings left, not even a penny of Ellie's severance money. And in less than a month, these new items could not have been bought on the wages coming in.

When Polly went off to the tiny brick lavatory built behind the house, Ellie fixed them all with pointed glances.

'I see things haven't changed,' she said to no one in particular as she dried a fancy china teapot and put it carefully away in the kitchen cupboard. 'Is she in debt again?'

'Aye,' Ben sighed.

'Ye'll not change her,' Tommy said in a hushed voice and they all looked at Jack

Martin, sitting on the end of the fender, his back to the unlit fire, his face hidden behind the open pages of the *Northern Echo*. The pages rustled slightly, but he remained as silent and detached as always.

'It's an obsession with her,' Margaret said, obviously feeling enough like a member of the family now to say her piece. 'As if she can't hold her head up high unless she's surrounded by what she calls 'nice things'.'

'Me mam was always used to nice things,' Mary piped up in her mother's defence. 'It must be hard for her not to want them again.'

'If only she would wait until we get ourselves on a proper footing,' Ben said, 'instead of landing us in more debt than we can afford to pay back, even with foundry wages.'

As they heard the rattle of the back door and Polly's footsteps in the passage outside, they fell into an uneasy hush. Her eyes darted sharply from one to the other of them as if she knew they had been talking about her behind her back. She pulled her mouth in and started wiping down the table.

'Well, then, Ellie,' she said stiffly as she wrung out the cloth in the sink and hung it to dry over the stove, which was burning brightly and heating the whole house. 'You've heard all our news. What about this job of yours? You haven't said much. Is everything all right at the Hall?'

'Oh, yes, Ellie.' Margaret gave her an enthusiastic smile. 'Tell us what it's like over there. Do you see a lot of the Rockwells?'

Ellie was relieved that they at last wanted to know about her life at the Hall. All through the meal they had patently avoided the subject as if it were taboo.

'Quite a bit, yes. Well, I work for Lady Rockwell, so it's only natural I'd see a lot of her. She's very nice, but I don't think she's happy. There's always a sad look in her eyes and she gets a bit irritable at times. Not with me, though.'

'And him? What about him? Sir Donald Rockwell.' Polly said the name as if it tasted bad on her tongue. 'Does he treat you right?'

'He hardly looks at me, Mam.'

'That's all right then. He keeps his hands to himself, does he?'

'Well, I . . . ' Ellie hesitated and saw an anxious frown pass over her mother's pinched face. 'There are rumours about him — you know, I hear the other girls talking. They say he's a bit of a flirt . . . '

'But you — he hasn't touched you in any way, has he?'

'No — no, of course not, Mam.'

'You keep yourself well away from him, do you hear!'

'Mam, don't look at me like that. Goodness, anybody would think I was a backward child. If he laid one finger on me I'd give him what for and no mistake, job or no job.'

'That's the spirit, lass!' The voice came from behind Jack's rustling newspaper.

'You hold your tongue, Jack Martin!' Polly flashed at her husband, but the only response she got for her pains was another rustle of pages and a loud sucking noise as Jack tried to locate the shreds of meat that were lodged in his teeth.

'And the son?' Polly pursued, putting her eyes through Ellie to such an extent she made her daughter flush with a guilt that was not justified. 'Does he ever try anything on with you?'

'No, Mam,' Ellie said thickly, and busied herself folding the tablecloth and putting it away so her mother couldn't see her face. 'Mr Rockwell's all right. He's nothing like his father.'

Oh, God, I hope I'm right. So why do I feel as if I'm lying to myself as well as my mother?

'Adam Rockwell?' Margaret smiled. 'He came to see me — you know — when Billy died. He seemed very nice, really. So ordinary. You wouldn't think he stood to inherit millions.'

'Aye, well, his father didn't have millions, as you say, when he started out.' Polly was staring out of the window as she spoke. 'He was a common quarryman who got a bit of learning that paid off. He got a job as an engineer and was clever enough to get himself a foundry, mainly because he married the boss's daughter. She was the one who had the money. Just like this new wife, by all accounts. Titles? Don't talk to me about titles. They mean nothing.'

Ellie was about to ask her mother how she knew all this about Sir Donald, but pulled herself up short when a cry was heard outside and running feet came pounding down the road towards their house.

'Mrs Martin! Mrs Martin!'

Polly rushed to open the door and they all crowded round her as a young woman, skirt muddied and torn, held up above her ankles showing stout workman's boots on the end of skinny legs almost bowled into her.

'What is it Mrs Foster? What's happened?'

The woman gasped for breath and stood panting before them, her eyes wild. 'Oh, Mrs Martin, there's been a terrible accident. It's your Archie.'

'Archie!' They all shouted the boy's name in unison. 'What's happened? Where is he?'

'He was playing on the slag heap with the other bairns — you know how they do? He must have slipped or tripped — I don't know, but he's hurt, Mrs Martin. He's hurt bad. That slag — it's cut him to ribbons.'

'Oh dear God, where is he?' Polly's face was as white as chalk.

'They've got him down at the Shawcross house. You'd better come quick.'

Polly had gone rigid. Her face went from white to red, then paled to a sickly parchment. She seemed rooted to the spot and couldn't move until Ellie took her arm and urged her forward.

'Come on, Mam,' Ellie said with a look at Mary who was almost as stricken as her mother. 'We'll all go with you. Mary, grab her other arm.'

Ben ran on ahead, while Tommy and Jack brought up the rear.

'I'll stay here and organize some bandages,' Margaret called out behind them.

Ellie prayed as she ran. She knew what it would be like. They'd heard the stories about children who fell victim to the cursed slagheaps. The heaps were made from iron-dross. Unwanted bits, shavings, splinters, that were emptied out in great hillocks all around the foundry area. Some of the older ones had, in the twenty years or so they had been there, finally grown a protective covering of grass. The newer ones were lethal. Falling on them was like falling on a hill of razor blades.

The last child who had slithered from top to bottom of a slag heap had died from loss of blood before they got him to hospital. Another child, a girl, lost an arm and was disfigured for life. At best the wounds became infected and often refused to heal. At worst, they died.

Margaret's bandages were never needed. Archie's injuries were too bad to bring him back home. They wrapped him in a sheet and Ben carried him, screaming in pain and shock, to the ferry. By the time they got him to the other side and into town to the doctor's surgery, the sheet was soaked in his blood and dripping a bright red trail for his family to tread in.

The doctor took one look at the now unconscious boy and ordered him immediately to the hospital. There was much shaking of the head by the doctors who attended him and they talked in a medical language that nobody understood.

After hours of waiting, the chief surgeon came to see the family where they were gathered in a small waiting area off the ward. All the Martins were pale-faced and sipping hot, sugary tea which the nurses had kindly provided. Archie had been in surgery for just under two hours, though it seemed like for ever.

'How is he, doctor?' Polly was the first to rouse herself sufficiently to speak to the man in his green theatre-gown smeared with Archie's blood. 'Is my son going to live?'

The doctor licked his lips and flexed weary shoulders. He was tired of having to patch up these foundry children and sick of having to impart bad news to their devastated parents. Something should be done about those blasted slag heaps. How many injuries and deaths was it going to take before the necessary action was taken?

'He's going to survive, Mrs Martin.' He reached out and placed a reassuring hand on her shoulder; instantly she moved away from it. The surgeon gave her a look, then addressed himself to the family in general. 'Archie's had a narrow escape. It's a miracle you got him here before he bled to death. He wouldn't have been the first, I assure you.'

'Can we see him, please?' Ellie said in a thin, wavery voice as she swung her legs to the floor and tried to rise from the bed she had been ordered to rest on. The room swayed beneath her feet until Ben pushed her gently back again.

'There's no point just yet. He's under deep sedation and he won't wake up until tomorrow. It's best that way. He has more stitches in him than my mother's cross-stitch sampler.'

'Poor little bugger!' Ben groaned and received a sharp look of censure from his mother.

'Some of his wounds were quite serious. The cuts went deep and in some instances the jagged metal gouged out the flesh.' The doctor stopped to allow the family time to assimilate the facts. The mother and the younger sister looked on the point of collapse. The father remained curiously silent throughout, but his eyes were haunted like those of a man with a lot to worry him. 'I'm very much afraid he will be scarred for life. He'll need careful nurturing once he gets out of hospital.

'These accidents often affect patients drastically. Archie may never recover completely from what happened to him. I've seen patients in similar circumstances go through stages of sorrow and anger. We can't tell at this stage. They're all affected differently. I thought it best to warn you what you can expect. Don't be too harsh in your judgement of the lad. For a while, he's going to look at himself and think he's some kind of freak. In fact, that kind of attitude could last for a very long time. Perhaps all his life.'

'He's only ten,' Ellie whispered through the lump in her throat and fumbled for Ben's hand, clasping it tightly when she found it.

★　★　★

The moment Ellie and Mary got back to Rockwell Hall, they received a summons to go immediately to the library where Lady Rockwell was waiting to speak to them.

'What do you think it's about?' Mary's voice shook with fear as they hurried through the house, still dressed in their travelling clothes, having had time only to wash the dust from their hands and faces.

'How should I know?' Ellie was uncharacteristically sharp in her reply, but she too was worried. She was worried about a lot of things and Mary, with her constant moaning on their journey, had got on her nerves.

'Do you think we've done something wrong?'

'Don't be ridiculous, Mary! How can we possibly have done something wrong? We haven't even been here over the weekend.'

As they crossed the grand entrance hall and approached the door to the library, Mary hung a pace or two behind Ellie, determined not to be the first in the firing line.

The door was ajar, but Ellie raised her fist and was about to rap her knuckles on the thick oak panel when it swung open and she gave a little gasp on seeing Adam Rockwell standing there.

'Come in, Ellie,' he said, his expression disconcertingly grave. 'You too, Mary.'

Lady Rockwell was installed behind the huge desk where Ellie had only ever seen Sir Donald or his son sit. The woman's face was pale and drawn, but she gave the two sisters a gentle smile as they came into the room and took up position before her.

'You wanted to see us, your ladyship?' Ellie said hesitantly, her glance flitting momentarily to Adam, who had come to stand by his stepmother's elbow. His face gave nothing away, but the eyes that looked upon her were not exactly unfriendly. She licked her dry lips and waited.

'First of all, Ellen . . . Mary . . . ' Lady Rockwell looked from one to the other, her eyes large and sad. 'I want to say how sorry I was to hear of the terrible accident to your young brother. How is the poor child?'

'Archie's going to be all right, madam,' Ellie told her. 'He's out of danger, but he has to stay in hospital for a while.'

'Rockwell . . . the foundry, that is, will take care of any bills,' Lady Rockwell announced, with a quick glance up at Adam, who nodded his agreement. 'This is a terrible thing to have happened. Terrible. Is the boy in much pain?'

'They're keeping him sedated, madam, but he did manage to raise a cheeky grin before we left. Archie's a tough little lad. It'll take more than a few scars to knock him down.'

Adam turned and strode over to the window, but not before Ellie saw the anger crowding in on his features. He punched a fist into his palm.

'Those damned slag heaps! They've claimed too many young lives.'

'Adam, please!' His stepmother threw him a warning look and turned back again, smiling, to the two Martin girls. 'Something will be done, I'm sure, but in the meantime, we'll organize some compensation for the family. It's the least we can do.'

'Thank you, madam. That's very kind of you.'

'Now, Ellen,' Lady Rockwell said, finally. 'My stepson here tells me that he has offered you the post of secretary and is expecting your decision this morning.'

Ellie heard a suppressed exclamation from her sister and felt a sharp nudge in the small of her back as Mary pushed up closer behind

274

her. She cast a glance in Adam Rockwell's direction, but he had turned to the window and was now standing with his back to the room.

'Yes, madam, that is correct,' she replied. 'And, if it won't upset you too much, I'd like to accept Mr Rockwell's offer.'

After a short pause she thought she saw Adam's shoulders relax. He turned and smiled, slowly nodding his head in agreement.

'Well, Ellen,' her ladyship sighed again and seemed to swallow with difficulty, 'I'll be sorry to let you go. You haven't been with me very long, but you've already proved your worth. However, I realize that Adam . . . that Mr Rockwell's need is perhaps greater than mine. We certainly do have need of a secretary . . . ' She looked up at Adam, ' . . . but I shall never forgive him for poaching my personal maid!'

'Oh, madam . . . ' Ellie stepped forward. 'If my leaving you causes a problem I — I'm quite happy to stay on.'

'Nonsense, girl!' It was Adam who spoke. 'You're far too talented to waste your life as a lady's maid. I'm sorry, Cynthia. I don't want to demean the job of lady's maid, but there are many young women who could do the job equally well. To find someone who can use a typewriting machine and do the book-keeping is like finding gold in a chalk-pit. You did say you understood bookkeeping, did you not, Ellen?'

Ellie could not remember whether she had mentioned it or not, but she nodded her head anyway. 'Yes, sir. Professor Graham taught me simple book-keeping. I quite enjoyed it.'

'Heaven be praised, for I detest poring over columns of figures that refuse to add up, subtract, divide or anything else they're supposed to do.'

Ellie pressed her lips together, suppressing a grin at his expression of profound relief.

'May I make a suggestion, madam?' She turned again to Lady Rockwell.

'Yes, of course, Ellen.'

'Well, could I ask you to give Mary here a sort of trial run as your lady's maid?' She saw her employer suppress a shudder and continued quickly. 'She's very quiet. She wouldn't chatter or gossip out of line. And she's an excellent needlewoman. Much better than I am at turning up a hem or . . .'

'Oh, all right, all right, Ellen! Until I find someone else. Is that understood? It is just to be a temporary arrangement, Mary.'

'Oh! Oh, yes — yes, thank you, madam!' Mary's face had become animated and her eye came out of its corner and just for a second looked almost normal.

'It is not me you should be thanking, but your sister here. Anyway, Ellen can spend today showing you where things are and explaining your general duties. Ellen, you will report here to Mr Rockwell tomorrow morning at eight-thirty sharp.'

Ellie looked up and caught his eye, her heart missing a beat as she saw a familiar twitch of humour lifting one corner of his mouth.

'Do I — I mean — am I — er — responsible also to — er — to Sir Donald?' She didn't know why she should feel so awkward mentioning the man's name and put it down to the fact that she was perhaps coloured by her mother's strange attitude towards him.

'I don't think Sir Donald will be involving himself in much more business,' Lady Rockwell said steadily, her fingers clasping and unclasping rapidly as she spoke. 'My husband, Ellen, is not a well man.'

'Oh, I'm sorry, madam,' Ellie said, showing a genuine concern, though it was for Lady Rockwell's feelings rather than for the health of her husband. 'I didn't know he was ill.'

'My father,' Adam said, obviously not sharing his stepmother's emotion, 'had a stroke during Saturday night. He, like your brother, is in hospital and partially paralysed.'

'Oh, how awful!'

'Yes.' Lady Rockwell rose and straightened out the creases in her skirt. 'Now, run along Ellen and take Mary with you. I will inform the household of the new arrangements and you will both commence your new duties tomorrow.'

★   ★   ★

'He seems a bit better today, don't you think?' Margaret gratefully took Tommy's arm and was glad that he, unlike Ben, remembered to walk slowly. She was beginning to feel heavily pregnant and the extra weight she carried tired her out easily.

'Aye, you're right, lass, but I don't know how the devil that lad manages to raise a smile, the way he looks. It's no wonder me mam's reluctant to visit him. It must churn her up something awful to see her youngest son all torn and battered like that.'

They were on their way back from visiting Archie in hospital, being the only members of the family who could go on a regular basis, though Ellie and Ben went whenever they could, as did their father. However, their mother, Polly, seemed to lack courage and was only persuaded to visit at weekends when someone else could go with her.

Polly's fear of hospitals was doubled by the horror of having to look upon her young son's scarred countenance, see the pain-filled eyes and listen to the moans he could not stem when the pain-killing drugs wore off. They had thankfully stopped the morphine, which had given him wild hallucinations and affected his usually docile temper with violent, uncontrollable outbursts of rage.

'Even so, Tommy,' Margaret said, thoughtfully, 'I wish your mam would see her way to go in more often. The poor little lad must miss her terribly. She is his mother, after all.'

'Aye, there is that.' Tommy patted her hand, then squeezed it, smiling gently into her face.

Margaret felt her heart lift. They were so different, the two older Martin brothers. Ben was big and burly, both in stature as well as in temperament. Larger than life, she always thought him. He was kindness itself and she owed everything to him, though the passion she had enjoyed, thinking she was in love with him, had soon abated in the light of Tommy's mild devotion and deep understanding for how she was feeling at any given time. There had been no need for words between them. How they felt for one another was obvious. The trouble was, neither of them wanted to hurt Ben.

Margaret had made the baby her excuse for not allowing Ben to make love to her. He had been so understanding. For a few nights he had continued to share her bed, without touching her, other than holding her close, then turning from her when the urge to enter her became too insistent. However, he eventually drifted back to the room he shared with his brothers. He said little, voiced no recriminations, but his eyes were full of remorse and she was sure he had guessed the truth.

'So, Tommy, what is it you're making in that shed of yours that's such a big secret?' Margaret asked, trying to lighten the dull mood that had descended on both of them. 'I hear you banging away in there and I know you turned Mrs Dawson away the other day, telling her you were too busy to take on more work. She was very disappointed not to get that kitchen cupboard she wanted for Christmas.'

Tommy looked away from her and pulled a face, then looked back and grinned. 'Ach, that old witch is always wantin' something. The trouble is, she always wants it for nothing. Besides, it's true that I'm busy just now.'

'Would it have anything to do with this?'

She grinned back at him and patted her swollen belly.

Tommy looked down at the precious mound she indicated. He licked his lips, bit on the side of his mouth, then grinned again.

'Aye, all right, Margaret, hinny. You've guessed. It was supposed to be a surprise. At the rate I'm working it'll be a surprise if it's ready before the young 'un arrives.'

'Oh, Tommy! What is it? Tell me, please!'

'Ach, it's nothing special, but every baby needs a good solid cradle to rock himself to sleep in. Maybe this little fella is going to need one more than most, him not having a dad and all. I just thought I'd like to — well, you know . . . '

Tommy wasn't one for much talk and certainly not when the talk got into intimate areas that he was still young and inexperienced enough to be embarrassed about.

Margaret leaned hard against him, went up on her toes as they walked and kissed his cheek. He was so thin and fragile-looking that she felt he might disappear in a cloud of dust if she was too demonstrative with him.

'Tommy Martin,' she breathed happily. 'You're a lovely person and I . . . '

'Aye?' His glance was quick, but it didn't need words. She took his bright eyes for a sign of encouragement to continue.

'I'm very fond of you, Tommy, you know that, don't you?'

'Aye, I do, lass.' Tommy smiled shyly and patted her hand.

They fell into silence until they were almost back at the house and they saw Ben sitting morosely watching them from the doorstep. It was cold, with winter coming on ahead of itself, but there he was, oblivious to it, staring into space and looking as though he'd been having words with the devil himself.

He got to his feet as they approached. 'So, you're back! How's our Archie?'

Margaret could hear Tommy swallowing, trying to lubricate his dry throat sufficiently to speak. She spoke for him.

'They say he's making good progress — or as good as he can in the circumstances. He was asking when you were going to see him.'

Ben gave her a flat stare. 'I don't suppose I can count on you coming with me, can I, Margaret? It seems, these days, that you'd prefer to keep company with me brother.'

Margaret bit on her lips and tears welled up in her eyes. She reached out and held on to Tommy's arm to stop him walking away.

'That does seem to be the way it is, Ben,'

she said softly. 'Tommy and I — we have something to say to you.'

'Aye.' Ben nodded, his face full of understanding mixed with personal loss. 'I had a feeling it was coming to this.'

12

Ellie had been working as secretary to Adam Rockwell for about four months and not once had he taken advantage of her, as he had tried to do on the day of Sir Donald's birthday. It was as if the incident had never taken place between them, which was fortunate, since Ellie loved her work. Her darker side, however, often wished that their growing friendship could have a more intimate side to it. If only she had been born a lady, she thought with a sigh.

'What's putting that frown on your face, Ellie?'

'What . . . ? I mean — I'm sorry, Mr Rockwell?' Ellie squinted up into the sunshine, into Adam's face so close to hers.

'Good gracious, Ellie, you were miles away. Something came into your head that wiped away that lovely smile of yours.'

They were walking together over the moorland adjacent to the Hall. It was something they did on a regular basis and she enjoyed it immensely, especially when Adam pointed out wild flowers and animals and told her their names. Sometimes, he sketched while she sat reading. Once she caught him sketching her and he had laughed self-consciously and quickly turned the page.

Today, cold though it was, with frost hardening the earth and crunching under-foot, they had stayed out longer than usual and now they were heading back home.

She looked up at him, shading her eyes from the setting sun's glare. 'Oh, I was thinking of so many things.'

'What kind of things?'

She shrugged and pulled her coat more closely about her. The air was turning more chilly and damp as evening approached. 'All the things that have happened since we came to Rockwell.'

'Such as?'

'Oh, you wouldn't be interested. You know — family stuff mainly.'

'No, really. I'd like to hear about it. Heaven knows, nothing much happens in my own family. I might as well enjoy hearing about yours.'

Ellie took a deep breath. She gave a small laugh and felt suddenly stuck for words. 'You know, moving to Rockwell . . . '

'Well? Go on!'

'The day I dressed up as a man and tried to get work.'

He gave a lopsided grin. 'You might have

got away with it, if I hadn't sketched you less than a month prior to that.'

'On the Quayside! Yes, I remember that. I was so embarrassed.'

'You looked quite beautiful, Ellie. There was no way I would ever forget that face of yours. It was engraved on my memory.'

'Oh, please, Mr Rockwell! You're making me blush!'

'It's the prettiest blush I've ever seen on any fair maiden!'

Then they were both laughing and his arm had snaked companionably around her shoulders as they walked. She wished he would never remove it.

'What else were you thinking about?'

'Oh, I don't know,' she said. 'The first day at Northend, my two elder brothers both falling in love with the same girl.'

Tommy and Margaret had got married last month, a week after Margaret's baby was born.

Ellie smiled ruefully. 'Poor Ben. He's still in love with her.'

'And Archie? How's that little brother of yours?'

Ellie swept away a rogue tear that had overflowed, helped by a gust of keen wind as they rounded the hill that was the last lap of their journey back to the Hall. 'His injuries refuse to heal. I think he suffers a lot more than he lets on.'

'He's a brave boy.'

Ellie nodded. 'He's a Martin. We're made of pretty stern stuff.'

They were a few hundred yards away from the Hall when the sky darkened above them and thunder growled. Within seconds there was a deluge of rain and they were running blindly through the storm.

Ellie didn't see the deep rut that caught her toe and sent her sprawling face down in the mud. She lay there panting, her breath all but knocked out of her. As she struggled to raise herself, a pair of strong hands lifted her. She took a step and winced. Before she could protest Adam had her in his arms and was carrying her the rest of the way.

'I'm all right, honestly, Mr Rockwell!' She gasped as pain shot through her ankle and saw him grin.

'The Martin pride, eh? Well, you can just put it to one side for once. I'm not putting you down until we get you home and see what the damage really is.'

She thought he would take her into the kitchen for Mrs McKenzie to see to, but he didn't. He marched through the entrance hall and straight up the stairs, leaving a trail of wet, muddy footprints behind him.

He did not, as she then expected, head for her room, but took her directly into his own suite of rooms on the first floor. Pushing the door open, then shutting it with a thrust of his foot behind him he took her and laid her gently on a couch by a fire that was already lit and warming the room nicely.

'Mr Rockwell — really, I don't think — you shouldn't do this . . . '

'Be quiet, girl, and let me look at that ankle!'

He was pulling off her rain-sodden coat as he spoke, throwing it to one side on the floor where it lay steaming before the heat of the fire. Then he lifted her leg and his fingers fumbled numbly with the laces that had become knotted.

'Damn!' he swore. 'You women do wear some complicated apparel!'

The boot finally came off and he flexed her ankle, ordered her to wriggle her toes, which she did with only the slightest discomfort. 'See, Mr Rockwell! It's nothing. I'd better go and — and help Mrs McKenzie with the dinner.'

She started to get up, but found herself being pushed back with a firmness that came as quite a surprise. 'Mrs McKenzie is visiting her family this evening.'

'In that case . . . ' Why was she feeling so

breathless? Was it the fall? Had it shaken her up more than she had imagined? 'In that case, they'll need my help even more in the kitchen.'

Adam was slowly shaking his head. 'My father and Cynthia are out to dinner. Grace too. I imagine they have already left since they have to travel quite a distance to Wolsingham. I believe they are even staying the night. So, you see, my dear Ellie, no one has need of you.'

'Oh!' Ellie saw the reflection of the firelight flickering in his dark eyes, saw the indecision on his face turn to determination and she felt a small rise of panic beneath her breastbone.

'No one, that is, except me.'

Ellie swallowed hard, her eyes falling from his face to the rise and fall of his broad chest as he struggled slowly out of his damp coat and threw it to join hers on the floor.

He turned and warmed his hands at the fire, then began massaging her ankle, letting his thumbs drift to the sole of her foot, pressing, stroking in such a sensuous fashion that she had to call out to him to stop, thinking that she could not stand any more of it without making an utter fool of herself.

'It's very kind of you, Mr Rockwell, but I think I should go back to my own room now. Will you be — I mean, can I get you anything

— you know — dinner?'

She was speaking in such a breathless, hopscotch fashion she must sound ridiculous. He smiled and shook his head.

'Ellie, I'm sorry. I'm obviously frightening you and it's the last thing I ever want to happen, believe me.'

His voice was soft and caressing like a velvet glove. It mesmerized her.

'I'm not afraid of you,' she murmured and tried once more to rise from the couch, but he was sitting on the edge of it, blocking her way, and he was much too close for comfort.

'I'm glad to hear that one of us isn't afraid of what's happening here,' he said gruffly, a catch in his throat. 'Because I have to admit that I am more than just a little afraid just now.'

'I — I don't understand — sir.'

'Ellie, you can't possibly be unaware of the way I feel about you. My God! I've been fighting it for months, trying to dampen down my passion . . . '

'Your — your passion?' Ellie shrank back against the cushions, hardly daring to recognize the true meaning behind his words.

'Don't be afraid, Ellie.' He was moving in closer, his hand caressing the side of her face, making her quiver with uncontrolled ecstasy. 'You've been in my mind from that first moment on the Quayside, though I didn't recognize it for what it was then. Not for a long time. What I feel for you, Ellie, is very profound.'

Ellie stared at him. She knew she should be pushing him away, telling him to leave her alone. She knew that. Instead, she raised one trembling hand and traced the lines of his face, feeling the soft smoothness and the masculine roughness of his skin, the warmth of his slightly parted lips beneath her exploring fingertips.

'If I'm afraid,' she said huskily because her own emotion was blocking her throat, 'it's because this is so new to me. I don't know what to do.'

'You've really never been in a situation — I mean like this, with another man — with *any* other man?'

'You are the first, Adam.' She had used his first name without thinking. It felt good on her lips that were already vibrating, waiting for his kiss.

But he didn't kiss her. Not right away. He drew her to him so that she could feel the beat of his heart against hers, feel the heat emanating from him. His face nuzzled the side of her neck and he murmured into her ear. 'Oh, my love! How could I have waited so long?'

He rose and pulled her with him. He started opening the tiny buttons at the neck of her woollen dress.

'No!' She grabbed modestly at his hands, her cheeks aflame and her heart palpitating with a mixture of emotions. How she wanted him to touch her, hold her in his arms as a lover — the kind of lover she had always dreamed of having, but he was Adam Rockwell. He was forbidden fruit — and so was she.

'This is not a mild flirtation, Ellie,' Adam said, taking her face between his hands. 'You should know that by now. If I was going to take advantage of you, I could have done so long ago. You can't pretend that you are not aware — that you don't feel something too.'

'No, I can't deny that.' She gulped on her words, mind and body fighting one with the other for control of her emotions. 'But you're my employer and I don't belong in your world any more than you belong in mine.'

'I thought like that too — once. Now, I see things differently.' His lips descended, slowly, purposefully, filling her with yearning and terror. He emitted an agonized groan that ended in a whisper against her mouth. 'I want you so much, Ellie. Can you say honestly that you don't want me too?'

Ellie caught her breath, the words that

would send him away from her taunting her lips, but when she spoke she did so from her heart and knew it was right.

'I do want you, so much ... ' she whispered.

'No more words, my darling,' Adam gazed at her, his expression softening, his arms clutching her to his chest, cradling her, then giving her the kiss of a lifetime that would never be forgotten for it was the sweetest rapture that ever took hold of her senses.

She stood, swaying dizzily and he laughed softly as he grasped her, steadying her. He had to bend to find her lips again, his arms crushing her to his body until she felt every muscular mound, every bony contour.

He lifted her from the waist, raising her a foot from the ground so that her face was on a level with his. He kissed her again, softly; agonizingly sweet butterfly touches of a mouth that could be so firm, yet so softly persuasive.

'You're like a tiny, fragile bird.' He laughed against the top of her head as he set her down on her feet again. 'I'm afraid of damaging you.'

'I may be small,' she said with a pert smile, 'but I'm not that fragile.'

'Ellie ... ' His breath caught and he pushed her back from him, shadows flitting over his face. 'I want so much to make love to you, but . . . '

'But what?'

'Since you have no experience of lovemaking, I'd hate to frighten you off. I'm told it can be quite traumatic for a virgin bride on her wedding night, if she has not — tasted the fruit beforehand.'

Ellie put her hand up and stroked his cheek. 'There's only one way to gain experience, Adam. Everything has a first time and — I don't think I will be frightened off. Not by you.'

'I'll be as gentle as I can be, but I'm afraid that the intensity of my feelings might scare you or — or hurt you, or . . . '

She shook her head and smiled up at him. When she spoke her own passion was thick and cloying in her throat. 'I think you'll find that I'm more than ready. Anyway, men don't own the sole right to be passionate.'

The room spun as he whisked her from her feet and in a few hasty steps he had placed her before the high, double bed in the next room, which was chilly because the heat of the fire had not yet reached there. Ellie shivered, though it was perhaps more from anticipation than from the cold.

His fingers, as he slowly undressed her, shook slightly and his smile beneath the intense gaze of his eyes, wavered. Obviously, Adam too was a trifle nervous and it came as a surprise to her.

'You're cold, my love,' he said, seeing her shiver as he slipped the straps of her chemise down over her naked arms and his hands cupped her full breasts as if scooping up some long-lost, priceless treasure. 'But I'll soon warm you.'

He bent and kissed each of her stiffened nipples, his tongue flicking in and out at them with delicious effect. She didn't want him to stop but she was as impatient as he was to satisfy the driving desire that gripped her loins.

With impatience she watched him unbutton his shirt, his trousers, but when he came to his underwear, he grew more desperate and ripped them off with a grunt and a growl. Then he was standing before her in all his naked glory and she felt her eyes widen with the wonder of it all.

Although she had lived in close intimacy with her parents and her three brothers, Ellie had never once seen them naked beyond the age of eight or nine. She opened her mouth, drew in a gulp of air and gagged on it as Adam took a step forward and pressed himself against her, his hands at her back, exploring, sliding over her rounded buttocks, pulling her in to him. And all the while his mouth left a trail of kisses on her head, her brow, her temples. Then he continued down, kissing her neck her shoulders. He lifted her on to the bed as easily as he would a small child and kissed and licked her all over until she wanted to cry for mercy because she couldn't stand so much bliss.

He knelt over her, soothing her, stroking her, touching and gently probing the most private part of her that had ached for him for so long.

'Oh, Adam!' she sobbed, turning her head to one side and shedding tears of happiness into the pillow.

'I'll stop now if you want me to, Ellie,' he whispered in her ear. 'Just say the word. It's up to you.'

'Oh, Adam — don't . . . ' She swallowed with difficulty as her throat blocked up and he backed off, rigid and grey with anticipation. 'Don't stop, please!'

She had expected pain and there was some, but it was bearable and soon eased as he slid into her inch by inch, careful not to force the way. He was a big man and a powerful one and she sensed that it was difficult for him, holding off the way he was doing. This made their first lovemaking even more special to her, proving beyond the shadow of a doubt that he was not taking her because of some vague animal desire, the way some men did with women they did not care for.

Then, when he was all the way inside her, and she was beginning to find some comfort, he did something that took her quite by surprise. He rolled over so that she was on top and smiled at the look of astonishment on her face.

'There! Perhaps now you can breathe without my weight on top of you. And you can control the situation much better from that position. Go on, Ellie. Move. Move the way God intended you to move.'

And Ellie moved and cried out in exultation as her senses soared and her whole being vibrated with the ultimate pleasure of two bodies joined in love and passion.

It was over too soon. After their mutual climax had abated and she thought she would die from the sheer joy that was bursting her heart, Ellie slumped against Adam's chest and wept softly.

He was lying with his eyes closed, his lips curved into a vague smile. His hand came and touched her head, stroked her back, now glisteningly warm with the effort of their lovemaking. 'You're not unhappy, I hope?'

She raised her head slightly, shook it and kissed the broad chest with the dark veiling of masculine hair. 'I don't think I'll ever be unhappy again.'

He pulled her off him, laying her at his side and turned to face her, head propped up on one hand, while his other hand traced the curves that flowed the whole length of her body.

'You're the most beautiful thing that has ever happened to me, Ellie,' he told her simply. 'Don't ever . . .'

A soft tapping at the outer door made Ellie jump and Adam look up with a scowl of impatience. Ellie grabbed at a sheet and pulled it up to her chin.

'Who can it be?' she whispered and he shook his head as he got out of the bed and slipped on a heavy quilted-satin dressing-gown, tying it about him as he strode off to answer the summons.

Ellie heard muffled voices, then silence. When Adam reappeared he no longer looked happy and relaxed. His eyes, when they regarded her were dark and brooding and she knew there was something dreadfully wrong.

'What is it?' she asked, shivering suddenly beneath the covers of his bed.

'Ellie — it's bad news, I'm afraid.'

'What? Your father — your stepmother . . . ?'

He shook his head and was suddenly fumbling about the room, climbing back into his clothes. 'Get dressed Ellie. Quickly.'

'What is it?' She heard her trembling voice go up a fearful octave.

'There was a message from the hospital. The new maid couldn't find you, so she came to me . . . '

'Couldn't find *me*? Oh, Adam, tell me, please . . . ' She was frantically looking for her own clothes and her hands seemed almost paralysed with fear as she found them and clutched them to her naked bosom.

'It's your brother — Archie.'

'Archie! Oh, dear God, not another accident!'

'No, not an accident.' Adam picked up her stockings and handed them to her. 'Something about an infection. Ellie, you must prepare yourself for the worst. The message said that the boy was — dying.'

★   ★   ★

Ben and Tommy were standing, caps in hand, heads bowed, at the foot of the narrow bed, Margaret with them, while Jack stood behind Polly where she sat close to her youngest son on the only visitor's chair provided. Mary stood on the other side of the bed, sniffling into her crumpled handkerchief.

Polly raised glacial eyes as Ellie was

ushered in by the ward sister, but her eyes and the half-grimacing death-mask smile went beyond Ellie to the tall figure of Adam who stood behind her.

'This is family business,' she stated flatly and there was a definite cutting edge to her voice that annoyed Ellie even while she was trying to find sympathy for her mother.

'Adam — Mr Rockwell was kind enough to bring me here, Mam,' Ellie said with a glance of apology at Adam.

'I thought there might be something I could do to help,' Adam said.

'He's not welcome here!' Polly's voice rose and Jack gripped her thin shoulder, but kept his silence.

Ben turned and nodded at Adam. He stuck out his hand and Adam clasped it. 'Sorry about me mother, Mr Rockwell, sir. She's upset. They say — '

'Be quiet!' Polly hissed, her gaze fixed on the pallid little face that could just be seen above the hospital quilt. 'Leave us, Mr Rockwell. Leave us to mourn in private.'

'Eeh, Mam, our Archie's not dead yet!' Mary cried out and the boy in the bed gave a sudden twitch and mumbled incoherently. 'You shouldn't say things like that!'

'He's dying. They said so, didn't they? And the Rockwells killed him as good as if they took a knife to him. Just like they ruined my life all those years ago.'

'Mam, stop it! Mr Rockwell . . . ' Ellie started to protest, but was cut short.

'If ye think this one's any better than the other one, Ellie, then ye're deceivin' yerself.'

Adam touched Ellie's arm and bent forward to whisper to her: 'I'll wait for you outside, Ellie.'

She nodded and moved to stand beside Ben who put an arm about her shoulders with a wobbly smile and she was grateful for his being there. She stared across at Archie and although her heart sagged with grief she couldn't prevent the selfish wish that he had chosen another day to die. Not this day of all days, the happiest in her life.

A few minutes later a nurse appeared. She looked down at Archie, pulled back his eyelids, checked his pulse and gave a little shake of her head. 'I'm sorry,' she said with a swift glance around that encompassed every-one present.

As she pulled the sheet up over Archie's lifeless face, Mary ran out of the ward sobbing. Margaret touched Tommy's shoul-der then went after her sister-in-law. Ellie was clinging on to Ben's hand and she could feel him straining not to give way, see the tears brimming in his eyes, blurring his vision, just as hers were.

Her father gave a huge gulp and turned his face to the wall. She saw his shoulders shake up and down as he tried to suppress and get rid of his grief all in one go. But her mother remained rigid in her chair, staring ahead into a void that was her own private place. Only her hands were animated as her fingers wove some ritualistic pattern, jerking, pulling, stroking, hooking themselves into the material of her coat, plucking at it relentlessly.

Jack moved away from the bed and as he passed by Ellie, he pressed a hand on her shoulder. 'Ye'll be coming home with us th' night, lass? Yer mother will need ye.'

★   ★   ★

Outside, it was beginning to snow from a purple sky. Adam was waiting, pacing up and down on the cold, wet pavement. When he saw them, he came forward anxiously. 'Well?'

'Archie's dead, Adam,' Ellie told him and was aware of her mother's stabbing glance. 'I have to go back home with the family. At least until the funeral.'

He gave a nod and his eyes were dark, searching hers, sending her unvoiced messages. She tried to smile back at him, but it didn't quite work. He took her hand and squeezed it.

'I understand, Ellie. Of course you must go, but — you will come back, won't you? I'll be waiting.'

'Yes, of course.'

She would have given anything to be able to spend more time with him right then. Being separated in such a way, so soon after they had made love for the first time, was cruel. She needed the comfort of his arms around her, his strength to help her get through the next few hours. Instead, she was sending him away and she was going to go back to the house at Northend and face her mother's wrath or her silence. It didn't matter which. One was as bad as the other.

Almost as if it had been arranged, the ferry was empty except for the Martins, which seemed to pinpoint even more acutely the reason for their all being abroad together.

The house was cold and cheerless and seemed even more silent and empty than when Ellie's grandfather had died. Jack and Polly sat down at the kitchen table. They faced one another, saying nothing, their eyes never meeting. Ben set to lighting the fire that had gone out while Mary got out cups and saucers and filled the kettle.

Ellie paced the floor, feeling superfluous.

She was suddenly aware of her mother's eyes following her. Surely, she thought, Polly wasn't girding her loins to give yet another lecture about her foreboding with regard to the Rockwell family. Even for Polly that was taking things a little too far on the day her youngest son died.

'Close the curtains, Ellie,' Polly said and, when Ellie had complied, she clasped her hands on the table in front of her and lowered her head over them. 'I want to talk to Ellie alone.'

Tommy and Margaret exchanged glances and quickly left. Ben got up from his hunkers in front of a fire that was just beginning to blaze. He frowned curiously at his mother, then at Ellie. He jingled some change in his pocket. 'I'll go and see what they've got up at the home farm, shall I? Mary, you can come with me.'

'I've got a headache,' Mary told him with a dry sniff. 'I'm going to bed.'

'Please yourself, lass,' Ben said and left the room with another glance at Ellie that seemed to have a warning in it.

'Jack, if you please . . . ' Polly glared at her husband.

'What is it, woman?'

'This is not for your ears either. I need a few minutes with Ellie — just the two of us.'

Ellie saw her father's eyes waver, saw his chest heave as he gave a sigh of resignation. He picked up an *Evening Chronicle* and went out through the back door.

'I'll be in the lav,' he called over his shoulder. 'Give us a call when it's safe to come out.'

'Right my girl,' Polly said when she and Ellie were finally alone. 'Sit you down there and I don't want to hear a word out of you until I've finished what I have to say.'

'Mam, if this is about . . . '

'Sit down, I say!' Polly banged her fist on the table. Crockery rattled.

'Yes, Mam.' Ellie sat, feeling uneasy, trying to quell her anger at her mother's attitude.

'It's about them Rockwells.'

'Yes, Mam, I know what it's about, but this is not the time to start on about them again, surely.'

'Will you hear me out, our Ellie!'

Ellie had not heard her mother's voice raised to such an extent. Despite her constant anger and displeasure, Polly had always managed to keep her voice at an unemotional level. Normally, when she spoke, it was with a flatness, a coldness that often struck a chill to the bone. This emotional outburst was something new.

'Go on then. I'm listening,' Ellie said

evenly and gave a nod of encouragement.

Polly closed her eyes for an instant and rocked slightly in her chair, all the while plucking at fingers that were never still.

'It makes me ill to know what's going on between you and that Rockwell man. When Mary told me what she suspected I didn't want to believe her. But then you turned up with him in tow at the hospital and I knew that it was true. You've let him touch you, our Ellie, haven't you? You know what I mean.'

Polly opened her eyes and Ellie could see the accusation in them. She swallowed quickly and squared her shoulders, drawing on her inner courage.

'Yes, I know what you mean, Mam,' she said defiantly. 'And I know you don't approve. You're shocked because I've allowed a man to make love to me. Well, I'm not ashamed.'

Her mother's hands curled into tight little fists. One of them came up to Polly's face and she bit on a knuckle as if to stop herself from crying out in horror at what she was being told.

'It's a wicked sin to let *any* man touch you like that before marriage, Ellie. You know that. I've drummed it into you plenty, haven't I?'

'Yes, Mam, but — '

'It's wicked! You've committed a sin and you'll go to Hell!'

'I love him, Mam!'

'You can't love a Rockwell!'

'I can't help myself. Adam loves me, too. We were meant for each other.'

'No! It's not possible. It — it's sick, Ellie. You're sick if you crave for sex as much as that and can't hold off. I raised you to be good and respectable and all you've done is make me so ashamed I'll never be able to lift my head if people find out what you've done.'

Ellie was beginning to lose patience. She got to her feet, pushing her chair away, leaning her hands on the table and peering into her mother's stricken face.

'Mam, this is ridiculous! Just because he's a Rockwell — rich and well educated. You're a bigger snob than they are! I would have thought you'd be happy that I've found somebody I love who's worth having.'

'Worth having! A Rockwell!'

'I don't care that Adam's a Rockwell,' Ellie fumed. 'And I don't care what you have against his father. I love him and that's all that matters.'

'I'll tell you what I've got against Donald Rockwell, my girl. I used to work for him years ago, just like you do. Oh, not a fancy high-falutin' job like you've got, but he was the boss and anything he wanted he took. It didn't matter to him that a girl was young and innocent.'

'Mam, what are you saying? Are you saying that Sir Donald . . . ?'

'Aye! He took me all right and if you think I was willing you think again. He took me against my will and not just one time, neither.'

'Adam's not like that. He hates his father for what he is.'

'I don't give a sod what that young man thinks. He has no right to abuse you . . . ' Polly's words tailed off and she seemed to entertain a thought that was almost too painful for her, then she continued in a low voice. 'Haven't you noticed how alike your Adam is to our Ben? Oh, the colouring is different, I'll grant you that, but in everything else physical they are almost identical. They could have been twins, only they were born a few years apart.'

Ellie's forehead creased into a deep frown as her mother's words sank in. 'You don't mean . . . ?'

'Aye, I do mean that, Ellie. Sir Donald Rockwell is Ben's father, not Jack Martin. And . . . ' Polly hesitated, her troubled eyes darting about, not wanting to look at Ellie. 'Look in the mirror, lass. Are you and Ben not like peas in a pod? As I say, Donald Rockwell took what he wanted from me, when he wanted it. Now, do you understand why I didn't want you going anywhere near them?'

Ellie felt a sudden chill grip her as if an icy wind had suddenly blown through the room. Electrical impulses of shock coursed through her. Her knees gave way and she sat down again heavily. 'He — Adam — he's my brother?'

Polly's chest heaved. She took a long time to answer and when she did there was the trace of a wry smile twisting her thin lips. 'You work it out, lass.'

'It's not possible — say it's not possible, Mam, for pity's sake!'

Polly got up and walked slowly to the door. With her hand on the knob, she didn't even turn her head when she spoke again.

'I'm going out now, Ellie. I can't take any more.'

Ellie stared uncomprehendingly into space. She didn't know how she could sit there so calmly, seeing the fire flickering in the grate, counting the flames. There were dishes in the sink that needed washing. One of the cups had a crack in it and should be thrown away before it spread germs. She wondered when Archie's body would arrive and thought about what kind of flowers he might like on his grave.

Then she wondered what Adam was doing at that precise moment and what he would do when she told him what her mother had just divulged. That was when she broke down and cried and choked on her sobs and went on crying long after Jack Martin, the man she had known all her life as her father, came back into the room, thinking he had been forgotten sitting out there in the dark, cold lavatory.

13

Adam's hands were shaking as he read again and again what Ellie had written. One of the workers from Northend had been trusted with the delivery of the letter on Tuesday morning. He felt sick to his stomach. When he tried to walk across the floor of the library he found his legs to be useless.

Ellie had been strong in his thoughts when the letter arrived. He could not get her out of his mind. It was a sweet torture waiting for her to return to him so that he could again take her into his arms and love her as he had never loved any other woman.

And then this bombshell had exploded, obliterating his happiness as surely as any bullet could shatter the brain or the heart of a man. A bullet would have been easier to tolerate, for there would have been nothing to feel afterwards, nothing to see. Only eternal darkness. This way, he would have to survive with all physical organs intact, but his soul destroyed.

Adam pulled out a deep drawer in his desk and removed a sketchpad that he had filled over the last few months. They were all sketches of Ellie. The first, earlier sketches had been merely head-and-shoulder portraits drawn from memory after that morning when he first met her on Newcastle Quayside. After that, he had made drawings capturing her every mood. They leapt out of the pages at him like living images. He could hear her laughter, her husky voice, smell the faint lavender that perfumed her fine skin.

He snapped the book shut with an angry movement and sat staring at it, his eyes aching, tears stinging behind his lids. He didn't hear the shuffling footsteps hesitating in the open doorway, approaching him. His father was almost on top of him, leaning heavily on his walking cane, before he realized he was there.

'Father!' Adam jumped to his feet and stood swaying, one hand to his forehead, the other clutching the edge of the desk, supporting him. 'Is it true?'

Sir Donald frowned and his dark eyes became small and bright and suspicious. 'What are you talking about? Is what true?'

Adam picked up Ellie's letter and threw it across the desk. Sir Adam scooped the pages up, turned them over in his hand and scrutinized them.

'Ah!'

'Well? What do you have to say? I want the

truth, Father. I'd already guessed about Ben Martin, the way that woman went on and the way you so readily handed out jobs to her men as if you owed her something.'

'I owed her nothing!' Sir Donald dropped the letter and sank down into a chair. Since his stroke he had been paralysed down one side and his speech was slurred, but his wits were still as keen as ever. 'It was an expediency until I could figure out what to do about the situation. The woman was black-mailing me. I couldn't afford for your stepmother to find out.'

'Heaven forbid that you should lose Cynthia's financial support!'

Sir Donald leaned forward, tapped his fingers on Ellie's letter and gave a soft chuckle. Saliva trickled down over his chin. Adam looked at the father he had always hated and felt nothing but disgust.

Sir Donald raised rheumy eyes to Adam's puzzled frown. 'You have read the last page, I take it?'

Adam started to shake his head, then stopped. He looked down at the pages of the letter spread out before him. He had gone no further than Ellie's news about being his half-sister, not being able to bring himself to read further. Now, he picked the pages up, re-sorted them, found the last page.

Ellie's handwriting was in neatly formed script, though he detected a shake of the hand here and there, a smudge from a fallen tear:

After my mother delivered her terrible secret to me, she left the house and did not come back. They found her body floating in the river. She will be buried tomorrow, alongside Archie. My family is distraught. They do not understand why she should have taken her own life. The doctor says her mind must have been unbalanced at the time because of my brother's death and all that led up to it. I believe that my mother's mind has been unbalanced all her life — or at least since she was taken by your father when she worked at the Hall twenty-five years ago.

Adam, I have so many things in my heart that I cannot say, must not say to you. I realize that your heart will be just as torn as mine by such a devastating revelation. What has gone between us will always remain. I do not know how I see it or might see it in the future. It is too close yet to judge. You will understand when I say that I cannot continue to work at the Hall, that I must leave Rockwell. Please do not try to see me — it would make matters more difficult to bear.

My sincere wish is that you find happiness, my dearest Adam. You are so deserving of it. I have no idea how to finish off this letter. My heart is breaking, but I must say goodbye — for ever. Your Ellie.

Adam drew in a raw, sobbing breath. The words on the pages blurred. He turned away and marched to the window so he could have his back to his father, not see the supercilious, triumphant smirk on the man's face. Even in his invalid state, Sir Donald had managed to have the last laugh over his son.

'I knew about the death of Catherine Durham,' Sir Donald said slowly and clearly. 'I gave Whitfield instructions to throw them out this morning.'

'Where have they gone?'

'Who knows? They can find work in another town, another pit or foundry. I want no more truck with them.'

Adam spun around, his face suffused with anger. 'You tried to break their spirit when they first came here by giving them jobs beyond their means, putting them in accommodation not fit to house pigs. They overcame all the disadvantages, at their own cost, and they survived. They proved they were worthy of anything the Rockwells could throw at them. I won't have you treat them like rabid dogs.'

'You have no choice. They've already gone.'

'And if I find them and bring them back?'

'That would be ill advised, my boy. I still own Rockwell and if you cross me I might find it necessary to give the rest of your inheritance to someone else. Whitfield himself, perhaps. At least he is loyal to me. He's a foundryman, like I am. He doesn't fill his head with ridiculous dreams like some frilly-minded female.'

'What about Ben? He's done everything I've asked him. He's as strong as an ox and a good worker. The men like him — and he's your son too. For God's sake, Father!'

Sir Donald looked up from beneath dark, overhanging brows, one of which now sagged permanently over his eye. He was no longer smiling, but had a fierce expression fixed on his lopsided face.

'I want nothing of him! Do you hear me?'

'You're despicable!' Adam folded the pages of Ellie's letter and put them carefully in his inside breast-pocket. He came around the desk, brushing past his father's shoulder on his way to the door in just a few long strides.

'Where are you going?'

'What do you care? When have you ever cared for anyone but yourself?'

As he passed through the doorway into the hall, Lady Rockwell was coming out of the lounge, an expression of great concern on her face.

'Adam! What's happening? I heard raised voices. You haven't had a dispute with your father, have you?'

'No more than usual! Tell me, Cynthia — why should I stay here at Rockwell? What is it about all this . . . ' his hand swept the great hall, ' . . . that keeps me a prisoner here. So many times, I've wanted to walk out, turn my back on the whole lot, but I can't! Why is that?'

Cynthia looked at him kindly. 'Because, Adam, it's in your blood and one day it will be yours to run as you see fit. Because you care for those working men out there — and their families. You know what things would be like if they didn't have you to fight for them.'

As Adam stormed off, he couldn't help recognizing the truth in what Cynthia had just said. His inheritance was far more important than power and money and that was what made him stay. With Ellie taken away from him, what else did he have left?

'Well, as I live and breathe, I didn't expect to see you back here!'

Ellie gave a trembling smile and wished her heart would stop its frantic beating. Professor Graham's old housekeeper was standing inspecting her with a very uncertain look in her eyes.

'It's nice to see you again, Mrs Renney,' she said, trying to sound confident, but it was difficult the way she was shivering and clenching her teeth against a sudden attack of nerves. 'Is — is the professor at home please?'

'Aye, he is, but he's entertaining at the moment and I don't like disturbing him, but . . . ' Mrs Renney put her head to one side and licked her lips. 'You don't look well, lassie. Why don't you come in and I'll make you a nice cup of tea while you wait?'

'That's very kind of you, Mrs Renney. I think I may have caught a chill. It's such a cold day and . . . '

She stopped speaking as a door down the hall clicked open and a small confusion of voices emerged, followed by the tall, slim figure of Professor Graham and two rather sophisticated women, one of whom Ellie recognized as the professor's cousin. The second woman, whom she put to be about forty, was speaking rather animatedly and hanging on to Nicholas Graham's arm, laughing flirtatiously.

At that point the professor looked up and saw Ellie standing shivering in the doorway. He became suddenly very shy and mute and seemed to have difficulty taking his eyes from her.

'Er — Mrs Renney, would you be so good as to see our guests out — thank you so much. Good afternoon — er — ladies . . . '

The two women looked a little put out as if he had cut them dead, handing them over to the housekeeper, and Ellie could see the unvoiced question in their eyes as they passed her. Mrs Renney gave her a little shove and suddenly she was standing before him and he was gazing down at her with disbelief written all over his face.

'Ellie!' He said her name a little breathlessly. 'Ellie, my dear girl! Do come in — come in. How are you? You look cold and pale and . . . '

He took her hands in his and gripped them hard, then he was drawing her into his study where the fire was lit and the atmosphere was warm and cosy. Everything looked so agonizingly familiar. It was, she thought, like coming home.

'I hope I'm not disturbing you too much,

Professor Graham,' she said in a small voice, reaching out to warm her hands at the fire and, at the same time, noticing Adam's portrait of her, framed and hanging on the wall where there had once been a mirror. 'Oh!'

'You left it behind,' the professor told her with a reticent smile as he saw her looking at it. 'I had it framed so I could look at your lovely face every day and pretend . . . Oh, my dear, you must think me stupid, but you see — Oh, well, never mind.'

Ellie blinked at him, then turned and looked once more at the portrait. 'I didn't think you would remember me with such — such fondness.'

'Dear Ellie, I could never think of you with anything other than — *great* fondness,' Professor Graham said, looking at her more closely, now that he had recovered from the unexpected sight of her. 'Do sit down. Will you take a glass of sherry with me? You look tired?'

Ellie sat down gratefully. He was right. She was exhausted, but it was more a mental exhaustion than a physical one.

'Thank you.'

He handed her a rather large amount of sherry in a wine goblet, though he himself took a small schooner. 'Drink this, my dear.

You look as if you need it. I've put a spot of brandy in it to warm you through.'

She smiled at him and sipped the sweet, fiery liquid. Her body was still trembling, but her heart had calmed itself now that she knew he was not going to turn her away without hearing her reason for being there.

'You've lost weight,' she remarked. 'Isn't Mrs Renney looking after you properly?'

He gave a short laugh and sat down opposite her on the other side of the fireplace. 'The woman complains all the time that I don't eat enough, but really, I haven't had much of an appetite for anything — not since . . . ' he cleared his throat loudly, 'well, not for a long time. But you, dear girl — let us talk of you! What brings you back here just when I had given up hope of ever seeing you again?'

Ellie hardly knew how to say what she had come there to say. She was so afraid of incurring his disapproval, of turning him against her. It would be no more than she deserved. It had taken a long time to make the decision and find the courage to confront him. She did not want to lie to him. He was too good a man to deceive.

'Last month,' she began, then took a deep drink of her sherry and began again. 'Last month, I buried my mother and my little brother on the same day.'

'Oh, my dear girl, how awful for you, but how did that come about?'

'It's a long story, Professor. You may not like what you hear, but I want to be honest with you. I've always been honest with you. You know that, don't you?'

'Yes, Ellie. It was always one of your many qualities that I admired. Please — go on.'

So Ellie continued, slowly, hesitantly, unsure of how far she dared take her story without shocking and disappointing him so much that he would not wish to have anything to do with her. He listened intently to her every word as she explained as simply as possible what had happened to her and her family from the day she had left him.

It was when she reached the point when Adam had made his love for her known that she stumbled over her words, but he merely nodded and told her, gently, to go on. When she hesitated again and felt her cheeks burn with embarrassment, he came to sit by her, taking one of her hands in both of his.

'Ellie, did you care for Adam Rockwell?'

'Yes,' she said, the tiny word coming out as a croak. 'I cared for him very much. It was — my feelings — they were too strong . . . '

'You became lovers?'

She closed her eyes, ran her tongue over

her dry lips and drew in a great, deep breath. 'Yes.'

'I see.' The professor's grip on her fingers slackened slightly so she drew her hand away, feeling her shame and his disappointment.

'No, I'm afraid you don't see,' she said softly and his eyes flickered over her face that was dark with pain. 'It was something I can't explain. It was as if we were both caught up in something that neither of us could control.'

'But you allowed him to — to take you? He did not force himself on you?'

'There was no force, Professor. I was a willing lover. More than willing, if I'm perfectly honest.' She heard the professor sigh deeply, felt him begin to move away from her, so she reached out and touched his arm to stay him. 'It only happened once and it will never — can never happen again.'

Professor Graham's eyes narrowed. 'What are you trying to say Ellie? Are you saying that you no longer love him, that you have perhaps realized the error of your ways?'

'No,' she shook her head and, with the utmost difficulty, took her courage in both hands and faced him with the final truth. 'After — after it happened, we were informed of a shocking fact that had never been divulged before. The fact that — that Adam

Rockwell and I are — that we share the same father.'

Professor Graham's face paled, then a rosy flush appeared high on his cheekbones.

'My God! And you never knew this?'

'Of course not!' She spoke perhaps a little more sharply than was necessary, but she was annoyed that he might doubt her word. 'If I had known that Adam was my brother, do you think I would have — could have . . . No, Professor Graham. That would have been quite out of the question.'

He now took hold of both her hands and was staring down at them, shaking his head and murmuring half to himself. 'Oh, my poor, dear Ellie! How you must have suffered and I — I thought I was the one with all the suffering to bear when you left me.'

'I can't bear that you think badly of me,' Ellie said. 'I know you did when I turned down your proposal of marriage . . . '

'No — no, Ellie! I didn't think ill of you. After all, I was a fool to expect such a young girl as yourself to want to marry me.' He swallowed hard and went on. 'This ugly business with young Rockwell — it's unforgivable that you didn't know — but you must put it all behind you. What is your situation at present?'

Ellie explained briefly how the family had

gone to live with her father's three sisters, though it was hardly an ideal arrangement. Tommy and Margaret had found rented accommodation close by. Ben had been fortunate enough to secure a gantryman's position in another foundry down in Yorkshire.

'And you, my dear? What of you?'

'I cannot think straight,' Ellie told him. 'My life seems to be in such turmoil. My three aunts are not happy at having their lives interrupted by us and they make constant reference to the fact that I shall have to find work. I didn't know which way to turn. I couldn't approach the Rockwells — couldn't ask Adam to . . . Well, I — I wondered if you — if you knew of anyone looking for a secretary or a companion or a lady's maid or . . .'

'Or a wife?' Professor Graham got up and paced the floor with one arm tucked behind his back. He paced three times, then turned and fixed her with a meaningful stare.

Ellie flinched and gave a violent shake of her head. 'Oh, no! Please, don't think that I . . . I haven't come to beg you to take me back, Professor. I came because — because I felt that you were the only friend I could turn to.'

'I'm not reprimanding you, my dear.' His

voice was softer now, more like the kind professor she had known nearly half her lifetime. Suddenly, he drew himself up erect and flexed his shoulders. 'Ellie, my offer still stands.'

'Your offer?'

'I asked you to marry me once. You turned me down. I would like you to go away now and think things over very carefully. Take as long as you like, but do please come back and let me know your decision.'

'My — my decision?'

'Whether or not you are going to become Mrs Nicholas Graham.'

'Oh!'

'I cannot promise you fun, or excitement — I am no longer a young man, Ellie. But I do love you with all my heart. I think you already know that and — surely, it counts for something?'

Ellie breathed in deeply and held it, then let out a quivering sigh through slightly parted lips. 'It counts for a great deal, Professor. Perhaps more than I deserve.'

'Then you'll consider my proposal once more?'

She smiled and nodded and he nodded back, satisfied with the arrangement.

★   ★   ★

Cynthia Rockwell looked up from her embroidery with a start as a door banged loudly down on the ground floor. She put down her canvas and needle and hurried to the window in time to see Adam stride across the courtyard as if his heels were on fire. She rapped loudly on the window, but he either didn't hear her or he ignored the sound.

She made an impatient 'tch' and tapped her foot. For days she had been trying to catch him to talk about the new social proposals for the foundry-workers' families. Somehow, he had never been available. He no longer appeared at mealtimes and was very often to be heard returning late at night or in the early hours of the morning. And the grunts that emanated from him in the darkness of the house, together with his clumsy stumbling on the stairs, meant only one thing. Something had happened to drive Adam to drink.

Cynthia crossed to the fireplace and pulled the bell-pull at the side. As she waited her attention was caught by a mounted rider heading over the moor at a gallop. She recognized the broad frame of Adam and the powerful way in which he controlled his horse. Nobody sat a horse quite like her stepson. He became one with the animal. It was magic to watch.

Today, however, he rode like a madman, driving the poor stallion as if he wanted to break some mythical barrier of time and speed.

'Did you want to see me, milady?'

She spun around and saw that the housekeeper had entered the room without her noticing.

'Oh, Mrs Mac! Do come in and close the door, would you? Now, I apologize for this, but I feel you might be the only one in this house to know what is going on with my stepson.'

'Mister Adam, milady?'

'He's acting strangely. He's rushing about like a mad thing and won't stay in one place long enough for me to speak to him. I've questioned Sir Donald, but he insists on remaining mute on the subject. I know they had another argument, but it's more than that, I'm sure.'

'Are you asking me to be indiscreet, milady?' Mrs Mac was plainly agitated.

Cynthia fixed the older woman with a challenging eye. 'Yes, I am! If there is something worrying Adam, then I should know about it. I mean . . . Oh, come along, Mrs Mac. You can trust me, surely.'

'Well . . . ' The housekeeper had one hand to her face and was averting her searching eyes. 'It's really not my place to talk about members of the family, but I'm worried about Mr Adam too. It's ever since that letter was delivered. You know the one I mean, milady. From the Martin girl — Ellie.'

'Oh, that was so sad. Those poor young women, losing two members of their family on the same day. It was tragic, Mrs Mac. And there again there's a mystery. I sent a message of condolence, only to be told that the family had left Northend. Just like that! Left — and not a word. I didn't expect that of Ellen Martin. She seemed such a sensible, responsible type of girl.'

'Aye, milady. I agree with you on that. A nice girl. A bit on the flighty side, but then I'm old-fashioned. Anyway, it's since Mr Adam received that letter from her that he's gone off half-cock — if you'll pardon the expression, milady.'

Cynthia nodded. The letter had arrived three days ago. It was addressed personally to Adam and he had refused to let her read it, reading out what he considered to be the salient parts, though she knew there was more to it than he had admitted. The little boy, Archie, had died and the mother — that dourfaced, sparrow of a woman — had committed suicide. Thrown herself in the river. Ellen had written that she and her sister, Mary, would not be returning to the Hall.

It had been sad and unexpected news. On the other hand, with Ellen gone Cynthia could relax a little more. Adam had been too close to the girl he had promoted to be his secretary. Too close and too interested. She had seen the way his eyes followed her about, devouring her. And the girl was not impervious to his attentions.

So, there was something of his father in Adam after all. Now they were back where they started and would have to find replacement staff, which was always a tiresome task. Perhaps Adam would do better by hiring a male secretary. She would certainly feel more at ease knowing that temptation was not exactly at his fingertips.

Cynthia sighed. 'Thank you, Mrs Mac. We won't speak any more of this. I shall take it upon myself to find out exactly what the problem is.'

★   ★   ★

Adam felt the wind whipping his face like iced birch twigs, felt the dull thudding vibration of the horses hoofs pounding through him as the animal raced over hillock and hedge. If he had been riding on a winged

Pegasus he could not have travelled any faster. He refused to see the dangers of such an unwise flight. In fact, he almost welcomed the possibility of getting hurt. He courted death and did not care how or when it came.

When the horse finally slowed to an exhausted trot, its body quivering and flecked with foam, he sat slumped in the saddle. His eyes stung and he realized they were filled with tears. When he raised his head and gazed out at the distant horizon, he realized that he was looking north. Ellie was out there somewhere. So near and yet so impossibly far away.

After reading her letter as many times as it took to let the truth of her words sink into his confused and traumatized brain, he had sought out his father yet again and flung his question in the old man's face.

'I want to know if it's true? Are you also Ellie Martin's father. Ellie Martin, the sister of Ben who is beyond doubt your son? Tell me, Father! No lies or I swear I'll see you rot in hell!'

Sir Donald had been taken aback at this verbal onslaught, but after a moment he shook his head and laughed and the saliva from the paralysed side of his mouth bubbled and dropped in foamy globules.

'If that's what the little slut tells you, then it

must be true, eh? How should I know? I was simply — shall we say — entertaining myself. The girl does bear a strong resemblance to your half-brother, does she not?'

'Animal! Dirty, filthy animal!' Adam's fists beat down on his father's desk.

Sir Donald laughed again, a dry, mirthless sound. 'And my blood flows in your veins. Don't ever forget that, my boy. Come on, Adam. Forget the Martin girl. What was she to you anyway?'

What was she indeed? *Everything* was the word that came into his head and what he wanted to scream at his father. Everything.

The horse had come to a halt and Adam drew in a ragged breath.

'Oh, Ellie — *Ellie!*' He shouted out her name across the moorland and it came echoing back to him on the wind. A cold, empty, painful sound.

Part II

14

Ellie could not, in all honesty, say that her marriage to Nicholas Graham was unhappy. He plainly adored her and she, in her turn, was very fond of him.

He had done his best, she knew, to make her forget the unhappy circumstances by which they came to be married. On the surface, it would appear he had done a good job of erasing the affair with Adam Rockwell. It was deep down, beneath her light steps and her ready laughter that Ellie continued to hurt to such an extent she believed that her heart would never heal.

In the years following her flight from Rockwell, there had been stories in the newspapers about the foundry and the men who ran it and worked there. Ellie read these reports avidly, hoping to see mention of Adam. She tried to pretend that she was simply searching for news of her half-brother. There was nothing wrong with that. The wrong was in the way her heart squeezed or flipped every time Adam's name did appear.

Like this morning. *Concern over the failing health of iron-baron Sir Donald Rockwell, continues to mount as he struggles to overcome yet another stroke. For some time now, the foundry in Wearside has been running in the capable hands of Sir Donald's son, Adam, 32. The heir to the foundry is as yet unmarried, but there has been speculation . . .*

'Is there anything much of note in the *Journal* today, my dear?'

Ellie quickly folded the newspaper and laid it beside her on the sofa as Nicholas came towards her. Her hands, she noticed, had become quite clammy and she wiped them discreetly down her skirt.

'It's all very boring, I'm afraid,' she said and glanced across at the sunlight filtering in through the window. 'What a beautiful day. I think I'll go for a walk.'

She wanted to get out of the house, breathe some cleansing air, empty her head of all brooding and unhealthy thoughts.

'An excellent idea. I'll accompany you, if I may.' Nicholas stood, one foot raised on the brass fender, firelight flickering in his gaunt face. He took down his favourite pipe and filled it, all the time watching her. 'You don't mind, do you, Ellie? It will do us both good to get away from this house, if only for an hour or so.'

'Of course I don't mind, Nicholas!' she

exclaimed, colouring slightly because she hated lying to him. Usually, she enjoyed his company, but today she wanted to be alone.

'Good. Run along and fetch your cloak while I tell Mrs Renney to organize a late lunch. Wear your warmest clothes, my dear. It's very cold.'

'Yes, Nicholas.'

'And this afternoon, I plan to take you into Newcastle to see that artist fellow — Salter. You remember?'

'Oh — I — yes, but . . . ' Of course she remembered. How could she possibly forget? Freddie Salter was Adam's best friend. He had come to the Hall once for lunch and spent the afternoon sketching her as she chatted to his frail but pretty wife.

'Ellie, you're not listening!' Nicholas touched her arm and she blinked up at him, realizing that her mind had slipped away into itself while he was talking.

'I'm sorry?'

'I was saying that I think it's time we asked Salter to do your portrait in oils. With Christmas and our anniversary approaching, I'd rather like to offer myself this luxury, if it would not tire you too much to sit still for as long as it takes.'

Ellie sighed and tried to give a light laugh, but it came out rather like a pathetic squeak.

'I have to say I don't relish the thought of staying still for hours on end, but if it will please you, Nicholas . . . '

'Then it's settled. As a matter of fact, I've already made enquiries of Mr Frederick Salter and agreed a price. We'll go and see him directly after lunch.'

★   ★   ★

'Are you quite well, my dear?' Nicholas was looking quite concerned as Ellie came into the room, her arms full of Christmas decorations. They were to dress the tree together, then go into Newcastle to Frederick Salter's tiny artist's studio, which was now in an attic in Grey Street.

'I'm perfectly well, thank you.' Ellie smiled and started sorting out bundles of tinsel garlands and shiny glass toys for the large fir tree that stood in the corner of the room. Christmas was her favourite time of year. She could hardly remember a time when she had not enjoyed the festive season. Except, perhaps, that first Christmas after she had left Rockwell Hall. But she refused to let herself think about that. 'What do you think, Nicholas. The star or the fairy?'

'I beg your pardon?'

'For the top of the tree!'

'Oh! Do as you please, dear. I don't mind at all.'

'The star then.' She had always liked a star taking pride of place rather than rather plump angels that hardly looked right or real. She climbed up on the steps she had brought from the kitchen. In her haste to get the tree dressed before they had to go out, she had quite forgotten her weak head for heights. On the top step she wobbled precariously and let out a small cry.

'Good Lord, Ellie, do be careful!' Nicholas's hands came up to grab her and lift her swiftly to the floor. He continued to hold her tightly and as he stared down at her she recognized barely masked anxiety in his eyes. 'Are you quite sure you are well, Ellie? You appear to be quite — um — giddy.'

'No! It's all right, Nicholas. I never could stand heights. Perhaps it's better if you do the top of the tree while I stay on the ground.'

He was still holding her, still gazing questioningly into her eyes. 'You don't think that perhaps . . . ? I mean, is it possible that . . . ?'

Ellie sighed. She knew immediately what was going through his mind and she felt almost guilty that she was going to disappoint him yet again.

'Am I pregnant, do you mean?' She gave

him a small, sad smile and shook her head. 'No, Nicholas. I'm so sorry, but — no. Everything is — well, as it should be — for a woman who is not pregnant, that is.'

'Ah! I had hoped, but — well, no matter. Perhaps I am expecting too much of myself. A small miracle. It would have been such a wonderful Christmas gift from you to me.'

'To both of us, Nicholas.' Ellie pushed away from him and turned back to the tree, filling her hands full of decorations and draping them on the green boughs smelling so freshly of pine. 'I, too, would dearly love a child. Really! But if it's not to be, then we must be content with each other. But don't give up hope. There's plenty of time yet. I am, after all, only twenty-seven . . . '

'And I am over fifty! My dearest girl, you have no idea how old I feel at times when I look at you dancing and singing about this old mausoleum like a wood nymph.'

She saw his stricken face and patted his hand as she squeezed around him to pick up some bright red baubles and some silver bells. 'A man is only old when they lay him in his grave,' she told him with a light laugh and he gave her a grateful smile. 'That's what my granddad used to say. He was much older than you and he still had a twinkle in his eye.'

'Dearest Ellie. Not a day goes by when I

don't thank God for you.'

She blew him a kiss and heard his sigh, then they continued the work of dressing the tree in silence.

* * *

Professor Graham dropped Ellie off outside the studio and went on to his club in Dean Street. She mounted the dark stairs with their yellow electric lights that gave no more illumination than candles. There were eight flights of stairs and ninety steps in all, which she had counted now seven times up and seven times down, which was the number of sittings she had given.

The portrait was supposed to be a Christmas gift for Nicholas, but it had taken so long to execute it was now well into February. She had not expected it to be such a time-consuming exercise and she was uncomfortable sitting still in the cheerless, cold and badly lit attic with a man who did not even offer her entertaining conversation as he worked. In fact, Mr Salter preferred to work in comparative silence, except when he scolded her gently for shifting her position.

He did allow her a ten-minute break half-way through the sessions, during which he talked volubly and he often made mention of Adam, whom he had known practically all his life. And then she would lock a benign smile on her face and try not to probe him with questions that would betray her heart.

Breathlessly, she reached the top landing, having run all the way, which she could do easily when Nicholas was not with her. Without thinking, she grasped the brass knob and pushed open the door that bore Freddie Salter's sign claiming that he was a portraitist and landscape artist.

There was a clink of glass upon glass and a mutter of male conversation, but she was already inside before she registered the sounds. Otherwise, she would have knocked and waited politely.

'Oh, I'm sorry, I . . . '

Adam had been sitting with his back to the door, one haunch perched on the end of Freddie's work table. He turned, glass of wine in hand, and she saw it spill over his fingers as he jerked to his feet.

'Ah! Do come in, Mrs Graham.' Freddie sang out. 'Of course, there's no need to introduce you two . . . ?'

'No — no, of course not,' she said, choking on her breathlessness and her beating heart that was galloping even more recklessly than ever.

'Good afternoon, Ellie.'

'Adam.' She inclined her head and felt his eyes burning into her with such an intensity she thought she would bear the marks of it for evermore.

'You look well.'

'Thank you, I'm very well.'

Her body tingled and her ears were on fire. She put a self-conscious hand up to one of them and gave a quivering smile. 'It's so cold and wet today.'

'Perhaps we could persuade Freddie here to break out another bottle of wine.' Adam's cheeks dimpled. He looked perfectly relaxed again after the initial shock of seeing her so unexpectedly. 'It isn't good French wine, but it will help to warm you. How about it, Freddie?'

'Yes, of course. I'll go and get a bottle.' Freddie looked from one to the other of them with an uncertain twitch to his mouth and disappeared into an adjoining room, closing the door behind him with a resounding click.

Adam came a step or two towards her. Ellie felt she should back off, but her feet were rooted to the spot.

'You look wonderful, Ellie. More beautiful than ever. Marriage must agree with you.'

'Yes — um — yes, we're very happy. Thank you.'

'Are you? Truly happy? Does he treat you

right, your professor?'

Ellie took a deep breath and cast about, looking for something to latch on to to help her out in this very difficult conversation.

'It's such a bore having to sit for Mr Salter. And I have to wear the same dress every time I come. People must think I have nothing else to wear.'

She looked at him and laughed. To her own ears it sounded like the laugh of a stranger. He drained his glass and regarded her over the rim. With an almost staggering step, she headed for the nearest chair and sat down heavily before her knees gave way completely.

'Don't!' she chided him without looking. 'Don't look at me like that!'

'How should I look at you?'

'I don't know, but not like that. Not like . . . '

'Like what?'

'You know what I mean. Please — this is difficult for me.'

'And for me.'

'Have you married your Miss Dunstable yet?' she asked quickly by way of changing the subject.

He threw back his head and gave a hollow guffaw. A single sound that expressed totally his feelings for the luckless Miss Dunstable. 'You should never believe what you read in the newspapers, Ellie. They like to invent stories to entertain their readers.'

'So, you are not married — to Miss Dunstable?'

'I'm neither married nor engaged to Stella Dunstable — or anyone else. On the other hand, you are married. You couldn't wait, it seems, to recapture your precious professor.'

'That's unfair.' Ellie's eyes slid over him, then returned to Freddie's cluttered palette and jars of brushes. 'As you well know, he had asked me to marry him long before . . .'

'Yes?'

'Before we met.'

'Are there children?'

'No — not yet.'

'Ah!'

She didn't quite know what he meant by that and was about to ask him, but Freddie Salter came back with a new bottle of wine, already opened and a clean glass, which he handed to her.

'There we are, Mrs Graham. It's not as bad as Adam here says, but he's been spending a lot of time over in France lately, so he's acquired a palate for French wine. Personally, I prefer German white, when I can get it, but there's no accounting for taste, is there?'

'I must go,' Adam said, his eyes still riveted on Ellie's face. 'It was good to see you again,

Ellie. Please give my regards to your husband and tell Ben that if he ever tires of Yorkshire to come and see me.'

Adam nodded at Freddie and left without a further word. How, she wondered, did he know that Ben was in Yorkshire? Giving herself a mental shake, Ellie drank deeply and managed to smile warmly at the artist.

'Well, Mr Salter, where is my portrait? Have you finished it already? I thought I was needed for a final sitting.'

Freddie Salter looked uncomfortable. He poured himself another glass of wine and drank half of it back in one gulp. It looked to Ellie that it was the last thing he should be doing, for he had already seemed quite merry on her arrival. Adam, for his part, however, had looked as sober as ever. All except his eyes, which had a wild look to them, much the way they had appeared the first time they met.

'The portrait! Ah, yes! Now, there we have a problem.'

'What kind of problem?' Ellie was still listening to the echo of Adam's feet on the stairs growing ever fainter. In her mind she followed him as he descended each floor and was with him when he stepped out on to the street and turned his collar up against the wind and the rain. 'I'm sorry?'

Freddie was frowning at her because he had blurted out something and she had not been listening. Now he had to repeat it and he was having the greatest difficulty.

'I will repay every penny your husband has paid me, Mrs Graham,' Freddie finally said in a rush of words that tumbled over themselves in their haste to get out of his mouth. 'I will even pay him for the time you have wasted and the discomfort you have suffered and the inconvenience of it all.'

'I don't understand you, Mr Salter. What has happened to my portrait? You said yourself it was nearly finished.'

'I'm afraid I was not at all pleased with my work and when an artist is dissatisfied he has a dissatisfied client.'

'But . . . where is it? Let me see it. I'm sure it isn't as bad as all that. Perhaps if I sit today, you might get it right.'

Freddie was shaking his head adamantly. 'Too late, I'm afraid. The painting has been . . . I got rid of it. There was no point in my keeping it you see.'

'Oh, but my husband put so much store by this painting, Mr Salter. Could you not do it again?' Ellie had made the suggestion, but in truth she was relieved when she saw him shake his head again. The thought of having to agonize her way through seven more

347

sittings was more than she could bear. Especially with the risk of having Adam turn up out of the blue, as he had done today.

'I'm sorry,' was all Freddie could say and he kept on repeating his apology, looking genuinely remorseful.

Ellie looked about her, half-expecting her unfinished portrait to emerge from the shadows, but there was no sign of it. 'Very well,' she sighed. 'I will do a little shopping and then call for my husband at his club. Perhaps you could lend me an umbrella? It's raining rather heavily out there.'

'Yes! Yes, of course, Mrs Graham. Please — take this . . . '

'I will, of course, return it to you . . . '

'No, please! Keep it. It — it's the least I can offer you . . . '

Ellie ran down the stairs, clutching the long black gentleman's umbrella. Outside, the street was wet and greasy with the footsteps of a hundred people who had passed that way in the last few hours, but she only wanted to catch sight of one of them. She stood in the rain, the umbrella still furled, looking to right and to left, but Adam was nowhere to be seen.

15

Adam was wandering aimlessly through the kitchen-gardens, looking from time to time in the direction of the moorland where he and Ellie had walked together. Six years had passed and not a day went by when he did not find her in his thoughts.

He gazed at the house, the gardens, fondled the ears of his two dogs, Dougal and Scallion, and wondered if he would ever see them again after tomorrow. He did not regret his decision to leave the foundry, but there were things he would undoubtedly miss.

The crunch of wheels on the gravel drive in front of the house caught his attention. He hurried to meet his visitor, thinking it to be one of the coal barons who had demanded a meeting with him in the face of the war that had just been declared.

But it was a woman who alighted from the motor car. At first he saw only a stranger. A tall, heavily-built woman with greying hair. She stood, looking around her, eyes shaded from the warm September sun by a gloved hand. There was something familiar in the way she moved, so silkily smooth, no jerky movements. And she did not wear a fashionable dress of 1914, but a flowing caftan.

'Adam!'

The husky voice was unchanged.

'Sarah? Good Lord, is it really you?'

Sarah Wells put her hands on her hips and beamed at him. He couldn't remember the last time they had met, but it must be some years ago when she announced she was planning to go to visit cousins in America. They had exchanged letters and postcards for a while, but then they had stopped and he had been too preoccupied to worry about it.

'I didn't think you would recognize me, Adam. I'm afraid I've grown a bit between head and ankle. What do you think of this grotesque spectre from your past, eh?'

'I do believe I detect a slight American accent,' Adam said, coming forward to envelop her in a fond embrace. 'What happened to you over there on the other side of the world?'

'You won't believe it! I got married! To one of my many cousins.'

'Well, that's good news, Sarah.'

'You're not jealous?'

Adam laughed. 'No, not a bit — well, maybe I am, but I'm determined to keep a stiff upper lip. We British are like that, you know.'

'If all the newspaper reports are accurate, I'd say the British are going to need that stiff upper lip. Do you think this damned silly war will last, Adam?'

He shrugged. 'Who knows? There are some who think it'll be over in a few days, but whatever happens it's succeeded in throwing everybody into panic. I have a meeting in a few minutes with pit directors, fellow foundry-owners, government officials . . . '

'You're not going to do anything silly, are you Adam? Like joining up and going out there to fight the Germans?'

'Freddie Salter and I leave for France tomorrow, Sarah.'

He saw her face stiffen. Her eyes regarded him sharply. 'You fool!'

'We're not joining up exactly. We're going out armed with sketchpads and pencils and cameras.' He saw her frown and laughed. 'We won't be there to fight as soldiers. We're going as correspondents of a sort. Journalists, if you like, but most of our reporting will be on the artistic side — you know, capturing the images of our fighting forces.'

'And the foundry? Who will be in charge. I thought the place couldn't run without you.'

'My father is no longer capable, it's true,

but I have a good man to see that things run smoothly in my absence. I'm sure he can manage things for a few weeks.'

'Not Whitfield!'

He smiled and shook his head. 'I got rid of Whitfield long ago.' Adam looked down at a scar across his knuckles and remembered the day when he and Whitfield had fought, fist to fist. The men who were loyal to Adam had reported how sadistic and cruel the fellow was, but what had driven Adam into a rage was the way Whitfield had taunted him in front of the workers, accusing him of incest. Where the man had got his information from he didn't know and didn't care. Adam sent him running, all bloodied and with his tail between his legs.

'Then you'll come home, safe and sound?' Sarah was pressing him.

'That's the plan, yes.'

'Good boy.' She patted his cheek and as she did so the sun fell on her face and he saw how much she had aged. It shouldn't have been such a surprise, but this was the first woman he had ever slept with and he had thought himself madly in love with her once. Now, she cut a rather maternal figure.

She put an arm through his and led him away from the house where he could see the twitch of an upstairs curtain at the window of his father's room. The old man rarely came downstairs any more, but nothing much escaped his notice even so.

'Do you have time to walk with me for a little while before your meeting?' Sarah asked him, steering him still further away from the house.

'Do I detect a conspiracy?' he asked with a chuckle.

'Maybe,' she said in a low, secretive voice. 'Maybe not. You'll have to judge for yourself.'

'Goodness, I'm intrigued. And here I was thinking you'd just come to chew over old times.'

'The old times are gone, Adam. At least some of them are. Certainly for me. For you — well, there may still be hope. You're still young. There's time for you to build a future.'

'Sarah! What is all this? Are you going to tell me or not? And when am I to meet this famous husband of yours? You did bring him back with you, did you not?'

She smiled wanly and shook her head. 'Harvey died a few months ago.'

'Oh. I'm sorry.'

'Don't be. He was okay, but five years was enough with the old reprobate. He left me all his money, so I won't speak too ill of him.'

'Sarah, you're incredible.'

'It's odd, you know, but here I am on the

wrong side of the half-century, a widow, no children, alone in the world — and for the first time in my life I'm completely happy. It's crazy, but true.'

'You must come back when I have more time, Sarah, and you can tell me all about your adventures in the States.'

'What I came here to tell you, Adam, won't wait. I may be wrong, but I guess you've already suffered too long because of the wrongdoings of others.'

Adam's steps faltered. He turned and looked at her, one hand resting loosely on her shoulder. 'What are you talking about, Sarah? What wrongdoings?'

She took a deep breath and chewed on her bottom lip. 'Adam, the first thing I did on getting back home was look up my old friends. A lot of them are your old friends too. One of them is a particularly close friend of your stepmother's, who just couldn't wait to tell me something she had found out.'

'Who?'

'Constance Witherspoon.'

'Sandy hair, rosy-cheeked and wheezingly plump?'

'That's the one. Oh, she's all right. A bit blinkered in her opinions and rather naïve, but she is apparently your stepmother's listening ear. Cynthia, it seems, has been keeping a certain fact locked inside her and feels quite guilty, but cannot bring herself to tell you about it.'

'Sarah, you've lost me.'

'The thing is, Adam, if she told you this great big secret of hers, she might lose you completely.'

'She doesn't have me!'

'Perhaps not, but as long as you're a free man there's always the hope that you will one day turn to her. It's about that girl you were so taken with. The one who is now happily married to a professor.'

Adam stared at her, his face turned to stone. 'You'd better tell me, Sarah,' he said at last, his eyes flickering back to the courtyard where more motor cars were arriving. 'But make it fast. This is one meeting I can't afford to be late for.'

★   ★   ★

'Gentlemen, we have spent two hours arguing over the future of iron and coal and I, for one, do not feel that we are any further forward. Why not?'

Adam was on his feet, addressing the meeting, resting heavily on his hands which were placed flat on the board-table around

355

which twenty men sat, each with the same grim expression.

'It seems to me, Rockwell, that if this bloody war goes ahead we all stand to lose, no matter what we do.'

Adam turned a fierce look on the man who had shouted at him from the bottom of the table. 'War is always a question of loss rather than gain, Foulkes! Most of all, we lose the lives of our men, women and children. What good is a country without people to run it?'

'But the percentages are already reducing. We can't afford to let them get so low that we start making a loss.'

Adam sighed. 'During the first ten years of this century, the Rockwell Foundry saw growth in the production of pig-iron of sixty per cent, where it reached its peak. It started to slide soon after and has continued, but not to an important extent. Let's not be greedy, gentlemen. Until the scientists come up with something better than iron and steel, or until the coal seams run out completely, we will be in business and reaping the rewards for some time to come.'

'But the shares have crashed. People are running scared.'

'People always run scared when war is announced. It's going to be tough, I can guarantee that, but we'll survive as long as we don't set our expectations too high.'

'There's talk of the government demanding that we hand over our scrap. Can you see them paying us for that?'

Adam shook his head and sighed. 'I, for one, will welcome the opportunity to turn our slag heaps into something more useful than death-traps for unwary children.'

'Aye! They'll turn them into death-traps for the Germans! Knives, swords, bayonets!'

There was a ripple of laughter and a cheer or two. Adam ignored it, his mind already racing ahead to what he planned to do as soon as he could tear himself away. Slowly and deliberately, he gathered together his papers and ledgers.

'Gentlemen!' He raised his voice and slammed the gavel down twice, three times on its block and the room fell into silence. 'I think we all know where we stand on this issue. We may lose some profit along the way, but this war cannot be won without us. You must take care of your own consciences, but Rockwell will be pledging its slag heaps as a donation towards the war effort. I declare this meeting closed.'

There were more murmurings as he left the table and strode purposefully to the door, indicating on his way the sideboard with drinks set out, the crystal decanters and glasses sparkling in the filtering rays of the afternoon sun.

'I have a pressing engagement, gentlemen. Please help yourselves to drinks.'

He could not get away quickly enough. There was a tightness in his chest and his pulses were racing so that the whole of his nervous system was on edge as if it were overloaded with energy and might explode at any minute.

Without stopping to knock, Adam burst into Lady Rockwell's private sitting-room. He found his stepmother sitting with his sister, the pair of them involved in the execution of a large tapestry that was fixed tautly in a long frame that rested across their knees.

'Why, Adam! What new disaster has brought you in such terrible haste? My dear, you look awful!'

'If I look awful, as you put it, then it's all your fault, Cynthia!'

His sister stood up quickly, her face paling. The tapestry fell to the floor, pulling itself out of Cynthia's hands, needle and all.

'I'll leave you to talk in private,' Grace said, making for the door.

'No, Grace! You'll stay, if you please,' Adam shot out a hand and gripped her arm as she tried to pass him. She winced with the unexpected force of it, but no longer attempted to leave. 'What I have to say needs a witness and who better than my own sister who has been shunning me because of what she mistakenly believes I have done.'

'There's no need to speak to your sister like that, Adam,' Cynthia's voice was low, controlled. Her eyes, however, were bright with anxiety.

'There is every need, Cynthia. And I will speak to you in the same manner.' Adam strode about the room and the eyes of the two women followed him closely, exchanging worried, furtive glances behind his back.

'Adam, do sit down and stop acting like a caged animal.' Cynthia retrieved the canvas from the floor and put it to one side. 'Whatever it is you would be better calming yourself before you speak.'

'If I had come to you two hours ago, Cynthia, you would have seen me less calm than you see me now. In fact, I might have been driven to the point of murder, because all I could think of at that time was to place my hands around your haughty throat and squeeze the life out of you.'

There was a small cry of alarm from Grace. She took a step back from him, but he was there, taking hold of her, pushing her into the seat she had just vacated.

'Stay where you are, the pair of you!' Adam

growled. 'Six years ago, having thought I would never know happiness with any woman, I found myself in a situation that showed promise beyond my dreams. To put it in the romantic terms that you ladies appreciate, I was deeply in love with the most wonderful person.'

'Your secretary?' Grace responded caustically. 'That little miner's daughter you found among the workers?'

'Grace — please!' Cynthia reached out and touched her stepdaughter's hand. 'Let him speak.'

'Yes, Grace,' Adam shouted, unable to keep the tone of his voice at a moderate level. 'Let him speak, by all means. Why, Cynthia, when you could have spoken, did you keep your silence? When you knew what agonies I was in, thinking that Ellie was my half-sister? You knew, damn you, that it wasn't true. Your stepmother, Grace, was so bloody jealous she could not bring herself to let me go to another woman.'

'How did you find out?' Cynthia's breasts were heaving, but she was still able to behave with inbred decorum.

'Sarah Wells told me two hours ago.'

'Sarah Wells! That trollop you used to visit when you were a young man and couldn't control yourself?'

'She has one quality that you do not possess, Cynthia. Honesty. And in my eyes, that makes her a better woman than you. Between Ellie Martin's mother, my father and, above all, you, dear stepmother, we just didn't stand a chance, did we? Warped, twisted minds, all of you. You took my happiness and that of Ellie, and you screwed it up like a piece of unwanted paper and threw it in the fire.'

Cynthia looked down at her hands and he saw her throat constrict as she swallowed.

'I'm sorry, Adam. You've no idea how bitterly I regretted what I did, but at the time I was — I was driven by my own hopeless desires, my own miserable life here at the Hall. It was wrong of me to let you go on thinking that Ellie was your sister, but I didn't think it was such a serious affair. After all, she was hardly more than a servant. I thought you would get over it quickly, forget it . . . '

'You had no right, Cynthia, to toy with my life! No right at all!'

A muffled sound from behind him made Adam spin around. Sir Donald was standing in the open doorway, the paralysed side of him drooping and distorted. The normal side was bright with angry understanding. He moved into the room with an unsteady shuffle.

'You — know?' His one bright eye fixed itself on Adam's face.

'Yes, Father,' Adam said, suddenly feeling calm, his emotions having exhausted themselves. 'Why did you let me believe that you were Ellie's father? What had she or I done to you to deserve such treatment?'

'N-not . . . ' Sir Donald was struggling to speak through uncontrolled saliva and a tongue that was thick and immobile in his mouth. 'Not the — the girl — not her fault. The woman — Catherine Durham. The girl's — mother.' He tapped his temple with a shaking finger. 'Bad blood. She blackmailed me — made me feel bad. Should have . . . ' He struggled to swallow and swiped at the saliva drooling down his chin. 'Should have chased her off — stupid bitch. She — she thought she was — in love with me. Ha! The idea! All these years — the love and the hate — it all congealed inside her. She didn't want her daughter — the girl, Ellie — didn't want her to be part of my family. Ironic, eh Adam? It was — it was the only opinion I shared with the crazy woman . . . '

A bout of breathless coughing arrested his uncertain flow of words. Grace rushed to his side to guide him to a chair, but he pushed her away from him and went to sit down unaided. Cynthia poured him a glass of lemonade, which he clutched and drank deeply, spilling most of the sticky citrus juice down the front of his shirt and smoking-jacket.

'Six years,' Adam said coldly. 'Six years I've suffered in the knowledge that I made love, albeit unknowingly, to my own sister. And now, when it's too late, you tell me that there is no blood-tie between Ellie and me. I hope you're very happy to know how you have ruined my life, Father.'

Sir Donald looked up, his coughing over, and laughed wetly. 'You could have discovered the truth if you had tried, Adam.'

The old man lay back wearily in his chair. His eyes closed and his breathing became instantly heavy as he slipped into a deep slumber.

'What does he mean? How could I have found out?' Adam looked pleadingly at Cynthia.

'It's a question of mathematics, Adam,' Cynthia told him, fetching her shawl to drape over her sleeping husband. 'At the time when Ellie would have been conceived you were enjoying a tour of Europe with your parents, which lasted some months. Ask Mrs Mac, if you don't believe me. Our old housekeeper accompanied the family at your mother's request.'

'Mrs Mac knew about this?'

Cynthia shook her head. 'No — no, Adam! She knows nothing, but if questioned she would be able to remember when you, your mother and your father were travelling through France and Spain and one or two other countries. It would have been impossible for Sir Donald to father Catherine Durham's second child. The fact that she resembles so strongly your half-brother is, I suppose, a coincidence of heredity.'

'And there is no possibility that Ellie is my sister? No doubt?'

'None whatsoever.'

Adam drew in a deep breath. 'Then I must go to her, at least give her the relief of knowing the truth.'

'She is, by all accounts, Adam, a happily married woman now. Best leave well alone.'

Adam spun on his heel, calling out over his shoulder in an urgent voice. 'I *must* go to her! Don't you realize? She has suffered too, all these years. She must be told the truth. If I don't do it now I may never get the opportunity again. After tomorrow — I could be dead!'

He stormed out of the house, calling to his driver. The man appeared from the stables in shirtsleeves, riding-boot and polishing-brush in his hands.

'Jenner! Does my motor have a full tank of petrol? I need you to drive me to Newcastle.'

Adam was in the habit of driving himself, usually, but today was different. He could not trust his disturbed equilibrium to get him past the foundry gates in safety, let alone all the way to Newcastle.

'Aye, Mr Adam, sir, but I'll need to wash and change me clothes . . . '

'Forget that, Jenner. This is urgent. Get the car. Now, please?'

Jenner gaped at Adam for a second, then literally dropped the boot he was polishing and went off at a gallop.

★ ★ ★

Ellie was alone, Nicholas having gone to give a lecture. She was tapping away at her old typewriter, deep into transcribing her husband's newest work when she vaguely heard the jangle of the doorbell followed by the sound of voices. Students often called to see the professor, so she thought little of it until Mrs Renney appeared, clearing her throat loudly.

'There's a gentleman to see you, Mrs Graham. I told him that the professor wasn't available, but he insisted on seeing you personally.'

'Oh, who is it, Mrs Renney?'

'A certain Mr Rockwell.'

Ellie's fingers stumbled over the typewriter keys and half a dozen letters jumped up and jammed themselves against the paper.

'Mr Rockwell?' she gulped, feeling the blood drain from her cheeks.

'Aye. And he looks a bit wild in the eye. Would you prefer that I ask him to come back when the professor's at home?'

'Mr Rockwell is — an old friend, Mrs Renney. We cannot possibly turn him away.'

As she spoke, the door behind the housekeeper swung open and Adam himself appeared, obviously too impatient to wait any longer.

'I apologize, but I just had to see you and . . . ' Adam stopped himself and glanced pointedly at the housekeeper.

Ellie, her heart thundering, took the hint. 'Thank you, Mrs Renney. I'm sure you're eager to be off to see your brother in hospital. Please give him my good wishes for a speedy recovery.'

'Will you not be needing anything, Mrs Graham?' Mrs Renney asked with a questioning glance at Adam who was standing there staring at Ellie, his chest heaving and looking as if he could not contain himself any longer.

'That's quite all right, Mrs Renney. I can

make a pot of tea later, if necessary.' She came forward, extending her hand in polite greeting. 'It's so good to see you again, Adam. Do sit down and tell me what brings you here?'

Despite her heart's erratic behaviour, she thought she conducted herself fairly well in the circumstances.

'Well, if you don't mind, Mrs Graham,' the housekeeper was saying contemplatively, 'I'll be off then.'

'Yes — yes, of course. I hope you find your brother improved.'

Adam took her hand and held on to it with a desperation she felt vibrating all along her arm and into her chest. His eyes were black, fiery orbs and they sank into her.

'Ellie!' was all he seemed capable of saying. 'Oh, Ellie!'

Neither of them noticed the departure of Mrs Renney, who left the room quietly, closing the door behind her.

'What is it, Adam? What's happened?'

Now his eyes seemed damp and glistening with tears that he struggled to hold back. He shook his head as if trying to rid himself of all that was going on in there.

When he finally spoke, his voice was an unsteady croak. 'Perhaps I shouldn't have come.'

'But you are here and you're frightening me.' Ellie pulled away from him and he reluctantly let go of her hand. She went to the sideboard and her hands shook uncontrollably as she poured him a measure of whisky and a small sherry for herself.

He took the whisky she offered and sat down with it beside her on the sofa. He studied the glass a long time before raising it to his lips and drinking it back, draining it in two desperate gulps. Then he put the glass to one side and his head dropped into his hands with a sound that resembled a sob.

'Adam, you seem to be in some kind of distress or shock.' Ellie put a hand on his arm and he enclosed it with his hand, holding on to her as if he were afraid she might disappear. 'If you can't tell me about it I can't help.'

He took a deep breath and met her gaze. 'Ellie, I don't have much time. I leave for France tomorrow . . . '

'You're going to the war? But you can't Adam! You don't have to. You're not a soldier. You . . . '

'Hush!' He placed his fingers against her lips to silence her and she tasted salt, smelled his warm skin and remembered how it had been before their lives together had been shattered.

'Oh, Adam!' She clamped her lips tightly together and blinked back her own tears.

'It's all right, Ellie. There's no danger. I'm going with Freddie Salter. We're going as artists, not soldiers. Neither of us has much to lose anyway. Freddie has nothing to live for since poor Clara died trying to give him a son and me — well, I hardly need go into my reasons, do I?'

Ellie dragged her eyes from him and stared into the flickering flames of the coal fire that crackled and sparkled and smelled of oil and soot. She counted the pieces of glowing coal, tried to see pictures as she had done as a little girl. She tried to keep her mind away from Adam and what he was trying to say to her. Whatever it was, she knew she was going to be hurt yet again. Terribly hurt.

'Please, Adam — don't go into all that. I can't bear it any more than you can. You were right. You shouldn't have come here. If it was just to say goodbye, then a letter would have sufficed . . . '

'No! Ellie, that's not the reason!' His voice was raised and he turned and gripped her shoulders, pulling her towards him, his fingers hurting like steel vices, his closeness scaring her. 'It's true I'm going to France. It's even true that, if things go wrong and this damned silly war continues, I might never return. No, listen to me, Ellie. I was all prepared to leave without a word to you, but in the last few hours I've discovered something that — something that changes everything.'

'What do you mean?'

'Ellie, today I found out that I am *not* your brother. Half-brother — quarter-brother, whatever. There is no blood-link between us. None whatsoever. They lied. Your mother, my father. My stepmother too by omission. We are no more related than the King of England is to the Queen of Sheba!'

Ellie opened her mouth and gulped in a huge breath. She felt her eyes widen and her body prickle with the shock of his words as if the blood had turned to champagne in her veins. She wanted to laugh, to cry, to run barefoot about the town, screaming out the news. What she did was give a tiny grunt and slump towards him, quivering as his arms slid about her and he buried his face in her hair.

'Talk to me, Adam. Say something — something normal. This is too much for me to take in. My mind is whirling about inside my head like a spinning-top.'

He tightened his hold on her and she felt his heart beating against her shoulder. 'I had a long meeting to endure before I could come to you, my darling. I almost didn't make it through the afternoon.'

'Please — it won't sink in. Tell me something else, something I can believe in. How's your sister? Is she married yet? And Sir Donald . . . ?'

She heard his low-throated chuckle. 'Grace is as miserable as ever. I doubt she will ever marry. My father suffers stroke after stroke, but keeps on going, though a lot of the stuffing has been knocked out of him. He can't chase young girls any more. Not even captive ones, though I've seen that good eye of his roam from time to time when nurses are required to wash and dress him. He has a bedroom on the ground floor now, which saves him falling down the stairs. It also saves Mrs Mac's poor old legs every time he rings for service. Ellie, do you still love me?'

There wasn't a second's pause. Ellie's jaw tightened and words tumbled fearfully out of her head. 'Ben is a soldier — did you know that? He's already out there fighting for his country. In Belgium, I think. And Tommy? Do you remember my other brother, Tommy? He isn't very strong, but he's good with his hands and does fine woodwork, so he's helping to build boats. He and Margaret are living in Portsmouth, would you believe? They have a nice little house and a garden and two lovely children and — '

371

'Do you still love me, Ellie?'

'Mary got a job in a munitions factory and she's going out with a sailor. And my dad is doing fine, though he doesn't much care for living with his three sisters. They nag him all the time. I thought about asking him to move in here, but I don't think it would be fair on — on Nicholas.'

She felt and heard Adam swallow hard. 'How is your husband?'

Ellie ran a tongue around her dry lips and sighed. 'Nicholas is such a nice man. I couldn't do anything to hurt him. Oh, Adam!'

He stood up suddenly and Ellie felt her body sag limply against the cushions. She watched Adam walk a few steps away from her. He stopped at the fireplace, rested his hands on the mantelpiece, lowered his head as if in deep thought. When he turned round, she saw the glisten of tears. He blinked them away, closed his eyes tightly, then opened them again and they were filled with the same pain that was searing her heart.

'This is too hard, Ellie,' he whispered huskily. 'I shouldn't have come. I should have waited — written to you from France. It was foolish of me to think — to hope that . . . '

Ellie got briskly to her feet and, not totally conscious of what she was doing, but unable to stop herself, she threw herself bodily into his arms with a little cry, burying her face into his chest. His arms tightened around her, lifting her so that his mouth could find hers.

It was a long kiss that seemed to have no end. Even when their lips separated, the embrace was somehow unfinished.

'My heart has been breaking for six years, Adam,' she said through dry sobs. 'Now, seeing you like this, I feel that even my soul is shattering into millions of tiny pieces. I don't know what to do, what to say!'

His hands were tangling in her hair, his fingers tracing patterns on her face as he kissed her again, such a bittersweet kiss that melted her core and set her heart racing afresh.

'My God, Ellie, I want you so much. You can't deny me this one last chance to make love to you. Please — please don't turn me away now.'

With what seemed like superhuman strength, Ellie pushed him away from her. She was shaking her head, trying not to read the expression in his eyes.

'We can't — I can't — not here . . . ' She stepped back and the separation was a physical pain inside her. 'Not in Nicholas's home, Adam. I couldn't do that to him. I just couldn't!'

Adam looked about him. He had not been

in this house before, had not noticed the personal things dotted about the place. Things like family photographs, ornaments, trinket boxes, the pipe rack with its complement of well-smoked pipes. It was the personal property of another man. And so was Ellie. He had no right expecting her to give herself to him.

'You're right,' he said thickly. 'But Ellie, I can't go like this. I must go, but I must also take something with me. Something of you that I can hold on to. Something good and happy that I can remember when — if — things get bad. I have no one else. Only you.'

Ellie shook her head, confused, trying desperately to solve the situation and failing miserably. 'Adam, I don't know what to do.'

'When is he — when will the professor be back?'

'I'm not sure. He's giving a special lecture in the town hall and afterwards, I believe, there's to be a reunion with his colleagues and some of his old students.'

'Ah, yes! I believe I received an invitation. Freddie will no doubt be attending. He'll drink too much so I will have to pour him on to the train tomorrow. He's a nervous traveller so if he's still a little drunk it won't be a bad thing.'

They were both trying to act rationally. It wasn't working. The atmosphere was charged with suppressed emotion that begged to be set free.

'Would you like another whisky?'

He declined with a small shake of his head. 'Get your coat, Ellie. Let's walk together. God help me, but I can't let you go so easily.'

16

Ellie rushed upstairs and grabbed the first coat she came to. It was light-weight and totally unsuitable for the freezing, damp evening air, but she didn't care. She wrapped a white silk stole around her head and slipped quickly down to the kitchen where the kitchen maid, Maud, was relaxing over a cup of tea and a sneaky read of a pink penny-romance. The girl jumped to her feet guiltily as Ellie approached.

'Maud, I'm going out for a breath of fresh air,' she told the girl lightly. 'It's so stuffy in the house at this time of year. If the professor comes back before me, please tell him that I won't be long and make sure that he has some supper if he hasn't already eaten.'

'Yes, Mrs Graham, but it's awful foggy out there th' night.'

'Don't worry, Maud. I'll be very careful.'

'You wouldn't catch me going out in the fog.'

'No, Maud. Well, good night. You may go to bed as soon as you've seen to the professor and washed up the dishes. Mrs Renney is staying the night with her sister-in-law, so make sure everything is clean and tidy for her tomorrow.'

'Yes, m'm.' The sulky-faced maid lifted a shoulder and shuffled her feet, as she always did when left with any form of responsibility.

Ellie ran back to the hall, where Adam was waiting. Outside in the road, Adam's driver stood smartly to attention, looking ridiculous in his shirtsleeves and corduroy breeches, his hands grimy and a smear of oil on his forehead. Adam acknowledged him with a short nod and told him to wait, but asked him to move the car to the next street rather than remain where he was. There was not even a suspicious glimmer in the man's eyes as he cranked the engine back into life.

They walked slowly, side by side, not speaking, not even touching. The air was becoming like dirty cotton wool. The fog had an acrid, sooty taste to it. Yellow headlights from vehicles appeared ghostly as they made their way slowly along. Sounds of footsteps, a voice here, a barking dog there, echoed eerily. The whole scene was unreal and Ellie found herself wondering if she was perhaps walking through a dream and would wake up and find that Adam and everything that had passed between them during the last half-hour had been nothing but imagination.

'What's that up ahead?'

The sound of his voice made her jump. She quickly looked up at him, resisting the temptation to reach out and touch him to make sure he was real.

'It's a piece of woodland. There are paths and trails. I walk there often.'

'Come on.' He took her hand and steered her in the direction of the trees.

The street had been deserted, but here in the woodland they might have been the last people left on earth. Hazy silhouettes of oak and birch and pine surrounded them. A thick carpet of fallen autumn leaves over a bed of sweet-smelling pine-needles cushioned their feet. There was a thick silence, the only movement being the vague milky swirls of fog that drifted wraithlike before them as they made their way down a dark, overgrown path.

They crept forward, like thieves in the night, thin tendrils of ivy and briars reaching out to trap their ankles, clinging on tenaciously to skirt and trousers like warning signs. *Don't go there, don't do this. Don't! Don't . . .*

A few minutes down the path it opened out into a clearing. There was a break in the canopy above their heads and a glimpse of a silvery moon could be seen peering at them like a ghostly face behind a filmy veil.

Adam stopped and looked around him,

listening, a small frown creasing his brow. Ellie shivered and he wrapped his arms about her, drawing her into him until their bodies formed one tight mass.

'You didn't answer me before Ellie. I'm going to ask you again. Do you still love me?'

She gagged slightly on the lump sticking in her throat. 'With all my heart, Adam. I've never stopped loving you, even when I thought it was wrong and sinful and . . . '

'That's all I wanted to hear,' he said, blocking her lips with his hungry mouth.

She opened up to him, feeling the lick of his tongue and the urgent pressure of his body against her. His hands gripped and explored and stroked her until neither of them could stand holding off any longer.

Breathing heavily, he took off his coat and laid it on the ground. They sank down on to it, two bodies, but already one soul, one spirit. There was no time for delicate, genteel acts of patience. Ellie groaned, urging him on as Adam tore off her clothing as quickly as he could. She heard material give and rip as he pulled at her undergarments. She didn't care. There was nothing to care about other than that brief, wonderful moment with the man she loved more than life itself.

He stroked her exposed breasts, licked and sucked gently on the small, hard nipples. She cried out and he moved down to her stomach, where his tongue flicked in and out over her heated skin, making her gasp and arch her back. He breathed hotly into the soft fuzz covering the pubic bone, then into the deep, dark cavern that was the doorway to her most sacred place. The doorway opened wide, nectar juices flowing, smelling like apricot and vanilla.

Adam could hold off no longer. He slid inside her as if oiled and moved against her with small, deep-throated groans as she gasped with the unbearable ecstasy of it all. They had waited six years for this and neither of them was going to be disappointed.

They came in a mutual climax that was an explosion of bright lights and undulating earth and then they sank against one another and laughed and cried together. Mostly they cried, because the magic that had been so short-lived was soon to be over. Perhaps for ever.

'You're shivering.' The words were whispered hotly in her ear.

'I'm not cold,' she said as he enfolded her in his arms and covered her lower body with his broad thigh. 'I don't think I'll ever be cold again.'

'I love you, Ellie. Don't ever forget that.'

'I won't — how could I — forget you, this

moment — our love . . . '

'One day . . . ' His voice faltered and she placed her fingertips against his lips, not wanting him to say the words she thought he was trying to say.

'Don't,' she said quickly, with a sharp shake of her head. 'Let's not say any more. Let's just — just live on this day, this moment — for the rest of our lives if necessary.'

He nodded, kissing her fingers. 'You're right, but if there is to be a tomorrow for us, I need to know now that you'll belong to me, somehow — somewhere.'

Ellie swallowed hard and gave a trembling smile. 'Oh, Adam, I've always belonged to you. I always will, no matter what . . . nothing can ever part us.'

'Not even death?'

'Stop! Don't even speak of that. You mustn't.'

'It's a possibility, Ellie. It's a reality.'

'I don't want to think about it. Not now. I'm too happy.'

'Then don't.'

He struggled to sit up, disentangling himself from her body and their array of clothes. For one brief wonderful moment he hung over her, gripping her face between his two hands, gazing lovingly into her eyes. Gently, he kissed her eyelids, the tip of her nose, her cheeks, her mouth. She heard his breath catch in his throat, then he released her and was standing up, pulling on his clothes haphazardly, handing her things to her as he came across them.

'It's time to go, my sweet.'

'No!'

'I must. You know that. You too.'

He didn't tell her to think about her husband, about Nicholas. There was no need. Her heart was already aching with the hurt she would inflict upon that dear man if he ever found out what she had been doing in his absence.

Adam walked with her to the top of the street. Beneath the light of a street-lamp he stopped, turned her face up to his so that he could see it for the last time. He squeezed her hands, but did not kiss her again. That would have been too much for either of them to bear.

'Go,' he said. 'Don't look back, I beg you. I won't be there. I will never stop loving you, Ellie.'

Her heart felt as if it were swelling and breaking through her chest wall as she forced herself to walk away from him, each step an unbearable distance. She reached the white-painted gate of the house where she had been first a scullery-maid, now the mistress. A light was shining dully through the heavy wine coloured velvet curtains of the sitting-room. Nicholas was home.

Ellie gripped the wooden struts of the gate, her knuckles turning white like the gate itself. She allowed her eyes to slide to the side, dared to look up the street, but Adam was gone. There was only the yellow gaslight beneath which they had stood, and the swirling fog dancing in clouds all around. Somewhere in the distance, growing fainter, she could hear the echo of his footsteps. Even further away, a dog howled. It was such an eerie, lonely sound.

'Ellie, is that you?' Nicholas' voice floated out from the sitting-room as she stood in the hall, quickly brushing dead leaves and soil and drying mud from her person, adjusting the buttons of her dress which she had, in her nervous haste, fastened up all wrong.

'Yes, Nicholas!' She went to the door, tried to act normally. 'Goodness what an awful night! Have you been home long?'

He looked tired and drawn. There was a flatness about his eyes that were usually so bright when he saw her after they had been apart for even an hour. He seemed barely able to lift his head.

'Where have you been?' he asked and even his voice had an edge to it that was not usual.

He spoke like a man in a dream, almost sing-song and not at all real.

'I'm sorry, Nicholas. I didn't mean to be so long. I went for a walk to — to pass the time . . .'

He looked at her properly for the first time and his eyes widened perceptively.

'Good God, Ellie! Look at the state of you? Did you have an accident? Your clothes are filthy and your face is all puffy and flushed.'

'Oh!' She looked down at herself and grimaced, trying to make it seem less than it was. 'I made the mistake of walking through the wood. I got lost in the fog and fell down. I did feel such a fool. It was a good job there was nobody to see.'

'You were walking in the wood alone?'

Ellie nodded, swallowing drily, already feeling guilty to her fingertips for telling him a lie. 'Yes.'

'Maud tells me you had a visitor and left with him.'

Damn the girl, Ellie thought, gathering her wits about her swiftly. 'Yes, that's right, Nicholas. It was — Adam Rockwell.'

'What! That fellow? He came here? Why the devil did he do that?'

'Oh — um — he came to see you actually — well, both of us . . .'

'Really?'

'He — um — he came to say goodbye.' She put a hand to her temple where a vicious migraine had started to throb. 'He's joining the war effort — going off to France tomorrow with the artist, Freddie Salter.'

'But why the devil should he . . . ?'

'Look, Nicholas, I'm sorry, but I have the most dreadful headache. If you don't mind, I think I'll take a bath and go straight to bed. Have you eaten?'

'I wasn't hungry.' Nicholas rubbed a hand over his face. He looked drained and her heart went out to him, but she dared not go to him as she felt she should. 'I became ill during the lecture and left early.'

'Ill?'

'Oh, it was nothing. A slight malaise. I'll feel better for a good night's sleep.'

'I'll make that appointment with the doctor in the morning,' she told him, hanging on to the half-closed door so that it hid a good deal of her dishevelled appearance.

'Yes — yes, my dear. You go and have your bath. I shan't disturb you when I come up. I think perhaps I'll sleep in the guest bedroom tonight, if that's all right with you?'

'Yes, of course, Nicholas, if that's what you want.'

'I think so. Just for tonight.'

Ellie spent a long time soaking in the bath,

which she had scented with essence of lavender. She breathed in the perfume and felt her body slowly relax, but her mind kept wandering out of control. First she was back in the wood with Adam, then she was at home with Nicholas. Her imagination kept taking over and she thought of herself following Adam to France, then she felt sad and guilty because Nicholas would be so hurt and lonely without her and he didn't deserve that. But then, none of them deserved the fate in which they found themselves.

She heard Nicholas come upstairs and lay quiet in the cooling water until the low temperature forced her to get out and briskly towel herself dry. Then she slipped between the sheets of the big double bed, grateful that Nicholas had chosen tonight to sleep in the other room.

★　★　★

Ellie and Nicholas spent a quiet Christmas alone in a small hotel in Rothbury. It had been Ellie's idea to get her husband away from work and the busy festive season his sister organized every year, which tired everybody but her five boisterous children and the lady herself.

After five days, Nicholas seemed a lot

better for the enforced rest and their pleasant, daily walks in the fresh country air. He had consented to see the family doctor, but would tell her nothing of the outcome other than his having been ordered to rest. Ellie suspected that there was a more serious side to his physical problems and intended to speak to the doctor personally as soon as the opportunity arose.

'I think I'd like to go home now, Ellie,' Nicholas said one morning, touching her cheek with the back of his hand in an affectionate gesture that had made him so dear to her. 'You must be finding life a little boring, nursemaiding this decrepit old man of yours. Why don't you invite a few people over at New Year?'

'Wouldn't that tire you too much, Nicholas — and by the way, I *never* think of you as an old man.'

He laughed softly and his grey eyes caressed her. 'You're very kind, my dear, but I'm well aware of my limitations and how well you tolerate them. Come on. It's time you had some fun. You've been looking a little peaky yourself lately.'

Ellie felt a ripple of butterflies in her stomach and she automatically put a hand down to calm them. There was nothing for it. She was going to have to tell him soon. If she went on blocking it out of her mind much longer the fact that she was pregnant would announce itself in no uncertain terms without her having to say a word.

She and Nicholas had been hoping for a child for so long. It was ironic that the baby she now carried inside her was not his, but Adam's. She could have kept the true identity of the father secret, had it not been for the fact that she and Nicholas had not even come close to making love for at least five months. The news would shatter him.

'Well,' she smiled at him brightly and squeezed his hand. 'If you're sure it won't be too much for you, it would be really nice to see my family again. That is, if they'll come.'

Since their wedding day Ellie had not seen her family together in one group. She knew it was difficult for them to accept Nicholas. He wasn't one of them and never would be. They didn't dislike him — who could possibly dislike Nicholas Graham? But he was as far removed from their working-class lives as they were from his comfortable middle-class one. Ellie herself sometimes felt that she was straddling the fence that separated the two classes, though in all honesty she was far nearer to the professor's background these days than to her own roots.

She wrote letters to her father, and to

Tommy and Margaret, asking them to come for lunch on New Year's Day. Her second brother and his wife were back in the north-east for a few days' holiday and would be grateful for a break away from the three maiden aunts.

'We can't invite my father,' Ellie said with a sigh, 'without inviting my three aunts. They would be very put out and poor Dad would never hear the end of it.'

'Then you must invite them also.' Nicholas smiled at the face she pulled. 'Don't worry, Ellie. They are bound to be on their best behaviour when they are in your home. Like difficult children, people are often seen to be exemplary when faced with strangers. We'll invite my cousin and his wife. John is a flirt and Pauline would make the Princess Royal feel inferior. Between the two of them those three old girls won't stand a chance.'

It was good to see him laugh again and look quite like his old self, even if it was to be short-lived once he found out about the baby.

As soon as Ellie realized that she was pregnant her mind had flown back to her mother and how Sir Donald had given Polly an address and money to buy an abortion. Well, now it was Sir Donald's son who was the father and Polly's own daughter the mother of the unborn child. History had repeated itself in some way, but her circumstances were very different and whatever this baby was going to cost her — even to the extent of losing Nicholas's love and respect — she was determined to keep it. She might never see Adam again, but he had left her with the most precious legacy on earth.

In the end, the girls — Rose, Mabel and Priscilla — declined the invitation for New Year's Day, which was a relief to all. Ellie's father arrived, looking dapper in a new suit and smelling of soap and talc and nobody would have ever thought he was an old miner. These days he hired himself out as a gardener and happily fell into discussion with Nicholas and his cousin about the best way to prune roses and fertilize vegetables with compost made from kitchen waste.

Tommy coughed a little when he got overheated or excited, but on the whole he seemed much better and claimed that living down south beside the sea had worked miracles for him. Margaret was blooming and well into her third pregnancy. They had left the children with friends, so the couple were enjoying a second honeymoon.

'Have you heard from our Ben?' Tommy wanted to know. 'We had a letter six weeks ago, but nothing since.'

Ellie shook her head. She had heard from

Ben around the same time. He had talked of his unit, the Northumberland Fusiliers, being posted to France. It was a short letter, badly written. Ben was no scholar when it came to English and he wasn't one to communicate his thoughts in words of any kind, but Ellie got the impression that things weren't as rosy as he painted. The handwriting had been more shaky than usual and he had ended with the words, *I think about you as I hope you will always think about me, your affectionate brother, Ben.*

Margaret opened her capacious bag and drew out some newspaper-cuttings, which she spread before Ellie on the kitchen table as she was basting the crisp coating on the leg of pork while Mrs Renney saw to the vegetables.

'We'll have to make the most of this,' Ellie said. 'By all accounts food is already getting scarce.'

Margaret nodded solemnly over the papers in her hand. 'Yes, there are notices going up in all the shops on the High Street at Felldene. It's the same back home.'

'What's that you've got there, Margaret?' Ellie nodded at the papers as she continued basting.

'I saved these for you,' her sister-in-law said proudly. 'Dad was all set to throw them on the fire, but I thought you'd want to see them, since you used to work for the Rockwells.'

Ellie's hand jerked and she spilled hot fat over the table, burning a finger in the process. She rushed to the sink and poured cold water over the burn while Mrs Renney muttered about the dangers of having people in the kitchen who didn't know what they were doing.

'Mrs Graham, why don't you take your sister-in-law back into the sitting-room and let me get on with things in here? It's all done bar the shouting and I'll do that an' all just as soon as it's time to come to the table.'

'Sorry!' Margaret giggled and grabbed Ellie's arm. 'She's a bit of a battle-axe, isn't she?'

'Oh, she's all right,' Ellie said, wishing she had grabbed a glass of water because her throat was dry and she felt slightly sick. Whether it was the heat of the kitchen, the stress of entertaining so many people or the mention of the Rockwell name, she wasn't sure, but when she saw those newspaper-cuttings and saw the drawings of soldiers fighting at the front bearing the name of Adam Rockwell, it was as if someone had thrown ice down her back.

By the time she reached the sitting-room and the crush of bodies and the hum of animated conversation she was feeling quite dizzy. Margaret sensed immediately that something was wrong and pushed her quickly towards a vacant chair. She sank down on it gratefully, going first hot, then cold.

'You're not — you know . . . ?' Margaret whispered in her ear as she plumped up a cushion at Ellie's back. 'I got the feeling you were the minute I saw you.'

'Please, Margaret — don't say anything!'

'He doesn't know yet?'

Ellie gritted her teeth and shook her head, glancing fearfully at her husband who turned to look at her at that precise moment and she saw his face blanch.

'Ellie? Are you all right? You're as white as a sheet.'

'She's just feeling a bit faint,' Margaret said, then quickly followed it up with, 'It's stifling in your kitchen and she scalded herself with some hot fat.'

'Oh, my poor love!' Nicholas was beside her at once. 'Are you badly hurt? Let me see.'

Ellie smiled and held up her scalded finger, which everybody inspected with much sympathy. She was almost grateful for the huge red weal the hot fat had left.

'It's nothing, really, but I'm such a coward and then Mrs Renney started to fuss and I just — well, I came over all funny.'

'I think she was just looking for an excuse to get out of the kitchen,' Margaret grinned and everyone laughed and went back to where they had been before her entrance had interrupted them.

All except Nicholas. He perched on the arm of her chair with his hand protectively on her shoulder. 'Are you absolutely sure you're all right, Ellie? Perhaps you should go and rest on your bed for a few minutes.'

'Oh, Nicholas, please don't fuss. Everybody's fussing over me today. I don't know why.'

'Because you're so precious to us, my darling. Now, no more accidents, eh? Promise me that?'

'I'll do my best,' she said, smiling up at him while her insides churned.

Mrs Renney excelled herself that day. The meal she produced was superb. No one would have guessed that there was a war on. Nicholas broke out the best bottles of wine in his cellar and everyone got a little merry on white Graves from the Domaine de Chevalier, a rich ruby-red Château Haut-Brion, a sweet yellow Muscatel and a vibrant, sparkling champagne that produced giggles from the women and discreet belches from the men.

Ellie laughed to see her father grinning

from ear to ear as he sampled everything that came his way. By the end of the meal his eyes were glazed and his ears looked like glowing red jug-handles.

'Eeh, our Ellie!' he said, staggering over to her as he was about to take his leave with Tommy and Margaret. 'I've supped a bit today an' no mistake. Ye're not ashamed o' your old dad, are ye, pet?'

She gave him a tight hug and felt her heartstrings twang. 'Go on with you, Dad. It's about time you let your hair down.'

'It's been lovely, lass. Thanks for askin' us. It's good to see you so happy. I like that man of yours. I never thought I'd say it, but there you are. It never pays to judge harshly what you don't know nowt about.'

'Goodness, Dad, that's a long speech, coming from you!'

'Aye.' Tommy came and took Jack's arm. 'It's the drink talkin'. Come on, Margaret. Let's get this drunken bum home afore he disgraces us all.'

'Aw!' Jack's grin became even wider, but he allowed them to lead him away.

'The girls'll say more than 'aw' when they see the state their brother is in, Jack Martin. They'll have yer guts for garters.'

'Now look what ye've done, lad. Spoilt things good and proper.'

'Come on, Dad. We'll try and sneak you in the back way without them noticing.'

Ellie stood waving them goodbye. They were the last to leave and she was sorry to see them go. Now she had to go back and face Nicholas, wondering if she was going to have the courage to break her news to him while he was so relaxed and happy, or whether she should wait another day.

'Will they be all right, do you think?'

Nicholas was sprawled across the sofa, one hand covering his eyes. He had started to look tired just before everybody began to leave. The whole event had been successful, but perhaps a little too much for him.

'They'll be fine. They're walking down into the city centre and they'll get a taxi from there if there are no trams. The walk will help sober my dad up. Do you know, that's only the second time I've ever seen him the worse for drink?'

'He's quite a character, your father. I like him.' Nicholas struggled to a more upright position and winced slightly. 'Damn this indigestion! Sorry, Ellie. Look, I really should have driven them back, but I didn't think it was safe. Your father wasn't the only one to drink a little too much today and I . . . Aahh!'

He suddenly cried out and doubled up in

pain, clasping his chest and gripping the arm of the sofa.

'Nicholas!' Ellie rushed to his side as he slumped back, his face going from red to purple, then a terrifying shade of grey. She noticed the odd blue that came to his lips even as she watched. 'Oh, Nicholas! I'll send Maud to fetch the doctor.'

'No! Ellie, for God's sake, don't leave me! Don't leave me!'

He was fighting her, hanging on to her hand, bruising her wrist with the force of his grip. She pulled against him, but he refused to let go, so she screamed for Mrs Renney and Maud and the two women came running.

'The professor's ill. Fetch the doctor, please. Quickly!'

'But it's New Year's Day, m'm!' Maud squeaked and received a hefty slap from Mrs Renney.

'You know where the doctor lives, girl. Do as you're told and tell him to get here pretty damn fast too. Tell him it's serious. Very serious.'

The girl shot off, not even stopping to put on a coat. The old housekeeper approached cautiously and Ellie looked up at her pleadingly with tear-filled eyes.

'Oh, Mrs Renney! What shall I do?'

Mrs Renney shook her head sadly. She had lived a long time and was well experienced in sickness and death. She knew it was too late to do anything for Professor Graham.

'There's nothing either of us can do, hinny,' she said and knelt down heavily, one hand on Ellie's shoulder, the other on Nicholas's hand which was still grasping Ellie's wrist as if he was desperately trying to take her with him.

'Our Father who art in Heaven . . . ' the old woman muttered in a broken voice.

Ellie stared at her uncomprehendingly, then she turned to look again at Nicholas's face. His eyes were still open, but his features had relaxed. He was no longer feeling any pain. He would never feel pain again, or sadness, or hate, or love.

'Oh, Nicholas!' she sighed and laid her head against his chest where his heart had beat its last. 'Oh, I'm so sorry. Forgive me. I did love you, I really did.'

'Come on, lass.' Mrs Renney was struggling up from the floor. 'Stop that now. You have nothing to reproach yourself for. You made the professor a happy man. No woman can ask more from life. And no man can expect more than you did for him. It's just a pity he didn't know about the bairn.'

Ellie sniffed and blinked away her tears. 'You know?'

'Oh, aye. A woman has a certain look about her when she has a bairn inside her. She doesn't even know it herself at first, but it's there for all to see. You've had it for some weeks now, but it wasn't my place to say anything about it. These things are private between a man and his wife.'

'Oh, Mrs Renney. I — I was planning to tell him tonight.'

'Aye, well. Don't worry yourself about it too much, eh? What's meant to be is meant to be and nary the whole world can change it.'

When the doctor arrived some minutes later, looking flushed and flustered, he found the two women in the same position.

'Ah, Mrs Renney!' he said brusquely, putting down his black doctor's bag and taking out a stethoscope. 'What do we have here, hmm? The girl was so hysterical I couldn't make out a word she said to me. Is it Professor Graham or . . . ?'

'It's the professor, sir,' the housekeeper told him. 'And you'll not be needing them things stuck in your ears, neither.'

'Good Lord!' Dr Hargreaves bent forward at the waist and peered down at the professor. 'My dear Mrs Graham. How distressing for you!'

It was when the doctor gently removed Nicholas's fingers from her wrist and she could still feel the pressure of them that brought on a huge surge of grief and weeping. She had to be given a mild sedative and put to bed. Mrs Renney sat by her bedside, holding her hand until she finally fell into a deep, dreamless sleep. The last thought she had was a silent prayer of thanks that she had not been obliged to hurt Nicholas irrevocably after all. He had died loving her and took no recriminations to his grave.

17

Adam and Freddie transferred from the English fishing boat into the waiting French boat in mid-channel. As they approached Ostend the fishermen on board stowed them away beneath a tarpaulin that stank of seaweed and fish and engine-oil. Not that they would be using engines tonight with all the German troops on the Belgian coastline. Nevertheless, it was better to be prudent, as they well knew.

Wordlessly, the Frenchmen went about the business of their normal night fishing while transporting their human cargo as close to the beach as possible. There had been grins and clasping of hands and brief hugs all round for the first few minutes. They were old friends.

Now, the two Englishmen waited in anticipation, as they had done a dozen times before, for the word to slip overboard into the tiny dinghy that would take them on their final journey into the hidden bay out of reach of the enemy troops and exploding landmines.

Beneath the tarpaulin, Adam could hear Freddie breathing heavily and knew that his friend must be hearing the same sound emanating from his chest. There was the scratching of a match that flared into brilliant orange light between them. Freddie's fingers were shaking as he lit his roughly rolled cigarette and drew on it anxiously.

'The captain will have you hung, drawn and quartered if he catches you with that cigarette.' Adam grimaced good-humouredly. 'Aren't you scared you'll set us alight with all the fish oil there is around here?'

Freddie drew deeply on the cigarette, filling his lungs, holding it for as long as he could. His eyes narrowed in the eerie darkness of their hiding place, then he blew out smoky plumes slowly from his lips and his flared nostrils.

'At least we'd be warmer,' he said and gave a croaking cough from a chest weakened by too many winter nights sleeping rough in all conditions.

'For a while, yes,' Adam said, flexing his numbed fingers in the pockets of his stiff fisherman's jacket. 'But I have no fancy to become fish-fodder in a watery grave. Put the damn thing out, Freddie.'

Freddie took another long pull on his cigarette, then nipped the lit end between forefinger and thumb and stowed it away under his cap.

'This bloody war! Will it never end?'

'One day, Freddie. It has to. Nothing goes on for ever.'

'You've been telling me that for years. Does it ever occur to you that maybe you're wrong?'

'Never!'

There was a short silence, then Adam felt Freddie shifting restlessly at his side.

'I'm an artist, not a bloody soldier, not a spy or a partisan . . . '

'And you've been telling me that for years, but you're still here, still running risks, putting your life on the line for king and country.'

There was a long, low sigh from Freddie. 'Aye. Well, so are you, Adam. So are you.'

'We could call it a day any time and go back home. We've done our bit. We could tell them to stuff their secret messages they have us carrying through the lines under cover of diplomatic artists and war correspondents. We could . . . '

'Yes, yes, I know! We could do all that, but we don't, do we? Maybe we neither of us have any reason to want to go back home. Come to think of it, I don't rightly know where home is any more.'

Adam knew what Freddie meant. He felt it too. In different ways they had both lost that which was dear to them. At least, risking life and limb to save other lives in this war had some meaning. It stirred up the blood, gave them something worth living for. Something, perhaps, worth dying for.

They both jumped as the tarpaulin was pulled back and the black silhouette of Jean-Luc, the owner of the fishing boat, appeared against a pearly grey sky.

'It is time,' he told them in his staccato English. 'But this time no boat. You must swim. The moon this night makes too much difficulty. In a boat you will be seen. In the water the risk is smaller. *Bon chance, mes amis!*'

As they scrambled out, flexing their stiff limbs and glancing up at the brilliant silver orb of the moon hanging low above them, Jean-Luc thrust a couple of life-jackets at them. Adam slipped his on, making doubly sure the package he had brought with him from England was secure and watertight.

The package was the usual wad of new instructions to the men at the front. Several times a year he and Freddie transported messages both ways. They never saw the men who provided them. It was a safeguard against their being caught and forced to divulge the identities of their contacts.

'Now!' hissed Jean-Luc. 'We cannot go

further. We will be seen.'

Adam donned his life-jacket and pulled the strapping tightly around his waist, then staggered drunkenly to the rail of the fishing boat as it heaved about on the uneasy sea.

Freddie was hanging back, looking grey and sick. He had proved himself to be a poor sailor, but this time there seemed to be something else adding to his discomfort.

Adam grabbed at his friend's sleeve. 'Freddie? What is it, man?'

Freddie shook his head and blinked furiously as the wind and the salty spume tossed in its wake caught them full in the face. 'Adam, I can't . . . Dammit, *I can't swim!*'

Adam looked at him in disbelief. The thought that Freddie might not be able to swim had never occurred to him. They had never been obliged to put it to the test. So far they had been lucky, always running into trouble on dry land. The deepest water they had been in was only waist high — a canal they had waded across at night without too much difficulty.

'You must go now, my friends,' Jean-Luc urged, 'or it will be too late.'

Adam stared at Freddie: 'Can you dog-paddle?'

'No!'

'Have you ever watched a dog swimming?' Adam had Freddie by the shoulders and was shaking him, none too gently. 'All four legs beating the water.'

'I can't do it, Adam!'

'You'll do it. We have no choice. Jean-Luc?'

The Frenchman came forward, a worried expression on his dark, hook-nosed face. '*Oui, monsieur?*'

'Have you a length of rope?'

They found a few feet of stout hessian fishing rope and tied it around Freddie in halter fashion, tying the other end around Adam's wrist. Then Adam climbed up on to the boat's heaving rail. 'Come on, Freddie. I've got you and the jacket will keep you afloat. You won't drown, I promise. I won't let you.'

In a petrified dream, Freddie moved forward and slung one leg over the rail. Before panic set in, Adam nodded to Jean-Luc and jumped into the sea, at the same time pulling on the rope.

'Go, go, go!' was heard from the French captain before they hit the water.

He heard a short, stemmed cry from Freddie as they descended with a soft splash. He reeled him in, then set off with powerful breaststrokes, pulling the unfortunate Freddie with him.

At first Freddie floundered, swallowing water and gagging until he managed to get himself under control.

'That's it, Freddie! You're doing fine. Keep paddling. If you get too tired, turn on your back and float. I'll pull you behind me.'

There was a glugging sound from Freddie and his eyes stared wildly at Adam, but he seemed to be getting the hang of things, despite the choppiness and the cruel ice-cold of the briny water.

Long before they reached land the fishing-boat had turned tail and sailed out of their sight. They could afford to lose the two men in the water, but they couldn't afford to lose a boat. Boats were far too precious. Even old, rickety fishing-boats that leaked from every pore.

It was a long time before they felt sand beneath their feet. It must have seemed a lifetime to Freddie, Adam thought, as he hauled his friend up the beach, struggling through the soft, moonlit sand until they could find shelter among the rocks.

All the other journeys they had made had luckily been in the dark. Tonight, which was to be their last mission it was as luminous as a pantomime stage-set every time the moon broke through. Everything was etched in silver, down to the last pebble glowing in the sand.

'Oh, God!' Freddie was lying prostrate and coughing up seawater. 'Oh, dear God, just let me die!'

'Keep it down, Freddie,' Adam nudged him with a soggy toe. 'You can stop complaining. You're safe on dry land. Well, you're on dry land, anyway.'

Even the dry land bit was a misnomer. Adam turned his face into the cutting wind and felt the lash of icy rain. Well, there was no point in complaining. They couldn't get any wetter.

Freddie groaned and struggled to a sitting position, coughing some more.

'Ssh!' Adam's keen ears had picked up a sound. He threw himself bodily on top of Freddie and heard his grunt as they flattened themselves just in time to escape the sweeping glow of an arc lamp. From somewhere above them the nonchalant chatter of German soldiers told them how close they were to capture.

They waited an hour, cold, wet and shivering. As the wind rose, buffeting and howling loud enough to deaden any noise they might make, they made their move. The cliffs they had to scale were almost vertical, which was why it was considered by most a bad place to land. However, it also meant it was not so well guarded. They knew every foothold by now like the backs of their hands.

It wasn't far to the fisherman's cottage they used as a base, but it was all open ground. They had to wait until a cloud veiled the moon before they made each mad dash, flattening themselves to the ground as soon as the silvery light crept over the barren landscape.

At last they reached the cottage, its bright white-painted walls and blue shutters dulled to grey in the darkness. Adam rattled the rusting handle the required number of times and in the correct sequence. At the last rattle the door opened a crack, wide enough for them to slip inside.

There was no fisherman living there now. He had died with the first wave of German invasions. But his widow was Jean-Luc's cousin, a pretty, dark-haired young woman with three small children.

'I thought you were not coming,' Janine Poppe said, welcoming them with open arms, hugging them and kissing them as if they were close members of the family. 'The *Boches* were here not long ago. They frightened the children. It is stupid. All war is stupid. They were boys, playing at being men.

But they frightened my children. I do not like that.'

'What did they say? Did you learn anything?' Adam asked.

Janine swallowed and looked at him with the lovesick eyes he had had to steel himself against. 'They know about you, I think. They were searching for the English who are not soldiers. The English spies, they call you, but I think they now know your names.'

'Well, that's great,' Freddie breathed and sank heavily at one side of the big log-fire that warmed the whole cottage.

'I have something for you.' Janine smiled up at Adam.

'What is it?' he asked gently and she hurried off to her bedroom and came back with something clasped in her small hand.

'These,' she said, handing him papers that had once belonged to two British soldiers — privates in the British Army. 'These men were killed in the field just behind the house. I found their papers. I kept them for you. With these the *Boches* will not know that you are the men they are looking for. If you have identification I will place them on the bodies of those poor young men. No one will know the difference.'

Freddie gave a short, sharp laugh. 'They'll shoot us anyway, if we're captured.'

Adam shook his head. 'Maybe not, Freddie. But with these identities we'll stand a better chance.

Freddie shrugged his shoulders. He was past caring.

'Come,' Janine said, beckoning to both of them and leading them to the big kitchen table where she had set two places. 'I have soup — but first you must take off your wet clothes and dry them by the fire. It is all right. I have some clothes belonging to my husband . . . ' She glanced furtively at Adam and shrugged with a partially amused smile. 'He was not such a big man like you, Adam, but *tant pis, hein?* It is the best I can do.'

They drank the watery soup Janine had had simmering for hours and ate rough black bread, washing it down with strong rough wine that tasted of vinegar. Adam felt strangely emotional and wished he was back at Rockwell, an angry young man full of hate for his father, full of lost dreams for his artistic career and hopes of his rich inheritance — and Ellie. Always his thoughts came around to Ellie. Would there ever again be Ellie in his life? He thought not.

★   ★   ★

411

They slept until the first rays of dawn crept into the cottage. Janine woke them with the news that Rémi, the old postman, had called with the good news that the Germans had moved on. He gave them a map so they could find their way to the nearest British encampment.

Adam smiled at the thought of the old postman. Rémi must be at least eighty, but still had courage enough to fight for his country in any way he was able. Adam had never failed to be impressed by the bravery and the audacity of the French and the Belgians he had met over the past few years. But then, they had countries worth fighting for.

He crossed the room to look out of the window. The small panes of glass were misted over. The early morning was announcing itself like a grey shroud. A heavy curtain of rain fell, blurring the landscape and the distant view of the sea merged with the colourless sky. At least the wind had dropped overnight.

'Janine,' he said softly and the woman came to stand next to him, warm and expectant. 'This is to be our last trip. When this is over — all this war — I'm coming back to Europe . . .'

'Yes, Adam?'

He saw the hope glowing in her eyes and felt bad about it. He had not put it there intentionally. He wanted no woman sharing his life, unless it was Ellie.

'Perhaps in the south of France where it doesn't rain all the time,' he continued, trying to keep his conversation casual and impersonal. 'I believe there is plenty of land for sale down there. Good farmland and vineyards.'

'You will not stay here with us — when the war is over?'

Adam shook his head sadly. 'No. That would be impossible, Janine.'

'I see. Yes, I think I have always known. Your heart belongs to another. Is she beautiful?'

He stared out at nothing and Ellie's face stared back at him. 'Oh, yes, Janine. She is the most beautiful woman on God's earth.'

'Then you must go back to her,' Janine said simply, but there was a catch in her voice that he did not fail to notice.

'I don't know if that will ever be possible either, Janine. Besides, I may not live to see England again. I have the strangest feeling that . . . '

'Bah!' Janine struck the air between them with the wedge of her hand, then gripped his arms and turned him to face her. 'Such stupid talk, Adam! I expect this talk from

Freddie, but not from you! Never stop thinking about her, Adam. Draw strength from the love that you feel. She will guide you to safety — to happiness in the end. You do that, *hein?* If you do not, you are not the man I think you are, *mon amour!*'

Adam bent towards her and kissed her on both cheeks, then briefly on the mouth and saw her eyes fill with tears as she turned away and started bustling about the house preparing some food supplies for them from her meagre larder.

'Right, Freddie,' Adam said with a raw croak in his voice. 'Let's go.'

Freddie ignored him and went on stroking the cat. Adam listened to the animal's purr vibrating loudly in its gullet. He listened and waited, then when Freddie showed no sign of moving, he grabbed him by the arm and hauled him to his feet. The cat gave a squawk and ran for cover beneath the *chiffonier* with its motley collection of traditional blue and white pottery.

'Leave me be, Adam!' Freddie shouted, but Adam dug his fingers in and gave him a shake.

'I'll leave you be when we've finished the job we set out to do, Freddie, and not before. If that means I have to drag you all the way to the end of the war, then I'll bloody well do that. Now, are you coming under your own steam or not?'

★   ★   ★

They trudged through mud and driving rain, through fields and ditches and rivers and woods, skirting around villages and towns, narrowly missing the Germans at every turn. Rémi's map was impeccable. Without it they would have walked into certain capture, for the enemy lines had changed drastically and were strung out for miles across their usual route.

But at no time did Adam feel that Freddie was with him on this trip. His spirit had shattered once and for all.

'I'm getting out of here!' Freddie finally screamed the words above the sound of the shell bombardment all around them that was shaking the earth and showering them with stones and liquid mud.

Neither of them any longer had a watch so they could only guess at the time and it seemed as though a whole day had gone by since they'd left Janine's cottage. Either the Germans had renewed their advance yet again or Rémi had finally made a mistake, but they found themselves suddenly in the midst of a German brigade, which effectively cut them off from the British troops with which they were ordered to make contact.

'Hell!' Adam beat the sodden earth with his fist, sending up a shower of brown, watery droplets that spattered his face, stung his eyes and gave him a metallic taste in his mouth. 'So near and yet so far. We might as well be a million miles away from the British. I can almost smell them across that field, but the Germans are between us and them.'

'*I'm getting out of here!*' Freddie repeated, more urgently and rose unsteadily to his feet, his eyes staring and unseeing.

Adam lunged at the frightened man as he threw himself over the edge of the deep trench they were cowering in. He managed to grab hold of one foot and heave his friend back to safety. Freddie lay sobbing hysterically in the blood-reddened mud and the excrement as an army of panic-stricken rats stampeded over his prostrate body.

'Bloody hell!' Freddie screamed out as a shell exploded close to them.

'Keep quiet, Freddie!' Adam hissed at him. 'You'll get us both killed!'

On his knees, Adam started to crawl along the trench, dragging Freddie by the collar of his greatcoat as the air exploded with shrapnel in every direction all around them. One piece zipped across Adam's forehead and into his hairline, opening up the skin and drawing blood that ran into his eyes in a hot, blinding stream. Another embedded itself into his upper arm, but he kept on going until he could no longer feel his limbs moving beneath him. He kept on going, pulling Freddie with him, inch by agonizing inch.

If they could only make their way around the German stronghold they could deliver their new instructions and their mission would be accomplished.

Day turned quickly into night and Adam could no longer see where he was going in the long trench gouged out of the black Flanders landscape, yet the sky above him seemed to be on fire. A red and purple aurora borealis streaked with green and gold lit up the distant horizon. The air, acrid with the hot metal smoke of guns, burning bodies and rotting flesh filled his nostrils, making him cough and retch as he continued to struggle on.

Freddie's hysterical screams were silent now, thank heavens, and the gunshots and the mortar shell explosions had diminished to a few sporadic outbursts. Adam's ears were ringing with the sounds of battle, but there were voices not far away and they weren't English or Flemish. They had to get out of here. The *Boches* had won this round. They were cleaning up and preparing to retreat after the day's attack. The last thing they did would be to check the trenches to see if any live British soldiers remained.

Up to now, Adam thought, they had been lucky and it was hard to believe that they had been successfully dodging the Germans for nearly four years. Four years when they chose not to go back to England except to collect their instructions. When they did take leave, they spent short periods of time in the towns and villages further south where the Germans were not so active.

Both men had taken turns at being ill. Trench fever, dysentery, bronchitis and even the common cold had become part and parcel of their everyday lives. Even without the wholesale killing, Adam thought it would now be a miracle if either of them survived for much longer.

He and Freddie had started out at the beginning of the war full of enthusiasm, but enthusiasm soon waned when you were stiff with the cold and your bowels were out of control and all around you there was nothing but death.

The British government had decided that they would be better employed as spies and couriers rather than artists. For that they had been given honorary officer status. Freddie liked being saluted and addressed as 'Captain, *sir*!' That too, had been exciting. For a while. But all excitement loses its edge as time passes and the dangers grow.

Adam had watched Freddie's spirit gradually disintegrating over the past few months. His dream of making his name as an important artist recording images of a war that would be finished in a few weeks or months at the longest, had turned into an everlasting nightmare. And now that nightmare was about to end, one way or the other.

As the earth exploded all around them, Adam rolled with the force of the blast. The shell had come close, maybe the closest yet to destroying them. He lay winded for some seconds, his eyes tightly closed, thinking that this was the moment he should be praying, but he didn't know how.

He opened his eyes, squinting in the flurry of smoke and dust that was swirling all around him. 'Freddie?' His voice was hoarse. 'You all right?'

There was an answering cough, a choking whooping sound that told him his friend was still alive. He shaded his smarting eyes and peered in the direction of the cough. Freddie was lying face down, but his head was lifted, his eyes staring ahead, full of terror. Adam crawled towards him.

'Come on Freddie! Get to your feet, man!' he hissed in Freddie's ear as he lay panting and groaning, half-sunk into the mire of the shallow dyke. 'The *Boches* are only a few yards away. If we don't get away from here they'll find us.'

Freddie's head rocked helplessly from side to side. His eyes were starting out of his head and he looked like a crazy man. Adam drew back his hand in angry frustration and slapped him hard across the face as a new barrage of gunfire exploded close to them.

'*Can't!*' Freddie mewed like a weary child. 'Go without me. Leave me to die.'

'Come on, you bloody coward!' Adam yelled, on his knees now, not caring what he said, as long as it got Freddie moving. He started heaving at him to make him stand up. 'For Christ's sake, Freddie, get on to your damned feet and move or we're both dead men!'

Freddie gave a small laugh and raised himself a few inches on his elbows, then his eyes rolled back into his head as he passed out.

Which was when Adam saw that both Freddie's legs had been blown off below the knee. That last explosion had done the damage, but his own fatigue had been so great he hadn't even noticed that Freddie was hurt.

Adam allowed himself a moment's remorse, then he was spurred into action. Using the rope from the boat that they still carried with them, he improvised tourniquets and tied them tightly around what was left of Freddie's legs, hoping it would stop the bleeding enough to get him to a first-aid station or a hospital.

The gunfire above him was petering out. He ignored the pain of the shrapnel in his head and his arm as he heaved Freddie's inert body up out of the mud and slung him over his shoulder.

He didn't know where he was or where he was going. Rémi's map was lost somewhere in the mud and the slime beneath his feet. There was no going back, of that he was certain. To the right and the left and behind them the Germans had the stronghold. The only way to go was forward.

Black clouds scurried across the sky and obscured the moon. At least that was in their favour. By the sound of it, the military action was moving much further away down the line. The intermittent rain squalls were getting even heavier, coming down in impenetrable grey curtains. Not even the

Boches could see too well in such adverse conditions.

Adam went on walking, slithering and stumbling mile after mile. The trench came to an end with a morass of long-dead British soldiers, stinking as they rotted and decomposed. A stumbling dash across open meadows, bent almost double beneath Freddie's limp body, brought him tumbling down into a series of dykes around a broad stretch of farmland.

One dyke joined another and so on, just like the trenches, only they weren't so deep. Most of them were no deeper than three feet, but all were running with water and mud and slime. He felt nothing, not even his wounds. The cold and the wet numbed even his brain. Except in moments of weakness, when he cried out for Ellie, praying to a non-existent God to make her hear his voice, make her understand that in his last living moments he was thinking of her, loving her as deeply as any man could love a woman.

Freddie was no weight to speak of. He had never been a big man, but during the years of war they had shared together, he had withered away to a mere shadow of himself. And now he was minus half his legs and he would never know how Adam had cried after he had sworn at him and hit out at him in desperation.

A low bellow of a cow coming from the left somewhere made Adam turn in that direction. Then he was clambering up the banks of the dyke with his weightless burden and half running towards the dark, squat silhouette of a group of buildings.

As he neared the farmhouse he saw the faintest chink of light shining through a crack in the closed shutters. He put Freddie down as gently as he could on a pile of loose straw lit up by a sudden moonbeam from a clearing in the stormy sky. He was heartened by the slight groan that was emitted from Freddie's throat. His friend was still alive, but only just. If they could get help to him soon, he might survive.

Adam moved stealthily forward. There were only fifty yards to go to the main building. He stopped in his tracks as his brain registered a small warning sound. A pebble being kicked perhaps. Or the click of a rifle bolt being pulled back.

He stood, not knowing which way to turn. His legs had turned into useless things, as useless as Freddie's stumps. He could feel his bones turn to rubber and sink down deeply inside their covering of quivering flesh. Of all the times for exhaustion to overtake him, he thought, this was the worst.

Suddenly, there were voices and the sound of running feet. He could see, in a blur, two men running towards him. They seemed to be running blindly, yet that could not be possible. They wore the uniform of the German army, but they didn't seem to be armed and they looked scared. There was gunfire. He felt a searing pain in his leg, felt the world turn on its axis like a drunken ship on the high seas.

'*Merde! Arrêtez-vous!*' The shout from the house was in French.

The men ignored it and kept on running and Adam could only lie there and watch and wonder whether Freddie would ever walk again and if Ellie would still love him when she was old and grey and surrounded by her grandchildren, reading them fairy stories and whispering secrets of the long lost love she once had. And he wondered about the man she would eventually marry when the professor died and whether she would be happy.

Then the world stopped tilting and exploded. He felt the thrust of it lifting him high and throwing him backwards. As he rolled over and over, he saw two other bodies being tossed in the air at the same time like limp rags, arms and legs separating from the twisted torsos before being dashed to the bloody ground all around him.

Before they settled Adam's world became black and silent as the grave.

18

Ellie had been watching her daughter from the window for some time. There was an affectionate smile on her face, even though a lingering sadness dulled her eyes. Little Laura was so beautiful and neither Nicholas nor Adam was there to appreciate her. And it wasn't just a skin-deep sort of beauty either. She had the most adorable personality. Although she was an infinitely calm, obedient child, she also sparkled.

'Laura!' Ellie tapped on the window and the child turned her dark bronzed head and waved, her blue eyes shining. 'Come in now, sweetheart! It's time to get ready.'

'Where are we going, Mummy?' Laura was standing in the open doorway, swinging one leg like a pendulum. She was only three, but was already speaking like a much older child and was tall for her age. Ellie spent many hours talking with her, reading to her, teaching her the alphabet, while Mrs Renney tutted and complained that she would turn the child's brain with so much adult conversation.

'It's your birthday, darling and you

remember what I promised you?'

'The Quayside!' Laura squeaked and clapped her hands once, then held them tight to her chest, her face lighting up with the thought.

'That's right. Come and let me tidy up that hair of yours, then you must wash your hands and face and we'll catch the tram all the way into Newcastle.'

Laura put a hand up to her unruly mop of curls and giggled. 'It's just like yours, Mummy!'

It was true. She had Ellie's fine, springy hair and her big blue eyes, though both hair and eyes were a little darker in Laura. It was their saving grace. Her strong resemblance to Ellie did not lead people to wonder who the father was. It was taken for granted by all that she was Nicholas's daughter and Ellie was happy enough with that, though it pained her that the child would never bear Adam's name.

On many occasions recently, little Laura had asked where her father was, having met other children who either had daddies at home or still fighting in the war. It was no lie when Ellie told her quite simply and honestly that her daddy was dead, for that's what she truly believed.

It was nearly four years since that last

meeting with Adam and there had been no word since. She had not expected him to write. They had agreed that there should be no further contact between them, at least while she was still married to Nicholas. As it was, he had told her that his sister would contact her on a regular basis if there were any news of him. There had been no such contact. Then a year ago she had received an official note on Government-headed paper.

My dear Mrs Graham, I have the unhappy duty to let you know that Captain Adam Rockwell, government artist working in liaison with the British Forces in Belgium, has been reported missing, believed dead. Your name was among those mentioned to contact if such were the case and I have also been commissioned to send you the enclosed letters found in Captain Rockwell's kit. My deepest sympathies at your loss . . . '

The letter was signed by a certain Major Douglas F. Hughes of the Northumberland Fusiliers. The small bundle of letters mentioned and tied with a blue ribbon, were all addressed to her, having been written at regular intervals during the last three years, but never posted.

It had taken Ellie a long time to muster enough courage to open each letter and read the words scribbled in Adam's bold hand. He could not have posted them, she saw at once, since they were full of words and thoughts of love and passion and just reading them her cheeks burned and her heart beat a little faster. He was dead and yet she still loved him, still wanted him as much as ever.

'Ready, Mummy!' Laura, as pretty as a picture in a pink frock and matching bonnet with shiny black patent shoes, was tugging at her arm, dragging her back from her daydream.

'Let's see!' Ellie made quite a serious show of inspecting the little girl's hands, face and the soft baby skin exposed at her neck. 'Hmm. Yes, all right, young lady. You'll do! Let's go!'

It was strange, seeing the Sunday Market again. Funny and sad and it filled her full of nostalgia that tightened Ellie's throat and made her want to cry. There were not so many people these days. Old men and women and children, but no young men. Most of them were dead or missing or still out there fighting. The atmosphere was perhaps a little subdued, but that could be due to Ellie's own dull mood. She had to try and cheer up for Laura's sake, though her daughter seemed to be delighted with her surroundings and was already exclaiming ecstatically at everything and dragging Ellie from stall to stall.

Ellie sighed, recognizing the china stalls and the tangled puppies and mewing kittens and swearing parrots. And there was the toffee-apple kiosk and next to it a fat woman with a big laugh, twirling pink-and-white fluffy candyfloss. And Laura was ogling it all as if it were a magic universe.

They both sampled the candyfloss. It was just too good to miss and Ellie's mind shot back to the day when the professor had brought her here on her own birthday so many years ago — and where she had first met Adam. And over there was where he sketched the first likeness of her.

Ellie gulped as she saw a small crowd of people and glimpsed the tip of an artist's easel. There was a burst of applause and a young mother with her small son broke through the ring of people, carrying a pencil sketch and talking excitedly about sending it to the boy's father in France.

Ellie gripped Laura's hand and pulled her forward, pushing their way through the dispersing people until she reached the place where the artist was working. There was no one there now. Only the easel and his table with a collection of sharpened pencils.

'Mrs Graham? Yes, by God, it is!'

Ellie swung around at the mention of her name, her heart leaping about in her chest. Why she should have thought it could possibly be Adam she did not know. The man who addressed her was small and thin and bewhiskered. At least, she assumed he was small, though it was hard to tell since he was sitting in a wheelchair and appeared to have no legs from the knee down.

'Oh, I'm sorry! I — I mistook you for someone else.'

'That's not an easy thing to do, Mrs Graham.' Even though he was smiling up at her, she recognized the harshness in his tone, saw the animosity in his expression.

'You have the advantage over me, sir,' Ellie said, pulling Laura into her side and hoping the child was not staring too blatantly at her first cripple.

'Well, I can't blame you for not recognizing me. It's been a long time and, as you can see, a lot has happened since I painted your portrait. How is your husband, the professor?'

'Mr Salter? Freddie?' She looked more closely and could see now beneath the facial hair and the emaciated appearance the man who had been Adam's best friend.

'Well, at least half of him!'

'I'm afraid my husband died some time

ago,' Ellie told him, ignoring his self-pitying remark. 'Not long before Laura was born.'

'Ah! So, this is Laura. Well, Laura, what do you think of this funny old man, eh?'

Laura bit down on her lips, wrinkled her button nose and gave him an uncertain smile. 'What happened to your legs?' she asked and Ellie bent to shush her, but Freddie simply laughed.

'I woke up one morning and *pouf* they were gone. I think it must have been something bad I did when I was a little boy.'

'That's silly!' Laura fixed him with her big blue eyes and he blinked back at her with a curious frown.

'Yes, Laura. It is. You don't want to believe anything I say, unless I touch my nose and swear.'

'Mummy says it's not good to swear.'

'What! Not even words like — um — *sauerkraut* or *boudin*?'

Laura giggled and went to stand closer to the man in the wheelchair, completely unafraid of this strange phenomenon who spoke foreign words to her and looked like a broken pirate.

'I have a swear word that I say when I break things or fall over,' she whispered to Freddie. 'It's 'cabbage'.'

'Well, there you go! Pretty much what I say,

only my 'cabbage' is pickled.'

They laughed together, then Ellie saw a sudden change in the man's face and he seemed to withdraw into himself.

'Excuse me, Mrs Graham,' he said gruffly. 'Today isn't one of my better days.'

'Mr Salter — I wonder if . . . '

'Yes?'

'Would you paint Laura for me?'

'I don't do much painting these days.' His reply came a little too quickly, she thought. 'Just enough to keep me alive — though I don't know why I bother.'

'You shouldn't think like that! You have so much talent . . . ' Even as the words left her mouth, Ellie realized that they were probably wasted on him. After all, his life had been ruined in more ways than one. She didn't know how she would cope if their situations were reversed. 'Will you paint her? Please?'

She thought he was going to refuse, then he turned to his table and scribbled something on a piece of paper that he tore from the back of a sketchpad.

'Here's my address. It's not a studio. Just a room, but it's on the ground floor. Don't expect too much. It's a long time since I held a brush in my hand. In fact, I haven't done a portrait in oils since . . . '

'Since you painted me?'

433

He nodded. 'It was my finest work.'

'And yet you destroyed it. Why was that?'

He frowned, started to say something, then shook his head. 'Bring your daughter to me at that address next Wednesday. I'll get the place cleaned up so it won't be a shock to your finer senses.'

Freddie started to gather up his belongings. Ellie felt that he was dismissing her by doing so, but she hung on. There was something she had to ask him, but she was finding it terribly difficult and his offhand manner did nothing to encourage questions of a more personal nature.

As he turned and found her still standing there so hesitantly, a brooding shadow darkened his face. He inclined his head towards the scrap of paper she held in her hand.

'Well? Doesn't that date and time suit you?'

'What?' Ellie had already forgotten about the appointment. 'Oh, this? It's fine. We'll be there. It's just — I wanted to ask you . . . ' He didn't want her to speak. She could sense that. He was, if anything, willing her to go away, but she couldn't. She was rooted to the spot, blocking his passage. 'Were you with him — Adam — at the end?'

His frown deepened. She saw his throat constrict as he swallowed. For a moment she thought he wasn't going to answer her, then his mouth twisted into a grimace.

'Oh yes! Adam Rockwell, the big hero.' His eyes widened and she could see that he was angry and hurting. 'He saved my life, did you know that? Pulled me out of the mud and the filth, carried me for miles through enemy lines, got himself shot and blown up — and all for this!'

Ellie closed her eyes and drew a deep breath as he slapped his thighs. He had an expression of pure hate on his face, but she wasn't sure at whom it was directed. At Adam? At himself?

'He sacrificed his own safety for me,' Freddie continued, mumbling the words now, almost as if he were talking to himself. 'If he had left me there to die we might both be happy men today.'

'Then . . . ' Ellie gulped and wiped away a stray tear that had forced its way down her cheek. 'He's dead? He's really dead?'

Freddie squinted up at her, frowning as if he couldn't understand who she was or what she was saying.

'Adam?' He shrugged a shoulder. 'I never saw him again. They took me away. To a hospital. I remember seeing him lying on that dirty farm track. Him and two German soldiers — or what was left of them. It was a landmine. I was half-dead by then. It was months before I was sane enough even to remember the event. I made enquiries at the hospital, but nobody had heard of Adam Rockwell.'

Laura was tugging at Ellie's hand, turning up her sweet face and looking concerned. 'Mummy, why are you crying?'

'I'm not crying, sweetheart. I've just got something in my eye, that's all. Come along. We're going home now.'

'Just a minute!' Freddie called out after them. 'Mrs Graham — Ellie! He made me promise not to tell you, but . . . '

'What? Oh, Freddie, what is it?'

'That portrait I did of you. I didn't destroy it. Adam bought it.'

Fresh tears were spurting from Ellie's eyes, but she was smiling and she ran and kissed Freddie on his pale, flaccid cheek. 'Oh, thank you! Thank you for telling me, Freddie. It means so much to me.'

Freddie put his hand up to the spot her lips had touched. She heard him sigh. 'I'll see you on Wednesday, then.'

★   ★   ★

Ben stepped off the train at Newcastle Central Station and felt the chill of the northerly wind rushing through his inadequate clothing. The end of the war had not come too soon for him. Like so many of the lads he had fought side by side with, he had been broken in mind as well as body.

All the medicine and all the sympathetic smiles and encouraging pats in the world would never remove the memories that were indelibly printed on his mind. And the official recognition for bravery and the medals they had pinned on his chest would not bring back his left arm.

When he had written to Ellie and his father to tell them that he was coming home, he had omitted to mention the missing arm or the disfiguring scars on his face where he had been burned, or the pretty pattern of shrapnel scars that covered his back.

Glancing at the great station clock suspended from the ceiling above him, he was relieved to see that he was early. He cast about him, reluctant to go out of the dark, iron-grey place that seemed strangely safe, even with the hoot and screech of the trains, the hiss of steam and the smell of the coal and sulphur. It reminded him vaguely of the foundry and he was surprised at the pleasure he got from the memory of the days he broke his back humping pig-iron, or walked like a tightrope walker along the gantries, directed streams of molten iron and rode home on the ferry exhausted but satisfied with his life.

It had been short-lived, that part of his life, but it had made a great impact on him. And then there was Margaret, who went with it. Margaret whom he had loved with all his heart, only to lose her to his brother. How he had resented losing her to Tommy and now he was sad that he had not rejoiced in Tommy's brief happiness.

Ellie's last letter to Ben had announced the sad news of his brother's death. Tommy, who had ailed all his life, had finally succumbed during a bout of influenza, although she assured Ben that he had gone peacefully at the end. Margaret, of course, was devastated and had moved back to the north-east with her three children.

There had been photographs. A group taken of Tommy and his family only weeks before he died. Margaret, Ben thought, had never looked bonnier and the children were a credit to her. And then there was one of Ellie and Laura. They were like two peas in a pod. It was a shame the professor hadn't lived to be proud of his bairn.

'Ben!'

Ben stood up almost to attention as his name was shouted out by several voices at the same time. But it was Ellie who bore down on him first, throwing her arms about him and hugging him fit to burst.

'You're early! The train's not even due in yet.' She told him, laughing and crying at the same time.

'I wanted to get here before you, so I took an earlier train.'

Behind her, he glimpsed his father holding Laura by the hand and Mary, looking thinner than ever and a bit tight-lipped just like her mother used to look. His three maiden aunts were all looking morbid and snuffling into their handkerchiefs.

And Margaret was there, standing back, looking slightly uncomfortable, but she was there and that meant a lot. Her children were hanging on to her coat, more interested in the trains than the homecoming soldier they had never met.

Ben's vision blurred suddenly and he turned his head away, ashamed to be seen crying in a public place. Then Ellie gave a sharp exclamation and stifled it immediately. Her hand had found his empty coat sleeve.

'Oh, my poor Ben!'

They were crowding around him now, all of them reaching out, touching him, wanting to hold him. All of them crying and Ben's heart wanted to burst.

'Eeh, lad, it's good to have you back,' Jack

Martin's voice sounded old and frail and full of emotion. 'Please God that's the last this world will see of war.'

'Give us yer hankie, Dad,' Ben muttered, sniffing back suppressed sobs.

He fumbled with his dad's handkerchief and blew his nose loudly, then looked at the little lad who was standing looking up at him in some awe. Ben grinned and recognized the boy as Margaret's first child, the one she had been carrying that memorable day when the family arrived at Northend to start their new life.

'You must be Johnnie!' He grinned down at the child and was rewarded with a shy smile. 'My, yer a big lad now. I remember you when you were a baby, did ye know that, eh?'

Then he turned to Laura who was impatient to get the attention of the uncle she had heard so much about.

'Aw, Gawd, Ellie, she's beautiful!' Ben scooped the child up in his one good arm and hugged her to him. Laura laughed and hooked her arms about his neck, kissing him fondly on the cheek.

'Phew!' Ben blew out his cheeks. 'Such a welcome. It's all a bit much.' He put Laura down and squeezed Ellie's shoulder. 'I think I'm ready to go home now, lass.'

'Would ye leave us alone, ye little minx ye!'

Ben's scolding was draped in good humour as Laura bounced away from the newspaper he flapped at her. He had fallen asleep while reading and woke to find her tying pigtails into his hair, which had grown long and Ellie was constantly at him to get it cut.

Not only had the little girl twirled his hair into braids, she had tied an array of brightly coloured ribbons on to the end of each one, which had drawn an exclamation of horror as he regarded himself in the mirror above the fire-place.

'God luv us! I look like a bloody rag doll!'

Laura stopped her cavorting and drew in a huge, scandalous breath. 'Ooh! Uncle Ben! Mummy will be cross with you for saying things like that.'

'Will she then? Just go and do the same to her as ye've done to me and see what kind of language she comes up with, young lady.'

Ellie came into the room at that moment and burst out laughing at the weird and wonderful sight of her brother with ribbons in his hair. 'Well, aren't you a sight for sore eyes, Ben!'

'Get these things out will ye!' Ben was tugging at the braids, trying to look angry, but not being able to stop himself from laughing.

'It's a good job you didn't have your shoes and socks off . . . Oh! Oh, dear!' And Ellie covered her mouth as Ben looked down at his bare feet and saw that Laura had painted faces on the nails of his big toes.

'Aw! Where is she? I'll tan her hide for this!'

Laura's blue eyes appeared around the door and Ben made a play of chasing her. She ran off screaming merry blue murder and would no doubt let him catch her just so he could tuck her under his arm and run into the garden with her to the pond they had built together and threaten to throw her to the frogs and the fish.

Still chuckling over the incident, which was just one in a continuing complicity between Laura and her uncle, Ellie bent to pick up the scattered newspaper pages.

The name Rockwell jumped out at her from page three and as always Ellie's heart thumped uncomfortably until she realized that the article was about Sir Donald Rockwell who was reported to be 'very poorly' following another, probably final stroke.

What went through Ellie's mind as she read the short article was something that she thought would never have been possible, but over the next few hours it nagged and nagged until she had to give way and make a decision to act on it.

The next day, bright and early, she dressed Laura in her very best outfit and called up the stairs to Ben to tell him that they were going out. At the sound of her voice he appeared, sleepy-eyed and still in his dressing-gown.

'Where're ye goin' so early in the day, our Ellie?'

Ellie's jaws clamped tightly shut because she hated lying to Ben of all people.

'I have some business to sort out. It might take a while. There's a plate of cold cuts and some cheese in the meat safe in the kitchen. Can you manage till I get back?'

'Don't be daft, lass! I'm not exactly helpless. Anyway, I've got to start fending for meself soon or I'll go daft. Can ye not wait and I'll come with ye?'

'Sorry Ben, but this is something I have to do on my own.'

'Then leave the bairn with me. We'll be all right, won't we, Laura, pet?'

Laura looked up at him, chewing on her mouth, then looked enquiringly at Ellie who shook her head.

'No, this is something that involves Laura, too.'

Ben was coming down the stairs, his face full of curiosity. She knew she was going to have to tell him or he would be hurt because she had excluded him.

'Laura, go and wait for me at the gate and don't move from there, do you hear me. It's very important, today, that you don't get dirty, all right, sweetheart?'

'All right, Mummy. Can I pick some flowers to take to the sick man?'

'What sick man?' Ben wanted to know.

'Yes, all right, Laura,' Ellie smiled. 'But take some paper from your cupboard and wrap them up like the flower shop ladies do — and don't get any dirt on that coat please.'

'What sick old man?' Ben persisted as the little girl skipped away. 'Just where exactly are you going, our Ellie?'

Ellie looked down at her hands briefly, then faced him with the truth. 'I'm taking Laura to see her grandfather, Ben.'

'But me dad's not sick . . . '

'Not Dad. I'm going to see Sir Donald Rockwell.'

★ ★ ★

When Ellie rang the bell at the Hall and gave the maid the name of Mrs Nicholas Graham it had obviously rung no bells for Cynthia

444

Rockwell. When Sir Donald's wife appeared, swathed in dark-brown silk and pearls, her welcoming smile froze.

'Good morning, Lady Rockwell,' Ellie said into the startled silence of the vestibule, her stomach churning because her memories of the place were still so vivid. 'I apologize for this inconvenience, but it's absolutely imperative that I see Sir Donald.'

'Ellen! It *is* you!' Lady Rockwell was having difficulty recovering her composure. 'I'm afraid it is an inconvenience. You see, my husband is a very sick man. Far too sick to see visitors.'

'Too sick to see his only grandchild?' Ellie asked with a slight rise of her eyebrows.

Lady Rockwell's expression froze yet again. Her eyes slid from Ellie to rosy-cheeked Laura and she gave a small intake of breath. 'His *grandchild!* Oh, please, Ellen, you don't expect me to believe . . . '

'I don't expect anything from you, Lady Rockwell. It is because of you that Adam will never know his own daughter.'

'But you were . . . I mean — we thought it best . . . '

'Adam *loved* me. The love we had was precious and you destroyed it. You and your husband and — yes, my mother. Hate, revenge and jealousy all working together. It

445

was a strong combination, but not strong enough in the end.'

'My husband is dying. I won't have him upset needlessly. If you have come here today to blackmail him into giving you money — like your mother did before you . . . '

'I don't condone the actions of my mother. She allowed the past to destroy her. I'm not like her, I assure you. I simply want Laura and her grandfather to meet before he dies. Her father never had that opportunity.'

Lady Rockwell looked troubled. She drew her hands together as if in prayer and pressed them to her mouth. For a long time she stood there, immobile and silent. Then she closed her eyes briefly. 'You'll find him in the library.'

'The library?' Ellie was surprised. This did not seem a fitting place for a man who was dying.

Lady Rockwell gave a small, tight shrug. 'He insists on being there, though it was really Adam's domain. I think he has misgivings over the way he treated his son and now he's trying to atone by — well, no matter. Please, Ellen, do not stay too long. He is very weak.'

Sir Donald was sitting slumped in a large invalid chair padded with sufficient cushions to keep him upright. His head was tilted to one side and his eyes were closed, his mouth hanging open and dribbling saliva. As she approached, Ellie could hear the pneumonic rattle in his chest as he struggled to breathe.

'Sir Donald?' Ellie reached out and touched his shoulder.

Slowly, his eyes opened, showing the inside of the lower lids, bright red and dragged down on to his cheeks. He grunted, pig-like, smacked his lips and stared at her uncomprehendingly.

This, Ellie mused, is the man who relentlessly took advantage of young, innocent girls, who enjoyed my mother's body and planted the bastard seed that grew to be my brother Ben. This is the father of the man I shall love till I die and the grandfather of my only child. He deserves my hate, and yet he is so pathetic all I feel for him now is a kind of vague pity.

'Drink — thirsty!' The words were garbled, but Ellie understood his command and held a glass of water to his loose, impotent lips. Most of the liquid dribbled down over his chin and on to his chest where grey body hair curled against his pallid skin.

'Is this the sick man, Mummy?' Laura whispered.

'Yes, Laura. I know you won't understand today, dear, but I'll explain everything to you when you're a little older. I want you to know and remember this man, because he is your grandfather.'

'But I already have a grandfather! Your daddy is my granddad. Granddad Jack.'

'Well, sweetheart, everyone has two grand-fathers if they're lucky. This is your granddad — Donald.'

'He doesn't look very happy, Mummy.'

Sir Donald shifted uneasily and his head lolled in Laura's direction. He was able to lift a hand and point a finger at her, then turn jaundiced eyes on Ellie that seemed to ask a million unvoiced questions.

'Sir Donald, this is your granddaughter, Laura. She is Adam's daughter.'

He looked startled and began shaking his head in violent jerks from side to side. Ellie knelt down beside him and gripped his shaking hands.

'You?'

'I'm Catherine Durham's daughter. We knew her as Polly Martin, but you knew her long before that, Sir Donald.'

'Hmm — yes . . . ' He stretched his neck to look at something behind her and when she followed his gaze she gave a gasp. There on the wall was the portrait that Freddie Salter had sold to Adam. 'I know you — the portrait — it keeps me company.'

Ellie dragged her eyes away from the portrait. She took a deep breath and continued. 'My brother, Ben, is also your son.'

He made a sound that was half-way between a laugh and a whimper, then his attention was on Laura again, who was thrusting her posy of slightly wilted lupins at him. Slowly and with much effort on his part, he pulled one hand from Ellie's grip and reached, not for the flowers, but for the child's plump arm.

'My son, Adam . . . is dead.' He choked slightly on the saliva that wouldn't go down his throat. 'Adam's girl?'

Ellie moved to one side so that he could get a better view of Laura. Laura beamed one of her special smiles up at him and his face lit up as if some life were flowing back into his depleted body.

'Pretty flowers!' he said in a stronger voice. 'Pretty little girl.'

'I'm called Laura,' his granddaughter informed him importantly. 'Can I call you Granddad Donald?'

His cheek twitched, pulling up the misshapen mouth into a drunken smile. 'Granddad Donald? Yes — yes, little Laura — that's me!'

Then he was looking at Ellie again and his

face was running with rivulets of uncontrollable tears.

'I haven't come to beg anything from you, Sir Donald. I just thought it was important that you knew you had a granddaughter.'

'Beautiful child — I — thank you. Please — so tired — need to rest . . . '

'Yes, of course.' Ellie got up from her knees and drew Laura away, glad to see that the old man was still clutching the flowers they had brought him.

They were at the door when he called out weakly. 'Tomorrow — come back tomorrow. Beautiful child — my granddaughter! Thank you!'

The following day, Ellie returned to the Hall and this time she not only brought Laura, but Ben. Ben was nervous and fidgety at the prospect of facing Sir Donald as the man's son.

Almost as if Sir Donald expected Ben to be there with her, he welcomed them all with a tired smile and a fluttering of his fingers in their direction. He looked happy when Laura took the liberty of scrambling up on to his lap, much to Ellie's concern, but Sir Donald waved her away and listened to the little girl's excited chattering for a few minutes.

They had not planned to stay for long, so were surprised when Lady Rockwell, instead of showing them out, took them into the drawing room where a stranger rose to greet them.

'May I introduce the Martin family to you, Mr Davenport.' Lady Rockwell turned to Ellie and Ben. 'This is Sir Donald's solicitor. My husband has been making some adjustments to his will and there is another matter of importance we wish to discuss with you, Mr Martin.'

'With me?' Ben's eyebrows shot up and he glanced apprehensively at Ellie.

'Perhaps, Lady Rockwell, we could all sit down?' Mr Davenport suggested respectfully. 'This could take some time.'

An hour later, when they emerged into the afternoon sun and the great entrance door to the Hall was shut behind them, Ben let out a long, low whistle.

'I'm not sure I can handle all this, our Ellie,' he said as they started to walk towards the tall wrought-iron gates. 'First you break the news over me head that I'm the son of a bliddy — sorry — foundry-owner and now ... ' He gulped and shook his head. 'Now, Sir Donald's made over half the bloomin' foundry to me and wants me to go work for him. Tell me this is not a dream, huh?'

Ellie laughed lightly and squeezed his arm.

451

Laura was skipping along at the other side of him, hanging on to the empty sleeve of his jacket.

'That's the way I heard it,' she said, watching a car turn in and stop just inside the entrance.

'Well, if that doesn't beat the lot!'

Ellie wasn't listening. She was too busy trying to calm her heart when she saw a tall, dark figure step out of the car and take a few limping steps towards them.

19

'Adam!' Ellie cried, her voice raw with emotion.

He stopped in his tracks. She saw his look of disbelief, saw even at that distance, the pain of anxiety in his eyes. She propelled herself forward, leaving Ben and Laura staring after her, open mouthed.

Then he was running, awkwardly, but running and she could hear his gasping breath getting louder and louder as he neared her. It could not have taken more than a few seconds, but in that time she saw how very much brighter the sun was, how blue the sky, how green the grass. The birdsong was beautiful and deafening at the same time and her feet did not feel the ground beneath her.

'Oh, Adam!' He had stopped and she flung herself at him, her heart breaking as his strong arms enfolded her, crushed her, lifted her to her toes and kissed her hungrily like a starving man devouring his first, life-saving food.

'Ellie!' he croaked, his face buried in her hair.

Both their faces were wet with tears. He

swiped at his with the ragged sleeve of his topcoat and held her firmly at arm's length.

'I — we all thought you were dead!' she shouted at him as if it were an admonition, then bit down hard on her quivering lips and reached out to touch him to make sure he was real. 'But you're alive — you're really alive!'

He looked bemused and glanced over her shoulder at Ben and Laura looking on curiously. 'What are you doing here?'

'I — I . . . ' Ellie stumbled over her words, not finding the right ones, not knowing how to tackle the subject. 'Adam — oh, this is so difficult. I came to see your father.'

'My father! I should have thought he was the last person . . . '

'You don't understand — listen. He's dying, Adam.'

She saw the slightest twitch in his face which was gaunt with fatigue and she realized in that moment how thin he looked and how his shabby clothes hung loosely on him, much the way Ben's had done. She knew then that Adam's war had consisted of much more than just drawing pictures.

'That still doesn't explain why you're here.'

'I came, Adam, to show him Laura. I — I thought he had the right to see his only grandchild before he died, you see.'

Adam's eyes left her face little by little and slid over to where Laura was hanging on to Ben like a pretty, golden limpet. He blinked twice, then returned his gaze to Ellie, a frown creasing his scarred forehead.

'Yes, Adam.' Ellie gave a small nod of affirmation. 'She's your daughter. She bears Nicholas's name, but she's yours.'

His mouth fell open as he tried to assimilate this astounding news. He passed a hand over his weary face and she heard his breath catch. He blinked away more blinding tears and caught Ellie's hand, squeezing her fingers until they hurt.

'You must be both very proud of her,' he said thickly.

'Nicholas died before she was born,' Ellie said simply and felt his grip tighten even more. 'He — he never knew I was pregnant, Adam. I couldn't tell him because — because we hadn't been . . . you know . . . '

'So there's no doubt?' Adam was gazing again at Laura and she was smiling shyly back at him, not wanting to leave her uncle, but fascinated by this tall, handsome man who seemed to love her mother.

Ellie was in the process of beckoning Laura forward when the door behind them flew open and Cynthia Rockwell ran out, arms outstretched, eyes bright with tears.

'Adam — *darling*! I couldn't believe it was you!'

She pulled up short as she reached him, glanced painfully at Ellie and placed a sisterly kiss on Adam's cheek, squeezing the hand he held out to her.

'Cynthia . . . ' Adam swayed slightly and leaned on Ellie's shoulder. 'I think it would be wise for us to go inside. All of us. I could do with a stiff drink, something to eat, a bath and a change of clothes. Preferably in that order. Would you mind asking Mrs Mac to organize things for me, Cynthia?'

She gave him a tight little smile. 'Mrs Mac retired two years ago, Adam. We have a new housekeeper now, but I'm sure she will be happy to oblige.' She turned to Ellie and Ben. 'Well, I suppose you should all come back into the house and we can — celebrate Adam's homecoming together.'

Ellie saw Ben's eyebrows lift sarcastically as they followed Lady Rockwell. Adam was still leaning on Ellie like a crutch and she could sense how weak he was.

'I'm sorry about your husband,' he said softly in her ear as they made their way to the drawing-room where the solicitor was still gathering together his legal papers. 'The professor was a good man, even if he never approved of me.'

Ellie smiled. 'I think he had some kind of premonition, you know. He said he was afraid you might one day steal something precious from him.'

'Well, I didn't, but he'll never know how close I came to stealing you.'

'You did steal me, Adam. You stole my heart, my body and my soul. They're forever yours and always have been.'

'Do sit down, Adam, before you fall down,' Lady Rockwell commanded from the sideboard where she was pouring a rather large measure of whisky into a tumbler. 'And Mr Davenport — you might as well stay to dinner. After my stepson has had time to rest I'm sure you will want to sort out the necessary legalities with — my husband's two sons. Mr Martin, I suppose you will want a drink? I'm afraid we don't have beer.'

'Whisky will do fine, ma'am,' Ben responded.

'Cynthia . . . ' Adam took a long sip of his whisky and closed his eyes to savour it. 'Give my brother the same as me. And his name is Ben.'

'Who is he, Mummy?' Laura had sidled up to Ellie and was watching Adam in great fascination.

Adam forced his eyes open, pulled himself upright and smiled down at the small child.

'I'm your real daddy, sweetheart,' he said, and Laura's eyes swallowed him.

'But . . . ' She looked at her mother for confirmation. 'Two daddies!'

Ellie gave her daughter a small push. 'I'll explain everything later,' she said. 'Now, go and say hello to your father.'

Adam pushed his drink to one side and lifted the child on to his lap. He seemed almost afraid to touch her lest she should vanish like a bubble. As ever, it was Laura who broke the ice.

'Are you really and truly my daddy?'

'I am,' Adam said, his smile wobbling and almost coming adrift. 'And when I'm all clean and tidy again you can tell me whether or not you approve.'

'Does that mean 'like'?'

'Uh-huh!'

'But I like you now. Do you love my mummy.'

Adam's eyes flickered in Ellie's direction. 'Oh, I *do*.'

His reply seemed to please her, for she stretched up and aimed an impromptu kiss at his chin, giggling because it was so prickly. There was a loud commotion as the new housekeeper, a plain-faced, youngish woman, entered. She was followed by Adam's two excited, yelping dogs who were ignoring her sharp order to 'stay'.

'Dougal! Scallion!' Adam called out their names delightedly and the setter and the golden retriever pounced on him, tongues licking, tails wagging. And Laura squealed with glee and joined in the happy reunion.

A few minutes later, Adam was sinking back among the cushions of his chair, dead from exhaustion and too much unaccustomed whisky.

'If you will all excuse me,' he yawned and heaved himself to his feet, but then he held out his hand to Ellie and she took it, shyly aware that everyone was staring at the pair of them. 'Come with me, Ellie.'

He made no excuses, gave no explanation and she asked no questions, but simply went with him as he suggested.

'I'm out on my feet,' he said to her as they headed for his rooms on the first floor, 'but I can't bear to be separated from you for a single moment. Do you mind?'

'What a silly question, Adam.'

He closed the door behind them and, still swaying slightly, he pulled her into his arms and covered her face with kisses.

'Oh, my sweet love.' He gave an agonized groan against her throat. 'I never thought that there was the merest chance it would end like this. Four years of living like an animal in the mud and the filth with bullets and bombs going off all around me and most of that time I wouldn't let myself think about you, because you belonged to another man.'

'I loved Nicholas, Adam,' Ellie said honestly. 'I can't deny that. He was a wonderful man and, if he had lived, he would have been a wonderful father to Laura, I'm sure of that. Even knowing she was another man's child. But I never *belonged* to him, as you say. I wasn't *in love* with him. My heart was always yours.'

'I was as good as dead for a long while, Ellie,' he told her. 'I caught the blast of a land-mine that killed two young German deserters who had been seeking help at a Flemish farm. I already had a bullet in my leg and bits of shrapnel everywhere. The blast knocked me out, gave me a serious concussion. I was in a coma for some weeks, then when I regained consciousness . . . ' He stopped, swallowed loudly and tightened his grip on her. 'God forgive me, but I couldn't remember anything. Nothing! It was as if my life had never happened. And I was carrying another soldier's identity papers. It was months before I got any memory back and — Ellie, you were the only person I could remember for ages. You and the love I had for you. It gave me the will to live.'

'Oh, Adam! If only I'd known!'

He was staggering with her to the bed, his body moulding into hers. They fell upon it, softly, in slow motion. She cuddled in to him, held him to her as she would a weary child. He was asleep before his head met the pillow, but she didn't mind. She smiled at him, lying so peacefully. She kissed his mouth and he seemed to sense it, for in his dreams he smiled.

'No matter,' Ellie whispered. 'I can wait. We have all the time in the world once you wake up, my love.'

★ ★ ★

Sir Donald lived only a few days after his son returned home, but during that short time old wounds miraculously healed. Adam and Ben inherited the foundry as joint owners, but it was Ben who stayed in place as the new Iron master. Six months later he and Margaret got married and had two more children.

Mary later married Jenner, Adam's chauffeur, but they were not blessed with children. However, they seemed happy enough. Lady Rockwell continued to live at the Hall and became more and more involved in her work to improve social conditions among the foundry workers and their families. Adam's sister, Grace, never married, but stayed on to help her stepmother.

Ellie's father, Jack, lived to be ninety and happily spent his time pottering in his garden and visiting his grandchildren, of which there were many. His three sisters enjoyed the same longevity, though their lives remained largely unchanged, as did their characters.

As for Ellie and Adam, they left Rockwell and the foundry, with Ben's blessing, and bought a farm in the south of France where they spent many happy years growing lavender and grapes and providing Laura with two brothers and a sister, along with a menagerie of animals and an even greater lust for life.

In the evenings the family would gather together in front of the wide open *cheminée* or on the terrace strung with perfumed bougainvillea in pink and mauve. Adam sketched while Ellie played the piano and sang and neither of them looked back or dwelled too long on how their idyll might never have been. Sometimes, when the children had gone to bed, they would dance, holding each other closely beneath the star-studded velvet sky and make love to the songs of the crickets and the nightingales.

We do hope that you have enjoyed reading this large print book.

Did you know that all of our titles are available for purchase?

We publish a wide range of high quality large print books including:
Romances, Mysteries, Classics
General Fiction
Non Fiction and Westerns

Special interest titles available in large print are:
The Little Oxford Dictionary
Music Book
Song Book
Hymn Book
Service Book

Also available from us courtesy of Oxford University Press:
Young Readers' Dictionary
(large print edition)
Young Readers' Thesaurus
(large print edition)

For further information or a free brochure, please contact us at:
Ulverscroft Large Print Books Ltd.,
The Green, Bradgate Road, Anstey,
Leicester, LE7 7FU, England.
Tel: (00 44) **0116 236 4325**
Fax: (00 44) **0116 234 0205**

Other titles published by
The House of Ulverscroft:

GINNY APPLEYARD

Elizabeth Jeffrey

When Ginny Appleyard's childhood sweetheart returns after his racing season aboard the yacht AURORA, her hopes that he is bringing her an engagement ring are shattered, as Nathan disembarks with Isobel Armitage, the daughter of AURORA's owner. Nathan tells Ginny that he is following Isobel to London to pursue his dreams of becoming an artist. Already distraught at the tragic death of her father, Ginny is further devastated to hear that Nathan and Isobel are to be married. More heartache is in store for Ginny when she realises that she is expecting Nathan's child . . .

KEEPER OF SWANS

Joyce Windsor

In 1997, five acquaintances gather at The Glebe retirement home in a quiet corner of Dorset. Each is troubled by the shadow of events that took place twenty-seven years before. Against her better judgement, Bird Dawlish, proprietor of the home, takes in a widower, Hereward Parstock, who was once her lover. Connie Lovibond, Hereward's sister-in-law, who has never been satisfied that her sister's death was natural, is convinced that Bird and possibly Rita Parry, an old travelling woman, can help to discover the truth. The tragic death of Princess Diana heightens emotions and helps to bring about crises of love and violence that affect residents and villagers alike.

HALF MOON LAKE

Una Brankin

Grace grew up in the shadow of her widowed mother and her superstitious, overbearing neighbours in the remote town of Preachers Bay, Northern Ireland. One summer evening, a stranger knocks on their door, desperately seeking refuge. As Grace helps to nurse him back to health, she experiences at last the love that she has so innocently yet dementedly craved. Now, two decades later, Grace thinks back to her childhood and that steamy summer of 1976. And finally, the truth behind her lifelong reclusiveness, her relationship with her mother, and her first and only love, is revealed.